THE GIRL
IN THE
GREEN
DRESS

ALSO BY MARIAH FREDERICKS

STANDALONE NOVELS

The Lindbergh Nanny
The Wharton Plot

THE JANE PRESCOTT SERIES

A Death of No Importance
Death of a New American
Death of an American Beauty
Death of a Showman

YA NOVELS

The True Meaning of Cleavage
Head Games
Crunch Time
The Girl in the Park

The Girl in the Green Dress

A Mystery Featuring
Zelda Fitzgerald

Mariah Fredericks

MINOTAUR BOOKS
NEW YORK

This is a work of fiction. All of the characters, organizations, and events portrayed in this novel are either products of the author's imagination or are used fictitiously.

First published in the United States by Minotaur Books, an imprint of St. Martin's Publishing Group

EU Representative: Macmillan Publishers Ireland Ltd, 1st Floor, The Liffey Trust Centre, 117-126 Sheriff Street Upper, Dublin 1, DO1 YC43

THE GIRL IN THE GREEN DRESS. Copyright © 2025 by Mariah Fredericks. All rights reserved. Printed in the United States of America. For information, address St. Martin's Publishing Group, 120 Broadway, New York, NY 10271.

www.minotaurbooks.com

Design by Meryl Sussman Levavi

The Library of Congress Cataloging-in-Publication Data is available upon request.

ISBN 978-1-250-36751-8 (hardcover)
ISBN 978-1-250-36752-5 (ebook)

The publisher of this book does not authorize the use or reproduction of any part of this book in any manner for the purpose of training artificial intelligence technologies or systems. The publisher of this book expressly reserves this book from the Text and Data Mining exception in accordance with Article 4(3) of the European Union Digital Single Market Directive 2019/790.

Our books may be purchased in bulk for specialty retail/wholesale, literacy, corporate/premium, educational, and subscription box use. Please contact MacmillanSpecialMarkets@macmillan.com.

First Edition: 2025

10 9 8 7 6 5 4 3 2 1

For Victoria,
who told me "Zelda"
as well as many other brilliant things

It lies within the very nature of a mystery story that it must be told backward. The only possible beginning is the corpse. And then things are learned and told about the corpse and the creature that existed before it became a corpse, until at last we do not have a corpse at all, but a living and very human being to remember, with friends and enemies, with hopes and defeats, with sins and passions, and now and again, a few nobilities.

—Morris Markey

By the time a person has achieved years adequate for choosing a direction, the die is cast and the moment has long since passed which determined the future.

—Zelda Fitzgerald

The Girl in the Green Dress

PROLOGUE

HALIFAX, VIRGINIA
1950

It was a strange place to end your life—the front hallway of your home, right by the stairs that led to the second floor, where your wife and daughter slept. Strange time for it, too. Most people killed themselves well after midnight, when the goblins took over and it seemed morning would never come.

Such was George Abney's thinking as he stood in the narrow entryway of the Markey house on Beaver Dam Road. Halifax was a small town, barely eight hundred people. Abney had been its coroner for the last thirty years. In Halifax, death was not a matter of great mystery. The hows and whys usually amounted to old age and something gave out. There had been a few occasions when he had to write something more specific, the deceased being too young for the usual explanation. Eighteen-year-old Henry Dunk had run his car into a tree and himself through the windshield.

There wasn't any mystery about what had happened, but the coroner had kept quiet about the bottle of bourbon he found on the floor of the car. Pete Voorhies's stove had leaked gas; no one needed to know his head had been in it when he died. Martha Derwent's ailing husband had gone a little faster than expected, but no one would have wished him another day. In each case, Abney had written as little as possible in the report—*accident, accident, cancer*—and let everyone keep their secrets.

The body lay face down, toes pointed toward the door. No one who knew him would have said Morris Markey had any reason to wish himself dead. The town had been excited at his return, ready to welcome back the local boy who'd made it big as a writer. He'd started his career with the Atlanta newspapers before moving north, where he became a big deal at *The New Yorker*. (Abney did not subscribe, but he gathered the magazine impressed some.) He had served in the First World War, been a correspondent for the second. Even spent time in Hollywood. Morris Markey, people recalled, had always been a boy in a hurry.

He seemed a solid family man, married to Helen Turman of the Atlanta Turmans for nearly three decades. Last year, he'd come back South to take care of his mother—at least that was the story pieced together by the ladies who chatted with Mrs. Markey at the market and after church. Their daughter was marrying the Caldwell boy in the fall. Both families were said to be happy with the match—mostly. By any measure, the man was a success with a great deal to look forward to in life.

Now that man lay on the hallway carpet, belly down, arm thrown above his head, glasses askew, with a small, neat hole below his right ear. The rifle that had killed him lay on the floor beside him.

The rifle was owned by Markey himself. It had hung on two brass hooks on the wall of the very hallway where he died, placed there so a man could grab it the moment he heard someone coming in the house who shouldn't be. It was a .22 caliber, not particularly handsome or rare. But it would get the job done.

The matter seemed simple enough, if sad.

However, there was an issue of mechanics. Markey had been taller than most. His arms were long. But not so long, thought the coroner, that it would have been easy for him to shoot himself behind the right ear with a rifle four feet in length. He had fallen with his feet toward the door, which suggested he had been shot from behind, presumably by someone coming into the house. But there were no signs of attempted robbery, and neither the wife nor the daughter had heard shouting or scuffling.

Finally, anyone wanting to do the job properly would have put the thing in his mouth, and in Abney's experience, he would have gone into the woods or at least the garage to do it. Not a step beyond his own front door where his family would have to remember the sight every time they came home.

Which was why the police had been interviewing members of that family for the past few hours. It was a distasteful thing to contemplate. But Abney had been a coroner long enough to know sometimes it was the ones you loved the most that did you in. From upstairs, he could hear Mrs. Markey recounting her discovery of her husband's body to the police. Her voice was hoarse; she'd told the story several times. In the kitchen, another officer was talking with Sue Markey, but he didn't seem to be getting much out of her. Mother and daughter both insisted that Mrs. Markey had been upstairs when the shot was fired and that Sue Markey had been out in the yard. Sue Markey was particularly fierce in her assertion that her fiancé had been nowhere near the house at the time. The police were interviewing him at his house.

He heard his name called; the boys from the Danville morgue had arrived. Abney never liked to watch as they lifted the body onto the stretcher—the dumb acquiescence of the recently deceased gave his stomach a turn. So while the Danville boys did their work, he went to the dead man's study. If he could find evidence of suicide—a note or unpaid bills—he preferred to do so. It would mean the family couldn't collect the insurance, but Mrs. Markey would probably prefer that to a murder charge.

The study was a small, pleasant room with a fine stout desk placed near a wide bay window, presumably so Mr. Markey could look up from his typewriter and enjoy the view. Abney looked for bills, bank statements—evidence of money troubles. He found a bottle in the bottom desk drawer, but that wasn't unusual. Books crowded the shelves. Mr. Markey had a taste for crime novels, it seemed. *The Postman Always Rings Twice*—Abney had liked that one—and *The Benson Murder Case*. On the arm of a battered leather chair, an open copy of *The Great Gatsby*, the cheap edition they'd sent to the troops during the war. Magazines sprawled on tables: *The New Yorker, Vanity Fair, Esquire*. Flipping through them, he found the dead man's name again and again. BY MORRIS MARKEY. He had written a great deal about crime: the Hall-Mills case, the Lindbergh kidnapping, Legs Diamond, and the Starr Faithfull murder.

Had someone taken exception to something he wrote? Was that the real reason he had returned to Virginia after so many years back East? But these were old crimes. No one involved would be likely to shoot the writer decades later.

Abney went to the desk. On the blotter was a yellow legal pad crowded with handwriting. In the typewriter, a piece of paper, half curled around the platen. He examined the page, expecting to see a will or farewell. Instead, he read,

WHO KILLED JOE ELWELL?

A probe into the death of a man who glittered even in the ultra-Smart Set of 1920. Joseph Bowne Elwell was the last great practitioner of the discreet, deft amour.

Abney had never heard of Joseph Elwell, and he couldn't imagine why anyone would be interested in a killing that happened thirty years ago. Then he read the next line.

Was it suicide—or murder?

That, thought the coroner, was an excellent question.

Chapter One

**NEW YORK
1920**

"..."

At twenty-one years old, Morris Markey did not know how he meant to finish that sentence. His purpose was clear: to win the passionate admiration of the girl standing next to him in the crush of people who had gathered in the kitchen. He had come to this party to fall in love, and this girl with shining blond hair that swished alluringly over her trim jaw seemed a strong possibility. She had smiled when he suggested a trip to the North Pole might be a more efficient way to procure ice, then shared her concern that the gin came from the host's own bathtub—she knew the host; his habits were unsanitary. Markey was about to say he hoped the fellow's recipe called for more juniper oil and less glycerin because it was all a question of balance when another man popped up to ask the girl, "Say, weren't you at Bunny's last Tuesday?"

The girl said she hadn't been at Bunny's, and the other fellow said that was too bad, she missed a good time. Markey hadn't been at Bunny's either; he didn't even know who Bunny was. The interloper was the quick, buzzy type; he made his interest clear right up front. Markey could see the girl didn't mind that.

He was about to regain the advantage with a story of how in his first month as a reporter, he had been stabbed by a drunken lawyer in Atlanta—the punchline being that the *next* reporter had been shot. But before he could, the other fellow announced that he'd nearly had a story published in *The Smart Set*. Markey was about to say, *I believe in English "nearly published" means rejected*, but then the girl said, "What a *shame*," and there was nothing for it but to ask what the story was about and let the little blowhard have his say. In theory, the three of them were conversing. But the blowhard had the girl's full attention, while Markey got the occasional glance that he understood to mean, *Oh, are you still here?*

Then, just as he offered his "I—," the girl clapped a hand to her collarbone and laughed. Mr. Nearly Published had said something funny. Someone came through, drink held high, forcing them all to make way. When they resumed their places, the trio had become a duo. Leaving them to it, Markey shouldered his way out of the crowded kitchen to join the throng in the living room.

It seemed to Markey he had been to this party before. This one was on Perry Street, but it was the same crowd, the same gin, and the same loud, impenetrable conversation as the party last week at Sheridan Square and the one on Patchin Place the week before that. They all took place in squat brick town houses below Eleventh Street. At every gathering, he wandered through rooms packed with people locked in intense debate or exploding in shared mirth. Clearly, at some point, there had been a wonderful party attended by the entire world and he had missed it. Now they were all tremendous friends, and he was still introducing himself with a smile and a clammy handshake.

In vain, he looked for the people who brought him. He had tagged along with Eddie and Dottie Parker. Markey had first crossed paths with Eddie in France, where they liked to say Markey loaded the ambulance and Eddie drove it, hopefully arriving at the hospital with the same number of corpses. Eddie had gone back to his job on Wall Street. Dottie was a drama critic, and while she didn't drink much, Eddie did. One way or another, they seemed to end up in places where there were writers for her and liquor for him. Eddie sometimes asked Markey to join them, saying, "I can only take so many happy jackasses."

"Does that make me an unhappy jackass?" asked Markey.

"Well, sure, that's what we are," said Eddie, leaving it unclear who comprised the "we" or what the requirements were for joining the club. Other than unhappiness.

Settling on a cold radiator, he considered his defeat at the hands of the buzzy fellow. That incomplete *I*—what should he have done with it? An opinion? *I think* The Smart Set *is for pretentious juveniles.* A proclamation: *I write for the* Daily News. Neither would have impressed the girl. There was nothing but writers at this party; most were critics by nature and profession. And Markey had learned: The quality of paper mattered. Novels were first, of course. Then magazines, with their glossy, heavier-grade stock. At the bottom, newspapers, printed on cheap wood pulp. When Markey told people he worked for the *Daily News*, eyebrows rose and mouths went askew. *Too bad*, seemed the general consensus.

He suspected his looks were against him, too. His mother had always assured him that women wanted someone *big* who would make them feel protected. But Markey knew he looked not so much tall and strapping as overgrown, as if he'd hit six feet and not had the sense to stop there. Successful men in New York were pen and ink—a few bold strokes in a loose authoritative hand; sharp, definitive, they caught the eye. Beside them, he felt blurry. Blue-eyed with light brown hair, he was a type known as "nice-looking." The size of his ears suggested he had been hauled through childhood between the thumb and forefinger of exasperated female relations. The glasses didn't help. In France, he'd had to show off his inventiveness with cuss words before other men took him seriously.

Restless, he tugged at his collar and shifted his shoulders. It was a warm night, and there were too many talkers for the amount of oxygen in the room. Listening to the anxious gossip, casual bragging, and paranoid grievances of people desperate to establish a foothold in the word business, he tried once again to find an opening. People in New York liked stories about themselves, no matter how familiar. When all else failed, one could move from group to group, picking up information at one, passing it on at the next. Hearing on one end of the room that H. L. Mencken had launched a detective magazine called *Black Mask*, he mentioned it to people at the other end. From them, he learned that Robert Sherwood had been bounced from his job, replaced by a woman who gave the publisher's kid piano lessons and who knew what to the publisher. A few minutes later, he repeated that story to a couple who shared, in turn, that the ancient Edith Wharton had been seen at Scribner's and Scott Fitzgerald had burst into the offices to kneel at her feet.

This story he would not repeat. The man who took up the most space in the room was not even in it, and Markey felt mulish about increasing his reputation even a little. Fitzgerald's ascent to literary fame was miraculous and infuriating. It was a dizzying rise, so swift it was hard to believe, a gag where someone should shout, *April Fool!* And they'd all collapse in laughter, then sigh, *It would be wonderful if things like that really happened.*

Markey couldn't say he knew Fitzgerald, only that they had been in the same room on occasion at parties like this one. In those days, Fitzgerald was an ad writer with a novel he couldn't get published, grumbling about the gatekeepers and their lack of vision like the rest of them. "We keep you clean in Muscatine!"—a slogan for a steam laundry—had been the sole proof of his genius. (To his credit, he often used it as a jest when toasting their bright futures in literature.)

Then he'd sold that novel to Scribner's. Then he'd sold a story to *The Saturday Evening Post* and the movie rights to that story. Then *This Side of Paradise* came out and *The New York Times* called it "nearly as perfect as such a book could be." Scribner's proclaimed Fitzgerald the youngest author they'd ever published. He'd gotten married and been on a spree ever since. He also happened to be very good-looking.

Markey didn't begrudge the man his success. But he was aware he hadn't read *This Side of Paradise*, and there was a reason for that. He told himself he wasn't especially interested in the exploits of a spoiled Princeton boy. He mostly believed it.

They had had precisely one conversation. In the days of Muscatine, Markey had laughed sincerely at something Fitzgerald said and Fitzgerald noticed. Later the Minnesotan sought him out and said, "You write for the *Daily News*." Markey had braced for a joke about captions.

"They turned me down," said Fitzgerald cheerfully. "All the New York papers did. I went to every rag in town. Not a single one of them would give me a job."

Markey couldn't imagine anyone turning this man down for anything. Everything about him was expansive: his broad forehead, the bronze hair that flowed so beautifully from the center of his skull, the puckish charm of his green eyes. His mouth was thin, the lips paltry. The nose aquiline or witchy, depending on the angle. Otherwise the man was abundance personified.

Something occurred to Markey. "Had you been a reporter anywhere else?"

"Oh, no." Fitzgerald grinned at his own inexperience. No—Markey revised—his audacity.

"That might be it," he said.

"I'm sure it is."

The conversation had flickered, threatened to die out. It needed the fuel of curiosity, and Markey sensed it would only flow in one direction from here on. He asked, "What is it you want to be?"

"Me?" Mild surprise, as if it were obvious. "Oh, I want to be one of the greatest writers who ever lived. Don't you?"

Caught, Markey laughed. For a brief moment, he believed they had become friends.

"I suppose it's finding the right story," said Markey. "Being right there when the big thing happens and only you can tell people how it really was."

"I tend to write about myself," said Fitzgerald. "I'm not sure I could write about anything else." Then he catapulted off. A few months later, F. Scott Fitzgerald became the man everyone in New York was talking about, and they hadn't been in the same room since. Fitzgerald now lived in the rarefied world of hotels. Eddie had told him that "Scott and Zelda"—some thought her captivating, others thought her hell—had been thrown out of several establishments for their outrageous antics.

But in Fitzgerald's absence, people produced him anyway, competing as to who had the best story about the flamboyant couple. This evening, it was Dottie, who was regaling the crowd with a direct encounter. "I'd met him, but I hadn't met *her*." Tiny Dottie, holding sway—Markey couldn't actually see her; the crush was such that only a curling gray plume of cigarette smoke rising from the center of the crowd and bursts of laughter signaled her whereabouts. Markey would not say so to Eddie, but he found Dottie terrifying. Her contempt, even if directed at someone else, was unsettling. At some point, you knew it would come your way.

"*She* was sitting astride the hood of the taxi. *He* was sitting on the roof. You felt they were waiting for someone to take their picture—'Aren't they shocking, aren't they marvelous?' Well, maybe they were a bit marvelous. They both looked like they had just stepped out of the sun. Is she *the* most beautiful girl in Georgia *and* Alabama?"

Scott had reportedly made this claim. Dottie paused to let her audience know she considered the title of no great value, then said, "I wouldn't presume to know."

At last, Markey saw an opening. He had not met the famous Zelda, but as the only Southerner in the room, he could presume to know. Weighing words like *fresh* and *gracious*, he made his way to where Dottie sat. The room was packed tight, and it took time. He looked for Eddie and saw that his friend was deep in conversation with his drink. He and Dottie had snapped at each other earlier, something about the company she was keeping, and avoided each other all evening. Markey didn't like how Eddie was swaying toward an open window. He would check in with him later.

Making it to the outer rim of Dottie's circle, he deliberately exaggerated his drawl to say, "Pardon me . . ."

A strange shushing quiet greeted his approach. Her voice suddenly, startlingly clear, Dottie announced, "It's not the nose that makes him look like a parrot, it's the way he steps from foot to foot, mo*not*onously repeating things he's heard from other people."

Instantly, he understood that the shushing heralded the awkward, avid silence that occurs when the person being talked about suddenly appears. It was his nose she referred to, his monotonous voice, his inability to say anything original or interesting.

Curling her tongue between her teeth as if to chastise it, Dottie looked at him, brows raised: *Caught.* In her lap, she had a small plate with bits of cheese, a gherkin, and other cheap party fare.

Smiling, she held it out to him. "Cracker?"

She got her laugh. Markey knew he should return barb for barb. But he also knew a coup de grâce when he saw it. Raising a hand in farewell and surrender, he left the party.

Chapter Two

Morris Markey had tried to go home after the war. He had accepted his mother's joy at his return, his father's pride in his service. There had been some kind of dinner at the town hall. Markey smiled and nodded and said thank you. He observed the mayor patting the bottom of Miss Richmond. He listened to Floyd Napier and Matilda Swanson argue over dogs in the public park. He'd timed the waiters coming and going. It was crowded. As his father said over and over, "The whole town's turned out." He became increasingly aware of the press of bodies, the jostle of shoulders and elbows. He cringed at the assault of sudden, barking laughter, puzzled as to why no one else seemed to mind. He began to worry there were too many people and not enough air. It seemed a situation where something could go wrong, and he wasn't sure how you would get out if it did.

Somehow, he'd ended up sitting on a park bench, sweating and unable to catch his breath. His heart pounded so hard he was certain the muscle wall would give way. The wide avenue of the park was lined with statues of generals. He felt their disapproval.

One day, he drove his mother to the market. In line for the cashier, someone had given him a slap on the back that felt like a shove. Markey had turned on him, fists ready; he'd been made a fool of once before and he wouldn't let it happen again. Before he swung, he caught sight of his mother staring at him. She was frightened—not for him, but of him.

He announced his intention to become a reporter in Atlanta. Atlanta moved faster than Richmond, but he still found himself stuck and anxious. When someone told him all the writers lived in New York, he knew it wasn't true, but it was a reason to move on. The moment he'd stepped off the train, he relaxed. The endless crosscurrent of people dashing this way, that way, shouting, shoving, selling, acted on his nerves like a sedative. When he tried to ask directions and no one stopped or even slowed down, he knew he was in the right place. This was a city where people kept moving, and that suited him fine.

He took a job at the *Daily News*, a new tabloid based on the idea that most readers hate to read. The front page was made up of pictures of people of the moment with screaming captions like MOVIE STAR TO WED! and BRONX BABIES WIN! Markey lurked at the courthouse, trying to get in on the Bloomfield divorce. He haunted the precincts in hopes of the next brutal murder. But he didn't know the city yet. The accents were different and he missed cues. He ended up interviewing the winner of the paper's limerick contest and reporting on a Chicago delegation who dined with the Brooklyn borough president.

Still smarting from Dottie's gibe, Markey walked. It was three miles to his house, but there was no better way to learn a city than to walk it. He felt the fresh air would do him good—although he wasn't sure fresh air could be found in the city in summer. New York heat was not Virginia heat. Virginia heat was soft, easeful, the humidity freshened by the waters of the Chesapeake Bay and the Potomac. It enfolded you in a mantle of warmth, urging you to sit a spell—there was no hurry. New York heat clobbered you the moment you set foot on the pavement. It sapped your energy, gummed up your thoughts. As you stumbled to work, it blasted you from the concrete below, glared down on you from the reflections of hundreds of windows. And as bad as it was during the day, it was worse at night. At night, you lay in bed and it lay on you. Virginia was an old quilt, New York an anvil.

Staring up at the buildings, he imagined what was happening behind the curtains. Sex, fights, small joys and miseries—so many people in this town, and he could get close to none of them. He would have liked to talk to the kitchen workers wrestling garbage cans out to the curb or the police officer swinging his billy club in a wistful manner as he hummed Jolson's "Tell Me" to himself. But the *Daily News* was not interested in solitary policemen or kitchen workers.

The first time he heard his name, he ignored it, certain he had mistaken a newsboy's shout for someone calling him. Then he heard it again—"Markey!"—and risked embarrassment by turning. He saw Eddie weaving through the crowd. He'd meant to check on Eddie; now Eddie was checking on him. *Jackasses*, he thought in inebriated fondness, *we stick together*. The 33rd Ambulance Company had nicknamed Eddie "Spook" because he got pale when he was hungover—which was often.

Pulling alongside, Spook bent double to catch his breath. Hands on his knees, he swung to examine the back of Markey's pants. "Oh, yeah, Dottie took a bite out of you."

"I guess I annoyed her."

"Bah, we all do. Besides—*they* annoy *us*." Flinging his arm in the air, he shouted, "*They* annoy *us*!"

Having made the gesture, he stumbled, grabbed on to Markey for balance. Markey told him, "I'm not going to those parties anymore."

Spook swayed in grief.

"No," said Markey, earnest about his status as an outcast. "Being trapped in a room with people I don't know and probably wouldn't like if I did know . . ."

Spook put his nose to Markey's shoulder, took a deep, noisy breath. "I smell self-pity. Yeuch."

Markey gave it up. Together they lurched up to Markey's apartment at 237 West Seventieth Street, which was close to Spook and Dottie's on Seventy-First and West End. The area was new to affluence, its sheen spotty. The block itself seemed split down the middle between drab and deluxe. On one side, there were gracious town houses, often occupied by a single resident. On Markey's side, the same houses were chopped into cramped quarters for working people, ranging from large families whose lives spilled into the hallways and cranky older people who railed against the noise. Markey lived in the cellar apartment. The place had been passed on to him by a fellow he worked with at the *Daily News*. There had been a touch of *Better you than me* in the man's grin as he handed Markey the keys, and Markey's low expectations were not disappointed.

But as they turned onto his block, Markey was stunned by a vision: a gentleman in a silk top hat and tails, stepping out of a canary yellow roadster. The door to the roadster was held open by a uniformed chauffeur in olive green. The gentleman carried a silver-topped walking stick, which he swung idly like a bored conjurer. He was tall and arrow-slim. His sleek brown hair formed a clean, elegant line along his chiseled profile. His beauty and grace were such the grubby little street seemed transformed into a Broadway stage.

He lifted a laughing girl from the car. Alighting from the roadster, she raised her bare arms and shimmied. She wore a dress of green and silver shards, as if she had been showered in dollar bills, with just enough clinging to her body to avoid arrest. Around her shorn auburn hair, a headband with a peacock's feather drew the eye to her glorious, exposed neck. Markey stared. He felt sure he would step in front of a bus to protect that neck, the long, graceful arms, the sheer joy of her. She was a girl you'd do anything for because she'd make you feel you could do anything.

Aware that they had an admirer, the man turned in Markey's direction. He smiled—his teeth were shark white and perfectly even. With exactly the right amount of irony, he tipped his hat to them. Then he offered his arm to the girl, and together, they trotted up the steps of 244 and went inside.

Spook laughed. "Well, now you've seen Joseph Elwell—welcome to New York!"

Still dazzled by the image of the girl, Markey asked Spook, "Do you know him?"

"I know that car. A client told me Elwell brought it to Belmont. His horse lost, but all anyone remembered was that car. Fellow spent half an hour talking about it."

"He owns racehorses?"

"Owns racehorses, plays cards, invests in the market . . . any way you can make money without actually working, that's what he does. Supposedly, he once made $30,000 in a single night playing bridge. In his spare time, he teaches the game to socialites. But only if they're pretty and only if they're married."

"Well, then I'm quitting tomorrow and taking up bridge," announced Markey. He realized he was still a little drunk.

Spook's hand landed on his shoulder. "Ah, don't quit. You can't. You can't leave me."

Stooped—Spook meant to be collegial, but he was leaning hard—Markey said, "I can't see Dottie letting anything happen to you."

Spook's expression had been vague, sleepy with drink. But at this, his eyes popped and he let out a "Ha!" that echoed all over the block. Grasping Markey by the arms, he announced, "Good night, you walrus," and went stumbling down the block.

Markey watched him, wondering if he should insist Spook flop at his place. But there was construction across the street; the workmen started early, and Spook was unlikely to welcome the sound of hammers first thing. Walking to his own building, he stopped to look back at the Elwell house. It felt like a sign of sorts. In his hour of need, he had asked for a story, and the good Lord had delivered. Racehorses! Gambling! That transcendent, miraculous girl. If Markey could not make a story of that, he should go back to Virginia. *This* was New York, and he'd found it on his very own block.

And now he needed to go to bed.

His apartment was a single room with a temperamental toilet and a stove that sometimes worked. In the summer heat, he had pushed the bed close to the window to get what air could be had. Now he pulled off his clothes and fell onto his mattress.

Sleeping, Markey dreamed. Johnson was screaming. It was the howl of an animal half destroyed, aware only of pain and the impending end. Crouching, Markey patted the air as if that would quiet him. They were not supposed to be there—either of them. By all rights, Johnson should be dead, and Markey was only a Red Cross searcher, a fellow who came out after the battle was finished, gathered up what remained, and got it onto the ambulance. Yet here they were, trapped in a narrow ditch with the fight still going on. It was a tight, low space. Markey curled in on himself, trying to keep his head down. Johnson's screaming made it difficult to think, as did the rattle and ping of gunfire, the boom and sudden flurry of soil when a grenade landed. The whine of bullets was particularly distracting. Markey heard shouting in German, and his bowels turned to water.

He put a hand to his nose, a signal to Johnson, and when he didn't stop shrieking, he placed it over the wounded man's mouth, praying, *Quiet, quiet, quiet.* Johnson rolled in agony. The man was all but dead but begging to live. The gully was collapsing, earth piling high and hard all around them. Markey couldn't move up without getting shot; he couldn't stay put without suffocating. The bullets were flying closer, the vicious buzz of their approach so intense it hurt his ears.

Then the percussive pop of bullets faded, the smoke cleared. Even Johnson vanished. But Markey could still hear the screams, which he now realized could not be Johnson's and had never been Johnson's because they were too high-pitched for a man, and Markey understood he was not in France but in a bed with a pillow, and it was morning.

But a woman really was screaming. As Markey's brain reassembled itself, he understood he was hearing the word *murder*.

He scrambled out of bed, adjusting his spectacles as he went to the window. Across the street, a woman was shouting, "Help me, please, there has been a robbery, a man has been shot . . ."

She was standing on the stoop of number 244 West Seventieth Street.

Chapter Three

Markey snatched yesterday's clothes from the floor, keeping a sharp eye on the woman as he dressed. He had to get inside that house. If some decent soul got there before him or the police came, his chance would be gone. Hopping, he jammed his feet into a pair of battered brogans and clambered out onto the street, dodging cars as he crossed. Next door at 246, the carpenters had started their work, hammers banging. On the Elwell house, he saw a FOR SALE sign on the railings of the basement windows. Funny, he hadn't seen that before.

Carefully, he approached the distraught woman. "Pardon me, my name is Morris Markey, I live across the street. I served with the Red Cross. Maybe I could help?"

She was not the girl in the dollar-green dress. She wore sensible black, with an apron and sturdy shoes. There were tracings of age and labor along her eyes and mouth. Her skin was pale, but not in its first freshness. She had a married woman's weariness.

At the word *help*, she seized his arm. "Yes, please. Mr. Elwell is a good man, he does not deserve this. I am Mrs. Larsen, his housekeeper." Her voice was accented, with a lilt that had a pleasing firmness to it.

There were two doors into the house, the front entry and another leading off a small foyer with a black-and-white-tile floor. The doors were heavy, the windows frosted glass. As she led him inside the vestibule, Mrs. Larsen announced, "This front door was locked when I came. It is *never* locked. Come, through here . . ."

Markey entered to find the house as grand and silent as a cathedral. The luxurious decor of the entry hall reflected the city's old passion for French and the modern one for the Orient. The hallway was covered in a long rug of deep blue and reds. The wallpaper was cream, with a pattern of poppies in gold and navy. There were several mirrors, suggesting if one disliked the reflection in one, he might be pleased by the next. Smelling smoke, Markey breathed deeply to identify it. Tobacco, not wood. Someone had been smoking on this floor minutes ago.

The housekeeper stopped. "Here," she said breathlessly. "In the drawing room. This is where I found him."

She opened the door. Inside, Joseph Elwell sat slumped, his head resting on the back of a dark, heavy chair covered in crimson velvet. He was dressed in red silk pajamas.

There was a single bullet hole in the center of his forehead.

Markey stood transfixed. The sight of Elwell, majestic and ruined, felt strangely personal, as if he were meant to understand something having seen it. He wasn't distressed. Rather, he felt relieved, almost confident, as if the world had snapped back into focus. *Oh, yes, this is how things are.*

But this was a very different Joseph Elwell than the gleaming kingfisher of last night. For one thing, his head was bald except for wispy dark strands across the top. The hands on the armrests were wrinkled and spotted. His mouth hung slack, showing three teeth, listing sideways, brown rot creeping up from the livid gums. As Markey drew closer for a better look, Elwell's head suddenly jerked, his mouth working, the jaw spasmodic, the lips floppy.

"He is trying to say something," breathed the housekeeper.

Markey listened, but he could not make out words, only a thin whine with little breath behind it. The dying man's fingers twitched. The body did strange things at the end, fighting for life. It was a fight Elwell would lose, but still, Markey said, "We should get him to the hospital."

"Can't you do anything for him?" she pleaded.

She thought him a doctor; he'd implied as much by mentioning the Red Cross. "Not for a wound like this," he hedged. "I'll stay. You call the ambulance."

He felt her disappointment, but she collected herself, saying, "We will take you to the hospital, Mr. Elwell." She smoothed the collar of his robe. She was not squeamish. Markey admired that.

When the housekeeper had gone, Markey fished a small notepad out of his pocket. The bullet had gone through to the wall; the plaster was cracked and spattered with blood and brain matter. Near Elwell's chair, there was an ashtray on a small table, a cigarette still burning. That explained the tobacco smell. An ornate clock ticked away the last minutes of Elwell's life. Elegant figurines lined the mantel. A watch, gold by the look of it, was still on his wrist. The scene didn't read robbery to Markey.

An open letter lay on the dying man's lap, dotted with blood that had dripped from his brow. Leaning in, Markey copied several lines: *All horses are going good. Expenses pretty high for the month.* He remembered the FOR SALE sign. Elwell wouldn't be the first man to shoot himself over money troubles.

But if it was suicide, where was the gun? He glanced at the floor and under the chair, but found no weapon.

Straightening, he saw that grains of powder had embedded in the skin around the entry wound, but there were no burns, which suggested the gun had been fired at close range, but no more than four or five inches from Elwell's head. A suicide, you'd fire with the muzzle held to the skin; staring down the barrel of the gun was a hard thing. A discharged cartridge lay on the rug. From that and the diameter of the wound, he guessed the weapon was a .45 automatic. So, where was it?

And that wondrous girl in the green dress—where was she?

Making sure Mrs. Larsen was still out of earshot, he said in a soft voice, "Who did this to you, Mr. Elwell?"

Elwell's breath grew ragged, his shoulders hitching with the effort to breathe. His fingers rose stiff and splayed.

"The girl, Mr. Elwell—where is she?"

The gambler collapsed, hands dropping to his sides, head lolling. Markey's brain began to hum. Perhaps the girl had left before the killer arrived. Or perhaps she was somewhere in the house, lifeless, a victim of wrong place, wrong time. Or . . .

He recalled the slender, upraised arms. Mentally, he placed a gun into one shapely hand.

"They are coming." The housekeeper was back. "Has he said anything?"

"I'm afraid not." Drawing closer, he murmured, "Mrs. Larsen, what time did you arrive this morning?"

"I came at 8:35, a little late. I went to the kitchen to change, then I came to this room to clean. That's when . . ." She gestured to her employer.

"And you haven't seen or heard anyone else?"

"No."

He nodded to the front. "Do those doors lock automatically when shut?"

"No, you have to lock them from the inside or the outside with a key."

"Is there a back door perhaps? For deliveries?"

"Yes. But that is always kept locked. We had another burglary a few months ago. That time, they just took things. They didn't harm anyone." She looked sadly at Elwell.

To Markey's knowledge, burglars didn't usually strike first thing in the morning. The letter in Elwell's lap meant he had been sitting down when he was shot—a strangely calm posture for a man whose home had just been broken into. But not for a man luxuriating in the pleasant aftermath of a night spent with a beautiful woman. He might not even look up if she came into the room . . .

Markey felt tingling in his hands and the backs of his knees. He wasn't sure what had him more keyed up: the prospect of encountering a killer or being this close to a big story. A good-looking girl criminal could make a reporter's career, freeing him from limerick contests and borough presidents.

She could also blow a nosy fellow's head off. A shiver went through his groin.

"Does Mr. Elwell keep a gun in the house?"

"No. Why?"

"Because there's no gun in this room, Mrs. Larsen. Which means the shooter might still be here."

She gestured to the door. "The robber took it with him . . ."

Then she remembered the door had been locked and went still. Markey nodded: *Exactly.* "I think I should check, don't you?"

"This is Mr. Elwell's home," she said sharply. "You cannot go wandering about, looking through his things."

"I don't want to look through his things, Mrs. Larsen." Something of a lie—he very much did. "I just want to make sure we're the only ones here. I'm worried what might happen if they come back down and find Mr. Elwell is still alive."

"Oh." Mrs. Larsen looked at her employer. "I suppose then . . . yes. But please, *please* be careful."

He pressed her hands as a promise and went to the stairs. Laying his feet as carefully as possible on each step, he kept his eye on the railing of the next floor, alert to any sudden movement or sound. Catching the gentlest creak of wood, he imagined a dainty bare foot, the careful tread of a woman trying to avoid capture. He was aware of his own breathing, the hushed sigh of the wool carpet underfoot. To control his nerves, he composed headlines. *Ravished, She Took Her Revenge! Manhattan Mayerling—Bizarre Murder-Suicide on the Upper West Side.*

At the second-floor landing, he saw two closed doors, one on either side of the hallway. It seemed unwise to proceed without warning, so he called, "Hello? I'm not the police, I'm here to help . . ."

There was no answer. Hiding? he wondered. Or waiting?

Or dead. That was also a possibility.

Approaching the room that looked out on the street, he listened at the door, then turned the knob to discover a sort of reception area. He was intensely relieved to see no corpse. The room was sparsely furnished, offering no place to hide unless the killer were slim enough to conceal herself behind one of the enormous palms.

Crossing the hall, he opened the second door. Judging from the desk and bookshelves, this was Elwell's study. The contents of the bookshelves were largely ornamental: Chinese vases, exotic daggers, animal figurines. Among the books displayed: *Elwell on Bridge, Elwell's Advanced Bridge, Bridge Axioms and Laws.* Of course—like everyone else in New York, the murdered man was a writer.

There was an enormous cabinet in polished teak, with dozens of small drawers, each with a tiny brass handle. With his pinky, Markey drew one of the drawers open. Inside was a deck of cards, the one-eyed jack of hearts on top. Mystified, he opened another drawer to find another deck, this one still fresh in its box. Games were all around the room, he realized. Chess and checkers, as well as Puzzle Peg, a wooden Japanese brain teaser, a jigsaw featuring an aircraft—Markey thought it was the British Bristol. On the wall, a set of Ogden's Optical Illusion cigarette cards. Remembering the illusion Elwell had presented of himself the night before, Markey thought the dying man was quite the trickster.

Hands raised, he continued up the stairs, saying, "My name is Morris Markey, I'm a neighbor. Is there anyone who needs help?" If the girl was innocent, she might be too frightened to call out. If guilty, he didn't want her to feel cornered and do something desperate. He imagined her disheveled, snarling, gun pointed at his head. He imagined wrestling her for it, winning and pinning her to the floor. He would visit her in jail, take down her story, first the defiant lies, then the tearstained confession. Her dreadful life story, deprived childhood, a brute of a father. He would write articles that got her acquitted, sparking envy in fellow newshounds and sob sisters. He imagined taking her back to Virginia to meet his parents, his father saying, "Well, this is about what we expected when you went to New York . . ."

Coming to the top floor, he spotted a hatch with a string overhead. He didn't see how the girl could reach it without a ladder, and he didn't see one. Two bedrooms, one at each end of the hall. If he was going to find her—alive or dead—it would be here. Taking a deep breath, he entered the larger room.

It was precisely what his mother would imagine a degenerate's room to be. The bed had a lavender satin canopy. An enormous champagne bottle, now empty, stood atop the collected works of Oscar Wilde. There was a chair covered in crimson brocade, next to it an ornate cigarette box in the shape of a piano. When Markey raised the alabaster lid, wanting to see what the dead man smoked, the first few notes of "Yankee Doodle" sounded. Hastily, he let the lid fall.

A quick search revealed no body. An armoire held only clothes. Breathing more easily, Markey made notes. The bed had not been slept in—but it had been lain upon. The purple-and-black bedspread bore the imprint of Elwell's body, the lace boudoir pillows the indentation of his head. There was an empty hanger in the closet where the scarlet robe had hung, a set of evening clothes neatly folded on the chair. The dress shirt lay on top; Markey noticed the cuff had a gray smudge. Looking closely at it, he saw that it was not city soot but pencil. Someone had scribbled on it. Whatever the message, it had not been to Elwell's liking. He had rubbed out the words, leaving only a faint trace of a *Y* or *V*.

On the dresser he was surprised to find several items appropriate to a theatrical dressing room. Face powder, toilet water, hairpins, brow stick, rouge, peroxide, vanishing cream, and an array of perfumes. Mr. Elwell's hair, a rich brunet with red tints, sat on a polished wig stand.

A silver tray held a selection of tiepins and cuff links. No base metals for Mr. Elwell; the jewelry was gold, studded with diamonds and sapphires. There was also a money clip, strained to its limit with twenties. A thief could easily sweep up the lot and be thousands of dollars richer. Whatever the housekeeper might think, robbery wasn't the motive.

In the center of the room was a low, round card table, crowded with framed photographs arranged in concentric circles. Every single image, a beautiful smiling woman. Markey thought he recognized one or two of them—that blonde was an actress, the redhead the sort who got herself in the papers. Several of the women had been photographed in a state of undress. The pictures were inscribed. One woman whose beach attire revealed her powerful thighs had written, *Carlsbad, 1913.* Other messages were more personal. *I adore you!* from Dalla. *Swooningly yours*, vowed Amelia. And a simple *My darling* from Viola. Spook had mentioned Elwell's taste for lovely women, but this was peculiar. The collection felt oddly impersonal, like china dolls lined up on a shelf.

By the nightstand, he found the gleaming white teeth of last night in a water glass. There was a framed photo of a boy, perhaps ten years old; a son, most likely. Also on the nightstand, a matchbook of azure blue, the name RITZ-CARLTON stamped in gold. Markey felt sure Mrs. Larsen would have tidied it away, given the chance. That meant that Elwell had spent part of his last night on earth at the Ritz hotel. He had also, judging by a discarded program in the wastebasket, been to the *Midnight Frolic* at the New Amsterdam Theatre.

Examining Elwell's bedroom, he wondered: Had the girl in the green dress discovered these pictures and shot her cheating lover through the eyes? The undisturbed bedclothes and the false teeth argued against this being a place of seduction; this was Elwell's private chamber. But as Bluebeard might have said, women could get inside such rooms with fatal consequences. And there was another bedroom.

Crossing the hall, he positioned himself to the right of the door. "Miss? There's no need to be frightened." He showed his empty hands. "I'm going to step in now . . ."

As he entered, he saw at once this was a lady's bedroom. Everything was pink: the crepe de chine coverlet, the lace pillows, even the frilled lamp. A pair of pink pajamas was laid out at the end of the bed. The bed was made; the coverlet and pillows showed no sign of disarray. There was no blood on the floor, no body. But there was a closet. An excellent hiding place for a killer.

Markey steeled himself. The room was small; if the killer tried to shoot her way past, he would be an easy target. Careful to keep to one side, he opened the door. Then stood paralyzed by what he saw.

It was a treasure trove of intimate femininity: satin, silk, lace, feathers. Forgetting caution, Markey took in the sight of cascading robes and dancing teddies. A silver tray on a low bench offered other garments: filmy stockings, the delicate pooch of bra, the suggestive dangle of garter. He swore he could still smell the skin caressed by these garments, the teddy that clung to the waist, the lace of it brushing the buttocks. The garters that tickled the thigh, the bra that cupped the breasts. There was an array of colors—cream, red, black, pink. No green, he noted distractedly. Or silver.

Closing the door, he thought nothing about these rooms made sense. Two boudoirs, barely used. An all-but-dead body downstairs. Doors locked. No gun.

Going to the window, he drew his finger along the sill, finding dust. In none of the rooms had he seen an open window. The killer hadn't got out that way. There was the cellar to be checked, but he suspected the police wouldn't find anyone there either. Except for Mrs. Larsen and the dying Elwell, Markey felt he was alone in the house.

A siren told him the ambulance was near. He took a last glance under the bed, then hurried down the stairs, building his story as he went: lady in the dollar-green dress, face powder, Ritz-Carlton, playing cards, the lingerie (although he'd have to put that a different way). The women—Viola, Amelia, Dalla. That wooden head with the scalp of a wig.

Coming to the first floor, he saw Mrs. Larsen and heard the shouts of men outside. The story would remain his for only a few more seconds. Breathless on the landing, he said, "Last night, I saw Elwell with a girl in a green-and-silver dress."

Mrs. Larsen had been almost smiling with relief—he was unhurt; the ambulance was here. His announcement confused her. She stepped toward him as if to hear better.

"A girl in a green dress, I think she may have shot him. Do you know her name?"

The bell rang furiously. Distracted, Mrs. Larsen went to open the door. Two men stumbled in with a stretcher, and Markey knew the time for asking questions of Mrs. Larsen was done. The men were clumsy. One of them had a cigarette in his mouth. As they barged into the parlor, Markey called, "Gentle with his head, he's still with us. And mind where you step, there's evidence on the floor."

Mrs. Larsen was staring at him in dismay. He became aware of the notebook in his hand.

"You are not a doctor," she said slowly. "You never wanted to help. You only wanted to get inside. To *see*."

He decided not to add to his sins by lying.

Chapter Four

Outside, a crowd had gathered. Women stood on stoops, arms folded, craning their necks as if to see the truth of what was going on. The carpenters from next door had ceased hammering and come out to look. Jost Otten, the milkman, stood at a respectful distance by his wagon. Markey saw several of his neighbors out on the street. Arthur Griswold, who lived in the apartment directly above him, watched from his window.

He removed his hat as the stretcher was loaded into the ambulance. Out of the corner of his eye, he saw policemen headed toward the house. He also spotted two men in straw hats hurrying after them. He had been in newspapers long enough to recognize his colleagues. These two would be held at bay—but not for long. He needed to talk to the milkman. He needed to talk to the workmen.

He wanted to follow the ambulance to Flower Hospital—on East Sixty-Fourth, it was closest.

But first he needed to call in the story. There was a phone in his building; his landlady, properly approached, allowed tenants to use it. Mrs. Cecchetti was in the entry hall, watching the scene through the glass. She was an Italian woman in her early fifties, leery of anything that smacked of trouble. Removing his hat for a second time, Markey said, "Good morning, Mrs. Cecchetti. May I use the telephone?"

"Is it about across the street?"

He nodded.

"... Dead?"

"Yes, ma'am." She indicated the end of the hallway where the phone sat. Thanking her, he snatched it up and asked to be connected to the *Daily News*. For what seemed like ages, he listened to empty air; then he heard *"Daily News"* and answered, "Story." Told to go ahead, he said, "Headline: 'Joseph Elwell Mysteriously Slain' ... No, wait."

He revised: "'Elwell, Bridge Authority and Racehorse Owner, Mysteriously Slain in His Home.' Subhead: 'Gun Missing.'"

"... missing," the editor echoed.

"'Wealthy whist whiz Joseph Elwell was discovered by his housekeeper, Mrs. Larsen.'"

"That an *O* or *E*?"

"I don't know. '... by his housekeeper, Mrs. Larsen, at 8:30 this morning, a single bullet hole through the center of his forehead.' Now this I want in bold type. You ready?"

"Ready."

"'Every door and window in the house was locked.' New paragraph. 'The housekeeper said the doors were both locked when she arrived. But a milk bottle had been placed inside the vestibule, meaning the milkman was able to get in. Elwell was reading his mail when he was shot. One of the letters had yesterday's stamp on it.'"

"I don't follow," said the editor.

"It means Elwell opened the door to both the milkman and the postman. Which means he might have also opened his door to the person who killed him. He was sitting down, going through his mail when he was shot. That means he was killed by someone he knew. Someone he didn't fear. Possibly someone who was already inside the house."

"Who would that be?"

"I'm getting to that. Last paragraph. 'The police discovered photographs of several beautiful women in the dead man's bedroom. They want to speak with the ladies in question. In addition, they seek an auburn-haired young woman in a green dress who was seen entering the house of the murdered man just hours before the fatal shooting.'"

"Who's your witness for the sheba in green?"

"I am," said Markey. "I saw her go in at two o'clock this morning. He's got two bedrooms, one for guests, one for himself. My bet is she went to Elwell's bedroom this morning, saw the pictures, realized she was part of a harem . . ."

"And shot him through the eyes." The editor sucked his teeth. "Girls these days. Cutting their hair, drinking gin, killing people."

"It's good, right?"

"How you going to find this girl in green?"

"Elwell was at the Ritz last night, then he went to the *Frolic*. I'll head over to the hotel, see if anyone saw him with her. Also, he might have been in debt . . ."

"Pretty girl. Gun," said the editor and hung up.

For a few seconds, Markey basked in the satisfaction of a story well delivered. Then the difficulties of his mission became clear. He could not simply stroll into the Ritz-Carlton and demand to speak to anyone who had seen Joseph Elwell last night. Since arriving in the city, he had dutifully courted beat cops, morgue attendants, and one hotel maid, but she worked at the Elliott, which was hardly the Ritz. He had not yet begun wooing the higher-echelon doormen, bellhops, and stage door keepers. Now he would have to start. Who would have encountered Elwell at the Ritz? Waiters, musicians . . . A powder room attendant might remember the girl . . .

Murmuring ideas as he jotted them down, he was startled by a man shouting, "Hey, loudmouth! Keep it down, you think everyone wants to hear you talk?"

Markey looked up to see the angry face of Arthur Griswold, his upstairs neighbor. It was not the first time he had seen it, not the first time he had heard the complaint. The epithet *was* new; in the past, Griswold had called him "big feet." As in "Hey, big feet—watch where you stomp." Coming home, he often would find Griswold waiting to shout at him from his window. A long, milky man in his early forties with sparse hair, thin lips, and pale gray eyes, he talked fast, leaving Markey no chance to defend himself. It seemed to be accepted in New York: Someone could take issue with you for the most irrational of reasons. Question a man's right to be angry over a matter of mere proximity, and the city would fall.

"Every night I hear you," Griswold accused. "Now during the day, too?"

"I apologize for the call. But I don't see how you hear me at night, Mr. Griswold. I take off my shoes the moment I step inside the door."

"Last night, two AM, I heard you thump-thump-thump, clodding around down there."

"I'll try to be quieter," Markey offered, wanting to be done with the man.

"Don't *try!*" snapped Griswold and disappeared behind his door with a slam. Dispirited, Markey took refuge in his notebook. Who did he know who could get him inside the Ritz—a place for the successful and celebrated, the exuberant and extravagant?

The word *extravagant* reminded him: He did know someone in that world. A recent arrival, maybe, but one so gaudy in his beauty and success that no one questioned his right to go anywhere he damn well pleased. Flipping to a fresh page, he wrote *Fitzgerald*.

Where was America's favorite author staying now? Spook had said the Fitzgeralds were no longer at the Biltmore, but surely the couple's life was too glamorous to accommodate anything so mundane as house hunting. Why shouldn't they have landed at the Ritz? And the Fitzgeralds were said to be passionate theatergoers. Maybe they had crossed paths with Elwell and his lovely, lethal companion at the *Frolic*.

Taking up the phone, Markey called his friend at work. Spook at work was not an easy man to find. Markey was not sure what a stockbroker did, but he gathered that a lot of it was taking people out to lunch—at least that was the part at which Spook excelled. It took several calls to track him down at the Colony.

"Yes, hello, who's this?" Spook asked when he came to the phone. He had to shout because the room was noisy.

"Me—Markey. I'm sorry to interrupt . . ."

"No, no. Makes me seem important. The man in demand. What can I do for you, sucker, I mean supplicant, I mean pal . . ."

"Do you know where Fitzgerald's staying?"

"Oh, *God*—why?"

The *why* was two things: Why did Markey wish to know and why was Markey annoying him by talking about Fitzgerald. Markey should know, Spook seemed to say, that he was sick of the subject. For a moment, Markey considered telling Spook that Joseph Elwell, the wizard of whist and owner of yellow roadsters, had been murdered. But Spook got yakky when drinking, and he couldn't risk it.

"I need to talk to him about something for the paper."

Spook sighed. "They got tossed from the Biltmore because people complained about the parties. Then they went to the Plaza but got thrown out there, too. I think now . . ."

Markey held his breath.

"Now they might be at the Ritz, but you better get there fast before they set something on fire or dance on the tables or steal all the spoons."

"They did that?"

"Oh, they're just the funnest of the fun, the cat's pajamas, the bee's knees," said Spook with a bitterness that made Markey swallow. "Look, I have to part a fool and his money. Good luck with the boy wonder."

Markey replaced the receiver on its hook. Mindful of the wrath of Griswold, he crept across the hall and down to his room to fetch the good suit his mother had given him when he left home for a second time. Knowing that she had been equally scared for him on both occasions, he did not allow himself to worry that the suit was not good enough for the Ritz. It had been good enough for his mother, and that, he told himself, was all that should matter.

Chapter Five

The Ritz-Carlton was located on Madison and Forty-Sixth Street, a part of town where Markey felt shy about walking on the street, let alone into a luxury hotel. His first impression of the twelve-story building was of a bank vault, a massive and impregnable structure that contained infinite riches. Entering on the side street, he bumbled into an unexpectedly small foyer. The floor was covered with a floral Turkish carpet, the walls lined with mirrors. Towering palms brushed his ear. The sharp look of a sprinting bellboy told him he was not supposed to be there; the space was small precisely so riffraff should not linger. If he wished not to be seen as riffraff, he would have to keep moving.

And so he did, straight into a vast open palace so wondrous, he forgot to be blasé and stared open-mouthed at its beauty. Above him was a ceiling of glass and bronze. Surrounding him was a garden of palms and fragrant flowers. The walls were cream and pale green. Somewhere, a hidden orchestra played. White lattices enhanced the effect of a sumptuous greenhouse for the soul.

Dazed and spinning, he made his way to the front desk. It took some time for the clerk to look up from a notepad on which nothing seemed to be written. Markey wasn't sure of the correct way to request service. *Excuse me*? A polite cough? Tap the little bell to the right of the man it should summon? He waited, a pleasant smile on his face.

Finally, the clerk said, "Yes, may I help you?"

Markey stretched his smile. "Mr. Morris Markey to see—"

"I beg your pardon, who?" The clerk inclined his head.

"A . . . Mr. Morris Markey?" Hating the note of doubt, he asserted himself. "To see Mr. Scott Fitzgerald."

"Are you expected?"

"I am not. But he will know the name."

The clerk was not persuaded. Summoning a note of asperity, Markey said, "If you could call Mr. Fitzgerald's room."

The clerk raised an eyebrow and reached for the phone. After a moment, he barked, "Ah, yes, Mrs. Fitzgerald, a Mr. Morris Markey is at the front desk for you. Should I let him up?"

Markey panicked. The recently acquired Mrs. Fitzgerald would have no idea who he was. "Please say that I'm a friend of her husband's," he whispered. "I . . ."

What was the one thing Fitzgerald might remember about him?

"I write for the newspapers."

The clerk gave Markey a dark look; he was not supposed to be speaking. To the receiver, he said, "He says he is with the newspapers." A pause. "Yes, Mrs. Fitzgerald."

He set the phone down. "Room 1023."

"1023 . . . 1023 . . . 1023 . . ."

In the elevator, Markey repeated the number, terrified he would forget and have to face the desk clerk again. Arriving at the tenth floor, he discovered his fear was groundless. The Fitzgeralds were unseen but made their presence known. Through the richly carpeted corridors, he heard the scratch of a phonograph, the boozy moan of trumpets, and the lament of Mamie Smith as she sang:

> Now I can read his letters
> I sure can't read his mind
> I thought he's lovin' me
> He's leavin' all the time

A few guests had opened their doors, either hoping to locate the source of the disturbance or kill it with a glare. Smiling apologetically, Markey followed the music until he reached room 1023. The record was so loud, he pounded harder than manners dictated. For a short while, all he heard was Mamie: *Now I got the crazy blues . . . Since my baby went away . . .*

The door opened. A child beamed up at him. "Mr. Morris!"

It had been some time since anyone looked so delighted to see him. It was not, he realized, that she was so specially glad to see *him*, but that she seemed to have more capacity for delight than most people. He wasn't remotely surprised she'd gotten his name wrong, but her enthusiasm was unexpected—and infectious. He saw now that she was an adult—and indeed Southern, judging from the blithe way she dispensed with the *R* in his name. Rapidly, he added up the elements that had made him mistake her for a child: her bobbed golden hair, the eagerness in her green eyes, the fullness of her cheeks, the clarity of her brow. It was an uncommonly broad face, as if two people had been incompletely merged, possessing all the changeable vitality of double brains, double heart, double appetite and will. He saw why Scott had called her the most beautiful girl in Alabama, also why Dottie had tutted. Personally, he thought she deserved the title.

She was not entirely dressed. Covered, somewhat, in men's pajama bottoms and a silk robe that looped at the waist. A sudden gesture and it would fall open, and she seemed a girl given to sudden gestures. Had he interrupted them husband-and-wifeing? She was chewing gum, so he thought probably not. When she took his hand and pulled him inside, he felt both welcomed and joined in conspiracy.

The Fitzgeralds had not just taken a suite at the Ritz; they had taken it over. The living room was the size of his entire apartment. Small plates with the remnants of sandwiches, bits of cheese, smears of chocolate and caviar sat abandoned on side tables, chairs, the floor, the top of a grand piano. Flutes and highballs were everywhere he looked. The ashtrays were full, and most of the plateware held cigarette stubs. Near the gramophone, a pile of records had been knocked over, sliding like playing cards across the carpet.

From the other room, he heard a man's voice declaim, "And what are your plans now?"

His heart sank; another reporter was here.

But then the same voice answered in a lighter tone, "I'll be darned if I know. The scope and depth and breadth of my writings lie in the lap of the gods."

Mrs. Fitzgerald tugged on Markey's hand. "Scott's interviewing himself for some article. I'm trying to draw him out."

She marched to the gramophone—the heavy silk tie swung dangerously—and turned up the volume.

His anxiety escalating with the volume, Markey called, "Mrs. Fitzgerald . . ."

"Zelda, please!" she shouted.

"Zelda, I . . ."

A sudden bang made him jump; *gun* was his first thought. But then he saw it was simply a slammed door. Scott was with them. Ignoring Markey, he screamed "Turn it off!" at the exact same moment that Zelda snapped the volume to nothing. Husband and wife gazed at each other. Zelda rocked on her feet. Markey felt sure that something—highballs, gramophone records, bodies—would be hurled at any moment.

Was it possible Fitzgerald had become even *more* handsome? Like his wife, Fitzgerald was only partly dressed, wearing trousers and an undershirt. His feet were bare. His hair had probably been combed that morning, but in his temper, a lock had fallen over his beauteous man-of-genius brow. The eyes showed the bruising of late nights, but it hardly mattered. Not more handsome, thought Markey. It was just that now his looks belonged to F. Scott Fitzgerald, and it was better to look like F. Scott Fitzgerald than anyone else.

Hand out, he took a step forward. "Morris Markey. We met at a party a while ago, I don't know that you would remember."

Sensing her husband's ambivalence, Zelda said, "He's with the newspapers."

"I know," said Fitzgerald. "What I don't know is why he's here." Suddenly he smiled. "I don't *mind*—I just like to be kept informed."

There were teeth behind the smile, a reminder that fast chat was not only desirable; it was essential. If Markey was going to demand the attention of a man bold enough to interview himself, he had to earn it. He was suddenly conscious that he had not attended university, while Fitzgerald had gone to Princeton.

How he said it mattered. The words, also the tone, had to be right. He could not sound too eager for their interest. Settling his hands in his pockets, he said, "This morning I saw a man shot through the head. I thought maybe you might know him."

Zelda instantly dropped to the couch opposite him. Fitzgerald was more skeptical, but sat beside his wife, nonetheless. They looked like siblings, thought Markey. Their twinned attention was the most intoxicating thing he had ever experienced.

"Oh, my," breathed Zelda. "Was it Luddie?"

"Alec," guessed Fitzgerald.

"George!"

Husband and wife pointed to each other in agreement.

"It was a man by the name of Joseph Elwell." They did not know the name and their enthusiasm dimmed. "He was an authority on bridge. He was at this hotel last night. I'm hoping you saw him."

It sounded foolish even to him; hundreds of people passed through the Ritz on any given evening.

"I'm particularly interested in the girl he was with. She had reddish-brown bobbed hair, and she was wearing a green-and-silver dress that looked like shredded-up dollar bills. Her name might have been Amelia. Or June?"

Scott lifted his eyebrows to an unseen comrade. *The dullness of some people.*

"Viola . . . ?" tried Markey.

At this, Zelda sat straight up. "Not Viola Kraus?"

He didn't know, but it was an opening, and he said without hesitation, "Yes."

Zelda settled her chin on her fist, her elbow on her knee. "Was he very old? This man who was killed?"

Startled that she had seen Elwell's true age when he had not, he said, "Yes."

Zelda slapped her husband's arm. "We *do* know him! We met him last night at that party in the Japanese garden. Elwell . . ."

She looked back at Markey to confirm the name. When he nodded, she continued, "Elwell was there with Viola. There was also Viola's sister . . ."

She closed her eyes, murmuring, "Wait, I'll remember it, wait . . ."

Her eyes popped open. "*Selma!* And Selma's very strange husband, who sat there, staring at me. Viola's divorce had come through. They were celebrating. I remember wanting to tell Selma, 'You might as well go on and get rid of your husband, too, it's not like he adds anything.' Only we hadn't known them long and I thought it might be rude."

She smiled at Markey, alerting him to the fact that she knew very well it would be rude, but she'd wanted to all the same.

Keeping his excitement in check, he asked, "Does Viola Kraus have brown hair by any chance? Slightly red in some lights?"

"Why, yes, she does as a matter of fact. Viola's supposed to be the most beautiful girl in New York."

Oh, what a headline, he thought. *Most Beautiful Girl in New York Kills Card Cad.* "Was she wearing a green dress? With little shards of shiny silver material . . . ?"

But in his elation, he had missed that Zelda had expected a compliment; when a girl calls another girl the most beautiful, he rebuked himself, she counts on being contradicted. Back home, he wouldn't have made that mistake.

Now she gave Markey her profile, saying to her husband, "We all went to the *Frolic* afterward, *you* remember. There was that girl who wore nothing but balloons."

Fitzgerald shook his head, suggesting he was the last person his wife should expect to remember anything about last night. He looked longingly at the other room. Markey felt he wanted to get back to interviewing himself.

But Zelda had mentioned the *Frolic*, which Elwell had attended, judging by the program in the wastebasket. Determined to win her back, Markey turned to let her know she was now the sole focus of his attention and saw the green eyes brighten. "The *Frolic*—is that the Ziegfeld show at the New Amsterdam Theatre?"

"The New Amsterdam, yes! And . . ."

She withdrew, crossed her hands in her lap. "I don't know if I should say."

Matching her rhythm, he said, "Yet I feel you want to."

Fitzgerald rose abruptly. "*I* feel I should get back to work."

Zelda's eyes followed her husband as he stood. Her hands tightened in her lap. She was enjoying the game and he was leaving, not caring if it meant leaving her as well. Markey waited to see what she would do.

"Well, you go on, then," she said lightly. "Tell me where you're from, Mr. Morris."

"Richmond."

"Practically a Yankee." She dimpled to let him know she was teasing. "Why do you care so much if Viola wore a green dress?"

"I came home around two in the morning, and I saw Joseph Elwell go into his house with a beautiful girl in green. Six hours later, he was dead. It was early in the morning. The doors and windows were locked, so I can't think it was someone who came into the house . . ."

"But someone who was already *in* the house. Hm."

She looked away, gnawing her lower lip slightly as she pondered. She had remembered something, he could tell.

"What?"

"No, nothing." She turned back to him. "Do you really think Viola's beautiful?"

This time he was prepared. "Not the most beautiful girl in New York by any stretch."

Her smile broadened. "I don't remember what Viola was wearing, but she's staying at this hotel. She gave me her room number last night, said I must stop by. We *could* pay her a condolence call."

He wasn't sure what was more wonderful: the sudden proximity of Viola Kraus or Zelda Fitzgerald's use of the word *we*. Careful to maintain nonchalance, he said, "That would be the polite thing to do."

Suddenly Fitzgerald was back in the room. "It is not the polite thing. We don't know this woman," he told his wife. "You can't just call on her."

Markey tried to divine the source of the writer's irritation. Publicly, Fitzgerald delighted in an arrogant disregard for the old-fashioned. If it had been said, thought, or done before him, it wasn't worth a thing. Why so proper now? Then he realized: His wife had distracted him from himself, and now she had the nerve to be excited about something other than him.

Zelda frowned, calculating. "I believe I can get on the elevator. I believe I can knock on a door once, perhaps even twice. I *think* I remember her name . . . Yes, I do believe I can just call on her."

"You're going to go up there and accuse this woman of murder," Fitzgerald clarified.

"Well, that depends."

"On?" Scott and Markey said it at the same time.

"On if she did it or not." Zelda stood, the broad silk sleeves of her robe flapping like newfound wings. "You wait for me, Mr. Morris. I won't be long."

"It's Markey."

She pirouetted, confused.

"Morris Markey . . . is my name."

"Oh, is it?"

The news seemed to devastate her; for a moment, he thought she was so disappointed, she might give up on him altogether.

Then she said, "I suppose you can't help it," and shot off to the bedroom.

"How cheerfully she speaks of getting rid of husbands," said Fitzgerald.

Sheepish, Markey said, "She really would be helping me, if she could get me in to speak with Miss Kraus."

"No, you'd be helping me," Fitzgerald corrected, suddenly amenable, "by keeping her occupied. She gets bored when I write."

"I do get bored!" came the confirmation from the bedroom.

"Someone has to pay for the suite, my sweet," he called back. Turning to Markey, he said, "So you think pretty Viola shot her decrepit lover between the eyes."

Wary, Markey said, "Maybe."

"Why shoot your lover when you've just divorced your husband?" Fitzgerald began to pace, waving his forefinger like a metronome as he spoke. "Maybe . . . maybe Viola didn't shoot him. Maybe Viola's *husband* was jealous of Elwell. Resented him for stealing the woman he loves."

Suddenly he stopped, widening his eyes for dramatic effect. "He knows he's lost her, but he had thought he could win her back. Now—the final decree sends him over the edge. He sees them all laughing, drinking, celebrating the end of his marriage. *Celebrating* his broken heart! He sees his wife with his rival. It's too much, he cracks . . ."

Markey smiled uneasily. He didn't appreciate the most famous writer in the country nibbling at his story. He also felt there was a warning in Fitzgerald's tale of a spurned husband taking revenge. But then he realized jealousy was not a factor here. The regional bond aside, Fitzgerald viewed him as too beaky and shabby to enchant Zelda. Without the murder, Markey held no charm for her. It was the dead body, not his, that attracted her.

Fitzgerald was still chewing over the murder. Rubbing his thumb over his chin, he said, "Come to think of it, the husband *was* there last night."

"The one Viola Kraus divorced?"

"Yes, he's from Minnesota originally. But what's intriguing . . ."

The bedroom door swung open. Zelda appeared in a black suit and cloche. Markey was vague on the meaning of the word *chic*, but now he felt that if pushed to define it, he could point to Zelda Fitzgerald in this suit. The word *French* came to mind, also *expensive*. Her right to go anywhere she pleased was unassailable. In short, she had become the quintessential New Yorker. He had thought her eyes green, but now they seemed the silver gray of new coins, as bright as the gold hair curling along her cheek.

"Scott made me buy it," she said of the outfit. "It's the dreariest thing I own. Perfectly suitable for a bereavement call."

She waved a finger at Fitzgerald. "Never mind about the husband, you let me tell him about that."

Chastened, Fitzgerald took her hand, as if unsure of the wisdom of letting her go. "Alec begs audience, you know. And there's Bishop. Nathan, if you absolutely *must*."

"Those are all your friends. I want one of my own."

Their voices were low and intimate. Watching from the sofa, Markey felt they had forgotten he was there. Scott leaned in and whispered something in his wife's ear. She smiled, giving the slightest nod.

Then she presented herself to Markey. "Well, Mr. Morris Markey, shall we see if Viola Kraus is your green-gowned murderess?"

He stood, offered his arm. "By all means, Mrs. Fitzgerald."

"Zelda," she reminded him.

"Zelda."

Chapter Six

In the elevator, Markey remembered they were about to confront a woman who had possibly committed murder mere hours ago and whispered, "We should have a plan." Zelda shushed him. The cab bounced to a halt. She was out of the elevator the moment the gate was pulled back, moving swiftly in her black smock suit down corridors and around corners. He had to increase his stride to keep up, a thing he rarely had to do.

To her back, he said, "If she's just killed someone, she might be in a desperate mood . . ."

"Maybe she didn't kill him."

"Then what if she doesn't know he's dead? I shouldn't like to be the one who breaks the news."

"Shouldn't you?" This was tossed over her shoulder—query or accusation, he wasn't sure.

"But she won't know me. Who am I meant to be?"

Abruptly, Zelda stopped in front of room 1434. "You'll have to decide that for yourself, Mr. Markey."

Then she knocked several times in quick succession.

There was no answer. He and Zelda raised eyebrows. Markey wondered if Miss Kraus was fetching the .45 she'd used to kill Elwell. He was getting that light, fizzy feeling in the arches of his feet; there was a hissing somewhere, like a gas leak.

Then he heard a tremulous voice. "Yes? Who is it?"

"It's Zelda Fitzgerald, Miss Kraus. We met last night. I . . . I heard the news. I was calling to see if you were all right."

The door opened, and a petite brunette flung herself on Zelda, crying, "Oh, I can't *believe* it!" In her hand, no gun, only a sodden handkerchief. Clinging to Zelda, she swept them into her suite. The most beautiful girl in New York was a tiny thing with a shining cap of auburn hair and large brown eyes. Still in her pajamas, she wore a kimono of pink silk with gold and white blooms and had the darting restless energy of a hummingbird. At the moment, she was very pale, with delicate lines about her mouth and across her brow. Comparing her to last night's vision, Markey had doubts. She did resemble the girl in the photograph, the one inscribed "my darling." The hair color was similar. But the girl who had emerged from the yellow roadster had been taller, more . . . magnificent. However, it had been night, and he had been drunk and in the mood to be smitten. He looked for a discarded green-and-silver dress but did not see one.

Unlike the Fitzgeralds' suite, these rooms were immaculate. Each rose silk cushion on the sofa stood on point; the black lacquer surface of the piano gleamed. Heavy gold drapes had been pulled back and neatly tied with a navy-blue cord to reveal the panorama of the city. Everywhere, flowers of various stages of bloom: drooping roses, dazzling peonies, lilies of many hues. The carpets felt freshly vacuumed, the crystal ashtrays clean and sparkling. Either Miss Kraus entertained less or she tipped better. The divorce settlement must have been generous. Or she had family money. He tried to place her within his understanding of New York money. She had a fragile perfection that suggested she had been sheltered in the finest nests. But while she might refer to the palaces of Park Avenue and Newport as "Dickie's old hovel" or "Gertie's darling bungalow," he suspected she was not old money. She was a touch too vital; she hadn't been washed out by generations of cautious breeding. Which meant, perhaps, she was less secure on her perch, especially since her divorce . . .

The women sat on the sofa, hands clasped, speaking in fragments of shock and bewilderment. Seated on a chair to the right of the sofa, Markey thought their intimacy startling for two people who had met yesterday. Of course women were good at making friends. Or else Viola was keen to impress her audience with the depth of her anguish. On a nearby table, a photograph of the murdered man lounging at the beach in an elegant straw boater served as a makeshift memorial. Markey saw no newspapers in the room. Which meant someone had called Viola Kraus with the news that Joseph Elwell was dead. Or she knew it because she had shot him.

Aware that his first words could win or lose her, Markey inched forward. "How did you find out, Miss Kraus, if you don't mind my asking?"

Viola Kraus's neat little head jerked in his direction. "I'm terribly sorry." Her vowels became more clipped as she asserted her rank. "But who are you?"

Smoothly, Zelda came to his rescue. "This is Mr. Morris Markey. He's a neighbor of Mr. Elwell's and he was at the house just after it happened. He was so distraught, he raced over to tell me and Scott. So naturally, I raced right up here to you."

"You saw Joe?" Viola Kraus took a hard hold of his wrist. "Please—tell me everything. When I called the house this morning, Mrs. Larsen said Joe had been shot and they'd taken him to the hospital."

"Yes, that's right."

"But it makes no *sense*, who would shoot darling Joe? I keep thinking it must be a mistake."

With the Red Cross, Markey had written countless letters home to families. He knew how to confirm the worst with sensitivity, although if he thought bluntness would serve him here, he would use it. But he wanted Viola Kraus to see him as a friend.

"I'm afraid it's not a mistake, Miss Kraus."

Her lip trembled. "But they took him in an ambulance, that means there's some hope, doesn't it?"

"The wound he had, you wouldn't want him to survive it."

"Did he say anything?" she whispered. "Did he mention me at all?"

Concern for the dying man or fear that he had accused her with his last breath?

"He was unable to speak." He thought he saw her shoulders ease. "May I ask what time you telephoned? I was at the house around nine o'clock . . ."

She shrugged helplessly. "A little while ago. I . . . I only just got up. We were out very late last night."

"If you saw Mr. Elwell late last night, what did you need to say to him?"

A frost came over her as she began to suspect he wasn't a concerned neighbor. "We were to go away for a weekend of golf. Myself, Mr. Elwell, my sister, and her husband . . ."

Unseen by Miss Kraus, Zelda rolled her eyes wildly to remind Markey of the strangeness of Viola's brother-in-law.

"I called to tell Mr. Elwell that we would pick him up this afternoon. Only to hear . . ." She became tearful again. "What makes it worse is we'd had such a marvelous *time*." Again, she appealed to Zelda. "Wasn't it? A magical evening last night?"

"I do feel sad I didn't get to say goodbye to him and now he's dead. I remember seeing you and Selma when we left, but I didn't see Mr. Elwell . . ."

Viola Kraus withdrew. "No, that can't be. We left before Joe."

Perplexed, Zelda said, "Huh!" She widened her eyes at Markey: *Isn't that odd?* He widened his: *If you say so.*

"Yes, around two o'clock, I got tired and wanted to go home. Joe wanted to go on to another club. So we left without him."

Markey had left that wretched party where Dottie chopped his legs out from under him well after midnight. He calculated the length of the walk, the drag of Eddie Parker, drunk beside him. Then he remembered Griswold raging: *Last night, two AM, I heard you.* That meant he had seen Elwell with the lady in green minutes before.

Which did not square with Viola's account of Elwell leaving the *Frolic*, more than a mile downtown, after two AM. She was lying about the time she had last seen Elwell—why?

He looked at her again, trying to envision her barely clad in shimmering emerald and silver confetti. The images almost merged—but not quite. Wanting to be sure she was not the girl in green, he glanced at the bedroom. The money dress might be on the floor, laid over a chair . . .

He said, "I'm terribly sorry to ask. Might I use the facilities?"

To his disappointment, Viola pointed in the opposite direction of the bedroom. "Of course, there's a powder room down that hall."

There was nothing for it but to go. As he rose, he looked to Zelda, cocking his head to the bedroom. But she was preoccupied with a loose thread on her sleeve and missed it.

Then, as he entered the bathroom, he heard, "Miss Kraus, may I peek at your bedroom? Mr. Fitzgerald gets so particular about having the biggest suite, I suppose to accommodate his *genius*—frankly, I couldn't care less, but I'd love to tell him, once and for all, 'Yes, darling, yours *is* the biggest.'"

Shutting the door, Markey smiled. Incredible—the way she used that air of naughty frankness to do precisely what she wished. The flood of friendly babble gave no quarter. The drawl suggested to people up North, *Don't mind me, I'm not that bright*, flattering and disarming them. When he heard Viola Kraus laugh, "Go right ahead," he thought, *Oh, well* done.

As he searched the bathroom cabinet—finding nothing more incriminating than a bottle of toilet water—he heard Zelda exclaim over the magnificence of the boudoir. "Never mind Mr. Fitzgerald, Marie *Antoinette* would have fits. Well, I'm going to have to lie to him, that's all. I suppose there are worse lies women tell their husbands . . ."

Judging it to be enough time, he flushed and ran his hands under the tap. He returned as Zelda was settling herself back on the sofa. Their eyes met: She had not found the dress. Markey's suspicion was confirmed: Viola Kraus was not the woman in green.

But this raised the question: Did she know about the woman in green?

Sitting down, Markey said, "I confess, I did not know Mr. Elwell particularly well. But the times I did see him, I was struck by his extraordinary style and graciousness. He seemed a man who had everything."

"Oh, *yes*—Joe had a wonderful life. He was the most stylish man you could imagine, everyone adored him. He was laughing and gay, always going to parties. He had properties in New York, Newport, Palm Beach. His horses were going wonderfully well. L'Errant is running at Saratoga in a week's time, and everyone predicts great things. That's why this is all so . . . dreadfully unfair."

Then, perhaps feeling *unfair* was a weak choice of words, she amended, "Such a tragedy. Especially since . . ." She spoke slowly, looking down at her hand, flat on the rose silk surface of the sofa. "Especially since we were engaged to be married."

Zelda said, "Oh," and Markey sighed in sympathy. But he saw no ring on her hand. Sensing his scrutiny, Viola informed him, "Joe and his wife have been separated for years. Three weeks ago, he asked her for a divorce."

Remembering the photograph of the little boy by the bed, Markey made a mental note: wife, child, fiancée. Three was generally an unlucky number in relationships.

But Viola had more to say and she raised her voice to say it. "In fact, I think the police should speak with the about-to-be-*former* Mrs. Elwell."

"Oh, you think she shot him," said Zelda as if they were discussing nothing more serious than a pilfered cherry pie.

"I'm not accusing her. Only I think the police would want to talk to her, that's all."

"Because she's the killing type," said Zelda, wanting clarity on this point.

With sudden viciousness, Viola said, "She's a bitter, dry, stuck-up old thing. Related to the Roosevelts—or so she claims. She brandishes that boy of hers like an IOU."

Markey was careful not to react. But if Viola Kraus was capable of such spite against a woman Elwell hadn't seen in years, what might she feel if she knew about the laughing girl from last night? Was she aware that hers was not the only photograph in Mr. Elwell's bedroom?

Then Zelda said, "Here's what I wonder about: Victor."

The name, raised suddenly and without explanation, made Markey wonder if Mrs. Fitzgerald had confused her company. Then he noticed that Viola Kraus had gone still, like a deer hearing the cock of a rifle.

"It *is* fun, having men fight over you," Zelda added slyly. "But only up to a point."

Markey asked, "There was an argument?"

Viola said no as Zelda said yes.

The telephone rang, and Viola Kraus leapt up, saying, "If you'll excuse me." Markey mouthed, *Victor?* Zelda frowned, trying to make it out, then mouthed something that looked like *up end*. Markey had no idea what an *up end* might be and shook his head.

Then he recalled her words to Scott: "Never mind about the husband, you let me tell him about that." *Up end* meant husband. *Victor* must be Viola's newly divorced spouse, the one from Minnesota who had turned up last night. Markey knocked his fists together to suggest a fight, and Zelda nodded.

He heard Viola say, "Yes, yes, I think we should, if that's what Walter . . ."

Then she glanced over her shoulder. "I'm terribly sorry, but it's my sister."

"Of course," said Zelda rising. "We'll see ourselves out."

The most beautiful girl in New York smiled wanly, then went back to her call. Markey moved slowly, sensed Zelda doing the same. But Viola Kraus was waiting. She wanted them out before she said anything else. *Why?* was a reasonable question.

When the door had closed behind them, he and Zelda walked quickly without speaking. Only when they had turned two corners did Zelda stop short to demand, "Well? Was it her? The girl you saw in the green dress?"

He shook his head. "Unless you found that dress in her room . . ."

"No. But she's guilty, I know it." Resolute, she started toward the elevator.

Amused by her certainty, Markey called after her, "What's your evidence?"

She spun, catching him with her green eyes, and he felt as if a party had started. He could almost hear the blare of a brass band, shrieks of gaiety, the icy rattle of a cocktail shaker. Any moment, it would start raining dollars and confetti, and joyous crowds would burst through the sedate gold-flocked walls of the Ritz, hands in the air, dancing to the glorious despairing wail of Mamie Smith.

"Mr. Markey, have you ever had an orange blossom?"

Chapter Seven

"Start to finish, that woman told us nothing but lies."

In the Japanese tearoom of the Ritz, Zelda Fitzgerald held forth. Markey sipped at his orange blossom. At first taste, it burned, and he coughed, "This has gin. And vermouth, if I'm not mistaken."

"You are not."

He remembered now: She had handed a flask to the waiter as they sat down. "Does the Volstead Act not apply at the Ritz-Carlton?"

"Not for old and treasured guests."

He was about to observe that at twenty, she was hardly old, and could not be considered treasured by New York hotels, having been thrown out of several. But she had gotten him in to see

Viola Kraus, so she was a treasure as far as he was concerned, and if she wanted to drink gin in the afternoon, who was he to argue?

Getting out his notebook, he said, "Start to finish, give me the lies."

"Well, to begin with, last night was *not* a marvelous evening. Not magical nor sublime. Elwell and Viola Kraus did *nothing* but fight. Bicker, bicker, bicker all night long. Like two mangy old hyenas scratching at each other."

She took up her orange blossom. Humming lightly, she took one sip, then another.

"Mangy old hyenas," he prompted.

"It occurs to me, I don't know you at all. Before this goes any further, I shall have to interview you ex*ten*sively."

He was familiar with this tactic. In interviews, some people fired back question for question; it gave them a sense of control. "All right."

"Are you the youngest in your family?"

"Yes."

"I knew it. I am as well. The star always arrives last. What university did you attend?"

"None. Didn't even graduate high school."

"Mr. Markey, even I managed that. Although they did throw me out once, but then I went on a Saturday and they let me back in. Reason you left home? I suppose you know my reason."

"I believe I read something about it."

She blinked, reminding him she was waiting for an answer.

"Well, I signed up . . ."

She yawned dramatically. Despite himself, he was startled. Most people at least pretended respect for military service.

"Then I came here for work."

She dropped her head and snored. The word *brat* was on his tongue when she looked up. "I asked *why*, not what did you do?"

Suddenly he felt himself back on the park bench, thin on air, his heart about to burst. There was nothing about that experience Zelda Fitzgerald would understand, and he groped for a better, nicer truth. What had he hoped for, leaving home? Why had he made that leap?

He asked, "Back home, what's the longest hour of the day?"

She answered immediately. "Three o'clock on a Sunday afternoon."

"When you have to sit in the parlor and be still and be quiet . . ."

". . . and the air doesn't move, and the flies crawl, and the clock just *tick-tick-ticks*, and you smell the dust in the carpet and the polish on the table, and you think, 'Merciful God, will something please *happen*?'"

"Happen," he echoed. "When I was a kid, if you said you needed someone brainless to do something stupid, they'd say, 'Well, there's the Markey boy, he'll take a run at anything.' And I would, too. Just to get away from that Sunday afternoon feeling. It seemed to me most people do the same five things in life: go to school, get a job, get married, get old, and die."

On his notepad, he drew a line over and over so he didn't have to look at her. "And I guess I felt like I was more interesting than most people, so I ought to have a different sort of life."

Embarrassed, he waited for her to laugh at him. His family had. For weeks, they'd called him "Mr. Interesting."

"That"—Zelda leaned forward to tap the back of his hand with her finger—"is the right answer. Congratulations, Mr. Markey, you win the Kewpie doll."

Relieved, he said, "I'll settle for the lies of Viola Kraus."

She nodded, prepared to keep her end of the bargain. "You heard Viola mention Walter? That's her brother-in-law. Rich as anything, wants to write novels. He asked Scott to introduce him to his publisher. Can you believe it? Scott said it was funny right up to the moment he wanted to vomit."

He nodded in appreciation of Scott's wit, then steered her back to the point. "You said Viola and Elwell were fighting."

"Viola was in a mood and Elwell was playing her up. At one point, he got flirty with one of the dancers. Viola picked up one of the pencils they have on the table and wrote her name on his shirt cuff. 'There,' she said, 'you're mine.' Well, you don't write on a man's sleeve if you're sure of him."

Remembering the smudged writing on the pristine white shirt, Markey agreed.

"Then Elwell got talking about his horses and Viola told me, 'He cares more about those horses than he does me.' To which he said, 'They have nicer legs.'"

"I see why she was in a mood."

"No, she was sulky from the moment her husband showed up. By the way, you need to learn how to silently enunciate. *Ictor*," she said with scorn. "There's a *V. Vuh* . . ." She let her lower lip bloom under her teeth. Once, then a second time.

"And Victor is Viola's ex-husband," he said, taking care to exaggerate the *V*s.

"Victor von *Schlegell*—can you believe it?" She showed her tongue as she said the name. "People call him Von. He's blond, extremely Red Baron."

"Is he German?"

She shook her head. "American. He and Scott talked about the fascinating cultural sights of Minnesota—all one and a half of them."

"And Victor showed up at the divorce party last night."

She nodded.

"On purpose?"

"I don't know. He was with a pretty girl in black chiffon."

"Did Viola and Victor speak to each other?"

"He did to her. When they discovered they had come to the same place the night their divorce was final, he made a joke, saying that no matter what the law said, they just couldn't keep away from each other."

"Did Viola find the joke funny?"

"No, she did not."

Markey reflected. Viola had had a rough night. Her former husband had taunted her with another woman, and her hoped-for husband preferred horses to her. That could put a girl in a shooting mood.

"And you say the two men fought?"

"Mm, hm. Viola wanted to get away from Victor, so she and Elwell started to dance. Only Victor took his black chiffon lady onto the dance floor and started . . . almost following them around. At one point, he was practically stepping on their feet."

"Did it come to blows?"

"No blows," she admitted. "But there were some very ugly stares and curt words."

"What were those words? Did you hear?"

"I did. Victor von Schlegell said 'Joe.' And Mr. Elwell said 'Von Schlegell.'" She growled the greetings, giving them great menace.

"So they addressed each other by name," he said gently.

She deflated, shoulders slumping. He found he disliked disappointing her and offered, "It was the *way* they said it."

She nodded. "And Elwell didn't say just 'Von Schlegell.' He said '*Herr* Von Schlegell.'"

Dutifully he made a note of it, although he was not surprised that Elwell would use his rival's name as a chance to sneer. Anti-German feeling was still high two years after the war. Many Muellers and Schmitts had become Millers and Smiths. Berlioz replaced Wagner in opera houses. Dachshunds were dubbed "liberty pups," sauerkraut "liberty cabbage." Back home, the publisher of one newspaper had tried to get the publisher of a rival paper declared an "alien enemy" because his name was Goldbeck. It boosted circulation of both papers for a time.

Zelda said, "And then Von Schlegell did this." Touching two fingers to her forehead, she flicked her wrist in a sort of salute.

A predictable response to Elwell's *Herr*, thought Markey. He took another sip of the orange blossom; it really was very good. He could see getting a taste for it.

Wanting to get back to the lies of Viola Kraus, he said, "You seemed surprised when Viola said she left the club before Elwell did."

"All I can say is, as we were leaving, we saw her, but we didn't see him." He wrote down, *V says E after 2 AM, Z says No.*

Then he heard her say, "If Viola's not your girl in the green dress, that means Elwell met another woman at the *Frolic* and took her home, doesn't it?"

"Yes. But Miss Kraus is making a big, fat point of not knowing that."

"Well, of course she is. If he leaves with another woman, that embarrasses her and gives her a motive, doesn't it?" Zelda curled her legs under her. "Maybe Viola went around this morning to give him a piece of her mind. Maybe she stormed into the house and shot Elwell dead."

"But Viola was still in her robe and pajamas. Why would she change out of her street clothes? She didn't know we were coming."

Even as he said it, there was something about the vision of Viola in her gold-and-pink kimono that nagged at him. She struck him as theatrical, but so many New Yorkers did—it could be hard to distinguish affectation from dissembling. But she was a liar, that much he knew. What he didn't know was why. He finished his orange blossom, blinking as the gin gave his brains a good slap.

Zelda crooned, "Poor Mr. Markey—doesn't that mean your enchantress is the murderer?" The light in her eyes suggested the idea tickled her no end.

"Now we don't know that for sure. When I searched the house for her—"

"You went looking for a woman who shot a man through the head? She must have been quite the something."

"She was entirely quite the something," he admitted. "But she wasn't there. If she did shoot him, I can't figure out how she got out of the house; you need a key to lock the door. Also the bedrooms didn't make sense."

"How d'you mean?"

In an orange blossom haze, he had forgotten to whom he was speaking. Discussing bedrooms with a married woman—any woman—was unheard of. Or had been. Of all the things that were different after the war, girls were the most different, transformed from shy, cloistered creatures who peeped out at the world from behind lace curtains to bobbed-hair flirts who danced, kissed, and drank. But Zelda's interest was so frank and they'd already talked about so many unsuitable things, he plunged ahead, saying, "Elwell had two bedrooms. His own, where he had all these pictures of women and a wig and false teeth . . ."

She shuddered, which made him laugh.

"And makeup," he continued. "It was very strange. Most important, the bed hadn't been . . ."

"Utilized."

He tipped his drink to her. "Then there was this other room. Pink, frilly, a pair of lady's pajamas laid out, and . . . well, nothing had happened in that bed either."

Zelda thought. "You saw this girl in green when?"

"Two in the morning."

"And when was Elwell shot?"

"Probably around eight AM? You can't survive long with a head wound like that."

"So what were they doing for six hours if not getting tangled in the sheets?"

"I do wonder."

"Maybe she had a drink with Elwell and went home. Maybe

she's out there, lonely in the city, waiting for a nice long Virginia boy to sweep her off her feet." Her tone suggested this was both ridiculous and entirely possible. Then she added, "Or she's a cold-blooded killer, but that needn't be an impediment to true love."

Refusing the bait, he said, "All I know is she's one of the last people to see Joseph Elwell alive, which means she's either the woman who shot him or the reason he got shot. I want to find her and I want to talk to her."

"Sure you do. Her and her pretty little pistol."

"You *sure* you didn't see her at the *Frolic*? The dress looked like confetti made of money, like she had been bathing in ripped-up dollar bills . . ." He rippled his fingers down his front.

Zelda laughed. "No, I saw no such vision. But let's not forget Viola Kraus. Miss 'I left early and I don't know what my boyfriend was doing or who he was doing it with and I most certainly did not shoot him because he was running around on me.'"

"I won't, believe me."

In fact, he was pleased. The editor had demanded a pretty girl with a gun and now he had two: a tantalizing mystery woman and a society lady gone to the bad. At the moment, Viola had the edge. She had a motive and a statement that didn't hold up. More important, he had gotten the first interview with her. She was his story.

"Oh!" said Zelda, as if she had just remembered. "How many women have you been to bed with? Scott wanted me to ask you."

He managed to get out "I—" when a clock chimed two, saving him. It was time to sober up—past time. If he wanted his story in the late edition, he had to hurry. He put his hands on the arms of the chair, preparing to stand.

"Where are you going?" Zelda asked.

"I have to write my story."

"Well, but do you have to write it right *now*?" She looked forlornly at the empty glasses. "Scott's going to be working all afternoon."

Surprised and touched that she was sad to see him go, he said, "Just I don't know how long Elwell is going to be of interest. The story might not last more than a day."

"Oh, it'll last."

"How would you know that?"

She sat up. "Because it's a marvelous puzzle! A dead man inside a locked house. Where did the killer come from? How did he get in . . . or *she*? It's everyone's nightmare. You think you're in the safest place you can be, your own home, tucked up, ready for bed, with all the doors and windows locked. Then the grim reaper pays a call, only to disappear, leaving your cold, lifeless body behind. You were never really home, you were trapped in a place you *chose to be*."

"That's very evocative, Mrs. Fitzgerald."

She gazed avidly at him, waiting for something.

"And thank you very much for introducing me to Miss Kraus."

"Are you going to go looking for that fascinating girl in the green dress? Judging from your com*plete* failure to answer my question, I think you should."

"Of course I am, she's the last person to see Joseph Elwell without a hole in his head. But you said Viola Kraus was guilty."

"And she may be! The possibilities are endless, Mr. Markey. I don't think you should just write about this murder. I think you should *solve* it."

Her excitement amused him—and held him. Then he noticed the empty glasses on the table. He couldn't allow her to pay. But when he started fumbling in his pocket, she said, "Never mind that," and pulled an enormous roll of money from her purse. It was a gorgeous, gaudy thing, so fat it stretched her fingers to the limit. Peeling off bills, she looked like a gangster's girlfriend. He wondered if that was the point of the gesture.

She waved her fingers at him. "Give me your card. I might have another chat with Viola."

Handing it to her, he said, "My father would say it's not fitting to let a lady pay."

"My father, too. But we don't listen to our fathers anymore, do we, Mr. Markey?"

"I do, on occasion."

Then he thought of it: the thing she really wished to be thanked for.

"Thank you for the pleasure of making your acquaintance . . ."

At the last moment, he corrected himself.

"Zelda."

The *Daily News* offices were located at 25 City Hall Place. It was close to the courts, close to the jails, close to the mooncakes of Nom Wah Tea Parlor and a basement speakeasy affectionately called the Morgue. The paper was new, having come into existence the previous year, and the office had a shabby, fly-by-night quality, as if any moment they would be raided and shut down. The newsroom was a cramped space, seemingly created by someone shoving several desks through the door, filling the remaining spots with battered chairs that knocked into one another anytime someone pushed away from the table. Typewriters, used by scores of reporters in a hurry, were placed haphazardly; you either pulled the chair to the typewriter or hauled the typewriter to the chair. Markey worked himself into one of the seats, let his fingers hover over the keys. Then he banged out:

NEW REVELATIONS IN THE BRUTAL SLAYING OF JOSEPH B.

ELWELL

WIZARD OF WHIST SPENT HIS FINAL NIGHT WITH MYSTERY

WOMAN IN GREEN

He typed in a frenzy, informing readers that Elwell had been found in his scarlet pajamas, which hinted at sordid pursuits. Then the visit from the postman, the jewels and hundreds of dollars in the bedroom, the distress of Mrs. Larsen . . .

He paused a moment, considering how to present the housekeeper. *Devoted* suggested sex. *Loyal.* She would be loyal.

> Mrs. Larsen, his loyal housekeeper, discovered Elwell, all but dead, when she arrived at 8:35 that morning to clean.

He added money details. Racing stables, Palm Beach, Newport, yellow Packard. Made $30,000 in a single night playing bridge, luxury properties around the country. Then:

> "WE WERE TO BE MARRIED"
> SAYS PRETTIEST GIRL IN NEW YORK
>
> Elwell spent the last night of his life in the company of Viola Kraus—known to many as the most beautiful girl in New York—at Ziegfeld's *Midnight Frolic*. The couple was joined by Miss Kraus's sister, Selma Lewisohn, and her husband, Walter Lewisohn, who are . . .

His fingers froze. He had neglected to learn anything about the Lewisohns and didn't know how to describe them other than *rich*.

> . . . prominent members of society.
> Also present that evening was Victor von Schlegell, who had become the former husband of Viola Kraus that very day. Witnesses report that he joked to his onetime wife, "It seems we can't keep away from each other." Harsh words passed between Von Schlegell and the murder victim.
> We . . .

For a moment, he pondered the benefit of naming Zelda Fitzgerald as his witness. It would probably get him the front page.

But he was arrogant enough to think he already had it. Also, he didn't want the story to be all about the Fitzgeralds. Neutral *we*, then.

> We spoke with Miss Kraus, a diminutive brunette beauty, shortly after she learned the terrible news. Tearfully, the New York socialite recalled her beau as "laughing and gay, always going to parties. The most stylish man you could imagine." She suggested the police speak with the current Mrs. Elwell, whom she described as "bitter" and "stuck-up."
>
> ### SLAIN BY A WOMAN?
>
> One witness reports that the lovely Miss Kraus and the bridge impresario bickered that night. Elwell enjoyed the company of beautiful women. He kept a collection of photographs of lovely ladies in his bedroom.
>
> One such lady returned home with Elwell at two AM the night he died; she had amber hair and wore a green-and-silver frock. She was not Viola Kraus, and it must be asked: Did Viola Kraus discover she had a rival for Mr. Elwell's affections?

He frowned, briefly stuck for a final paragraph. Then hit upon the perfect thing.

> This we do know. On the night in question, Viola Kraus wrote her name on the dead man's cuff, saying, "There, you're mine."
>
> As a wise young lady of my acquaintance once said, you don't write your name on a man's sleeve if you're sure of him.

Mrs. Fitzgerald—Zelda—would like that, having the last word.

It was his habit to let a story rest for exactly three minutes. Sitting back, he stared at the wall, which was covered in recent front pages. The *Daily News* believed that you grabbed readers' attention not with words but with images. Each front page was a carefully curated selection of the faces of the famous and infamous, with a few sad-eyed orphans and salt-of-the-earth laborers thrown in for moral fiber. Fitzgerald had made the cover more than once. Today's favored few were Douglas Fairbanks and Mary Pickford, Columbia students getting up to collegiate high jinks, an ancient Henry Cabot Lodge, and a derailed subway in the Bronx.

Markey knew if he wrote this right, Elwell and Viola Kraus would take over the entire front page. It would be all his. And maybe, if the story lasted, his name would be right there beside theirs: Morris Markey, the only man in New York who had the story everyone in the city wanted to hear.

Tearing the sheet out of the typewriter, he took it to his editor for approval. Gus Schaeffer was a wrung-out rag of a man who hadn't really approved of anything besides a stiff drink in decades. Still, as he read, Markey thought he looked less disgusted than usual, and he ventured, "I thought I could get my name on this one. Since I got the interview with Viola Kraus."

"No bylines."

"Edna Ferber has a byline."

Schaeffer looked up. "Are you Edna Ferber?" He went back to reading. "Fine, put Ferber's name on it. You don't want yours on it, believe me."

"Why not?"

Schaeffer indulged himself with a brief but colorful discourse on the quality of the Southern intellect, a thing he did not believe existed. Then he said, *"Lewisohn."*

"What about him?"

"You don't know who Walter Lewisohn is?"

"Well, clearly I don't, so why don't you tell me?"

"Walter Lewisohn slid out of his mother a millionaire. His old man, Leonard, made a fortune in copper. Walter went into banking, increasing the family fortune considerably. He's a member of the New York Stock Exchange. One of his sisters married someone high up at the US Treasury, another a member of Parliament. His wife is an opera singer. These are substantial people, Markey. Wealthy people."

"People like reading about wealthy people who do awful things."

"That they do." Gus Schaeffer actually smiled as he tossed back the pages. "But cut out all the 'we' and 'I' stuff. No one cares what you think."

Markey said, "We'll need pictures. Elwell, Viola Kraus. A sketch of a girl in green. And I want to talk to the chauffeur. Maybe he caught her name."

Schaeffer pointed to the door. "The police are talking to the press first thing tomorrow at Elwell's house. Go find out what they don't know."

CHAPTER EIGHT

"Gentlemen, let me state this clearly. A woman did *not* shoot Joseph Elwell."

Standing at the back of a large crowd of reporters, Markey fumed. Captain Arthur Carey might not have been the stupidest man he ever saw, but he gave the competition a good run for its money. The head of New York City's Homicide Bureau stood preening on the stoop of Elwell's house. He was a plump man with bright blue eyes and a habit of framing his thoughts with a folksy *Here's how I see it*. He liked newsmen who gave him good press, responding to their questions, bestowing scoops. Markey had not been in town long enough to court him, and he had come today knowing it was going to be a challenge to get his question answered. But he had not expected Carey to dismiss his story of a glamorous murderess out of hand. It was a frustrating start.

Carey spoke at length about cigarettes and carpenters. One of the cigarettes found at the scene had been a blend specially made for Joseph Elwell. A second had not. That cigarette was still damp at the time it was discovered, suggesting it had been in the killer's mouth shortly before the murder. Markey, who had only seen one cigarette, was puzzled. It was possible he had missed it. But it was also possible one of the policemen who had crowded into the house had tossed one aside without thinking. Now that he recalled, one of the orderlies had been smoking when they came in.

The carpenters next door did not recall hearing any shots. The theory was that the banging of the hammers had confused the issue. Markey, who had been woken many times by the hammers, thought this likely.

Jost Otten, the milkman, had been interviewed. He had arrived at the house at 6:30 and found the front door unlocked, the inner door locked. The mailman, Charles Torrey, arrived at 7:25 and found the same.

At 8:35, Mrs. Marie Larsen arrived to find both the front door and the inner door locked. Here Carey paused to let the reporters do the calculation. Markey wrote down: *7:25 to 8:35, Elwell lets someone in the house. Someone he does not fear. Someone able to lock the front double doors because they have key.*

None of the three were considered suspects. Torrey had been delivering mail in the area for a quarter century. Six-thirty was considered too early for the shooting, which cleared the milkman. Mrs. Larsen's husband and a neighbor had confirmed the time she left her apartment.

Everything else Carey reported—the make of the bullet, the reputation of the dead man, the lingerie in the pink bedroom—Markey knew. In fact, Markey wondered if some of the facts Carey was passing off as the results of his investigation had been taken from his article. It was a strangely reciprocal relationship, between the press and the police. More than once, he had seen a fantastical theory, written to fill space, presented the next day as a new lead in the case.

"And now, lads," said Carey, "I have time for a few questions."

A roar went up. Markey stayed quiet. There was a rhythm to these sessions, and he would have to buck the beat to be heard. He let three questions go by. When he sensed Carey was about to say, *That's all for today*, he stood on tiptoes and bellowed, "Are you going to interview Viola Kraus?"

It was a gamble. The pack had been ready to let Carey go; now they might pile on. But Markey had asked the right question and they stayed silent, awaiting the answer. Thrown—and irritated—Carey said, "I don't have . . ."

Markey called, "Are you aware that Mr. Elwell spent the night with a woman in a green dress?"

Carey gave him a hard stare. But he was enough of a showman to sense that he was in danger of losing his audience. Affecting an air of breezy candor, he said, "I never knew it to be a crime for a lady to wear green in the city of New York."

Patronized, the press turned mutinous. Other voices rose, demanding, "How about the photographs of women in his room?" "Do you have the name of the woman in green?"

"A woman"—Carey shouted down his challengers—"could not have shot Joseph Elwell because the weapon in question is a .45-caliber automatic. That gun is far too powerful for a lady. The recoil would send her across the room. It would be impossible for a woman to manage such an expert shot with such a formidable weapon."

Markey, who had shot a .45, thought this a sweeping statement. Remembering the raised arm of the lady in green, he thought she looked strong enough to manage the shot less than half a foot away. Even a petite woman such as Viola Kraus could do it. But he didn't want to get tangled in a debate over the strength of the fairer sex, so he shouted, "Will you be interviewing Viola Kraus's former husband, Victor von Schlegell?"

"We will be interviewing those persons deemed to have information about this case," said Carey. "Those persons will be identified by us, not by the press. Good day, gentlemen."

Afterward, Markey lingered, picking up bits of information from the jeers and complaints that followed any press hearing. The atmosphere was aggrieved. Reporters liked the woman angle and did not want it snatched away so quickly. One *Herald* reporter was pushing the notion that a soldier had shot Elwell as the .45 was army issue, only recently available to the public. But everyone else was trying to pin names on Elwell's ladies. Having cornered the market on Viola Kraus, Markey was popular, with fellows wanting to feel out where he was headed next.

One of them was Hal Meyers, also with the *Daily News*, who sidled up to ask, "Think Carey means it when he says a woman didn't do it?"

"I can think of a good reason for him to say so in public." Markey disliked Meyers. He was the kind of reporter who felt he wasn't getting anywhere unless he shoved another fellow aside. But he was one of Carey's pets, so Markey threw out his own question. "I wonder where the funeral will take place."

"The family's not saying, but I'd wager New Jersey. That's where his folks live. You think Viola will show?"

The same question was on Markey's mind. But the news that the funeral would be in New Jersey wasn't meaty enough to warrant a trade. "I wouldn't, if I were her."

Just then, a particular woman caught his eye as she left number 244. Her head was down, but the plainness of her black straw hat and white collared dress revealed her as Mrs. Larsen. A few reporters drifted her way, shouting the odd question. She fired back, "If I have anything to say, I say it to the police," and kept going.

Markey waited until she had turned the corner. Then, touching the brim of his hat, he said "Gentlemen" and ambled down the block as if he were making his way to the drugstore to call in his story. Once out of sight of his colleagues, he ran to catch up. "Mrs. Larsen, I owe you an apology."

He meant it. It seemed one thing to mislead Viola Kraus, because Viola Kraus had everything in the world and was herself dishonest. But Mrs. Larsen had only wanted to help a dying man, and she had trusted Markey when he said he wanted the same. He had taken advantage of her decency and he regretted doing so.

Also, there was something else he needed to know: the name of Elwell's chauffeur.

"I would have done something for him if I could have," he said.

She turned, examining him from under the brim of her hat, as if he were the bottom of her shoe and she had stepped in something. "But instead, you go through his possessions and tell people things they have no right to know."

"It might help find the person who killed him."

"And the women—do they have no right to privacy?"

"Not the woman who killed him, no."

Deliberately casual, he added, "I was talking to Mr. Elwell's chauffeur, Mr.— Sorry, his name escapes me. But you know the man."

He smiled tentatively, inviting her to supply the driver's name. She gave him a scathing look. "How old are you?"

"Twenty-one."

"Do something else. This is not a way to live."

Her contempt was so strong it made Markey flinch. As she walked away, he wondered how he could go from feeling so full of himself to lower than a worm in just five minutes.

Smacked by Mrs. Larsen, he was left with his second option for finding the chauffeur: finding the yellow roadster. There was only one garage in the area where one might store such an ostentatious vehicle and that was the Chatsworth, a few blocks west of Elwell's house. Built to serve the new apartment buildings that were rising along the river's edge, the twenty-story Chatsworth offered shelter to cherished Packards and Cadillacs when their owners weren't using them to travel to the North Shore or Saratoga.

Markey found the garage attendant in a booth, half hidden behind the *Daily World*. The hand that held the paper was a dark, well-creased brown, the voice when it inquired "Can I help you?" Mississippi by Markey's ear. He asked the gentleman how he liked New York winters, if he had found anywhere that served a decent plate of greens. Had he moved alone or with family? Told family, Markey said, "That's better. Myself, I get lonely. You have kids?"

The gentleman had two, a boy and a girl. He observed it was hard to get them what they needed up North. Back home, it wasn't to be had. Here, it could be had, but for a price. It took some haggling. But Markey got the name and address of Elwell's chauffeur, and the garage attendant's children would get some of what could be had up North.

The chauffeur was William Rhodes. He lived on Sixty-First Street and he had a wife. This Markey had not expected, thinking that the man would have the same louche habits as the master. Katherine Rhodes had light brown curls, widely spaced blue eyes, and a welcoming manner that made him nervous on her behalf. He wanted to say she should not have opened the door to him so easily. Also, that she should rethink her choice of husband. William Rhodes—she called him Billy—was a strapping black-haired man with a smooth charm that hinted he got away with a lot.

Taking Markey into the parlor, Rhodes said with a cynical half smile, "Sure, you're the egg who found him."

"I'm afraid poor Mrs. Larsen found him."

Rhodes shut the door, then settled into a chair, legs apart, elbows on his knees. He sat hunched, clasped hands bobbing between his knees. Not a man who liked questions, thought Markey.

So he began with a statement: "You may not remember, but we crossed paths the other night. You were bringing Mr. Elwell home."

Rhodes sucked his teeth. "Can't say that I do remember."

"Maybe you remember his companion. She wore a green-and-silver dress?"

"He had a lady with him, sure."

"Did the lady have a name?"

"Probably, but I didn't catch it. I'm not good with names."

Markey smiled: *Of course not.* "But you picked them up at the *Midnight Frolic* at 1:30, something like that?"

"Something like that."

Satisfied, Markey wrote, *E met Girl at Frolic. Works there? Guest?* Hoping for her address, he said, "Late night for you—what time did you have to take her home?"

"I didn't. Mr. Elwell said he'd get his friend a taxi, so I went home. Where I stayed until ten the next morning. You can ask my wife."

Not unfamiliar with the inside of a jail cell and not keen to go back. "I'm not the police, Mr. Rhodes, just a reporter trying to sell papers. Rest assured, pretty girls sell more papers than fellows like you and me. Joseph Elwell had a lot of friends, didn't he?"

More relaxed now, Rhodes cracked his knuckles with a grin. "I guess you've seen the menagerie."

Markey remembered the photographs in the bedroom. "Is that what he called them, the menagerie?"

"How he treated them. You know how kids, when they get a pet, they play with it all the time, stroke its fur, give it little treats, want it in bed with them? Then a week or two goes by and they couldn't care less if it gets run over in the street? That was Elwell and women."

Remembering Viola Kraus's possessive scribble on the dead man's cuff, he said, "In my experience, neglected creatures turn feral."

"Some do, yes. They lash out." The driver nodded to indicate this was a shame.

"But how would this creature get in? Or out, for that matter. Mrs. Larsen said both front doors were locked when she arrived."

"Maybe this little creature had the key." Rhodes sat back in his chair, tipping it as he called to the kitchen, "Smells great, sweetheart."

His voice low, Markey asked, "Are you saying Elwell gave the keys to his home to a member of the menagerie?"

Settling all four legs of the chair on the floor, the chauffeur said, "No, I'm saying he gave keys to *several* ladies in his collection."

At the word *several*, the faces in the bedroom photographs fanned out like so many playing cards in Markey's mind. Genuinely astonished, he said, "That's risky, isn't it? What if one woman arrives when another's . . ."

"In play? Good question. Here's another good question: What if one of the husbands found that key and asked, 'Say, honey, what's this?' And didn't like the answer."

Rhodes, so cautious at the beginning, was now being rather free with his information. Markey wondered if he was being led. Changing the subject, he asked, "Did you like working for Elwell?"

"Better than some," said Rhodes.

"Pay good?"

"Good, not always regular."

From the kitchen, "Billy hasn't been paid in five weeks."

Rhodes shrugged. "Elwell was a high-low kind of guy. When he had it, you had it. When he didn't . . . you waited. He usually made it up to me."

Markey remembered Elwell's house, the stack of money on the dresser. He also remembered the FOR SALE sign and the bloodspattered letter: *Expenses pretty high.* Cards and horses would provide an irregular income. But Elwell had seemed flush at the time of his death.

Markey took in the way Rhodes sat, feet poised, ready to spring if provoked. He might have learned the servant's easy manner, but under that, there was a restless combativeness, a fist in search of a face.

"You won't mind if I put what you've told me in my article?"

Rhodes shook his head. "All going to come out anyway, right?"

"Right." Rising, he called, "Thank you, Mrs. Rhodes. I hope I didn't delay lunch."

She appeared at the kitchen door. "Not at all. You take care."

Rhodes had turned sullen. Either he resented Markey's questions about money—or Markey's attention to his wife. Opening the door, the driver jerked his jaw to the left as if he had something sharp to say but knew he should keep it to himself. The facial tic was familiar, also the anger. Going with his gut, Markey asked, "Where'd you serve?"

"I was with the AEF. You?"

Markey tapped his glasses. "Red Cross. Something, wasn't it?"

"Sure was."

Rhodes held out his hand. Markey shook it, then jogged down the steps. At the bottom, he turned back to ask, "Sorry, how many keys was it?"

". . . Maybe five?"

"But you're not good with names."

Rhodes stuck his hands in his pockets. "Never have been, no."

"All right. Well, if that changes . . ." Reaching up, Markey handed the man his card.

As Markey headed to the office, he wondered why a man as sophisticated as Elwell would trust his secrets to a man as wrong as William Rhodes, then stiff him on his pay. The whiff of violence came off the driver like cheap cologne. But maybe Elwell liked to live dangerously. A man who romanced several women at a time and gave them keys to his home had a taste for risk, as any gambler would. That meant any number of women might have had cause and means to shoot the philandering bridge master. But only two that he knew of had been seen with him the day that he died: the woman in green and Viola Kraus.

Commandeering a typewriter, he wrote,

> According to William Rhodes, the dead man's chauffeur, five of Elwell's lady friends were given keys to the house. Any one of these women could have gotten in. Or, if they are married, any one of their husbands.
>
> Did Viola Kraus have a key to Joseph Elwell's house? Did she use it to visit him on the fatal morning, hours after he had jilted her for another woman?

Hal Meyers jostled his way into the newsroom. Nagging another reporter out of his chair, he shouted, "Phone records show someone called the Elwell house at 2:30."

Markey felt the newsroom's eyes on him; since the Kraus interview, the Elwell story was seen as his. Hal was trespassing, but if Markey didn't see him off, Hal would be judged to have a right to it. Making a show of typing, he asked, "PM or AM?"

"AM, of course." Meyers smirked.

So, shortly after Elwell and his gorgeous companion got to his house, someone had called to check up on him. Markey felt he knew who. "Police give you a name?"

Meyers shook his head. "They've given her an alias: 'Miss Wilson.' Elwell also made some calls himself in the wee hours. Long distance."

Markey thought if he had a few hours to spend with the girl in green, he wouldn't waste them making phone calls. But it wasn't hard proof she hadn't stayed the night. Based on what Zelda had told them about the couple's bickering at the *Frolic*, it seemed likely Viola had made the 2:30 phone call to her caddish lover. Perhaps that was how she had discovered he was with another woman.

But Markey seethed that he hadn't gotten the story first. He strongly suspected Carey had asked which paper the tall, pushy fellow at the back worked for; hearing it was the *Daily News*, Carey had decided Markey needed competition and given Hal the Miss Wilson scoop. For consolation, he looked at his own typed-up piece. He still thought five keys beat a 2:30 phone call. But he didn't like the gleam in Hal's eye.

And the furies weren't done with him. Stopping by the New Amsterdam in the hopes that someone might know the woman in green, he was told off by a junkyard dog of a man who assured him it would make a bad day better if he could slit Markey's throat and watch the blood run down to his socks. Exhausted, he went home to find Griswold, his eyes aflame with rage, shouting from his window, "I got no sleep last night, thanks to you!"

Markey called up, "Mr. Griswold, I don't see how you hear me in my apartment, which, allow me to point out, is *below* yours."

"You slammed the door, you *woke* me up . . ."

I can't see that it matters since you don't do a lick of work anyhow. Markey bit his tongue on the thought. Maybe the man had been fired and that was why he had nothing better to do than watch people all day. There was a lot to watch. Since the murder hit the papers, gawkers had thronged the street wanting a look at the Elwell house.

Then Markey realized: Griswold was an early riser—and a light sleeper.

"Mr. Griswold, did you see or hear anything yesterday morning?" Forestalling the man's complaints, he added, "Me, I know. But before that. Did you see anyone around the Elwell house?" Griswold narrowed his eyes. "Maybe you heard the gun go off?"

"Who can hear a gun with you around? I'm going to complain to Mrs. Cecchetti."

Markey began climbing up the front stoop. "You do that, Mr. Griswold. Maybe she'll suggest we switch apartments. That way you won't be bothered by my feet on the ceiling."

It felt good to say; for a moment, the choleric Griswold was silenced. But when Mrs. Cecchetti knocked on his door a few minutes later, Markey was seized with worry. The parlor apartment rented for more than his; Griswold's complaints had money behind them. He was relieved when she extended a piece of paper, saying, "A young lady called for you. She didn't leave her name but said you can find her at the Ritz."

It felt heady to give the operator the number for the Ritz hotel. Still, as he waited, he wondered if someone was playing a prank on him. It had been that kind of day.

Then he heard, "I want to go to the funeral," and knew, no, it was her.

"Mrs. Fitzgerald, forgive me, *Zelda*."

"I read your article on Viola," she said. "I thought it very fine."

"How did you know it was mine?"

"You said you write for the *Daily News*. And it sounded like you. That's why I liked it—it didn't sound like all the other papers. And you quoted me, which made it infinitely superior."

"You've read *all* the papers on Elwell?"

"Mm, hm. That's why I want to go to the funeral. I want to get a look at Viola when she's right up close to the coffin. Where will it be? The papers didn't say."

He tried to envision Zelda in church. At the Ritz, she had been an asset. At a funeral, she might be a liability. "Somewhere in New Jersey," he hedged. "I have to find out where."

"How are you going to get out there?"

She made a salient point. He could go by train, but there was the matter of reaching the service. A taxi would be exorbitant.

"I might be able to borrow a car," she said, softly wheedling.

He considered. He needed to stay a step ahead of the likes of Hal Meyers. If he refused, Zelda could find out the time and place from Viola Kraus and come anyway. It would be easier to manage her if they went as a team. And if he said no and put her in the position of defying him, he would become her old father, and clearly she liked to provoke her old father. He wished he could turn her loose on Griswold.

"Do you know if Viola's planning to attend?" he asked.

"I'm not going to tell you until you say I can go."

He thought hard. "All right. If Viola is there, you've come as a kindness to her. If she's not, then we're a couple who took bridge lessons with Elwell." Given Zelda's jazz-baby allure, no one would doubt the lecherous Elwell would take her as a client. Markey would pose as the husband. Bluff, loudmouthed, provincial. Dottie would say it wasn't a pose.

On impulse, he said, "Say, you want to hear tomorrow's headline before anybody else?"

Over the line, an eager *mmm* as if something delicious had been offered.

"Viola had the key to Elwell's house. That could be how she got in and out." He didn't know why he wanted her to know it; he just did.

"*Well*," breathed Zelda. "I wonder what hymns they sing up here."

Chapter Nine

"I assume," said Fitzgerald, "that if you were trying to seduce my wife, you'd take her somewhere more festive than a funeral in New Jersey."

A round of drinks with a morgue attendant had revealed that Elwell's parents had smuggled the body to Ridgewood for burial that day. When Markey arrived to collect Zelda, he found Fitzgerald chilly. It was clear he had not expected to see Markey again and felt it was tacky of him to have reappeared. Markey was torn between saying of course he would take Zelda someplace more elegant and denying emphatically any thought of seduction. In short, he wasn't sure where he had offended: a lack of style or a lack of morals.

Zelda breezed into the room, saying, "Cemeteries have always had the most profound effect upon me. Not to *mention* the scent of lilies. I'm not sure I can be held accountable."

"Then I shall hold Mr. Markey accountable," said Fitzgerald.

Wanting to remind the writer that he had once thought him useful, Markey said, "May I ask what you're working on?"

Eyes on his wife as she adjusted her hat in the mirror, Fitzgerald said, "The story of a beautiful, hedonistic couple. He's rich and enjoys parties to an inordinate degree. She believes her beauty makes her more important than anyone else." In the mirror, Zelda raised an eyebrow. "He knows she's bad for him, but he can't help it. He's in her thrall."

"As he should be," said Zelda. "He wouldn't be much without her."

"She torments him with other men," Fitzgerald solemnly informed Markey.

Zelda gave him a gentle kiss. "Go write, darling. Shall we, Mr. Markey?"

As he and Zelda walked to the elevator, Markey was unnerved by Fitzgerald's resentment. He was about to suggest to Zelda that perhaps she should stay behind when she burst out laughing and said, "Your *face!*"

Shamed but uncertain as to whether the whole thing had been a performance, he waited until they were climbing into the Packard to say, "You're sure he's not upset..."

"Oh, don't fuss. He enjoys it." Irritated, she threw herself into the front seat, swinging her legs in and slamming the door.

Going to the other side, Markey got into the driver's seat. In a small voice, he noted the map lying on the floor by Zelda's feet; if she could be navigator and tell him how to get to Ridgewood, New Jersey, he would appreciate it. When she didn't answer, he knew she was still annoyed with him. With his foot, he nudged the map closer so it brushed her ankle. When they got to New Jersey, he would remind her.

Driving in New York was an entirely different proposition from driving as it was generally practiced. The only thing Markey could liken it to was riding with Eddie Parker during the war. The traffic had no rhythm that he could see, no pace. Some cars crept into a lane; others sped right out in front of you. When he drove in a way he thought sensible, he heard the furious honking of horns behind him. When he tried to move with speed and decisiveness, another driver screamed that he was a lunatic. Waiting at one corner, he looked over at Zelda, who seemed entirely unbothered. Only when he had edged the car out of the worst of the scrum and made it onto the ferry crossing the Hudson did he feel it safe to ask, "Did you see that someone called Elwell at 2:30 in the morning?"

"I did," she said eagerly. "It has to be Viola, right?"

Relieved she was back in a good mood, he said, "Did you find out if she's going to the funeral?"

"Miss Kraus is no longer speaking to me since she was quoted in a certain *Daily News* article. In fact—"

They had reached the Jersey side of the river. Markey edged them off the ferry and onto the road.

"—if she does come to the funeral, I'm worried she might throw something at you. An urn or wreath. I bet she flings herself on the casket." She spoke with the disdain someone gifted in the art of the grand gesture would show the amateur.

"She might not come," said Markey. "I imagine Elwell's son will be there, which means Elwell's wife will be, too."

"But if she doesn't come, isn't that suspicious? Since they were so in *love*?"

"Which is more scandalous," he agreed, "to be seen as a gate-crasher or suspected of murder?"

As he pondered that question, they passed a sign for a place called Ho-Ho-Kus. That sounded wrong on a number of levels and he asked Zelda, "Are we going the right way?"

"How do you mean?"

"You're the navigator."

She smiled at him in beguiling disbelief.

He pointed. "The map's right there. Just . . ."

But she was already shaking her head. He might have expected her to map-read, but she had never agreed to it, which, in her view, relieved her of the obligation.

Pulling up along the side of the road, he got out and laid the map across the hood. Zelda watched with great interest as he followed the vein from where he thought they were to where they really were to where they wanted to be. "We've overshot," he concluded. "But not too bad. I think we'll get there in time."

They did not get there in time. As Markey drove up to the church, he found the doors shut and the grounds empty, save for a solitary hearse. He heard the purposeful boom of the organ and a hymn being sung with the vigor of people who know the service has come to an end. Frustrated, he pounded the steering wheel.

"It's fine," said Zelda. "Better, even. This way, we can watch everybody as they come out. We'll see if Viola's here, then follow them to the cemetery."

There were several cars along the side of the road. Two cars and a truck were parked close to the church. Markey guessed they belonged to the minister and other church staff. He drew up behind the truck so they could still watch the church doors but not attract notice.

In a short while, the doors opened and the coffin glided out, followed by the minister. An older man in a dark suit came after, his hand rigid on the banister. A small, gray-haired woman clung to his other arm. From their age and debilitating grief, Markey thought they had to be Elwell's parents. He looked for the wife to follow, but she did not. Was the widow so bitter she had refused to come? Nor did he see Viola—or anyone resembling those ardent, playful images in the bedroom. Elwell's women, it seemed, had stayed away. Instead, there were neighbors and townsfolk—a conspicuously plain and sober group. He glanced at Zelda, a lone orchid among pine.

Then, when it seemed all the mourners had left, a woman emerged, dressed in black from head to toe, a veil over her face. She gestured impatiently and a boy appeared in a school uniform, a powder blue blazer with yellow piping. It was the child from the photograph, now about fifteen, with the odd angles and scrawniness of the suddenly grown. Mrs. Elwell looked forty years old, stout, handsome at best. Shopgirls would avoid her as someone both old-fashioned and thrifty—and they would feel her wrath for doing so. Markey wondered what had attracted Elwell to her. Nothing in her appearance resembled the fragile butterfly demeanor of Viola Kraus. He thought it strange the dead man's parents did not walk with his widow and child.

He had tried to be inconspicuous, but Mrs. Elwell spotted the car. She pulled her son close and gave them a hard stare, Zelda in particular, her eyes resting on the younger woman with a scorn that would have made any other girl sink in her seat. Zelda answered look for look as if she found the other woman's hostility predictable and tiresome.

"*That* is a woman with no joy," said Zelda when the widow had driven off.

"Don't you think it's odd Elwell's parents acted like they didn't know her?"

"I'd say they can't stand her, and I see why. Let's follow."

Markey let Mrs. Elwell's car get ahead, then rolled slowly down the road. What could the widow have done that was so abhorrent that the senior Elwells would snub her and their own grandson at a funeral? There were one or two things he could think of. Well, one.

"Zelda, didn't Viola say that Elwell recently asked his wife for a divorce?"

"She did. Why?"

"Because that could be a reason for the wife to shoot him."

"They've been separated for years. Why kill him now?"

"Money. She's got a boy to support. A new wife means new

expenses, maybe even more children. Miss Kraus is young enough. If Elwell's current will leaves everything to Mrs. Elwell and the boy, it'd be a good idea to shoot him before he had a reason to change that."

As he had expected, the widow led them to Valleau Cemetery. Through the high wrought iron fence, Markey watched the brief ceremony held at the gravesite. The parents stood at a remove from the widow, although Elwell's father brought the boy to his side. There was one man Markey could not place. He was dressed more expensively than the locals, but he wasn't family. His features were bland, the face round, his hair sandy. He wore circular glasses that reflected light, hiding his eyes.

After the casket was lowered, the mourners began to disperse. Mrs. Elwell lingered by the grave. Markey wondered what she was saying to her dead husband: *Forgive me? Good riddance?* The boy had gone a short distance with his grandparents before realizing his mother hadn't followed. Now he stood lost and caught between them. Then Mrs. Elwell finished what she had to say and began walking to her car.

Zelda whispered, "Here she comes."

Markey looked at Zelda in her pale turquoise dress with silver beading, her gold hair a burst of sunlight around her face.

"Zelda?" She turned to him expectantly. "I think I should approach Mrs. Elwell alone. Given her husband's proclivities, she may have strong views on attractive young women. I'd rather not antagonize her right off the bat."

"Oh, I can be very sweet with old cats."

"She's not a cat, she's a bulldog, and you know I'm right. Have a wander around the cemetery. I'll come when I'm done."

She threw herself against the seat in protest. Then she examined Mrs. Elwell.

"All right," she said finally. "She does look like she'd roll up that son of hers and stick him in her purse if I came near."

Getting out of the car, she called over her shoulder, "Don't leave me too long among the dead, hear?"

Markey smiled, then went after Mrs. Elwell.

Her car was the farthest from the gate. Mother and son walked, arms linked. But she walked fast, and the boy stumbled, unable to find his feet. Halfway down the dusty road, she stopped, fist clenched in frustration. Markey braced, thinking a slap was coming. But then she laid a soft palm on her son's shoulder. In that change of heart, Markey saw his way in. Her reaction to Zelda told him she saw herself as an upright woman; the sudden gentleness with her child, a mother first and foremost. And she was isolated. A strong show of support for the woman she believed herself to be might win her trust.

He called, "Mrs. Elwell?" She stopped, allowing him to catch up. "My name is Morris Markey. I'm sorry to intrude upon your grief."

"There's a simple answer for that. Don't." She had that old Yankee demeanor that took pride in avoiding fripperies or trivial conversation.

"Yes, ma'am. But I lived across the street from your late husband and I thought you'd like to know that he kept your son's portrait by his bedside." He addressed the boy directly. "You were not forgotten. You were . . . recognized."

The boy nodded, holding his eyes wide in a show of dry-eyed manliness. Markey read the badge on his blazer: PHILLIPS ACADEMY ANDOVER.

He took a step back. "That was all I wanted to say. I'm sure it's a confusing time. A sudden death brings so much grief to the widow." He was careful to give her that title. "So many overwhelming considerations . . ."

He avoided the words *money* or *will*. His mother had said Yankees were practical about money, and while many might not be, Mrs. Elwell was, because she said to her son, "Richard, go wait in the car."

Then she lifted her veil to face him. "Who are you really?"

"I did live across the street from Mr. Elwell."

"And."

"I'm a reporter with the *Daily News*." Then, before she took his head off, "Mrs. Elwell, you and your son are being ignored. You're not part of the story. In situations like this, that can be financially perilous. Anything you have to say, I'm ready to listen."

The word *listen* caught her; she gave her assent by not moving. Markey got out his notebook. "You were separated from Joseph Elwell but not divorced, is that correct?"

"It is."

"How long did you live apart?" He had learned, when interviewing suspicious people, to start simple and dull. Say almost nothing, laying one brief, comforting phrase after the other, letting them step closer and closer to confiding in someone they'd all but forgotten was there. Repeat their words as much as possible so they mistook you for an echo of their own thoughts.

She said, "I have not laid eyes on my husband in four years."

A smart woman, she knew perfectly well she was a suspect. Before he could come at her from a different direction, she went on the offensive. "You said you saw a photograph of Richard by my husband's bed. Was that a lie?"

"No, ma'am."

"Would you be willing to say publicly you saw that picture in his room?"

"I would. May I ask why?"

"Joseph Elwell owes me a great deal. I mean to collect."

Here it was. The money. He waited.

"His success is entirely my doing," she told him. "I come from a fine family. My cousins attended Groton with Franklin Roosevelt. Mr. Elwell Sr."—she spat her father-in-law's name—"was a clerk for an insurance company. When we wed, many felt I was marrying beneath me. But I saw that Joe had a gift. I took him to

Newport and Hyde Park. I introduced him to the Vanderbilts, suggested that they engage Joe as a teacher to their son. In society, you must know how to play bridge. I made it known that if you wanted to win, you had to learn from Joseph Elwell." She raised her chin. "Do you think that son of a clerk would have seen the inside of Marble House without me?"

Markey had never heard of Marble House, but he knew the right reply. "No, ma'am."

"I made him. Because of me, he was invited to join the Studio Club in New York, where wealthy men indulge their taste for gambling for high stakes. Through such connections, he began to dabble in horses and real estate. He commanded considerable advances for his books on bridge. Books I coauthored, although I received no credit."

She had been speaking with a certain lofty pride, but the words *no credit* seemed to undo her and she fell silent. Sensing she needed to recover her dignity, Markey said, "You know, I don't play much bridge. Could you explain its appeal?"

"It is an intimate game. You play in pairs. You must be able to read your partner's signals, which may be as delicate as a sniff or the raising of an eyebrow. The intuitive side of it appeals to women. It is a game husbands can play with wives."

"What was the appeal for Mr. Elwell?"

"It's also a game for the striver. Success is only partly due to the cards you've been dealt. If you bid cleverly and you have a good partner, you can score a lot of points from a poor hand." She smiled briefly. "For a short time, Joe and I were good partners. Then he found others he liked better."

"And that caused the separation."

"Yes. To put it bluntly, Joe was a chicken chaser. He said that women over thirty should be chloroformed. Once he began putting his bizarre notions about women into practice, it was impossible to continue living with him."

"I can imagine."

She had given him several reasons she might have killed her husband, so many that Markey wondered if she would be so free with her grievances if she had shot him. Zelda's question of why now was apt. But he could think of two reasons: money and Viola Kraus.

"Your son attends Andover. I assume that means Mr. Elwell was generous in the settlement."

"You would be wrong." She looked away, embarrassed. "After we agreed to live apart, I did a very foolish thing: I underestimated Joseph Elwell. I was arrogant enough to think without me, he would fail. He offered to pay me a monthly sum as well as Richard's education if I signed away my rights to future earnings—including the proceeds from any sale of property gained during our marriage. The monthly sum was paid by his father, who refused to send payment until I acknowledged receipt of the previous month's."

So the parents' animosity went back before the murder of their son. Curious, he said, "The family's treatment of you strikes me as unkind."

"His father disapproved of our marriage. He disliked that I— Never mind. But for years, his parents watched as their son withheld money from his lawful wife and their own grandchild and said nothing on our behalf. As you say, we have been ignored."

The paltry settlement and stingy payments could mean Elwell was worth more to his wife dead than alive—if she inherited. Which she would not if he remarried. It was time to raise the subject of Viola Kraus.

"May I ask why you did not divorce him, given his cruelty toward you?"

"Joe didn't want a divorce," she said bitterly. "As long as he was technically a married man, he couldn't be sued for breach of promise by any of his women friends."

"Oh, but—" Markey affected surprise. "Well, surely you're aware that he intended to marry the socialite Viola Kraus."

A flicker of anxiety, but she smiled through it. "I was not. Nor do I believe it."

"Miss Kraus says he asked you for a divorce three weeks ago."

"That may be what Joe told her. That does not make it true."

"Viola Kraus *is* considered the most beautiful woman in New York."

"Miss Kraus has been considered by some to be the most beautiful woman in New York even back when she was Mrs. Von Schlegell. How long do you think she has held that title? How long can she continue to hold it?"

He asked, "Do you have keys to your husband's home, Mrs. Elwell?"

Her manner became steely. "Don't you try to make a vengeful wife out of me. I've given an account of my movements that morning to the police. At least two people saw me leaving my house at 8:15 AM. I arrived at an appointment with my attorney, whose office is on the East Side, at nine precisely."

"Why did you see your attorney?"

"That's a private matter. The point being, I could not have left my house at 8:15 AM, been at my attorney's at nine, and had time to kill my husband in between."

"Has your husband's will been read, Mrs. Elwell?"

"Enough. You may return to your vulgar companion."

She turned toward the car. Markey saw the boy watching from the back window.

"You're worried your son's been cut out, aren't you? You and he both? For Viola Kraus?"

Mrs. Elwell took a sudden step toward him. "You won't have to look far to find a woman who wanted to kill Joseph Elwell. He had a gift for making us suffer. As with all talents, he was good at it because he enjoyed it. This isn't the first time someone's tried to kill him. In Kentucky a few years ago, some poor broken thing shot at him with a pistol. She missed. Clearly the woman who visited him on June 11th did not. I say brava to her."

Chapter Ten

Zelda had told him not to leave her too long among the dead, so he expected her to be at the cemetery gates, waiting eagerly to hear about the widow. But she was not. In fact, it took some wandering to find her, which he didn't appreciate as it was hot. Mrs. Elwell had given him plenty of good stuff, although he wished he'd pinned her down on the issue of inheritance. But the widow and her son had upset him. There was something about the boy's bony, too-visible wrists and lumpish Adam's apple that made Markey angry. In his view, the kid had been cheated. The father had rejected him. The mother's love was tied up with hatred of her husband and a desire for money. Removing his jacket, Markey tipped his hat back on his head to swipe his wrist over his brow. It really was scorching. And he really was annoyed.

Moving around the graves in search of Zelda, he nearly stepped on a small, inset stone that read "Jack Albrecht, PFC Co F, 108th Infantry Division." Someone had placed a small flag on the grave; it hung limp and unmoving in the baking sun. Looking at it, Markey felt the buzz of memory like so many flies. The day the recruitment parade came to Richmond, flags had waved wildly up and down Main Street. There had been a band, women singing, "*A-mer-i-ca, I raised a boy for you. A-mer-i-ca, you'll find him staunch and true. Place a gun up-on his should-er. He is read-y to die or do.*" Crowds of people had turned out, Markey among them.

A man in uniform had ridden by in a truck, shouting through a megaphone as he pointed wildly into the crowd. "You, young man, and you, yes! I see you're ready. How about you, young fellow?" Their eyes had met. Convinced the man meant him, Markey had leapt forward, thrilled to have the whole town witness his moment, only to be turned down for poor eyesight. Furious that fate had conspired to keep him out of the Big Thing, he had immediately signed up for the Red Cross.

After tramping some distance, he found Zelda standing in front of a mausoleum with a look of such wild disapproval on her face, Markey thought to ask if she would like him to fetch a sledgehammer.

"Who would ever want to spend eternity in such a place?" She gestured to the squat, boxy structure of gray stone. "You might as well be buried in a Sunshine biscuit tin."

Shading her eyes, she gazed over the flat, tidy landscape. "I've never *seen* such a mediocre cemetery. There's no beauty here. Not a single remarkable story. Flat, dull stones for flat, dull lives."

She marched through the gravestones, stopping to peer at them as a teacher might stop at the desk of a student she suspected of cheating. "'Wife of.' 'Mother of.' 'Wife of,' 'wife of.' All these beloved wives, as dead and buried as when they were aboveground."

Already in bad humor, he found her theatrics aggravating. "It's no terrible thing being beloved."

"Oh, nobody loved these women, they just put 'em in a box and forgot about them. That Mrs. Elwell should lie down beside them right now. Bitter old martyr who expects people to admire her for breathing."

So that was why she was in a mood: the judgment of Mrs. Elwell. "Well, she's had a rough time. Elwell cheated her out of money, ran around with younger women."

"Bet they were prettier and livelier, too," she said flippantly.

"She built his career, basically wrote his books for him." Why he was defending the viperous Mrs. Elwell, he didn't know. But Zelda was young and lively and pretty, and the widow was not. It seemed an unfair fight.

"'Here lies Widow Elwell,'" Zelda proclaimed. "'Wrote books on bridge and annoyed people.'"

"What would your tombstone say?"

"*Lots.*" She walked ahead of him, arms swinging.

"Not 'Beloved wife of F. Scott Fitzgerald'?"

"That—but more than that. I intend to live the life of an extravagant. I do like to think about it, what people will say about me. How they'll argue whether my eyes were blue or green. How much they'll get wrong . . ."

"What'll they get wrong?"

"Well, if they stamp a 'beloved wife' on me, I will rise up from my grave and tear the tongues from their mouths. What about you? What do you want on your tombstone?"

Thinking of PFC Albrecht, he said, "Anything later than 1918 does me."

Turning, she peered at him. "I don't think that's true," she said after a moment. "I don't think that's true at all."

It wasn't, and he was surprised she could see it. But he wasn't prepared to tell her the truth, so he shrugged.

"Scott was in the war, you know. Well, it was over before he had to go, but he was at a training camp in Montgomery and we met at a dance. He looked *very* handsome in his uniform. So wonderfully clean."

Markey couldn't remember feeling clean a single minute in France. "I'm sure he was."

"I used to think about him going off. How we'd write and how people might read our letters one day. I imagined how I would feel if anything happened to him . . ."

"Well, nothing did, and that's a good thing."

He had interrupted her fantasy bereavement. Maybe it was unkind, but he didn't particularly care to hear how handsome and clean Fitzgerald had looked in his uniform at some dance.

She resented it, he could tell. Kicking at the grass, she said pointedly, "The aviators from Taylor Field used to fly over my house. They'd perform aerial stunts for me, it was great fun. I kissed one of them once. He had a mustache and I'd never kissed a man with a mustache before. His plane crashed into another doing a trick. Right over our house. Armistice Day—goodness, I was so full of confetti, I could have birthed a paper doll."

Astonished that she would follow such a story with a joke, he stopped in his tracks. She stopped, too, saying, "Well, what?"

"What was his name, the young man with the mustache. Do you even remember?"

"I do, as it happens," she said evenly. "His name was Lincoln Weaver, and you can bet he's not buried in some biscuit tin nobody visits. Not everyone's meant to live until they're old and pointless. I want to be very young *always*. Young and irresponsible." She threw the word *irresponsible* directly in his face.

"You know, there's really only one way to be young always."

"I know it. I said to Scott, we'll *just* have to die when we're thirty."

She twirled as she said it. The sight of her, vibrant with youth, engorged with appetite, spouting off about the worthlessness of long life spun him into a fury. He tried to put his feelings in order. She was young and spoiled, given to melodrama; he should laugh her off, say, *Well, we'll see when you're thirty.* But he couldn't. There was something in her vicious contempt for living past the time of deeds that struck a nerve so deep he wanted to scream her into oblivion.

A mosquito whined at his ear. Flicking at it, he felt the need to be away. Muttering "Well, that's fine," he pushed past her. It did him good to move, to feel his feet hit the ground hard. He was probably stomping on a few graves as well, but what did they care; they were well out of it.

Then, from behind, he heard her shout, "Isn't that what you went to war for? To *do* something? To be as big as you could and have everyone in town say, 'Did you hear about the Markey boy? Oh, my, isn't he splendid?' Didn't you want to be *interesting*?" Fists at her sides, she added, "And don't you dare give me all that bunk about duty."

He had been about to do exactly that. Now he had the disquieting realization that had she been in his town, he would have gladly done a loop-the-loop over her house. He absolutely would have done it. And thought it well worth the crash.

For a while, they walked to the car in silence. Then Zelda stopped by a headstone. "That's why it's important, if people are brave and startling and beautiful, that we tell about 'em, fix them in people's minds so they *matter* . . ."

As he drew up beside her, she looked at him so intently she might have taken hold of his hand. "I just think it's awful not to matter."

He looked at the grave marker. The stone had disintegrated with time. The cherub's front curls had been knocked off; the tip of its nose and chin were gone. The word *tell* struck him, also *matter*. He had thought the same when he wrote to those families. Nobody had given him the job. He just felt something ought to be said by someone who had been there. And the writing had calmed him down.

He gave something like a nod to Zelda and they started out of the cemetery.

As they passed the newly dug grave, she asked, "Isn't that why you're writing about this murder? So Joseph Elwell will matter to people?"

"Truthfully? I think I'm writing it so I matter to people."

She let out a great whoop of a laugh and curled her arm around his like a vine. Her warmth was a sudden reprieve; he felt his neck ease, his jaw loosen. The sky, he noticed, was quite blue. It was a fine summer day.

As they left the graveyard, she said, "By the way, I talked to the parents."

She had switched subjects so fast, he was fogged. "You spoke to Elwell's parents?"

"While you were wrestling with the old cat, yes. I made up a story about tripping on the curb and how he carried my packages to my door. I said he reminded me of my sweet old grandfather."

"You told them a man who was dallying with a dozen women was like your sweet old grandfather."

She took his hand, pointed her toe, and swept it along the ground. She appeared to be dancing. Which somehow did not surprise him.

"Whenever you want to charm someone, tell them they're the opposite. Don't praise their good qualities, praise them for qualities they don't have but want. If someone's stupid, you go on about how clever they are. Ugly, they're the handsomest thing you ever saw. Works best with boys, but parents, too. Now, for a start, they *don't* care for their daughter-in-law. She was a divorced woman when she met Elwell . . ."

Ah, that was the *never mind*, he thought. Mrs. Elwell must have worried two failed marriages would make her less sympathetic in the public eye.

With a pirouette, Zelda continued. "They think she led him

into a life of profligacy and gambling. So they are very pleased that she gets *nothing* in the will. Neither does the boy. It all goes to them, the parents. Who are convinced, by the way, that a woman murdered their son."

She did a final spin, landing up against him, eyes bright with triumph. "*Now*—who do we think that woman might be?"

Chapter Eleven

"I am astonished. I am amazed. I am *impressed*, is what I am. I am truly and sincerely . . ."

Zelda grinned from the passenger seat. "You're talking a lot."

"I'm excited. I talk a lot when I'm excited." He looked at her. "It's extraordinary. You're . . ." Repeating the word seemed inadequate, so he shouted it: "*Extraordinary!*"

They were rolling down an open country road lined with trees on one side, open field on the other. Markey was driving at a lower speed, partly so he could hear Zelda and partly because his father had always stressed that people in too much of a hurry usually ended up somewhere they didn't mean to be. But he felt so exhilarated, he was tempted to let her rip.

"The parents say who they think the woman is?" he asked.

Zelda shook her head. "But they have their suspicions, you can tell. Tell me more about the widow. If she did kill her husband, I'll think better of her."

Not taking his eyes off the road, he said, "She wants her share of the estate all right. But she has an alibi. She was seeing her lawyer at the time."

"Do you believe her?"

"The police believe her. At least she says they do. She also said Viola was lying when she said Elwell asked for a divorce. Or else Elwell was lying to Viola."

"How would the widow know?"

"Because, according to her, Elwell was a chicken chaser and Viola's not so young anymore." Markey suspected this was true. He remembered his impression that the late nights were beginning to show around Viola's eyes and mouth. He had assumed she and Zelda were the same age but now realized Viola was older, possibly by a decade. Dangerously close to the age of being put down, by Elwell's reckoning.

Zelda's lips bunched in a moue of feigned disapproval at the older woman's cattiness. She sat—lay, really—stretched out with her feet on the dashboard, twitching them this way and that as if she were conducting an orchestra with her shoes. Her dress had been wrapped snugly about her legs; now it fell free like an unfurled flag, forming a delicate hammock between her thighs. As brazen as her posture was, he could not call it flirtatious. She was not inviting him to consider her body in the slightest. Her pose was entirely unfeminine; she resembled nothing so much as himself at twelve, lounging on the porch, feet up on the white-painted balustrade, gnawing on his thumbnail. When she threw an arm over her head, he thought how splendidly at ease she was. It would take a great deal of pressure off a fellow, this confident nonchalance. Her affect suggested we all have these sacks of flesh and bone—there's no need to be so precious and terrified about it. He felt he might ask her, *What is it like? Do you think we might do it once so I get a feel for it?* And she would respond, with complete naturalness, yes or no.

The car swerved. He thought it best to return to the Elwells.

"More importantly, if the will leaves everything to his parents, she's got no financial motive for killing him. In fact, she's almost worse off than before. The grandparents'll look after the boy"— Zelda nodded to confirm this—"but given their opinion of her, Mrs. Elwell could be in a tough spot."

She raised a finger. "But did Mrs. Elwell *know* that she and her son were cut out of the will before the murder?"

It seemed to him that what Mrs. Elwell did or didn't know about her husband's will mattered less than that she had a solid alibi. Yes, Elwell had cheated on her, ignored their son, and manipulated her into a bad position financially. But she seemed genuinely dismissive of the idea that her chicken chaser of a husband would remarry, and Markey would take her word on that before he took Viola's. Mrs. Elwell was a shrewd lady and Viola wasn't.

"Can't you make this car go any faster?" Zelda asked.

"It only has two speeds."

"And you're going the slow one. *Faster.*" She actually wriggled in her seat as if willing the car to wake up. He set his hand on the throttle, recalled his father's warnings.

"I guess your friend wants his car back."

She shrugged. "You just drive like a poky old woman, that's all."

Deeply affronted, he stared at her, then shoved the throttle all the way down. The car lurched, then accelerated. Zelda threw her hands in the air and cheered. Her hair blew straight back from her face, revealing its fine, bold lines.

"Who is your friend, anyway?" he asked.

"Never mind."

"Is he a friend of *Mr.* Fitzgerald's?" She had called him a poky old woman; perhaps that was why he found himself playing the role of the stern older brother.

"I like to go fast," she offered by way of explanation.

He coughed; she must know that fast girls were called "speeds." "You shouldn't say that."

She drew closer. Draping her arm along the back of the seat, she fixed him with those green eyes she so wanted remembered. "I like to go fast."

"Well . . ." His mind was rather blank and it took him a moment. "In that case, I think you should sit back down, because I wouldn't want to hit a rock and send us both through the windshield."

"Oh, but imagine the brief but glorious flight." She rolled her shoulder, deliberately vampish. He laughed, liking her best when she admitted it was all a bit of a put-on.

He declared, "I think the widow's a dead end. The police are satisfied she was with her lawyer, and I believe her when she says Elwell had no intention of marrying Viola. Especially since you say he was being awful to her that night at the *Frolic*."

"And you still think Viola was the one who called Elwell at 2:30 in the morning?"

"Who calls that late except someone who has every reason to know he was still awake? What it *doesn't* prove is that she knew he was with another woman . . ."

"Unless Viola saw them leave together, which I still think she did. *Or* the lady in green answered Elwell's telephone for a joke. I do that at parties. 'Hello, you've reached the White House. President Wilson's on the toilet, I'm afraid.' The lady in green would be able to tell us if you put any effort into finding her."

"I asked about her at the theater. Brutally unhelpful is how I'd describe it."

Zelda continued spinning the story. "One way or another, Viola finds out she's been jilted. She stews for hours, then the next morning goes to the house, a gun concealed in her purse, and shoots Elwell dead for playing around on her."

"Except Viola was still in her pajamas when we saw her."

Zelda waved a hand as if to say, *Well, if it's not how I said, then I don't care.* For a while, they drove without talking. Markey brooded on Viola. Perhaps, in her rage, she had thrown a coat over her night things? That seemed unlikely. But even if she was not the killer, she could still be the cause.

He asked Zelda, "Can you think of anyone else who might object to Elwell's cruelty to Viola?"

Keenly examining her thumbnail, she asked, "How do you mean?"

"What would your father do if someone toyed with your affections?"

"Usually it was the other way round." She curled up on the seat. "What would your father do if someone toyed with *your* affections, Mr. Markey?"

"*If* I were a young lady delicately reared, as I'm sure you were, then my father might get out his shotgun and remind the young man of his responsibilities."

"Viola's father would be too old to be shooting people."

"But other men in her life." Recalling the chauffeur's sly insinuation about husbands, he asked, "What about her husband, Von Schlegell? Do you know if Elwell was the reason they split up?"

"I don't. She got a lot of money, though. Doesn't that mean it was his fault?"

"What's he do? Is he a gambler as well?"

"Business something. Oh, I remember. Rubber, because Scott kept asking him, 'So you're in rubbers.'"

"You said Von Schlegell and Elwell argued, that there was ill will between them. If Von Schlegell knew Elwell had no intention of marrying Viola, that'd be hard to take from a man who broke up his marriage. And if he saw Elwell leave with the woman in green . . ."

"He couldn't have seen that. He didn't come with us to the Frolic."

"Oh." His story of a jealous husband demolished, he said, "What about Viola's brother-in-law"—he struggled to remember the name, then recalled Schaeffer's grotesque remark, *Walter Lewisohn slid out of his mother a millionaire*—"Walter Lewisohn?"

Briefly, Zelda stuck out her tongue. "Lewisohn's all over Scott anytime we see them. Scott says the most awful things to him, but with a lovely smile so he never catches on."

At the invocation of her husband, she stretched, a private smile on her face. Markey sensed she was done with thinking about other people for the day.

They were back in the city now, and he had to concentrate so they didn't get killed. Zelda was deep in thought, so deep she seemed almost asleep. Approaching the Ritz, they passed a newsstand, and Markey was startled to see Viola Kraus, all limpid eyes and curling mouth, glaring at him from the front page of his own newspaper.

As Markey pulled the car up to the curb, Zelda announced, "There's only one thing for it. We'll have to go back to the *Frolic*."

"What do you mean?"

"You, me, and Scott. It's the only place I can think they would all be. Viola, the Lewisohns, and your goddess in green."

"Viola's in mourning, supposedly. Would she go to a show?"

"If I were Viola and *I'd* found out my beau was seeing girls behind my back, I'd get myself out in public and act like I hadn't a care in the world. And the Lewisohns are mad about theater. Selma sings opera, or so she says. But it'll have to be tomorrow. Tonight we have things. I'll let you know what time."

Markey knew what terror felt like. But he hadn't known it was a feeling that had so many *shades* to it. Or that one could feel it standing on the sidewalk outside the Ritz, contemplating an evening out with a beautiful girl—the most beautiful in Alabama and Georgia and, hell, you could add New York as far as he was concerned—and her husband, who happened to be F. Scott Fitzgerald.

"How will you get the car back?" he asked because it seemed the only safe thing to say.

"Oh, we're driving it back to the owner on Long Island tonight. He's having a party."

"But then how will you get home?"

She smiled, as if the question were quaint. "I don't know. Somehow!"

She trotted up the steps of the Ritz and disappeared through the revolving doors.

Chapter Twelve

Zelda didn't call the next day. She didn't call the day after either. Markey wrote up his story on Mrs. Elwell, the will that left everything to the parents, and the police belief that the widow was in the clear. He wrote a poignant portrait of Richard Elwell in his too-small school uniform and tried to keep the story of Viola Kraus and the Woman in Green alive. To his annoyance, there was now a plethora of mystery women in the papers. His very real Woman in Green had been joined by the *World*'s Woman in Black, the *Tribune*'s Woman in White, and the *Herald*'s Woman in Gray. Which showed such a lack of imagination and initiative he could spit.

Then, on the third day, Zelda left word that he was to meet her and Scott at the Ritz at eleven PM, and a whole new set of troubles took hold.

As he dressed that evening, moving quietly so as to not upset Mr. Griswold because he didn't have the time or patience to fight with him, Markey reminded himself that had anyone predicted six months ago—six *weeks* ago, six days—that he would be attending the scandalous and exclusive Midnight Frolic in the company of Scott and Zelda Fitzgerald, he would have worried that person was drinking grade-A rubbing alcohol. One part of his mind recognized that this was a magnificent gift, the sort of opportunity that transformed one's life. Another part dwelled on the fact that he was simply not prepared. He had no idea what occurred in the rarefied realm of the wealthy, beautiful, and notorious, but from bits and pieces gleaned from the newsroom and his parents' fears, he imagined it was pretty much everything. The night was going to be test after test. What, exactly, was he willing to try? Would he inject morphine, snort cocaine, remove his clothes, swing from a chandelier, pleasure two ladies at once? What was the correct response to a homosexual overture in such a setting? What if a married woman approached him in the smiling presence of her husband? Surely he would be expected to say yes to anything. He imagined Scott giving him that wry, pitying smile, Zelda a look of wide-eyed surprise and disappointment. Neither of them would speak to him again. Worse, they would tell everyone.

Maybe they would be raided and arrested before he had to take off his clothes.

He was somewhat relieved when he met Zelda and Scott in the lobby of the Ritz; there was no air of malicious anticipation, no giggling glee to indicate they had planned his humiliation. If anything, Scott seemed puzzled, asking in the taxi why they were returning to the *Frolic* when they had been a few days ago.

"Because we're looking for Viola, Selma, and Walter," Zelda explained.

"I see," said Scott, unwrapping the foil from a bottle of champagne. "I don't, but go on."

"Viola Kraus was the companion of Joseph Elwell," said Markey. "She would say fiancée, his widow says otherwise. The Lewisohns—that's Selma and Walter—are her sister and brother-in-law. All of them were with Joseph Elwell on the last night of his life."

"Elwell is the man with the wig and the bullet through his brain. That you're writing about." Fitzgerald's brow creased as he eased the cork out with his thumbs.

"Yes."

"And you think one of these rich people killed him?"

"Well, not because they're rich . . ."

"Oh, almost certainly because they're rich. The rich aren't like you and I."

The cork popped. The Fitzgeralds exclaimed in delight as it hit the ceiling of the cab. Markey lent his handkerchief to catch the overflow, then accepted a swig from the bottle, which was finished in remarkably short time. Zelda rolled down the window and Fitzgerald pitched the bottle out on the street, where it smashed in front of revelers standing outside a club. Far from minding, they cheered its destruction. They waved wildly at Scott, shouting their love, for him, for *Paradise*. He shouted back that he loved them, too. Markey heard a girl shriek Zelda's name, followed by happy screams as the thrill of seeing her, being *this close* as she passed, ran through the crowd. He leaned forward to see how she was taking it. Lips parted, she gazed through the open window, rapt and enchanted by the sight of people enchanted by her. She was, he thought, looking especially ravishing in a dark red silk dress with delicate lines of black beading that sparkled when she moved. It was a pirate's dress, he thought, and it suited her.

Scott, resplendent in black tie beside her, raised a flask and cried, "*Frolic* ho!"

Although a Ziegfeld revue, the *Midnight Frolic* took place not in the New Amsterdam Theatre but on top of it. Something in between a theater and a nightclub, the Aerial Gardens sat nearly five hundred people in its tiered seats. Small tables ringed the stage, each equipped with a telephone so guests might call friends or especially attractive people at other tables. Applause was delivered by a wooden gavel at each table. Dancing was allowed during the intermissions. The performances were rougher, lewder than those in the Follies. It was a place to sample the new. Fanny Brice had sung here. Will Rogers had twirled his lasso and made snide remarks about President Wilson. Nijinsky had stopped by. For some, the highlight of the evening was the elevator ride up to the roof. You literally rubbed shoulders with all the best people.

To Markey's relief, the ambiance, while merry and risqué, did not seem pre-orgiastic; these ladies wouldn't risk their finery. True, there were glass catwalks overhead where Follies girls paraded, smiling, arms extended. Looking up, he discovered they were not uniformly equipped with panties. He knew he had gone quite red when Zelda laughed and said, "Be careful you don't get a crick in your neck."

As the Fitzgeralds took their places at the very front, Markey noticed a heavyset man standing at a remove, his eyes on the tables, pointedly not enjoying himself. Noticing Markey's curiosity, Scott said, "Oh, that's Nana."

"Nana," Markey echoed.

"That's right. Watch." Leaning back to address the waiter, he said, "We'll have three steaks, make sure it's a young horse this time, and three lemon crushes."

"I'd like orange," said Zelda.

"Orange for the lady," corrected Scott. Then he beamed at the thick-necked gentleman. "All right, Nana?"

"Is he a police officer?" asked Markey.

"We're not sure," said Scott, looking to Zelda, who shook her head, *No, not sure.* "He could be a stagehand playing the part of a policeman to keep the real policemen at bay. Or he could be a real policeman, in which case he's not terribly bright, so let's enjoy our crush. Tell me, what are your two top things, Markey?"

"That's what we've decided to call you," said Zelda. "Scott and I are the Goofos."

"We're past formal, and 'Morris' is . . ." Fitzgerald winced at the name Markey's parents had chosen. "So, Markey it is. What are your two top things?"

Then, seeing Markey was lost, he explained, "*My* top two things are good looks and intelligence. Those are the second-tier top things, the first-tier things being money and animal magnetism. But I have both of them, which is why I get the top girl."

Zelda obligingly cradled her chin on the back of her raised hands and batted her lashes.

"What are your top things?" Fitzgerald asked. His face was open; he seemed genuinely interested. Except that all Markey could think of was how much he didn't have any of the four top things as outlined. He could hardly claim animal magnetism.

"I think I'm intelligent," he began.

"You can't *think*. You must be sure. You either are or you aren't."

"I am."

"Good man. What else?"

"He's brave," said Zelda. "And he's interested in things. And he's kind." Markey smiled his appreciation, although he did recall what she had said about praising people's weak points.

"Those aren't top things," said Fitzgerald apologetically. "Not really. They're good things, don't get me wrong. I just don't know if they're *valued*."

His tone was earnest, as if he took Markey's qualities—or lack thereof—quite seriously. They would find something, he seemed to say, for Markey to be. Markey felt torn between thanking him and punching him.

Predictably, when the crush arrived, it was so strong you could run a car on it. Following Scott's example, Markey downed it in one, then coughed. The next one went down more smoothly, and by the time his eyes had stopped watering, he was almost enjoying himself. He smiled benevolently at his hosts, these two ravishing children with their flasks and nanas and top things. They were playing a game of coming up with rhymes for animals. Scott had proposed turtle, to which Zelda promptly answered, "Girdle." He said, "Birdle." She said, "Objection!" Scott launched into a serious explanation of the fabled birdle, a creature of the Amazon that migrated to its nest, following the great river.

Zelda said, "I'll allow it, barely. You do one, Markey."

Put on the spot, he struggled. Then it came to him. "Hurdle. Hurtle. Oh, and fertile." Zelda applauded enthusiastically, Scott cynically. Then they turned back to each other.

Markey felt humbled by their infatuation, the way their excitement grew as they conversed, agreeing and building on what the other had said. They looked as if they had just discovered each other and could not believe their luck. Their gaze never broke. Seated a foot apart, they swayed and arched in a harmonious flow as if tethered by a sinuous elastic band. They were rather wonderful, he thought to his drink, and when he thought they weren't looking, he raised his glass to them.

But of course they were looking. Zelda burst out with "Sweet!" and Scott instantly became knowing and ironic once more. Even so, he patted Markey's hand and said, "Let's have another round and then we'll look for your murderer." When Markey held up his hand to indicate enough, Scott drank his. He talked of his time at Princeton, his poor grades, the clubs to which he'd been accepted, the ones that had refused him. For a man with the world at his feet, Markey thought, he did seem to brood on the matter of *getting in*. Being accepted by the right people. Markey also noted that Zelda had not touched her drink. She was staying behind, he thought—a lonely endeavor on two points, risking the companionship of her husband and the fellowship of alcohol. Not wanting her to be lonely, he said, "Do you see Viola anywhere? They'd be in the front row, wouldn't they?"

"Yes, they would," she said quickly, twisting in her seat.

But as they began the search, the lights went down and the show began. Streamers were thrown by a frantically happy parade of dancers overhead as the crowd cheered the start of the festivities. The band swung into action, the brass proclaiming its power with the undeniable force of a bouncer's fist. There was nothing to do but sit and enjoy the naked flailing limbs and the bright, stiff smiles of the dancers. At a certain point, champagne arrived at the table—a gift from an admirer, the waiter murmured into Scott's ear. Scott's arm shot into the air; he had recognized the sender. In a moment, he was off to say hello. Zelda lit a cigarette.

At one point, girls sauntered through the theater to have their balloons popped by patrons' cigars, applause and laughter greeting every burst, oohs of anticipation rising as the gentleman extended his hand and the girl twitched in supposed fear and modesty—*What shall happen to my balloon?* Markey thought this was in bad taste. There was a cruelty to it he didn't like. With the first pop, he flinched. He hoped now it was over, the point had been made. But there seemed to be an endless stream of girls, countless balloons exploding, the voices of the guests rising to a shout. The noise was unbearable, surely a sign that something awful was about to happen, annihilation was near . . .

"Markey, are you all right?"

Startled, he saw Zelda reaching across the table for him.

"You've gone all fidgety."

Had he? He became aware his shoulders were around his ears, his neck ached, his fingers were tight on the edge of the table. There was an ugly hissing in his ears. Through his legs, an electric current hummed.

"I've never cared much for balloons," he managed.

"The girls aren't hurt," she promised.

He smiled, grateful for her mistake, pleased that she thought him the sort of man who worried girls might be harmed. "No, I know."

"It does seem a bit mean," she tried. "And . . . *loud*."

She watched him carefully as she guessed. He nodded, admitting loud was the problem. But his shoulders had eased. Breath was coming more easily—now that he'd remembered breathing was generally a good idea. The buzzing in the arches of his feet and the back of his knees subsided. The hiss faded. He let up on the table; holding tight no longer seemed essential to survival. Zelda poured him a glass of champagne and he drank it. He wasn't sure it helped, but it was something to do so he didn't scream. Then the girls receded and some comedy act with a singing dog came on and everyone went back to table-hopping. Markey looked for the girl in green, but did not see her. Of course she wouldn't be wearing that particular dress. The new short hairstyles made it hard to tell girls apart. But he felt sure he would know her once he saw her again.

He felt Zelda's fingers rapping the top of his hand. "They're here . . ."

Still disoriented, he said, "Who?"

"Viola. And Selma and Walter. What do you want me to do? Should I wave?"

"I . . ." The opportunity was right there, but he still felt panicked and scattered. How would he dissemble?

The telephone on their table rang. Markey spasmed, as if jolted by an electric shock. But Zelda's eyes went wide and eager as if a cascade of diamonds had been sluiced onto the table.

"Let's answer!"

For some reason, he thought it dangerous to answer, so dangerous he couldn't quite get the words out. Zelda snatched up the telephone, said, "Hello?" Her eyebrows jumped; it was them. "Of course! You come right on over . . . No, I'm sure he'll be back shortly."

Scott had been asked for. As she promised his return, Zelda looked about the theater. Markey looked, too, but did not see him. Hanging up, she said, "Well, I've got another writer for them, anyway."

"You do?"

"Yes! I've got *you*!" She shook her head: *You are ridiculous.*

"I think it's best if we don't mention that." Hopefully Viola was not a reader of the *Daily News* and had not seen his articles quoting—and accusing—her.

In the next moment, Viola and the Lewisohns were upon them. Viola and Zelda exchanged the breathless, excited pleasantries that seemed the custom in New York. Viola nodded in his direction, murmuring "Howdyoudo," but took the seat at the farthest remove from his. He rose to introduce himself to the Lewisohns. They shook his hand limply, disappointed that he was not Scott Fitzgerald.

In the dim light of the theater, he examined Selma Lewisohn. Zelda had said she sang opera, and befitting that profession, her looks were dramatic and severe, lacking the fey, kittenish appeal of her sister. Her face was long, slightly heavy through the jaw, her dark eyes sloping, her mouth full but discontented. Still, she had a certain powerful eroticism. Medea, he thought, or Lady Macbeth, those would be her roles.

A potato with legs was his first impression of Walter Lewisohn. He was a short man with round glasses and an expensive suit. His thinning brown hair was heavy with oil. All that wealth, thought Markey, and still he resembled a picture Markey might have drawn as a child—blobby circles with stick limbs. After shaking Markey's hand, he flapped like a penguin, arms lifting and falling against his sides. "Zelda," he said by way of greeting. "Zelda."

He seemed to count seconds, then asked "Where's Scott?" in the belligerent tone of a diner whose meal has not yet arrived.

"He's been called off somewhere," said Zelda. She patted the chair. "But sit down and tell us: How *are* you? I was so sorry to hear the news of Mr. Elwell."

"Terrible," barked Lewisohn. Markey, keenly aware when he himself felt not right, thought, *This man is off.* He felt Selma Lewisohn assessing him. She was definitely the elder sister. Wanting to ingratiate himself and get a sense of her, he said, "Mrs. Fitzgerald tells me you sing opera."

"Yes," she said, and left it at that.

"Madame Selma is a wonder," announced Lewisohn. "You will not hear a finer voice anywhere."

"Madame Selma" rolled her eyes. Markey did not blame her. Even as he praised his wife, Lewisohn's attention had been firmly fixed on the shapely legs passing overhead. His head was tilted, his mouth open. He looked like a spectator of a fireworks display.

Viola reached for the champagne bottle. Markey saw that she was taking great pains to be indifferent to him; clearly she didn't want her family to know they had already met. Wanting her trust, he played along. "I'm very sorry for the loss of your friend, Miss Kraus. Do the police have any suspects yet?"

"Oh, yes," Selma answered for her sister. "You're looking at three of them."

Zelda affected shock. "But that's crazy."

"Why is that?" asked Markey. "Because you were the last people to see him?"

"I—" said Viola.

Her sister interrupted, "We were *not* the last people to see him. He wanted to meet those other people, so we left without him. Remember, Viola?"

"Oh, yes, I suppose I was a bit tipsy."

Markey tried to remember. Had Viola mentioned other people when they spoke at the hotel? No. She had only said Elwell wanted to go somewhere else and she was tired. Selma was trying to steer the guilt elsewhere.

"Did you tell the police about these other people?" he asked Mrs. Lewisohn. "The police should be talking to them, not troubling you in your grief."

Selma Lewisohn saw the trap and said coldly, "I don't know who they were."

Then she gave a pointed look to her younger sister. Viola bit her lip, and announced in a high, strained voice, "I was never engaged to Joseph Elwell. And I did not appreciate you saying that I was in your article, Mr. Markey."

The reversal was so extreme, Markey had to check his faculties; was he drunk? No, he was not. The surprise on Zelda's face reassured him they had heard the same thing at the hotel.

The mood at the table had become distinctly chilly. Selma Lewisohn asked him, "What did you say you do?"

There was no point in denying it. "I'm a reporter for the *Daily News*."

Lewisohn pointed to him, demanding of his wife, "This is *that* reporter?"

"Apparently so," said Mrs. Lewisohn.

Lewisohn swung his finger in Markey's direction, leaning in so close it seemed he meant to shove it up his nose. "What you wrote is irresponsible. Worse than irresponsible, it was boldfaced *lies*."

The richly clad Lewisohn posterior was rising from its chair. Wanting to hear their new story, but also protect his nose, Markey said, "Forgive me, Miss Kraus, your sorrow seemed so genuine . . ."

"I was *sad*, of course."

Here she broke off, looked to her sister and brother-in-law. They were controlling the new stage of the story, thought Markey.

"But your insinuation that Viola was a woman scorned is ludicrous," said Selma. "Neither she nor I knew the man well. We were light acquaintances, if anything."

"Not well at *all*," said Lewisohn. "And if you write anything to the contrary, I will not just sue. I will not just have you fired. I will have you broken."

The threat silenced the table.

"He was old enough to be my *father*," said Viola, as if she had suddenly remembered her lines.

Markey looked to Zelda, who was thoughtfully sipping her

crush. She met his eye and they agreed: If they pronounced Viola's claim hooey, they wouldn't get to hear more.

"Let me correct the story, then," he said. "How did you become acquainted?"

"*I* knew Elwell," said Lewisohn as Viola piped up, "I met him as a child in Palm Beach forever ago."

"You were business associates," Markey said to Lewisohn as if he now understood.

"That's right. I advised him on certain things. Art acquisitions. Real estate."

"Walter helped Joe find his house," said Viola eagerly. Selma shot her sister a look. That was not supposed to have been divulged. Or she was not supposed to refer to her "light acquaintance" as Joe.

"Bernard Sandler, the owner of the house on Seventieth Street, has his office near Lewisohn Brothers," explained Selma.

"We were getting our shoes shined one day, and Sandler mentioned he needed a tenant," said Lewisohn expansively.

Markey very much doubted Lewisohn had his shoes shined by anyone other than his valet, but he left that alone. He hadn't realized that Elwell's house was rented. The gambler had not put the house up for sale, his landlord had. And yet Elwell had still been very much in residence. A tenant who refused to leave could be a nuisance.

He looked back to Viola, who was taking a long drink of champagne. That she had changed her story so dramatically suggested she was capable of lying on a grander scale than he previously had suspected. He had been surprised at their luck, finding Viola and the Lewisohns at the *Frolic* so easily. He had assumed the allure of the Fitzgeralds had drawn them to their table. Now he wondered if they had come specifically so Viola could change her story.

Just then a waiter passed their table, carrying a tray full of glasses and a bottle. Hurrying, he came just a shade too close, and Walter

Lewisohn became aware of him. Furious, Lewisohn pushed away from the table and followed. Neither wife nor sister-in-law seemed surprised by Lewisohn's sudden departure. Zelda widened her eyes; he was meant to notice the awfulness of the Lewisohn marriage. He nodded to say: *Noted.*

They heard Lewisohn screaming profanities, a clang, then the crash of a tray and glasses. Markey looked in the direction of the sound and saw Lewisohn smiling meanly as he stood in a pool of shattered glass and spilled liquor. The young waiter looked distraught. Markey guessed the cost would come out of his pay.

"Selma," said Viola quietly.

Selma sighed. "Yes, I suppose so." Rising, she said, "If you'll excuse me . . ."

Half rising himself, Markey said, "Of course."

When the Lewisohns were out of earshot, Zelda said in a reproachful tone, "Viola."

Viola fiddled with the clasp of her jeweled clutch. "Mrs. Fitzgerald?"

"I'm surprised, is all. You were so heartbroken."

Markey said quietly, "I distinctly remember you telling us you were engaged to Joseph Elwell."

Viola pulled off one glove, twitched her hand at him to show naked fingers.

"Yes, but you said you were waiting for him to divorce his wife."

"I was upset, Mr. Markey. I really don't remember what I said."

"That's all right, I do."

If she had not been so blatant in her assumption that she could change the past to suit her present, as if reality were a pair of old curtains, he would have been kinder. At least better mannered. But Fitzgerald was right about the rich: They were different. They didn't treat you as they would treat people like themselves. So he needn't either.

"Who did Elwell leave with that night?" he asked. "I have a feeling you know very well."

"I don't remember. I . . . I was tired."

Zelda pounced. "Before you said you didn't know because you left before he did."

"No, I said he wanted to go somewhere else." Viola had begun to look around the room for her sister.

Markey said, "So you called him at 2:30 in the morning because you were worried about him?"

"No . . . I didn't, I . . ."

She was on the verge of panicking. Drawing closer, he said, "Come on now, Miss Kraus, you knew all along Elwell spent the night with another woman. Maybe you even know her name. I'm sure the police would be grateful to know it . . ."

"Mr. Markey?"

Selma Lewisohn had returned to the table. Without her husband.

"I wonder if you would do me a kindness. I cannot find Mr. Lewisohn. Would you see if he is anywhere backstage?"

Viola said, "Selma . . ."

"And if he is, remind him that we are waiting for him."

On the surface, Mrs. Lewisohn was exerting the time-honored privilege of a lady. She was in distress; as a gentleman, he must assist her, her husband being not only absent but the cause of that distress. Of course what she was really doing was interrupting his questioning of her sister. But she could have done that in any number of ways: taken Viola back to their table, brightly changed the subject, even demanded that he stop. Instead, she was siccing him on her husband, who was no doubt making an ass of himself. Why?

He was intrigued enough to say, "I'll try, Mrs. Lewisohn. If you'll cover any breakage," he added, reminding her that her husband had already threatened him once.

"I would be grateful."

As he stood up, Zelda said, "Keep an eye out for Scott." Her tone was carefree, but she was chewing on her thumbnail. She didn't like the turn events had taken.

Weaving through the crowded club, Markey followed busboys and balloon girls here and there until he found a way backstage. In a place that advertised as the promised land, the promise being that anything goes, it was relatively easy. He was nicely dressed, he wasn't too intoxicated, and he lacked the arrogance of the truly rich. When he approached a middle-aged man whose bored demeanor and indifference to naked flesh suggested he was in charge, the stage manager instantly recognized him for what he was: a clean-up man.

"I'm looking for a gentleman who's making a nuisance of himself," he said. "Someone you can't toss in the gutter."

The manager nodded toward a narrow hallway that led to the dressing rooms, with the instruction, "Paws off the girls." It wasn't hard to find Walter after that. All he had to do was follow the shouts of "No, Walter, I said no!"

The corridor of dressing rooms was cramped and crowded with performers. Men in evening wear tied their tap shoes. Ladies tugged at their bodices and pinned feathered headpieces more securely. A parrot squawked; a ventriloquist dummy lay sideways over a chair, its wooden mouth agape. A terrier in a clown suit skittered in and around feet. A juggler kept his hands loose by tossing three balls in a continuous loop. A small clutch of people had gathered at the third door. Markey asked a gentleman in tights who stood with his foot behind his head, "Is there an ugly rich man in there?"

He nodded. "Good luck getting in."

Markey discovered what he meant. It was easy enough to turn the knob and crack the door ajar. But it was immediately slammed shut. Markey caught a glimpse of black wool and greasy hair.

He called through the door, "Your wife would like to leave now, Walter."

The door opened. The banker stared up at him furiously. "What did you call me?"

"I thought last names were best avoided."

"Get him out of here!" The voice was feminine and angry. At first, Markey couldn't tell where it was coming from; the tiny room looked empty. Then he saw one of the curtains was quite bulky. Below the hem, a lovely pair of calves and bare feet.

Lewisohn said, "Tell Selma I'll be a moment."

Markey sensed that this would have to become physical. He wished someone else would take on the task. But when he looked around, everyone seemed to be waiting for him to do it. "No, she said now."

In graphic terms, Lewisohn specified a lack of interest in his wife's wishes. In equally graphic terms, the girl behind the curtain told Lewisohn to leave. Lewisohn started to close the door, but Markey put his shoulder to the wood. Leaning heavily to give the shorter man some idea of what was coming, he said, "Both ladies want you to leave, it seems to me."

"It seems to *you*?"

"Yes, sir."

"*You?*" Now Lewisohn was bubbling with laughter. "Who the hell are you?"

Markey said he was the man his wife had sent, but the millionaire was laughing too hard to hear him. His amusement was such, he bowed under the weight of it, dropping his head, hands on his knees as he howled. He could not catch his breath and could only manage ". . . you . . . you . . ." before succumbing to his own mirth.

Markey found himself smiling. Lewisohn's laughter blocked out all sound, all dissonance, and all worry. The hissing had stopped. The snapping electricity that had threatened to burn him alive a short while ago surged to his hands and found its purpose. He took a moment, assessed the man's center of gravity. Then he slapped the millionaire's left ear and seized his nose, hooking a finger up one nostril. Keeping hold of the ear, he pulled Lewisohn's head in, Lewisohn instinctively following because he didn't want his nose torn. A solid kick to the knee tumbled him to the floor. The thud was deeply satisfying. Markey resisted the urge to land a blow to the ribs; he didn't want any grounds for charges later on. Instead, he reached down and took hold of one arm—the pits were warm and damp. The acrobat took the other. As they dragged Lewisohn from the room, Markey called to the curtain, "I apologize for this . . ." A long slender arm waved farewell, its middle finger raised high.

Thankfully, by the time Lewisohn recovered enough to scream obscenities, the bouncers had arrived. They were nice bouncers, polite, but they knew their business and escorted the millionaire back to his wife and agreed with her that it was time to go home. Lewisohn was allowed to stand on his own. He began to hum. Selma and Viola collected their things. Markey stood braced, one hand gripping a nearby chair. But Lewisohn's expression was genial. Stepping forward suddenly, he clapped Markey by the arm like an old friend.

"I'm going to gut you," he promised.

Markey waited for Selma to say, *You'll do no such thing.* But she either hadn't heard the threat or she hadn't remembered her pledge of gratitude. Or meant it.

Viola, on the other hand, was watching everything, her eyes bright and avid. Markey met her gaze, then looked away, disturbed.

"Markey?"

He had been so intent on the Lewisohns, he had forgotten the Fitzgeralds. Hearing concern in Zelda's voice, he was about to assure her he was fine. Then he noticed she was looking not at him but at the stage, where Scott stood nearby, removing his white tie, grinning feverishly as he watched the chorus girls. The tie dispensed with, he shrugged off his jacket and threw it to the floor. Then he flipped his suspenders from his shoulders and began undoing the buttons of his trousers. He clearly had every intention of joining the unclothed ladies onstage.

He said to Zelda, "Shall I?"

"I think so, yes."

Markey had some experience in stopping men from going where they wished. In operating rooms, he had held men down when they were out of their minds with pain, had lugged them onto stretchers, even stopped them running toward the bullets because they wanted it to be over. He was bigger than Scott, but the writer's determination to be onstage seemed formidable.

Scott was down to his underwear and garters when he reached him. The bronze hair was dark with sweat, the girlish mouth distorted with inebriated glee. Ready to leap, he looked feral—and incompetent. Hooking his arm under Fitzgerald's, Markey said, "Zelda wants you."

Scott peered at Markey as if he barely remembered him. He tried to twist away, insisting, "My friends are waiting for me."

"Yes, they are," said Markey, sliding an arm around the writer's neck. "Over there."

He started dragging Fitzgerald away from the stage, not easy when the writer was struggling to escape. People leapt up to avoid having their chairs kicked out from under them. Some cheered and applauded. Others looked annoyed. Apologizing to everyone and no one as he went, he deposited a giggling Fitzgerald into the seat next to Zelda, who said, "Did you find his jacket and pants?" It was his night, apparently, to be an errand boy.

But when he went to fetch them, he discovered the clothes had been snatched up as souvenirs. Returning to the table, he allowed himself to wonder if Fitzgerald pulled such stunts because he drank too much or because he liked to imagine people sighing, *So unconventional—he must be a genius!* As he made his way through the crush of people, he looked for the Lewisohns. They were long gone. He had failed to find the girl in green. He told himself it was tiredness and the late hour that had him feeling despondent.

He found Scott and Zelda by the coat check. Scott was fast asleep on the floor. Zelda was asking if she might have something from lost and found so that America's most distinguished man of letters didn't have to go home in his underwear.

In the taxi, Markey and Zelda sat Scott between them. At one point, the cab stopped suddenly short, jolting Fitzgerald awake. Drunk, dazed, he looked around, as if unsure whether they were starting the night or ending it. Then he began to cry.

"It will never be this good again. Never. Life will never be . . . this perfect again."

With a long, agonized shudder, he closed his eyes.

Chapter Thirteen

"That was *bizarre*," announced Zelda.

Coming back from the bedroom where he had laid Scott on the bed, Markey paused to ask "Which part of it?" before falling on the sofa. Water, he needed water and lots of it. The thought of food made his stomach swim. His arm ached. Looking about the suite, he saw the floor was strewn with newspapers with articles cut out. Picking one up, he saw that the Fitzgeralds were keeping a record of their adventures. No doubt tonight's exploits would go straight into the scrapbook.

Zelda was wide awake. Pacing, she asked, "Did you take his shoes off?"

He nodded.

"Good. Viola changing her story like that. Saying she barely knew the man after weeping to us about her lost love. Do you want spinach?"

"Not in the least."

"I crave spinach." She took up the telephone. "Yes, hello, room service." To him, "You want anything, a clubhouse sandwich? I feel you should eat. Yes, hello! I'd like a plate of spinach, please."

She looked to him, inquiring. Feeling the world had gone mad, he decided to give in. "Eggs. Scrambled."

"And a plate of scrambled eggs with toast . . ."

He nodded. Toast was a good idea. "Water."

She widened her eyes: *Yes.* "And a bottle of seltzer water. If you could manage a bottle of champagne, that would be divine. Thank you. You know—"

She returned to the sofa, falling on it.

"When Walter said he was going to gut you, you should have knocked him down."

"I did. When we were backstage."

"Oh! I'm sorry I missed that."

He accepted the compliment of her interest, but he felt disturbed by the evening. That Viola and the Lewisohns knew his name and face was not a comfortable thing. And for all the drama of the past few hours, he had no story for tomorrow, and as Schaeffer had often told him: no story, no pay. Lewisohn's invasion of the chorus girl's dressing room was too hot; Schaeffer wouldn't touch it. There was Viola's sudden change of heart regarding Elwell, but Markey didn't want to do her the favor of spreading her phony story. But how to prove it was phony? The lie was so bold, he would need fresh evidence to challenge it.

There was a gentle knock at the door. Crying "Food!" Zelda ran to open it. She ran well, Markey noticed, her stride powerful and sure. The food sailed into the room, borne aloft on a white covered cart, pushed by a uniformed waiter who lifted each of the silver domes to reveal steaming hot eggs and spinach. He indicated the freshly made toast, the small pots of jam and butter. He poured the seltzer, opened the champagne. Signing the bill with a flourish, Zelda thanked him. Seated on sofas on either side of the table, they ate. She had some of his eggs; he ate some of her spinach. He had never realized how good spinach and eggs were together.

Zelda poured champagne into coffee cups. "I looked for your lady in green. I didn't see anyone who matched your worshipful description."

"I didn't see her either. Maybe I'm wrong and Elwell met her somewhere else. Picked her up off the street. Maybe I'm just wrong about everything."

"You're gloomy."

He nodded, admitting it. The worst of it was he didn't actually believe he was wrong, just that he couldn't prove he was right. Chewing, he brooded: How to get *at* them? How to break down that fortress wall of wealth and influence? A bit of toast fell on the floor. Hungry, he looked to retrieve it and saw a headline from his own newspaper: ELWELL'S MYSTERY PARAMOUR! Hal Meyers had been poaching again.

Furious, he snatched up the paper, and read the headline out loud, adding, "'Police are investigating the movements of a mysterious woman who is said to be a frequent visitor to the Elwell house. She had stayed overnight on several occasions, leaving items of intimate apparel behind.'"

Lowering the paper, he told Zelda, "You know how the police found out about that intimate apparel? Me, that's how. Hal Meyers wouldn't even have this story except he's Carey's pet." He realized she didn't know or care who Hal was, but he felt the need to make the point. Also, the need to knock Hal Meyers across a room.

Zelda stretched and reclined against the pillows. "Oh, we get *loud* when we're gloomy."

"No, but listen to this: 'District Attorney Swann refused to identify the lady, calling her only "Miss Wilson." The DA added, "To protect the honor of womanhood, we have decided to withhold the girl's real name for the present."' Honor, my . . . posterior, he's talking about a girl who goes to a man's house, stays overnight, leaves her undergarments hither and yon, and he's blabbing about honor."

"Hither and yon—oh, dear. Hither is one thing, yon another, but hither *and* yon, that just won't do."

He understood that he was being serious and she was no longer in the mood for serious. Still, he said, "The DA has to know Viola is Miss Wilson. If he doesn't know it, he's too dumb to walk upright. Someone needs to be looking at donations to Swann's campaign. I bet you'd find a big one from Lewisohn."

"Shush, you'll wake Scott."

She had closed her eyes. Markey looked at the remains of their meal. The toast rack was empty, the eggs and spinach just smears of green and yellow on the plates. The champagne bottle lay sideways, and the seltzer bottle had produced only a sad wheeze the last he tried it.

He placed his hands on his thighs, said, "Well . . ."

"Where you going?"

"It's late." He gestured to the door.

"You don't have to *go*." Her arm fell dramatically to the floor. Rolling over onto her side, she looked at him, head propped on her hand. One knee slid forward over the other, bringing her pirate dress high up on her thigh. "Just stop being noisy and pompous and tell me what you're going to do. Personally, it's starting to be my opinion that anyone who lets themselves be shoved around by creatures as ridiculous as Selma and Walter lacks the spine to shoot a man, even if he does wear a wig. How do you know Miss Wilson isn't your girl in green?"

He didn't. And he should have considered that possibility. Through the fog of the late hour, failure, and alcohol, Markey forced himself to sort through the possibilities, concluding, "I need to talk to someone who knows what went on in that house."

"Who would that be?"

"Mrs. Larsen. The housekeeper. But she's mad at me."

"Why, what'd you do to her?"

Hearing the amusement in her voice, he knew he was halfway forgiven. "I said I would help Elwell, but then I looked through his underwear drawer." That had been the complaint, as far as he remembered.

"His underwear drawer. What a terrible person you are, Morris Markey."

Her tone was such he thought he had never heard sweeter words. He pushed off his shoes so he could stretch out on the sofa. He needed to close his eyes for a moment.

Then he felt Zelda standing over him, her hands on his face as she gently removed his glasses. The red silk fell away from body as she leaned down.

"You're going to have to make it up with Mrs. Larsen," she told him.

"How?" he murmured.

But she was gone. For a moment, he fretted, wanting the smell and warmth of her back. Then she returned with a blanket. Throwing it over him, she said, "Try flowers, that usually helps."

Then, as she adjusted the pillow behind his head, she said, "What'll you do if you do find your dream girl in green?"

He opened his eyes, met hers. "Duck."

She smiled. "No, you won't."

Markey woke hours later to the sound of howling. Confused, he stared at his sumptuous surroundings, then sat up as Scott staggered into the room. Markey winced. His own head didn't feel any too good. But Fitzgerald looked dragged up from the grave.

"Zelda says I'm to take you to buy flowers," he croaked.

Markey couldn't imagine a crueler thing than making this man face daylight. "That's all right. I think I'm competent enough . . ."

"She doesn't think so." He fell onto the floor by the sofa, clutching his middle. "It is possible I'm dying. I feel I have to make that clear."

"It's clear." Tentatively, he indicated the phone. "Do you want me to call for some coffee?"

"Christ, no. I'm going to have a shower." As he got to his feet, he asked, "Who is the lady in question?"

"Mrs. Larsen. Elwell's housekeeper."

Fitzgerald's expression showed that he understood he was being punished for last night's excesses. Also, that he considered the punishment harsh indeed. Astonishingly, fifteen minutes later, he emerged dressed, hair combed, and smile restored. His gait was not the steadiest. But he was sprightly enough, saying they would go to the hotel florist's and thus avoid "the head-splitting presence of the sober, sensible man."

There was something flamboyant in the way he proclaimed his opposition to such a man that made Markey wonder. "Were you really that drunk when you tried to jump onstage?"

"It's in all the newspapers," the author tsked. "These wild, hedonistic youths . . ."

Irked to be seen as that gullible, Markey said, "You're a bit of a fraud, aren't you?"

The elevator was packed. As they squeezed in, Markey sensed a ripple of excitement over Fitzgerald's presence. It created a strange energy when someone was "recognized." As if they were all pallid and gray and Fitzgerald the only full-blooded human in the space. Markey resented being consigned to grayness, but it was hard to compete with Fitzgerald's bright plumage.

Aware that he had an audience, Scott said in a raised voice, "Do you think your 'peculiar institution' is why Southern women are so bad at housework? Zelda does not spin, neither does she toil, nor cook, nor clean. Not in the entire time I've known her."

"I don't think you married her for her housekeeping," said Markey.

"She says Northerners are far more sexually inhibited than Southerners. Would you say that's true?"

Markey looked to his fellow passengers for rescue. They looked eager to hear his answer. "I would say I have had neither the pleasure nor disappointment of discovering."

"So, just as inhibited," guessed Scott. "Or maybe more so."

As they emerged from the elevator—Markey noticed the crowd hung back to let Fitzgerald spring forth first—the writer asked, "Why are you buying a housekeeper flowers?"

"I upset her and I have to make it up to her."

"Ah." They were at the florist. Striding up to the counter, Fitzgerald said to the young woman, "This man needs to atone. Which flowers say to a girl 'I've been an ass and I want you to love me again'?"

Markey intervened. "I just want to say I'm sorry. She doesn't need to love me."

"No miracles necessary," the writer clarified. "A simple old-fashioned apology from a simple old-fashioned fellow."

"Purple hyacinth symbolizes regret and remorse," the florist told Fitzgerald.

"'Regret and remorse,'" he said dreamily, chin on his hand. "What hideous words."

"That sounds fine," said Markey. "May I ask how much?"

"No, no, this is on me," announced Fitzgerald. "Put a dozen hyacinths on my tab. And something for Mrs. Fitzgerald . . ."

The florist frowned, removing herself from the counter. The tab, guessed Markey, had become sizable. Digging in his pocket, he said, "It's my apology, I should pay."

He laid a few crumpled dollars on the counter. "How much will that . . ."

"Six hyacinths," said the florist crisply. "Any number of daisies and ragweed, though."

"Six is fine." He looked at Fitzgerald. "Did you want something for . . ."

Fitzgerald waved his hand. *No, and shut up.*

"Just the six hyacinths, please."

As they left, two young women bashfully approached Fitzgerald to ask for his autograph. He flirted pleasantly, signed, and sent them on their way. Seeing how the warm splash of attention restored the author's mood, Markey stated the obvious. "Must be nice."

"It's not terrible."

There was a wistfulness that reminded Markey. "Last night, is that why you said . . . ?"

He had been about to ask if Fitzgerald had meant it when he said life would never be this good again. Then he decided Fitzgerald probably wouldn't remember.

Hyacinths in hand, Markey went home to wash up and change. Reaching his building was now a challenge. As the police continued to interview witnesses at the Elwell house, hundreds of sightseers crowded the block, keeping an eye on who was called in. They passed along—or invented—updates, and advocated fiercely for their preferred culprit. A sham minister railed that Elwell had been killed due to "Sexitis! The abnormal overdevelopment of sex consciousness. The people in this city are money-mad and pleasure-crazed! America is on a joyride." Markey threw him a sarcastic amen. Then he was cornered by a gentleman who told him that Elwell sometimes engaged in underhanded signals and had been killed for cheating. Next a tottering fellow with rancid breath confessed that he had killed the gambler. The gun was at the bottom of the Hudson if Markey cared to look. When Markey asked why he had killed the bridge master, he said, "I didn't like his face."

Reaching his house, Markey saw Griswold at the window. The old crank had seemed less argumentative of late. But when Markey called, "See anything of interest, Mr. Griswold?" he scowled and withdrew into his apartment.

Since her loss of employment, Mrs. Larsen had been working at her husband's butcher shop. It was a thriving establishment with clean sawdust on the floor, fresh joints in the window, and a crowd of women who moved in and out, parcels of chops, steaks, and chicken wrapped in brown paper under their arms. Mr. Larsen attended to the customers. Mrs. Larsen sat at the cash register. When Markey walked in, she noticed him, as did her husband. When the last customer had been served, the butcher came out from behind the counter and said, "Yes, can I help you?" His accent was stronger than his wife's.

"He is here to see me," said Mrs. Larsen.

The butcher gestured to the hyacinths. "And he brings you flowers."

"They're an apology," Markey said nervously. The butcher was not a small man, and there were cleavers nearby. He proffered the flowers to Mrs. Larsen. "Please. I'm truly sorry for the way I took advantage of your trust when you needed my help."

A brief conversation took place between husband and wife. It was in Norwegian, so he didn't understand it. But he caught the name *Elwell* and the word *journalist*. He could see, from the butcher's darkening expression, these were not pleasant words. Mr. Larsen obviously shared his wife's aversion to the press. Markey felt it best to come clean.

"Mrs. Larsen, I'll be honest. I'd like to ask you a few things about . . ." He took a step toward her, intending to place the flowers on the counter. As he did, his head swam and he pulled up short; it had been several hours since the eggs and spinach.

Immediately, Mrs. Larsen was up. Her husband objected, and she argued. Gently but firmly. Then she said to Markey, "You come upstairs, you have something to eat. You ask your questions. Then you go. Understood?"

"Yes, ma'am."

The Larsens lived in an apartment above the shop. There, she cooked quickly in a small, light kitchen with a wooden table set for two. Markey noted the yellow curtains at the window, a gingham dishcloth, and a calendar on the wall. It was a peaceful space.

The sausages were excellent. "I can see why your husband does good business."

Then, as she poured them coffee, he leaned forward. "Mrs. Larsen, you cared for Mr. Elwell. Respected him. I saw that."

"He was a good man so far as I knew. A good employer."

"Then help me figure out who did this. The chauffeur told me Mr. Elwell gave five women the keys to his house. The police are lost, the DA's office is a mess. For better or worse, if we don't write about a suspect, nothing happens—especially if the suspect is rich."

A slight frown told him he was getting somewhere. "You had to know something about the women. The pictures, if nothing else."

"I knew many women admired Mr. Elwell. But as to who they were or what he felt about any of them . . ." She shrugged.

Trying to draw her out on the subject of Viola Kraus so he could expose the socialite's lies, he said, "He didn't mention he might be getting divorced? Or remarried?"

She looked exasperated. "'Good morning, Mr. Elwell.' 'Good morning, Mrs. Larsen.' 'I will have two fried eggs and a divorce, please.' I cooked. I cleaned. We didn't discuss his private life."

"You made him breakfast?" She nodded. "Was it always just him at the table?"

She hesitated, then admitted, "Sometimes there was a guest."

"Was that guest ever Viola Kraus?"

"No." Agitated by this small disloyalty, she wrung her hands. "Why does it matter? The police say a woman could not shoot such a gun."

"I've shot a .45 and I don't think it's impossible. Mrs. Larsen, on the last night of Joseph Elwell's life, I saw him with a very attractive young woman. She was tall, with auburn hair. They probably met at the *Frolic*. She moved like a dancer."

She smiled slightly. "This is your famous woman in green."

"Yes. Does she sound like anyone you might have seen at the breakfast table?"

"No, I am afraid not." She poured him more coffee. "Would you like to hear my theory on why it cannot be a woman who shot Mr. Elwell?"

"Please."

"Do you remember what he looked like that morning?"

The three teeth crooked and pointless in the slack, livery mouth. The sparse strands of hair over the age-spotted head. He nodded.

"No teeth. No hair. His face . . . pale. Without makeup. Had there been a lady present, Mr. Elwell would never have left his bedroom in such a state. When he had guests, he did not come downstairs until he was presentable. You understand?"

He did, and he felt the truth of what she was saying. But she had touched on something that had long puzzled him. "Didn't they . . . know?"

"Know what?"

"If a lady spends the night in a gentleman's house, I assume certain intimacies occur. A woman sharing his bed would know what he looked like, surely."

"But they are not sharing. The guest room—that is where the ladies sleep when they come."

"Are you saying he never . . . ?"

"Of course not," said Mrs. Larsen with full Lutheran fervor. "Of *course* not. Mr. Elwell was a gentleman."

Markey was skeptical. He remembered the lingerie in the closet— vividly.

Sensing his line of thought, Mrs. Larsen said, "Mr. Elwell was often out late. Sometimes his companion does not wish to return home because she has had something to drink and she does not wish her family to know. Or she is tired and her home is not close. Of course he provides the things a lady will need if she is staying the night. Soaps, hairbrushes, nightgowns."

He decided not to argue with her. If Mrs. Larsen insisted on believing she worked for an honorable man who wouldn't lay a finger on a nubile guest, he saw no point in disabusing her.

But he did ask, "So you never saw a tall auburn-haired beauty at the house?"

She shook her head.

"And you insist Viola Kraus was never his overnight guest?"

"I do."

"Then who was? Who did you see at that breakfast table, Mrs. Larsen?"

Perhaps sensing she had used up her denials, Mrs. Larsen was quiet.

"Who's your bet for 'Miss Wilson'?" he pressed. "The lady who stayed over many a night, leaving items of a personal nature behind?"

She stood and fetched a piece of scrap paper from a drawer. Returning to the table, she wrote two names, then pushed the paper toward him. "Princess Dalla El Kamel did not come often. But I have seen her here and she adores publicity. She will find the newspapers soon enough."

He looked at the second name. "And Mrs. Amelia Hardy?"

Marie Larsen permitted herself a small smile. "She said my coffee was weak. She is a very rude woman. Mr. Elwell didn't really like her, but she paid enormous sums for bridge lessons because she was in love with him. Many times, she was 'locked out of her home' and insisted on staying the night here."

"Would he have given keys to either the princess or Mrs. Hardy?"

She sighed. "It's possible. I think, for these women who loved him, it was easier to give them a key rather than affection. It stopped their suspicions. 'He gave me a key, he must love me.' I thought it unwise. What if their husbands found it?"

"That's what Rhodes thinks. That a husband of one of Mr. Elwell's lady friends found the key and went berserk."

She made a small tutting sound; she did not care what William Rhodes thought.

"You don't care for the man?" asked Markey, intrigued.

"I don't know him," she said. "Sometimes Mr. Elwell had him drive me home."

"He ever mention that he hasn't been paid in weeks?"

"Yes, once he mentioned it. He asked me to speak with Mr. Elwell. I said it would not be suitable for me to do that."

"You were always paid regularly, though."

"Yes. Always."

She moved the salt from one end of the table, straightened the milk jug. Adjusted his fork so it lay straight. They were the actions of an anxious person. "Mrs. Larsen?"

"I overheard . . ." She winced, then decided to go on. "Once, I overheard Mr. Elwell make a little joke with Mr. Rhodes about borrowing the car."

"Rhodes took the car out without asking?"

She nodded. "I think once he took his wife for a drive. Other times, he was running . . ."

She paused, unsure of how to put it.

"A taxi service on the side?" he suggested.

"Yes. That. Mr. Elwell noticed that the gas bills were higher."

"And maybe, rather than ask Rhodes to pay it back, he withheld his salary."

"I think maybe so. Mr. Elwell disliked discussions of money. Always he would leave my pay in an envelope on the kitchen table. Very discreet. And he did not like arguments. When the landlord came around to ask when is he going to move, because he wants to sell the building, Mr. Elwell would hide, saying, 'Tell him I am not here! Tell him I'm out!'"

He was also frail and middle-aged, whereas Rhodes was young, strong, and knew how to use his fists. "Why didn't he fire him?"

"I don't know," said Mrs. Larsen unhappily. "I wish he would have."

If antagonized, thought Markey, Rhodes could go straight to the husbands and cut a deal: information for cash. He wondered if the driver had a key to the house.

Then he looked at Mrs. Larsen, wondering how such an upright woman could defend a man whose habits were irregular, to say the least.

But before he could ask, she stood to indicate she was going back to work. "I don't know what the princess or Mrs. Hardy can tell you about who murdered poor Mr. Elwell. But I wish you luck. I hope you find the woman in green."

Markey hoped so, too. His next stop was the *Frolic*. Thus far, he'd found every door and mouth of the theater shut tight. He had tried presenting himself as a reporter keen to do a glowing article of New York's most fashionable venue and a young man in need of work. This time, he went to the ticket booth of the theater and claimed he was searching for his runaway sister.

"We had a postcard from her a while back, she mentioned she was working here. She's about so high, auburn hair, very pretty . . ."

The ticket seller shook her head.

"Her name is Alice, but she's probably changed it." He recalled the girl's loose-limbed grace. "Maybe she dances here? She always wanted to be on the stage."

"If she's changed her name, she doesn't want you finding her. I'd leave her be."

"Yes, ma'am, but this is breaking my mother's heart."

Her look said he had laid it on too thick. Knocking a stack of dollar bills on the counter to even them out, she said, "Well, you tell your mother that your 'sister' is doing just fine, and if she wants to see you, she'll write."

Markey opened his mouth, but she interrupted with, "I know New York is a lonely place. But I can't be giving out the names of the girls who work here to every friendless bird who asks."

So the girl in green did work at the *Frolic*. Grinning, he said, "I understand. Thank you."

CHAPTER FOURTEEN

Mrs. Larsen was right. The very next day, Princess Dalla Patra Hassan El Kamel, rumored to be the niece of the khedive of Egypt, did make herself available to the press. The reason she had not done so before now: She had been in jail.

The princess, it was said, had fled the palace harem when the khedive demanded she marry a very old nobleman of his acquaintance. She had, it was said, bribed the palace guards to help her escape to Cairo, where she boarded an Italian steamer. She came to America looking for love. The man need not be rich, she told the papers, only he should like the outdoors. She had tried to break into motion pictures, with limited success. In San Francisco, she had taken up with a mining engineer. Who then accused her of embezzlement. Also of the theft of a valuable pearl stickpin. She had fled to New York, where various businesses complained she did not pay her bills. She had been held at the Jefferson Market women's jail for five days. The beds there, she reported, were "very compact."

She was now at the Sherman Square hotel, where she was holding a press conference. Along with several other reporters, Markey spent an exasperating hour in the Sherman's lobby trying to extract anything of interest from the princess about the murder of Joseph Elwell. The princess was petite, with fashionably marcelled hair. Her eyes were large, giving her a startled expression, as if she could not quite believe all that had happened to her—understandable, thought Markey, as not a whit of it was credible. But he gave her respect. Playing a helpless harem maid in the fifth decade of life took a certain amount of dash.

Her English was selective. She was eloquent on the subject of the mining engineer, whom she called a pig. Precise in refuting the charges of theft: "Never would I have stolen such a cheap bauble." But when asked a question she did not wish to answer, she turned helplessly to her secretary, who translated the question however he pleased. This resulted in exchanges like "Did the princess have a key to Elwell's house?" "The princess prefers marmalade to jam."

The princess had studied the game of bridge with the dead man. But she was very clear that she could not have murdered him. "During this time, I have been held prisoner first in an actual prison and now here at this terrible hotel. Not since I was part of a harem have I known such a lack of freedom."

The bait offered, the reporters leapt at it, shouting inquiries about life in the palace, the scantiness of the clothing, how the ladies kept themselves occupied, all the old attention grabbers—as the princess had known they would. Markey could think of no original questions on harems and so he went to the office to dutifully type up his report.

Reading it, Gus Schaeffer said, "What about Viola Kraus and the Lewisohns?"

"I've run into a wall. Viola now says she hardly knew the man."

"She's been talking to a lawyer. And Lewisohn?"

"He ran amok in a dancer's dressing room at the *Frolic*." Scott in his skivvies trying to join the chorus line would be a good story. But whether because it would harm Fitzgerald's reputation or burnish his legend, Markey didn't feel like telling it.

"Lewisohn did say if I wrote anything more about Viola, he would have me—hold on, I have to get the order right . . ."

He recalled the snarling bowling-ball head, the finger in his face.

". . . 'sued, fired, and broken.'"

"Good, you're getting on his nerves. What else?"

"I talked to the housekeeper. She denies a woman stayed with Elwell that night—or any night—in the carnal sense. To hear her tell it, he was a nice, quiet gentleman who gave young ladies a cup of cocoa, a pat on the head, and a bed to themselves if they needed it."

"You believe that?"

"I believe that she does. I believe she's not stupid."

"What about the photographs?"

"Elwell's wife is a terrible social climber, maybe he was, too. Maybe he liked being reminded every morning that he hobnobbed with rich, glamorous people. Maybe he really did only teach them how to play bridge."

Gus Schaeffer looked disgusted. Markey sighed. "I did find out that the woman in green works at the *Frolic*. And I'm going to talk to Amelia Hardy. Her picture was in the bedroom. The police interviewed her this morning."

"Stay on Viola Kraus. Prove she's the Miss Wilson who made the 2:30 phone call. The family's closing ranks, that has to mean something."

Markey nodded. Leaving the office, he repeated to Schaeffer, "'Sued, fired, and broken.'"

"We'll send flowers to the hospital."

Mrs. Amelia Hardy lived at 200 West Fifty-Seventh Street. She had a ten-year-old daughter named Gloria, and the nanny had failed to come. When he arrived, Gloria was roller-skating up and down the black-and-white-tile hallway, screaming "Yah! Yah!" and brandishing a wooden spoon. Markey felt he was admitted solely so Mrs. Hardy could tell her daughter, "Mother has a visitor, go to your room." Gloria shouted "Yah!" and zoomed to the back, the heavy metal skates pounding like a coming headache. Markey wondered, in a contest of wills, who would win: Griswold or Gloria? He put his money on Gloria.

Mrs. Hardy had dark blond hair and the winsome pallor of a porcelain doll. Her nature was less winsome. She wished to make it clear: She had not seen Joseph Elwell in more than a year. She had also made this clear to the police, whose suspicion incensed her. She had adored Joseph Elwell—such a grand passion should be obvious even to the jackals at the police department. Originally from Poland, she spoke English fluently. In fact, her language was quite colorful for a lady who did not reside in a brothel. Markey gave up writing down her remarks. He couldn't print most of it anyway.

Finally, he managed to get in, as she obviously hadn't murdered Joseph Elwell, did she have any idea who might have?

"It was a horse," replied Mrs. Hardy.

Markey wrote *horse*, then stopped. Was the Polish woman implying a horse had shot Elwell? He knew some Europeans ascribed almost mystical powers to horses, but to credit one with the ability to fire a gun seemed far-fetched.

"Pastoral Swain," she added. "Joseph sold this horse. He didn't do it himself, you understand. He had the trainer do it for him. Joseph made more than $5,000 on the sale of that horse. Only"—she leaned forward to whisper—"he didn't pay the trainer his commission. All the money he kept for himself."

First his chauffeur, thought Markey, then his wife, now his trainer. Joseph Elwell seemed to make a habit of stiffing people. Not a healthy habit in the world of horse racing, which attracted its share of gangsters. Arnold Rothstein dabbled in ponies. The man who had fixed the 1919 World Series even had his own racehorse, Sporting Blood, as well as his own track in Maryland, where he won a great deal, as most jockeys were even poorer than baseball players, so easily bribed.

"That is where I would look," said Mrs. Hardy, "if I were searching for someone who wished Joseph dead. Someone in debt to gangsters who wanted to get out of it by doing someone a very dirty favor. The racetrack attracts criminals."

"Which trainer did he stiff on the commission, Mrs. Hardy?"

"Winfrey somebody. Carey."

"G. Carey Winfrey?" At the office, he had heard the name spoken with reverence by those who favored the track. He wasn't sure a trainer who could have his pick of horses would bother putting a hit on a man for $500.

Then, because he had never asked the question before, he said, "Why did you love Joseph Elwell, Mrs. Hardy?"

"Oh!" She pressed her arms to the sides of her bosom. "He was . . . oh, what a man he was. Handsome, charming, chivalrous."

"Chivalrous?"

She nodded.

"When he cheats his trainer out of money?"

"Who cares how a gentleman treats tradesmen? They are all thieves."

"I understand he gave you a key to his home."

"Yes, such was his regard for me."

"So you never felt that his attentions might be . . . divided." She frowned. "That there were other women in his life."

"Many women loved Joseph, including his awful wife. Because she would not let him go, he felt, for my sake, it was best that we part."

Mrs. Hardy's devotion to the dead man seemed genuine, if deluded. In the distance, he heard the creak of a door opening, the thud and buzz of roller skates. Gloria had gotten bored. Rising, Markey thanked Mrs. Hardy for her time.

"You should speak with my sister. She was once in very great danger and Joseph came to her aid. He was a Lancelot in our sordid modern times, too good for this world."

"I certainly shall. May I ask her name?"

"The Countess Szinswaska," said Mrs. Hardy with a flourish. "You may find her at the Plaza."

Markey wrote down the name. But after the princess's antics, he wasn't in the mood for another titled lady. Buying the midday paper to pass the time, he found a luncheonette and sat at the counter. The waitress looked at him oddly when he ordered eggs and spinach. With the first bite, he understood her doubt. It didn't taste the same. Maybe they had fresher eggs at the Ritz. It was also possible the company had something to do with it. He wondered how he might get back inside the *Frolic*. It would have to be at night; he felt sure the girl in the green dress was a performer. But he couldn't ask the Fitzgeralds; it was an expensive evening and clearly money was tight, judging by Scott's embarrassment at the florist.

Opening the paper, he saw in a gossip item that Zelda had gone swimming in one of the city fountains. He imagined her poised on the edge, ready to dive. Those fountains were shallow, the concrete floors slippery. He worried she'd hurt herself.

Going back to the office, he found himself wanting to write about Gloria and her roller skates rather than Amelia Hardy's accusation against the squalid denizens of the racetrack. Still, it was a lively theory, lending itself to the headline *Did Pastoral Swain Kill Joseph Elwell?* and various ruminations on his kingdom for a horse. He found himself stuck for details about G. Carey Winfrey, though.

Swiveling in his chair, he saw Frank Porter. Frank was always short of money, often putting the touch on you for a fiver till payday, which, if memory served, he usually lost at the track. "Say, Frank, what should I know about G. Carey Winfrey?"

Frank was a slow hunt-and-pecker who jabbed at the keys as if they'd wronged him. Not looking up, he said, "Trainer, works under Hildreth."

"Sam Hildreth who runs Rothstein's horse?"

Frank swatted another key—*Gotcha.* "Rothstein doesn't have a horse. Friends of friends of people Rothstein never met in his life have a horse. He just collects the winnings."

Markey swung back to the typewriter. He was typing when Hal Meyers burst into the newsroom, shouting for Schaeffer. This was not something one did unless the president had been shot or Mae West had appeared stark naked in Times Square. Even Frank stopped pecking long enough to say, "What's the noise?"

"They found a pink kimono," said Hal, breathless from his run up the stairs. Schaeffer emerged from his crypt and Hal repeated, "They found a pink kimono. In Elwell's house."

"Sure they did," said Markey, testy. "There was a whole closet full of lingerie . . ."

"Yeah, but *this* one was hidden in a box in Elwell's closet . . ."

"Something can be in a closet without being hidden," said Schaeffer.

Hal shook his head. "Somebody cut a hole in it. There's a piece this big"—he held his thumb and finger four inches apart—"missing. Gotta belong to Miss Wilson."

"Okay, who did the cutting?" asked Schaeffer. "Whose picture goes on the front page?"

"The housekeeper. Larsen. The DA's called her back in for questioning. Apparently, she's ratting out some mud-gutter blonde."

Mud-gutter blond. Markey tried to envision the color. Dark blond hair, like Mrs. Hardy.

Or brown with highlights. Like Viola Kraus.

Or auburn. Like the girl in green.

CHAPTER FIFTEEN

Up until now, the press had accorded Marie Larsen a certain amount of deference. She was a woman of middle age, married, sober, with a small gold cross around her neck. The Elwell murder was full of glamorous, faintly soiled ladies. Contrast was required. And so Marie Larsen had been assigned the part of the "Good Woman."

That her role in the case had shifted from loyal servant to suspicious character was clear when District Attorney Swann demanded she present herself not at the Elwell house, where she was comfortable, but downtown at his office, alongside criminals. When Markey got there, the cluster of reporters outside the building was sizable. Emerging from the building, Marie Larsen was blasted by a barrage of questions. Why did she hide the kimono? Who was she protecting? Was she Elwell's mistress? She was alone; her husband had not come, and Markey was distressed to see the housekeeper cringing, arm raised as if that would fend off the shouting. He waved to get her attention, but she was too frightened to look up.

In a panic, she broke from the entrance, racing down the side steps. The press pack followed, large and swarming. The men were excited, their movements reckless. Markey worried they'd trample Mrs. Larsen in their eagerness to catch her.

Moving to the perimeter, he shouted her name. Startled, she stopped—a risky thing—then caught sight of him. He signaled she should come his way. Putting her head down, she shouldered her way through. He put one arm around her shoulders, held the other straight to fend off her pursuers. At the next building, he hurried inside. The guard saw a man protecting an older woman on the verge of tears and stepped in front of the doors, denying the other men entry.

Settling Mrs. Larsen onto one of the polished wooden benches in the cavernous marble hall, Markey gave her a moment to collect herself. This she did by placing a hand on her clavicle to slow her breathing until she could manage "Thank you."

"You lied to me."

"I did not lie. You never asked about a kimono. And besides, you lied to me when we first met. Don't say you had a good reason, you had no good reason."

"Good or not, you must have some reason. Why hide the kimono?"

He desperately hoped she would not confess to being the owner of the kimono herself. It was not just that he liked and admired her, but that he understood her to be different from the succulent creatures Elwell squired about town. She was older. Sensible. She took care of people. In short, she reminded him of his mother, and he could not bear to think of his mother in a pink kimono.

He asked, "Did it have blood on it or . . . ?"

"*No.*" But the burst of annoyance seemed to rob her of her last bit of energy. "I hid it because the person who owned it asked me to."

"It didn't occur to you that person might have killed Joseph Elwell?"

"It did not."

"Did they also ask you to cut a piece of fabric from the robe?"

"No, that was my idea," she said quietly.

"What was so important about that scrap of fabric, Mrs. Larsen?"

"It had the woman's initials on it."

Astonished that she would confess to that level of deception, he asked, "Why not destroy it?"

She threw up her hands. "How? If I throw it away, men like you will go through the garbage and find it. It is summer, we are all dying of heat, I cannot make a fire and burn it. So when I found it under the bed, I cut out the initials and hid it in a box in Mr. Elwell's closet. I was going to say I had burned it ironing, but hoped the fabric might be saved."

Her report of finding the kimono under the bed puzzled him; he had looked there, expecting to find a dead body, and seen nothing. But there was a more urgent question.

"Whose initials were they, Mrs. Larsen?"

She shook her head.

"They'll find her eventually."

Her expression grew set. She was angry, frustrated, tired of the whole business. Finally, she said, "You know the initials."

He guessed. She made one small correction. At first, he didn't see why it mattered. Then he did.

"It's quite a favor you did her."

"I feel sorry for her. Her husband treated her badly, she is . . ." She widened her eyes and grasped the air. "Lost. She thinks if she talks to the housekeeper, it means that she is part of the household."

"So you did see her at the breakfast table. She did sleep over."

"Yes, although she says she was not there that night, and I believe her."

Markey believed her as well; the girl in green had taken her place, which Viola would have discovered when she called at 2:30.

"*When* did she ask you to hide the kimono, Mrs. Larsen? When she came to the house that day?"

"Yes, she was distraught."

"What time exactly?"

"I would say, maybe ten o'clock that morning."

Markey recalled his first sight of Viola Kraus, tearstained and inconsolable in her pink-and-gold kimono and too-tidy hotel room. No wonder the room had been so pristine. The maids had at least an hour that morning to clean it. Viola must have known that once the news of Elwell's death was out, the police would call on her. He had thought her not clever enough to change out of her clothes and back into her pajamas. He had been wrong.

"How did she know to come?" he asked. "The news didn't hit the papers until after noon."

"She told me she called the house and a policeman told her Mr. Elwell had been shot."

"She told me that *you* told her."

Startled, she said, "No, it wasn't me, I swear it. Why would she lie about that?"

"Because she didn't *call* the house at all. She knew Elwell was dead because she shot him and used her key to lock both doors." It seemed a thing Viola Kraus would do, lock both doors, childishly wanting to keep people from finding out what she had done. "She had a key, didn't she?"

"Yes."

He pounded his knee; another thing she had neglected to tell him. "Did Viola know what time you got to the house every morning?"

"Yes."

"So, she didn't have time to go up and get her things before you arrived. She kills Elwell, then has to run out the door before you get there. But she knows there's a pink kimono with her initials on it and she needs to make sure the police don't find it."

Mrs. Larsen shook her head. "This is all very elaborate planning for a woman who has not had to think much in her life. She is fond, foolish. I am not sure she is clever enough to work all that out."

"Maybe not. But her sister and brother-in-law are."

When she didn't answer, Markey knew he had won the argument. He felt no sense of victory. He was too upset that she had protected Viola Kraus. He told himself he didn't care why she had done it. Then he asked anyway.

Unable to look at him, she said, "It is not easy to own a shop in New York. The city takes more than its share." Folding one hand over the other, she added in a whisper, "And some men are smarter about business than others."

So she had taken Viola Kraus's money and lied for her. He shouldn't be shocked. Everyone had their hand out. Most people lied. He had thought her better than she was, and now he knew otherwise. It was hardly a tragedy.

He stood, wanting to be away from her. "You need to tell the police."

"I did tell them. Days ago." Seeing his shock, she said, "I am not lying now. I told them everything."

"So they do know Miss Wilson is Viola Kraus. Why haven't they arrested her?"

"They believe she is only guilty of romantic foolishness, not murder."

"And how much money did Walter Lewisohn pay them to come to that conclusion?"

"Enough that the district attorney will keep her identity secret."

"Maybe he will, but I won't. Viola Kraus can't shoot a man and get away with it because she has a rich brother-in-law."

"Please, I know you will not want to listen to me now." Unexpectedly, she grabbed his hand. "For your sake, do not put this in the papers. I do not believe Miss Kraus is guilty, but . . . even if she is, you would be making serious accusations against people who are not used to being held accountable. It is not safe."

He knew she was right to caution him. He knew he would be wise to listen. But he felt that surge of wild energy that went through him when the army came to town, asking for volunteers. He had leapt then, elated that here was his future at last. He should know better now . . .

But he didn't.

After he had turned in his article revealing Viola Kraus as Miss Wilson and seen Gus Schaeffer smile for the second time, Markey felt restless. True, his story would be the front page. He even had a byline of sorts, but it was not his name, only OUR INVESTIGATOR. He still felt the humming in his hands and feet, the need for an explosion of sorts. He looked about the newsroom but saw no one with whom he wished to celebrate. Some of the fellows had taken Hal down to the Morgue, but he still resented Hal snatching the kimono from him.

Zelda would want to know the latest right away, he told himself. And he owed Fitzgerald a thank-you for his help with the hyacinths.

But when he called at the Ritz, they were not in. He felt the man at the front desk took pleasure in telling him so. Leaving the hotel, he walked up to the first taxi in the line, knocked on the window, and asked, "Did you take Scott and Zelda Fitzgerald somewhere this evening?" It took four taxis before he got a yes.

They were not at the first party on Sixty-Third and Broadway. Or the second on Eighty-First and Fifth. But at Fifty-Seventh and Park, a gleefully inebriated young man in a tuxedo answered the door and said, "Oh, yes, they're here."

"Here" was a broad proposition. It was a five-story brownstone, and from the sound of things, every room of every floor was filled with revelers. Markey was startled to see a languid woman sitting in a straight-backed chair, her face impassive as the gentleman seated to her right caressed her bosom while a gentleman to her left slid a hand under her skirt. In a corner, two young men were spoon-feeding cognac to a terrier. A girl was trying to slide down the banister, only to repeatedly land on her rump. In the ground-floor parlor, a competition was taking place as to who could hop on one foot the longest while drinking. A young woman holding a telephone asked if he knew the number for the Russian Bear as she had a terrible craving for blintzes.

On the second floor, he found a room with people standing on tiptoe at the door. Then he heard Scott proclaim, "Until about five minutes ago, I was unaware there was anyone in the world aside from yours truly . . ." A jovial groan from the crowd and a theatrical "I beg your pardon" from a voice Markey recognized as Zelda's. Scott cried, "But you're not aside from yours truly, you are mine truly, me truly . . ." The babbling nonsense turned into a kiss, which was heartily cheered. When Zelda emerged, she said, "That was nice—what did you say your name was?"

Watching from the perimeter, Markey smiled more than laughed. They were being "Scott and Zelda," and he was disquieted by the ruthless intensity of the performance. Zelda had been at the gin. Her energy was high, her eyes glittering, she could barely stand still. She held on to Scott, pulling down on his hand, as she demanded, "Scott, tell 'em 'bout the time I rode on the roof of the taxi." "Scott, tell 'em what I said to that banker." "Oh! Tell the story about how I . . ." Far from minding the interruptions, Scott burst out laughing at the shared memory, pointing with glee at his wife, in total agreement that nothing could be more fascinating than the thing she had done, and it must be told immediately. Whatever narrative he had been spinning, he would switch, telling the story with great verve as Zelda listened, captivated by his recitation of her exploits. They were like some miraculous ventriloquist act. But who was the dummy and who the performer, Markey couldn't decide. It was not Zelda at her best, and he wished she'd stop.

Several tuxedoed young men stood around Scott, their proximity and mocking manner singling them out as friends—from Princeton, he imagined. Apparently, some had missed the Fitzgeralds' wedding, a situation that Zelda felt required a gesture. Markey watched as she bestowed kisses, some sisterly, some lingering as Scott waved his arms, shouting, "Everyone gets a kiss! They all get one each . . ." Near the line, a man was conversing with a woman. Zelda affected delight at seeing him and pulled him in for a kiss as well. Then she shoved him back, as if she disliked the taste.

But when that party game had ended, the men began to talk among themselves and Zelda drifted. Markey watched as she wandered, arms swinging slightly, smiling here, smiling there. But she found no other friends.

Then, she saw him and stopped dead. She looked right, then left, as if trying to assess: Was she at the right party? His presence would suggest not. Bemused, she approached, saying, "I didn't know you were here." Her voice was thready, her throat hoarse from party shouting.

"I bring news of the case."

Her eyes brightened.

"They found a pink kimono in Elwell's closet. Mrs. Larsen had hidden it. There was a monogram, she cut it off. But I got her to tell me what the initials were."

She waited, then punched his arm when he took too long to say it.

"V . . ."

"K!" she finished.

"No—better. 'VVS.' She and Elwell were playing around when

she was still married. The police have known for days, but they've been protecting her. But tomorrow morning"—he sketched the headline in the air with his hand—"'Revealed: Viola Kraus Is Mysterious Miss Wilson.'"

With a cry of delight, she grabbed his arm. Then he heard, "Markey! How'd the hyacinths go over?" Scott was with them.

Nodding, Markey said, ". . . Swell."

"He's figured out the whole thing," said Zelda. "And there's a pink kimono."

"A pink kimono!" echoed Scott. "That's good for business. Say, you should meet Phipps."

"Oh, yes, he'd love this," cried Zelda.

It took a while to find Phipps. As they searched, Zelda informed everyone they bumped into that Markey was a writer for the *Daily News* and he knew absolutely everything about that murder on Seventieth Street, and if they asked nicely, he might, *might*, tell them the latest. They finally found Phipps standing on a pool table and singing "The Prisoner's Song." At the word *murder*, Phipps jumped down and presented Markey with his full attention. Scott whispered, "'Twas a dark and stormy night . . ." Zelda elbowed him. "Let Markey tell it."

And he did. Stammering at first, discomfited by the elegance of the young man in front of him. When he came to the sight of Elwell in the chair, Phipps interrupted, "How d'you know it wasn't suicide?"

"There were no powder burns." Phipps cocked his head: *Say more.* "When you shoot yourself, you shoot at close range and it burns the skin. In this case, the powder grains were embedded in the skin around the bullet hole, which is different."

Phipps's eyes widened; then he called across the room, "Fellows, come listen to this. It's murder!"

Instantly, he was surrounded. Ordered to repeat his observation about the bullet hole, Markey did so. They demanded to know:

Had Elwell said anything? Were the women in the pictures naked? How much blood, exactly? Sensation seemed meat and drink to lovely, refined people. It made Markey uneasy; at one point, he lost the thread. But Zelda chimed in, "Then we went out to the funeral and met the widow. *She* was a horror," and he took up the story from there. When the chatter in the outside hallway grew loud, a girl opened the door and hissed, "Quiet! This fellow's telling us about the Elwell murder," which brought more people, until Markey had to stand on a chair to address the packed room. When he announced "Here's the thing nobody knows yet . . ." he felt the heat of a hundred people's energy fixed on him.

"The police found a pink kimono in Elwell's bedroom today. It was monogrammed. But someone had cut off the initials to protect the owner's identity."

Gasps throughout the room. Lowering his voice, he said, "I was able to find out what the monogram was."

The door rattled. Someone was trying to get in. A heavyset man shut it with his bottom. Markey glanced down at Zelda. "The initials were those of Mrs. Von Schlegell . . ."

He nodded to Zelda, who shouted, "Otherwise known as Viola Kraus!"

After that, things began to blur. He spoke to so many people, he no longer knew what he was saying. Barely able to hear himself, he understood from their expression that he was fascinating, witty, even a bit mysterious. How *did* he know all these things? Full glasses seemed to materialize in his hand as people sought to keep his vocal cords oiled. Food was pressed on him, and he tasted caviar for the first time. Later he would think how beautiful the girls had been, but he had been watching for Zelda, who'd gone off somewhere. He accepted invitations to dinner, to drinks, to weekend parties, offers to write this or that, without getting a single address or telephone number. They would find each other when it was time seemed to be the idea.

At some point, he woke up in a chair in a room he did not remember entering. A girl had fallen asleep at his feet, her head resting on his leg. A man sat cross-legged beside her, awaiting Markey's next word. Looking out the window, he saw the sun was well risen. His mouth tasted wretched; his throat was sandpaper. Raising a hand to indicate *good night* or *goodbye*, he lifted the girl's head off his leg—a miracle, and he had missed it completely—and laid it on the chair. Then he went to find Zelda and Scott.

He found them upstairs, fast asleep. They slept on their backs, their heads touching, arms and legs splayed. They were still dressed in their evening finery—Scott's black tie was only slightly askew. Crouching, he drew a finger down Zelda's arm, whispered her name. She mewed in her sleep, rolled over to curl around Scott.

Markey went back downstairs, stepping carefully over bodies slumped against the wall or curled up on the floor. Many were not wearing shoes, which puzzled him until he saw a great pile of oxfords, pumps, slippers, and brogans in the hallway. Someone—he felt he knew who—had been playing pranks. A young man lay near the door, apparently having collapsed as he was about to leave. It made opening the door difficult; Markey didn't want to hit the man's head.

It was an unspeakably beautiful day. He walked west through Central Park; in late morning, the lawns and pathways were quiet, the air still cool. Looking up at the city buildings that ringed the park, he danced a little. At this moment, most people in New York were either reading his article or talking about it. The whole city he now imagined as that crowd in the billiard room, mouths parted, eyes wide. If he died right now, it would be no bad thing.

As he wheeled onto his block, shouts and the thud of slammed doors interrupted his fantasy. Perplexed, he gave up his daydreaming to take in the scene. The hordes of murder tourists were still there. But they were strangely subdued. And rather than watching the Elwell house, they were watching his. There was an ambulance outside. A body was being carried out the front door.

His first absurd thought: Somehow, Elwell had opened his eyes, decided the hole in his forehead was no matter, and floated up from his coffin and back to his home. Then Markey saw that the curtains on the first floor were drawn. Griswold had not missed a second of the Elwell murder. If he was not keeping watch, it could only mean one thing.

Going to a police officer on the corner, he said, "Pardon me—I'm Mr. Griswold's downstairs neighbor."

"Then I'm afraid I have some bad news for you."

"Was it his heart?"

"Why do you say that?"

"He was a very angry man."

The officer nodded. "So, you didn't get along with him."

"I don't think he got along with anybody. He yelled at kids, women, old people—he was a yeller. Liked to get into people's business."

"A man with a lot of enemies, then."

"Why do you say that?"

"Because it wasn't his heart. Somebody shot him. Right between the eyes."

Chapter Sixteen

The officer asked if he'd be willing to identify the body; he preferred not to ask Mrs. Cecchetti. Markey climbed into the ambulance, where the stretcher was settled on the floor. The orderly flipped back the sheet. It was the same: a small dark hole in the middle of the forehead. They hadn't closed Griswold's eyes, giving him a rather startled look. He seemed about to say something, and if Markey had to write it, he'd put, *I always know everything. How did this happen?*

"That's him. Arthur Griswold." The sheet was flipped back.

Out on the street, he studied the first-floor apartment. Usually Griswold sat by his open window, making sure the world behaved as it ought to. A good shot from the other side of the block could have taken him out without too much trouble. On the other hand, the crowds milling about the street might have made it easy for someone to shoot and run off in the chaos.

"Where was the body found?"

The officer nodded. "Right by the window."

"And you're sure someone shot him?"

"Why? You think he's the type for suicide?"

"Not really. He wasn't a happy man, but he seemed to think well of himself. It was everyone else who was the problem."

"No gun was found," said the officer. "The windowpane isn't broken. I figure the guy wanted some fresh air. He opens a window, takes a whiff . . ." He grimaced to indicate the shot. "Did he sit by the window a lot?"

"He did." Markey cussed himself out for not having tried harder to interview the old snoop. "No witnesses?"

The officer shook his head. "No one's come forth. Gun goes off, everyone runs screaming. Landlady was sweeping the front hallway when she heard something fall in Griswold's apartment. She called to Mr. Griswold, and when he didn't answer, she used her key to open the door and found the body."

"Do you find it strange that two men have been shot in their homes on the same block in the space of a week? One in the morning, the other at midday? It seems excessive, even for New York."

"Depends on the block," said the officer. "Why? You know something?"

"Me? No," said Markey.

He headed into the building. People had gathered in the hallway, staring fearfully at the door to Griswold's apartment. Two residents, Miss Brewster and Mr. Siegel, were comforting Mrs. Cecchetti.

"Poor Mr. Griswold," she said. "So alone. Who would do such a thing? Do you think it was an accident?" She looked up at Markey.

There were times when being tall made him seem an authority, as if his height allowed him to see things others couldn't.

"Unless someone was cleaning their gun out on the street, I don't see how."

A ripple of alarm went through the little crowd. It was one thing to sense someone had been murdered, another to have it confirmed. Markey asked his landlady, "You didn't let anyone into the building, did you?"

"No, no one at all. Although people go in, they go out . . ."

Seeing her distress, he said, "No, of course you can't be at the door at all times."

For a moment, they all stood thinking of their deceased neighbor. Then Miss Brewster said, "Well, he *was* mean."

"Nosy," agreed Mr. Siegel

"Why do you say that?" Markey asked him.

Siegel said, "I have a regular poker game. Every Thursday at six, we take turns whose apartment. One week it's my turn. Griswold is standing by his door, watching as my friends arrive. And when they left, I came out on the landing—sure enough, he's watching my friends leave. I said, 'Busy night?' Then, the next week, I'm headed out and there he is again, standing by his door. 'Going to a meeting?' he asks. I say, 'Yes, it's the weekly gathering of the Pastrami Guild.' 'So you belong to a union,' he says. Which tells me what kind of man he is and I say, 'Actually, I work for the courts, which is how I know there are laws against harassment.'"

"Mean," affirmed Miss Brewster. "He once asked if I had ever been married. I said, 'What's it to you?'"

Markey asked, "Did he ever say anything about the murder across the street?"

Siegel shook his head. "But I avoided him."

Markey looked at the dead man's door, thought of Elwell's door across the street. One man was a dapper man of the world, the other a sour crank. Yet they'd each ended up with a bullet through the brain. Uncharitably, his first thought was that Griswold had screamed at the wrong person and got what he deserved.

His second: Griswold, the neighborhood scold, had seen Viola Kraus run out of the Elwell house, and she had killed him before he could go to the police. His article revealing her as Miss Wilson had just come out, putting her in fresh jeopardy. Clearly she had panicked.

But how did a woman who lived in luxury at the Ritz even know Arthur Griswold existed?

Unless he had tried to blackmail her.

He turned to his landlady. "Mrs. Cecchetti, I'm sorry to ask, but Mr. Griswold borrowed—"

What would be so small that it would allow him to open drawers, but not so fancy that he would be suspected of theft?

"—a pen from me. It's not valuable, but it was a gift from my father. Would you mind if I went into his apartment and got it? I worry the police will clean out his things and I won't get it back."

He thought to say he wouldn't take anything, but he didn't want to promise that. "I'd be happy to have you come in with me."

"I suppose so." She started toward the door, then drew up sharply. "There won't be blood, will there?"

Remembering Griswold's corpse, he thought there would be. "How about I go in first and you follow when I say it's all right?"

Nodding, she unlocked the door. Markey looked inside. Smears on the floor suggested they'd dragged the body through the worst of it. Someone had thrown a towel near the window.

"I think it's all right, Mrs. Cecchetti, but maybe keep your back to the front window."

Stepping carefully inside the apartment, his first thought was how bare it was. In the spacious front parlor, there was a card table and two wooden chairs. Leaning back to take in the kitchen, he saw little evidence of home cooking. One small pot and a percolator on the stove. One mug on the sideboard. Of course you wouldn't find much in his own apartment either; bachelors didn't tend to have the nicer things. But there was grime on the windowsill, rings of old coffee stains on the countertop. In spots, the floor was sticky under his shoe. The air tasted of dust. For a man with a mania for order, Griswold was slovenly in his housekeeping.

Mrs. Cecchetti, he could see, was offended that her best apartment had been treated so carelessly. Really, the parlor floor was a strange choice for a man who lived alone and cared little for his surroundings. Why had Griswold chosen these rooms when others could be had cheaper?

"Was Mr. Griswold ever married, Mrs. Cecchetti?"

"No. Not in the time he has been living here."

"And when did he move in?"

"Two years ago."

"Rent always on time?" Perhaps the man had run into financial troubles and pawned off the furniture.

"Paid in advance. Why?"

Momentarily stymied, he said, "It looks like he sold everything off. I'm worried my father's pen is long gone." This, the landlady understood, and she nodded. Then she went into the kitchen, exclaiming in horror at the state of the stovetop.

Markey looked for newspapers, books, letters—anything that might give some sense of the murdered man. But Griswold's apartment was as barren as Elwell's had been replete. A single notebook lay open on the table to a page with today's date. The last entry: *DA to interview Countess Szinswaska. Call B.* Out of habit, Markey wrote down the dead man's last words.

Quickly, he flipped through the diary. As he might have predicted, Griswold kept tabs on many people in the neighborhood: Jost Otten's lateness in delivering the milk was noted, as were the suspected political leanings of Mr. Siegel and the imagined proclivities of Miss Brewster. Griswold worried that Mrs. Cecchetti's nephew was an anarchist, that the mailman was stealing his letters.

Markey's arrival at the house was noted as: *Young man moved into apartment below. Reporter.*

But most of his recent entries concerned Joseph Elwell. Just like the death gawkers who gathered outside, Griswold had been monitoring the police investigation.

V. Kraus interviewed with BIL.

Chauffeur interviewed.

Garage attendant says VVS took car to Atlantic City day before murder. Police now unable to locate him.

VVS had to be Victor von Schlegell, who had not received much press attention thus far. Markey was curious that Griswold thought him of interest. Everyone had their pet suspects, of course. But if Griswold had seen Viola Kraus at the time of the murder, there was no mention of it here. He turned to the day of the murder.

E came home at 2 AM in company of new woman. Woman left an hour later.

Reading those five simple words, Markey smiled in surprise. The woman in green was innocent. As Zelda had suggested that afternoon of the orange blossoms, she had left the house long before the shooting. She had not killed Joseph Elwell. She wasn't a killer at all. Just a beautiful girl who worked at the *Frolic* and maybe he'd get back there someday . . .

Eagerly, he looked to the next entry; what had Griswold seen a few hours later? But disappointingly, Griswold, like Markey, had been awakened by Mrs. Larsen's screams.

8:45. Woke to hear housekeeper screaming. Hick from downstairs went, stayed half an hour. Police arrived 9:20.

Then, on a new line: *E died at hospital.*

Markey was struck by the fact that Griswold had been watching Elwell's house before the gambler was murdered. His reference to a "new woman" suggested he had seen others come and go in the past. Wanting to know if the two men had ever met, he turned back further, stopping at the first sign of E. In an entry for

February—*House dark for two weeks, housekeeper says E in Palm Beach*—Griswold had even taken the trouble to befriend Mrs. Larsen. Markey looked at the wide bay window, beginning to understand the appeal of an apartment that had such an excellent view of the street. If one wanted to watch Joseph Elwell, you could have no better spot.

But why did Griswold wish to watch Joseph Elwell?

His hand hovered over the notebook. He wanted very badly to take it. But the police would return and Mrs. Cecchetti might remember seeing it on the table.

Going to the bedroom, he found it equally spare, furnished with a single, cheaply constructed bed and a small nightstand with a drawer. The bed was made, the sheets and thin blanket wrapped tightly around the mattress. On the stand, a single book: *The Decline of the West*, by Otto Spengler.

Gently opening the drawer, he found it empty, save for a small pin. A somewhat squashed eagle sat atop a circle stamped with SECRET SERVICE. Around the outer rim the words AMERICAN PROTECTIVE LEAGUE. The eagle's head and neck were curved, making it look more like a serpent than a majestic bird. Markey had never heard of such a league, but remembering Mr. Siegel's complaint that Griswold had interrogated him about his union connections and the dead man's suspicious, judgmental nature, he thought it likely the badge belonged to him. Made of cheap tin, it struck him as pathetic.

From the other room, Mrs. Cecchetti called, "Mr. Markey, is this your father's pen?"

Pocketing the badge, he hurried back to see Mrs. Cecchetti holding up a pen. It had been lying by the notebook, he realized. From her expression, he knew she had seen him look at the notebook and that he'd ignored the pen beside it.

"I don't know how I missed that."

She didn't answer, just held it out to him. Markey took it with an embarrassed smile.

He knew more questions would provoke suspicion, but he couldn't help pausing at the door for a last look at the apartment. "Had Mr. Griswold paid next month's rent?"

"I can't tell you that, Mr. Markey."

Which meant he hadn't. Griswold was finished with number 237 Seventieth Street. Why? Because he had failed in his job? Or because he succeeded? He considered the brief references to himself—*reporter, hick*. He might have expected more complaints. Now he wondered if Griswold had shouted at him to keep him at a distance. Or maybe the man just liked shouting.

Getting out his notebook, he looked at the dead man's last words. *DA to interview Countess Szinswaska. Call B.* On the previous page were Markey's own notes from his conversation with Amelia Hardy. Without question, the countess was Amelia Hardy's sister. B—a person? A hotel? No, Mrs. Hardy had said her sister was at the Plaza.

He came out of the apartment to see Miss Brewster reading a copy of the *Daily News*. There was his headline: REVEALED: VIOLA KRAUS IS MYSTERIOUS MISS WILSON. A picture of Viola in a white dress festooned with feathers looked furiously back at him.

Chapter Seventeen

On his way to the Plaza, Markey read the midday papers, failing to find any joy in the fact that every one of them was chasing his story of Viola Kraus and the pink kimono. Goaded by the public unmasking of Miss Kraus as the mysterious Miss Wilson, Swann passionately defended his refusal to name her. In turn, the police accused the DA of concealing evidence. Viola Kraus had been invited back to testify; she would break her holiday in Newport to do so. Reading that the doe-eyed socialite was nearly two hundred miles from the city, Markey's heart sank. He tried to tell himself that just because Viola hadn't shot Griswold, it didn't mean she hadn't shot Elwell. But he couldn't make himself believe it. No doubt hordes of reporters would greet her at the DA's office. But he would not be among them. He wanted to speak to the Countess Szinswaska.

The Plaza was a lavish hotel, but its staffing practices were lax. It took Markey two conversations, one with the concierge, the other with a manicurist, to discover that the countess routinely visited the hotel spa at this time. Perspiring from the steam wafting through the gilded doors, Markey waited on a low bench in the hallway outside. When a dramatic-looking woman matching the description the manicurist had provided walked out, he stood up, hat in hand.

"Good day, Countess, my name is Morris Markey, I write for the *Daily News*. I spoke with your sister, Mrs. Hardy. I'd like to ask how it is that you know two men who have been shot through the head." He had it timed to eight seconds.

"You spoke with my sister?"

"Yes, ma'am. You can call and confirm that."

"I prefer not to speak with Amelia unless necessary. Did you say *two* men?"

"I did. Joseph Elwell and Arthur Griswold."

"I know no Arthur Griswold."

"But he knew you. Your name was in his notebook, an entry made on the day he was murdered. That was this morning, by the way. If I were you, I'd want to know more about Arthur Griswold so I could be sure I wasn't the next person to end up dead."

She inhaled slowly through the nose as she considered. "Have you met my niece?"

"I did. I thought her charming."

"I think she is a catastrophe. But you may buy me tea."

In the hotel café, Markey sat perched on a white-painted wrought iron chair while the countess lounged on the banquette. She was taller than her excitable china-doll sister, more European in her style. Every part of her was wrapped, from the dark cloche atop her head to the tight kid gloves of beige pink on her hands to the Patou suit giving her the look of a cobra that had risen from its coiled state. Her heavily lidded eyes regarded him with slumberous contempt. Her full mouth made him think of what she consumed; he imagined it would be live and wriggling. She looked very much like a woman who could commit murder and eat a pleasant meal afterward, chatting of the season at Deauville.

"Thank you for speaking with me," he said.

Slowly, she closed and opened her eyes to indicate his gratitude was appropriate. "You say you write for the *Daily News*?"

"Yes, ma'am. I've written a great deal about Viola Kraus."

"*Yes.*" Now the eyes stayed open. "I have enjoyed your articles. They are wonderfully tawdry. The murderous Miss Wilson and the mysterious woman in green. You are quite correct that a woman shot Joseph." She pronounced the name as they would in Eastern Europe, the *J* as a *Y*.

"The district attorney doesn't agree."

"But he is an idiot," she said matter-of-factly. "Over here, you are too chivalrous with a woman in a mystery. Most people defend her. It is not so on the Continent. There, where humanity is older and wiser, we say, '*Cherchez la femme.*' I frankly believe the woman is *always* to blame."

It was the perfect opening. But he felt she had come to the point too quickly. She had denied knowing Arthur Griswold. So he began with the other murdered man.

"When did you first meet Joseph Elwell?" She raised an eyebrow, indicating something was missing from his question. ". . . Countess?"

"I first made his acquaintance in Carlsbad in 1913."

He recalled the signature on the bathing costume photograph. "And you came to this country when?"

"Some time after. I don't recall."

The deliberate vagueness puzzled him. She could have said anything—he would have to take her word for it. Perhaps accuracy was seen as the obligation of the lower classes. Also honesty. It occurred to him that there were a lot of counts and countesses running about the city these days. Phony Romanovs, ersatz Hapsburgs, sham Bourbons. With the right clothes and a little hauteur, a waitress could pass herself off as an empress.

"You were born in Poland, is that correct?"

She nodded. "In Galicia."

"I hope your family made it through the war all right."

"Thank you."

Again, the aristocratic brevity. He was becoming more convinced that the countess's blood did not run as blue as she would have people think. He wondered if she was an actress. A member of the corps de ballet. Circus performer—who knew? Still, it was an entertaining act.

"When did you last see Mr. Elwell?"

"Not for some time," she drawled. "I believe it was 1918. I ran into him at a party. We talked of Palm Beach, which is a place I dislike. I can't say I knew him well at all. My sister was infatuated, but this you know."

And yet her photo had been in his bedroom. He recalled the strong thighs.

"So, you were not intimate friends?"

Now the cobra unfurled its hood. Sitting up, she stabbed out her cigarette. "Americans entertain a sort of childish curiosity in relation to a man's private life. They are inquisitive and greedy for intimate news. Elwell was no worse than most men, the only difference is that his affairs are being exposed—he has been found out."

"I assume you don't think your sister killed him."

A short sigh. "My sister was unhappily married. Her husband was in gas. From this, what can a woman expect? She was convinced Joseph Elwell would free her. But of course Elwell is not that kind of man. Nonetheless, she remains convinced of his nobility, even after he is finished with her. Now, that little Kraus person, she is very common. Do you believe she's Jewish? Her family called themselves Cross when they first came to this country. *I always say look for les bourgeois*. They lack sophistication and go positively off their heads when a love affair ends."

His conscience sore on the point of Viola Kraus, he felt the need to go on the attack in her defense. "But you were more tolerant."

She recoiled. "I?"

"When your affair with Joe Elwell ended."

"*I* never had an affair with him. He was my sister's folly."

"Then why did he keep your photograph in his bedroom? A rather racy photograph, if you don't mind my saying."

The news seemed to come as a genuine surprise. Raising her hands in a gesture of surrender, she said, "A woman cannot help who falls in love with her . . ."

"Elwell didn't seem a man to fall in love. More of a . . . collector. I'd imagine that would be pretty galling to a woman of your quality. To be one of many."

"I did *not* have an affair with Joseph Elwell."

"Then what was the nature of your relationship?"

Curling back up on the banquette, she said, "As I said, Americans. So greedy for intimate details. Fine, I will tell you. He had me arrested for being a spy."

Markey reached for his tea, then remembered he hadn't ordered any. The conversation had taken such a turn, he felt as if someone had wrenched the wheel of a car violently to the left and ridden them off the road. Was she joking? Was he expected to laugh, as a man of the world, and say, *But truthfully, Countess* . . .

"And were you?"

"Of course not!" she said, affronted, or doing a fair imitation. "During the war, anyone with an accent came under suspicion."

He didn't think the New York police would put a titled woman in jail merely because she pronounced her *J*s as *Y*s. But this was not the key point.

"Why would a bridge expert bother with spies? On what authority did he have you arrested?"

"He was part of the League," she said, as if it were evident.

Markey felt the tin badge in his pocket. "The American Protective League?"

She nodded.

His thoughts lurched in a new and uncomfortable direction. Until now, he had seen the Elwell murder as a love affair gone wrong, Griswold's membership in the League as further evidence of a squalid personality and Griswold and Elwell as entirely dissimilar men.

But both had been in the League. And now both were dead.

Fishing, he said, "I was in France during the war, I don't know much about the League."

"The APL," she explained. "Private citizens who were organized by the government to report anyone suspected of pro-German sympathies."

"Sounds like an idea that could go from bad to downright awful in a hurry."

"I was not partial to it. Some of them wore little badges."

He put Griswold's badge on the table. "Like this one?"

"Yes. But most of them worked covertly. Elwell was one of those."

"How long were you in jail?"

"Not long. But they had me under house arrest at my hotel for two months. My sister, who had no idea of Elwell's true nature or habits, enlisted his help. She saw it as an opportunity to demand his attention. But he called his friends in Washington *et voilà* . . ." She waved her cigarette. "I was freed."

"Why would he do that if he had you arrested in the first place?"

"I asked him that very thing. He insisted that, like me, he had been falsely accused. That he was not a member of any League and had never reported me."

"Did you believe him?"

"No. I know it was him who sent the police to my door. But as I was free, I saw no reason for ill will."

Markey was suspicious. Her attitude was remarkably magnanimous. True, a hotel made for a luxurious jail and the countess seemed in no danger of deportation now. And if she were a spy, she might feel that having been caught, she was lucky to escape the firing squad. But an innocent woman would resent the insult to her reputation, not to mention imprisonment.

Sensing his thoughts, she said, "I am a guest in this country, Mr. Markey. It is not in my interests to make a fuss."

"I wouldn't have thought Elwell was much of a patriot." She shook her head, unsure what he meant. "A man concerned with national affairs. Cards, horses, Palm Beach? He lived the life of a libertine, not a government agent."

"What better disguise for a puritan than excess and frivolity?"

"If Elwell was a puritan, he put on a pretty good show."

This she conceded with a tilt of her head. "What *I* heard was that he had invested heavily in Russia. When the Bolsheviks came to power, they nationalized everything and he lost a great deal of money. Then Lenin took Russia out of the war, and these two things became tangled in his mind: his financial disaster and a refusal to fight Germany. Also, he enjoyed power. He liked to be the man who knew everyone's secrets but kept his own. That pleased him greatly."

Her analysis struck him as sound. If the government wanted to ferret out traitors in high places, a man who moved among the rich and celebrated would be a decent choice.

He asked the countess, "Do you know of any other people who were arrested on Joseph Elwell's instructions?"

She shook her head. "It is not something that comes up in regular conversation. 'My dear, did they arrest you, too? Ghastly, isn't it?'"

Markey nodded at his own foolishness, even as he thought that if the countess was a spy, she would naturally refuse to name her associates.

"And you still say you never knew an Arthur Griswold?"

"I do. Who was he?"

"An unpleasant man who was shot through the head, same way that Elwell was. He was also a member of the League."

"Ah. Perhaps there are other people who were accused who were not released after a few months." She raised an eyebrow. "Or perhaps they are not as forgiving as I am."

He smiled. "I don't know, Countess. You don't strike me as a woman to cross."

"I am not. But I did not kill Joseph Elwell."

"How about your brother-in-law? Mr. Hardy the gas magnate? How'd he feel about Elwell?"

"Amelia may have thrown the affair in his face in one of her scenes. But I doubt he would have minded. Joseph Elwell made it a point to be congenial to the husbands. He would give them real estate tips. Introductions to well-placed people. Invitations to his Palm Beach house or the races at Saratoga. Usually, the husbands found these favors more valuable than their wives."

"And you still think a woman killed Joseph Elwell."

She had lit a fresh cigarette. Now she pointed it at him saying, "You think so as well. You say so in your articles. The pink kimono with the missing initials."

"Now I'm wondering."

"Don't wonder. We are tremendously vicious creatures, more so than you can imagine."

The word *imagine* and her theatrical tone prompted him to ask, "Is any of this true, Countess? Spies, the League . . ."

She regarded him through the haze of cigarette smoke. "Do you talk of your time in the war, Mr. Markey?"

"No."

"No," she echoed. "Because people wouldn't believe you. You barely believe it yourself. Sometimes, perhaps, you have dreams. But better they stay dreams. Better if you can feel you have returned home. Safe and sound to a place where life, if not always good, is not insane. America is such a happy place, isn't it?" She waved her hands in a phantom Charleston. "Better for all of us if we believe that to be the truth."

She stood. "Talk to the driver. The attractive one with the teeth. Ask him about Elwell's women . . ."

"I have."

"Ask him about Elwell's secrets."

Chapter Eighteen

As Markey rode the subway uptown, he marveled that his story of a society woman scorned had become a tale of wartime intrigue. He could think of no reason for the countess to reveal her arrest on suspicion of spying unless she was telling the truth. It didn't seem impossible that Joseph Elwell, a man who lived in the shadows of reality and pretend, might be drawn to a league of spies, except that he seemed like a man with no allegiance to any cause higher than a deck of cards.

But did the revelation that Elwell was an informant tell him anything other than that the dead man probably treated men as viciously as he treated women? The countess herself said that a woman had killed Elwell. Why shouldn't that woman be Viola Kraus?

Because Arthur Griswold was dead, and as hard as he tried,

Markey could not see the most beautiful woman in New York standing on West Seventieth Street and shooting him in broad daylight. Especially given that she had been in Newport at the time.

The countess's credibility was further bolstered by the fact that she had told him to speak with the chauffeur. When he had first spoken with Rhodes, Markey had the impression that the driver was both a veteran and a scoundrel. He had been confused as to why a man with a life as complicated as Elwell's would trust such a man. Now he wondered if Rhodes was just a driver. A man who betrayed as many people as Elwell did might need muscle for protection. Or intimidation.

But then Elwell had betrayed Rhodes by not paying him, and perhaps Rhodes had sold his talents elsewhere. Veterans down on their luck made good candidates for all sorts of rough work.

Calling at the chauffeur's apartment, Markey learned that Rhodes had a new job. "He's driving some vice president of the waterworks," said Katherine Rhodes. "Billy says the man spends most of his time at the Studio Club."

The Studio Club. Where had he heard of that? Mrs. Elwell—she had bragged that her husband had been admitted. A place for wealthy men to gamble in peace.

"I'm glad he found employment."

She smiled. "You and me both. It was nice of Mr. Barnes to set him up."

". . . Barnes?" As if he knew the name but could not place the face.

"He manages the club."

"That's right." Barnes—he remembered the initial *B* from Griswold's diary. Although *B* could also stand for *Billy*.

He touched his hat, prepared to leave, then noticed she was lingering at the door. "Is everything all right, Mrs. Rhodes?"

". . . No, not really." He saw tears brimming and reached for his handkerchief—a poor thing to offer, but all he had to hand.

Taking it, Katherine Rhodes said, "Ever since this happened, we've had police and reporters asking questions, searching the house, looking through our things . . ."

"I'm so sorry. What sort of things?"

"First it was a gun. Now it's a gray dress. I've never had a gray dress in my life. I don't know where people get these ideas."

Markey knew the reporter working the woman-in-gray story—he was one of the sadder newshounds—but he hadn't known he'd dragged poor Mrs. Rhodes into it. Or that the police had been smart enough to take a hard look at Rhodes.

Torn between sympathy and curiosity, he clarified, "Well, they didn't find a gun. And Mr. Rhodes was here the morning of the murder, wasn't he? He'd had a late night, I imagine he slept in."

Her eyes fluttered to meet his. "Yes, that's right."

He waited, giving her a chance to change her mind. When she didn't, he said, "So he's in the clear. I suppose the police think, given Mr. Elwell's reputation, that Mr. Rhodes had reason to feel protective . . ."

"Oh, I never even *met* the man. I wish Billy hadn't either."

Her misery was sincere. She might not know the truth, but she herself was not lying.

"If I see the fellow who wrote about you, Mrs. Rhodes, I'll have a word with him."

"They're writing about me like I'm some loose society girl. I'm not *Viola Kraus*, for heaven's sake."

Pained, guilty, he nodded and thanked her for her time.

It was early evening when he arrived at the Studio Club on Park and Eighty-First. Several Cadillacs were lined up outside, like so many shiny black beetles along the curb. Rhodes was sleeping in a car at the end of the block, his hat tipped over his eyes, arms folded. Markey rapped on the window, and he started, fear in his eyes, until he saw who it was. "Get out of here, I'm working."

"Talk to me and I'll get my friend to lay off your wife in print. Just a few questions."

The driver's expression suggested he'd prefer to throw Markey under the wheels of the Cadillac. But he opened the door. "Quick. I have to run him over to his lady friend in an hour."

Climbing in, Markey said, "Were you aware that Elwell was a member of the American Protective League?"

"Nope."

"Ever hear of an Arthur Griswold?"

"Never."

The driver's denials were ready before he heard the questions, but Markey hadn't expected the truth. He might not be lying about Griswold—you didn't have to know a man's name to kill him—but Markey found it interesting, the speed with which Rhodes denied knowing Elwell was a member of the League.

He glanced around the car's sumptuous interior. "You landed well. Your wife mentioned she was very grateful to a Mr. Barnes."

Eyes front, Rhodes said, "Barnes runs the Studio Club, likes to help veterans. He got me the job with Elwell. He recommended Mrs. Larsen, too, so don't go making anything out of it. You asked your questions, now get out."

"Just one more . . . were you blackmailing Joseph Elwell?"

Rhodes hitched his shoulders to remind Markey of their size and musculature. He was not a tall man, but his fists were considerable, and Markey guessed that, properly aimed, they would land squarely in his midsection, knocking the wind out of him and possibly his lunch.

"Just, if I drove a man who made it a habit to run around with other men's wives, I'd see an opportunity."

"If blackmail's the game, why shoot the goose who lays the golden egg?"

"Because the goose got tired of laying and threatened to go to the police. I think I'm right that you've done jail time?"

He asked it as casually as he might ask if someone had secretarial skills. Rhodes put his hands on the steering wheel, the knuckles high and visible. "Do I look like I'm sitting on blackmail money?"

Markey had to concede he did not. Mrs. Rhodes had been wearing a housedress that had been mended more than once, and she had been making a stew—a time-honored way to get the most out of a cheap cut of meat. Markey didn't know much about William Rhodes, but he strongly suspected that if he had extra funds, he would spend it on his wife. Because whatever mistakes he had made in the past, and was making now, he knew he was damn lucky to have her.

Unless he had a gambling problem. An unfortunate affliction for a man who drove for a gentleman connected to the racetrack. The sort of thing that left you in debt to all sorts of unsavory people, as Amelia Hardy had noted.

"Are you a betting man, Mr. Rhodes?"

"No. My old man was. Maybe bad luck is inherited, maybe not. I never wanted to find out."

There was a grim sincerity in his voice that Markey trusted. He didn't think he could goad Rhodes into spilling anything about who might have hired him to kill Elwell. But there was one more personal reason Rhodes might have shot the gambler.

"Your wife is a gracious and lovely woman. Did Elwell ever make a play for her?"

Rhodes bristled. "No, because he'd have come away in pieces if he'd tried. Elwell liked his women rich and connected. Katie wouldn't have interested him."

"But when we first spoke, you thought one of the husbands shot him. Why?"

"I said *maybe* a husband shot him. Truth is . . . they were all pals."

"How do you mean?"

The driver didn't want to be talking to Markey, but his disgust was too strong to keep down. "You know people like that. Too much money they did nothing to earn, so everything's a game to them. Your wife jumps in bed with another man, you've got two mistresses, what do you care? None of those husbands would have had the sand to do the right thing."

It matched what the countess had said, that Elwell's favors were worth more to these men than their wives' fidelity. What that signified beyond the poor morals of the rich, Markey didn't know.

He got out of the car. Leaning down, he said, "My apologies for mentioning your wife. I'd say in her you've broken your father's streak of bad luck."

"So long as your friend doesn't mention her or me again, we're good."

Markey smiled rather than answer. As he started up the street, he saw a fresh black car drive up to the Studio Club and discharge its passenger. The man was strikingly tall and slim. His blond hair was silvered, but with the brightness of youth. His jaw was clean-shaven, his aspect at once genial and ruthless. Oddly, he put Markey in mind of F. Scott Fitzgerald, that bright, clean Arrow Collar look.

As the man trotted up the steps, the doorman touched his hat. "Good evening, Mr. Von Schlegell."

So this was Victor von Schlegell, whom Zelda had likened to the Red Baron. Mrs. Elwell had said her husband got his start in real estate and horses at the Studio Club. Two men sleeping with the same woman—and they belonged to the same club. He glanced back at the car where Rhodes sat waiting for his new master. He, Elwell, and Von Schlegell were all connected through this place. And if the B in the diary was Barnes, Griswold might be as well.

But Griswold was hardly a wealthy businessman and there was no proof that the Studio Club was connected to the APL.

Walking home through Central Park, Markey tried to put an article on Griswold together. He could simply write it as *Second*

Shooting on Bridge Master's Block. But without more information about the connection between Griswold and Elwell, it was just another murder in the city. Did it matter that both men had been APL members? The war was over, so the League might be inactive now, aside from the busybody grievances of Arthur Griswold. The countess made for great copy, but her most colorful quotes accused women, Viola Kraus in particular. Markey didn't want to write another word about Viola Kraus.

By the time he got home, it was nearly eight o'clock. What he needed was an audience, someone to whom he could tell the story so he could hear it for himself. Ideally, someone who knew something of national politics. Zelda and Scott, he suspected, were not those people. And after his triumph at the party, it would be humiliating to confess he might have gotten the story wrong.

Since coming to New York, he had relied on one person to explain parts of city life he didn't understand. Eddie Parker was an imperfect guide, but unlike the Fitzgeralds, he understood that the time away meant there were gaps. It had been Spook, he realized, who told him about Joseph Elwell in the first place.

Finding his direction, he started walking to Spook and Dottie's apartment.

The Parkers had recently moved to Seventy-First and West End. They had also, from the sound of it, acquired a dog. Markey heard it as he stood at their front door. Then he heard Dottie shouting, "Shut up, Wilson, for God's sake." Markey tensed. She sounded in a bad mood.

She opened the door with one hard yank. Then announced, "*Not* what I was hoping for."

"I apologize."

"As you should. Come in anyway."

This was easier said than done. Wilson had left mementoes by the door. As Markey stepped over them, the dog looked eagerly at his leg, as if anticipating the chance to relieve himself again. He was a Boston terrier. Like Dottie, he was small and agitated, with a little head and prominent dark, shining eyes. Even his black-and-white coloring matched hers. He was an ugly thing, but likable, Markey decided, in his game attitude toward life.

He guessed, "Wilson for the president?"

"We're all good patriots here." Then, as a bird squawked in a cage by the window, she added, "That's Onan. So named because he spills his seed."

Markey nodded, thinking a great deal had been spilled in this apartment. Wilson had made the parlor his dumping ground in the purest sense; there was a strong odor of urine. Paper—news, typed-up sheets, blank—was everywhere. Moving boxes, still unpacked, were stacked against the wall. A small table seemed to serve as everything from dining space to work desk. Put simply, the place was a wreck.

"Eddie's not here," Dottie told him. "I have no idea where he is or when he'll be back."

She was distressed and unkempt—two things Markey had never seen her be. "Is he all right?"

"Oh, yes, he's marvelous."

The sarcasm landed as it was meant to, like a fist to the jaw. Markey nodded to admit he deserved it. "Are *you* all right?"

For a moment, her sharp features trembled. Then she breathed in through the nose, a long hiss of containment. "Why are you here?"

Understanding that she desperately wanted distraction, he said, "I came to ask Eddie if he knew anything about the American Protective League."

Dottie gawped; he had shocked her by being interesting. "The union busters?"

Two things less alike than the countess and unions, he could not imagine. "Are they?"

"Well, they are now. They hunt down socialists, anarchists,

pacifists, the IWW, all sorts of un-American desperadoes. During the war, officially, they were playing Swat the Spy, rooting out German sympathizers and draft dodgers." She gathered up the little dog, waved his paw at Markey. "Yes, Mr. Wilson, you had slacker raids, didn't you? Barging into restaurants, movie theaters, and people's homes, demanding to see draft papers? And if the men weren't carrying those draft papers, they got arrested, didn't they? Yes, they did. Jailed for weeks sometimes, however long it took for the draft board to check their status."

"This was the government?"

". . . ish. Mr. Wilson came up with the Espionage Act." She set the dog down, lit a cigarette. "Then a Chicago millionaire thought, why should the government have all the fun? Wouldn't it be swell if the average American could investigate his neighbors? He took the idea to the president, and Wilson said, 'Splendid idea, but all available funds are going to the war effort.' But the millionaire was happy to pay for the privilege and so the APL was born, a privately funded squad of dunderheads and bigots licensed to root out disloyalty wherever they saw it." She exhaled a plume of smoke. "Their first meeting was at the People's Gas Building, if you can believe it."

"And you say it's still in operation?"

"Not officially. But once you've given people a taste of power, they get to like it. Some of them are working with the Department of Justice to bring Bolsheviks to heel. Others have joined the KKK." She smiled thinly.

Her disdain made him feel defensive. "A German professor from Cornell did bomb the Senate. And German saboteurs blew up two million tons of munitions in New Jersey. Three men were killed."

"As well as a little baby, and that is terrible. It was also in 1916. It is now 1920. The war has been over for two years. For a few acts of sabotage, pretty inept ones at that, millions of American citizens have to live in fear that the nosy old lady across the street will have them arrested for eating sauerkraut? Or for being the wrong color south of the Mason-Dixon Line?"

Markey couldn't dispute that people being what they were could corrupt the noblest enterprise—and the APL might not have been so noble to begin with. Certainly not if it employed the likes of Elwell and Griswold.

"What's your interest in the APL?" asked Dottie. "I thought you were chasing down deadly divorcées."

"Elwell was a member. He had at least one person arrested. Now another man's been shot, and he belonged as well. I'm starting to think I owe Viola Kraus an apology."

If Dottie had something witty to say on the subject, she did not offer it. Instead, she went to the kitchen, coming back with two glasses and a bottle of Scotch. She poured with the concentration of someone sawing off a leg. He said, "I didn't think you cared for it."

"When Eddie drinks, he's awful. When I drink, he's less so." She pushed the glass toward him. "Do you know I never mention it to people? Eddie's time in France? Makes him seem as if he were too stupid to get out of it."

Stricken, he said, "*No, Dottie.*"

"Well, what did he get out of it?"

"He had an honorable war. He helped wounded and dying men—"

She interrupted. "Did you know he spent most of last year in a sanitarium?"

He had and had not known this. Spook made jokes about his time at the health spa to treat the twitches, and Markey had understood it had something to do with France. But he had not allowed the word *sanitarium* or *ill* or *sick* to enter his mind.

"And not for the drink," said Dottie. "For morphine."

"He's still taking it?"

She stared. "You *knew* he was taking it?"

Markey felt his next words, poorly chosen, could result in violence.

"During the war," he stammered, "once or twice"—a lie, he realized as he said it, but probably necessary. "He had to, Dottie. The ambulance had to get where it was going, and there were times with the shelling and the shooting . . . you couldn't move if you didn't block it out. It was medicine," he finished lamely. "But I didn't realize he was taking it here."

"'Warning: May be habit-forming.'" Dottie quoted the label on the bottle.

"Is he still taking it? Is that where he is now?"

"I don't think so," she said, suddenly exhausted. "Now we're back to the drink. Which he liked before the war, if we're being candid. Now he doesn't so much like it as . . ." Her expression darkened as she found herself unable to be funny on the subject. "He pours it down his throat as if it were water and he was stranded in the Sahara. Once, I came home and found him with his head in the oven. If only we had paid the gas bill that month."

Markey resolved never to dislike Dottie again, no matter if she disliked him. "I feel it would insult you to say I'm sorry."

"Not insulting. Just pointless." Then, as if it were no great matter, she added, "Maybe those slackers were onto something."

Because it was how he felt at that moment—or maybe it was the Scotch—Markey said emphatically, "No."

"Well, do *you* think it was worth it?" It was not a question, more accusation.

"I don't know what that means. I know if Eddie hadn't been driving that ambulance, men would have died. That has to be worth it to someone."

He meant it, but he knew to Dottie, in her empty apartment that smelled of dog leavings, it reeked of sloppy sentiment.

She said, "All I know is if your Mr. Elwell had dragged my

lovely funny Eddie out of a movie theater and sent him over there, I'd have shot him myself."

He felt she wanted him out, so he stood. But he couldn't help asking, "Does Eddie often stay out all night?" Spook had gone home the night of the Elwell killing, he told himself. At least he had meant to.

"Oh, we all stay out all night. I don't imagine any of us will have children; no one's home long enough to make them, let alone take care of them. As a matter of fact—"

A moment's searching, and she had her purse in hand and a small hat on her head. With a "Be good" to the dog, she lined up beside Markey at the door. He said, "Don't you want to be home in case . . . ?"

"Home is where the heart is not. *Venite*, chop-chop."

Going to the newsroom, Markey found it bustling. A young lady had gone berserk in her car, killing two men uptown, and something almost interesting had happened in the election. He had to wait twenty minutes for a typewriter, shoving to get to the open chair. But he had the story written in his head and he typed quickly.

> As the police search for the killer of Joseph Elwell, a second murder took place on West Seventieth Street. Arthur Griswold was shot and killed in his apartment early this morning. Arthur Griswold was not a well-liked man. Probably because he didn't like many people. His neighbors remember him as "mean," "nosy." He was often at his window, keeping an eye on the neighborhood. If someone came or went at a time he deemed unsuitable, he had something to say about it. His ears were sensitive, his eyes sharp, his judgment constant. Despite having no official title, such as police officer, elected official, or dog catcher, it was his job, he seemed to

feel, to divide the good people from the bad and to punish the bad. His job and his right.

Arthur Griswold was a member of the American Protective League. And he had a badge to prove it. According to at least one witness, Joseph Elwell also had connections to the League.

He wrote up what Dottie had told him about the APL. Inquired of readers why the APL should still be active, the war having ended. Wondered if the land of the free should set neighbor against neighbor, employing some to spy on others. He wrote about Arthur Griswold's empty apartment, a space where no life had been truly lived.

> Griswold was shot through the head, just as Elwell was. Possibly he did not know his killer. Which is funny, given that he knew everything about everyone. Or so he thought.

Then he took the story to Gus Schaeffer.

"What is this?" was Schaeffer's first question when he had finished.

"My neighbor was murdered. This is the report."

"What happened to Viola Kraus? Nobody cares about"—Schaeffer had to check—"Arthur Griswold."

"If nothing else, he's the man who lived directly across the street from Joseph Elwell. He was shot in a manner that's very similar."

"So you think it's a nut?" Schaeffer squinted, as if trying to see the story.

"No, I think either he saw who did it or it's something to do with the APL. Did you . . . read the piece?"

"No, I gazed upon it as a thing of beauty." He threw the pages back at Markey. "Cut it, all the little questions and 'I wonder' stuff. 'Man shot across the street from Elwell home. Police baffled.' Then get back on Viola Kraus."

"And the fact that he and Elwell were members of the APL?"

"Irrelevant. Worse than irrelevant, boring. I'm a member of the Loyal Order of Moose. If I'm shot tomorrow, you going to say it was because I was a moose?"

Markey paused. "No, sir, I wouldn't say that."

Then he took his article and cut out every last interesting detail. Except that Arthur Griswold was "an honored member of the APL."

He took the subway home. His feet hurt and his spirit ached worse. It was tiredness, he told himself. That's why he was suddenly feeling there might be worse things than going back to Atlanta and covering the dull squalor of local politics. Or quitting newspapers altogether. He had run a Boy Scout troop once. Knots, starting fires, camping. Good simple things. Except the thought of boys tramping through woods didn't feel so hopeful and happy as it once had.

How had the bridge teacher to society become a spy? Had he been approached by the government, wanting information on people like the countess, members of a class they couldn't reach—as he himself had enlisted the Fitzgeralds to get in to see Viola Kraus? Had Elwell gleefully thrown his companions to the wolves, delighting in the duplicity, the power, the bluff and double bluff? Or had he been full of patriotic fervor and a hunger to serve, as Markey had been in what now felt like a century ago?

He wondered if he should go in search of Spook. It would be a kindness to Dottie. Except he didn't have the first idea where to look. Spook was lost. How responsible was Elwell for that? *Warning: May be habit-forming.*

No, he told himself, Spook wasn't lost; he was on a bender the way a lot of people were these days, whether they served or not.

The Parkers' was not a happy home. Small wonder they both stayed away.

Trying to buck himself up, he remembered that only yesterday people had hung on his every word. Then he remembered that with every one of those words, he had accused a woman who was, in all likelihood, innocent. He thought of Zelda curled around Scott and felt desperately alone.

Number 237 West Seventieth Street was dark. Briefly, he adjusted his step as he entered his apartment. Then realized, with some sadness, that there was no need.

Johnson arrived swiftly that night. Markey felt the weight of collapsing earth at his knees, found he couldn't move his legs. Johnson was all but buried, the lack of air making him wilder. The dying man flung his hands up, gripping the edges of the ditch as if he might lift himself out. Frantic they would be seen, Markey pulled at Johnson's arms, half rising to pry his fingers off. As he did, he heard the whine of a too-close bullet, then the high ping as it struck a tree. The tree had chimes in it; there was a tinkling sound. A sudden spreading warmth filled his groin. Markey reached down and felt wet. The bullet hadn't missed him after all. *Johnson*, he thought, *I'm going now* . . .

Markey jolted awake to see broken glass on the floor by his bed. His first thought was *That's pretty, the way the streetlight hits it.* His second, *I haven't done that since I was a child.* Frantically, he patted his abdomen to make sure, touching not the thick, tacky feel of belly blood, but something thinner that cooled rapidly, smelling of ammonia rather than copper.

He had pissed himself. He touched the mattress, wondering how he would explain this to Mrs. Cecchetti.

The window had shattered—he understood that now. Frightened to leave his bed, he surveyed the room, expecting to see a rock or chunk of cement. Maybe a message wrapped around it. *Stop asking questions.* It would be a good story in the newsroom, where it was a badge of honor to be threatened. Lying in urine-soaked pajamas, he took some comfort in that. He would need the rock and the note as proof, though, and he didn't see it.

Shucking off his soiled pants, he carefully placed his bare feet on the floor. His body felt like a beehive. In his head, the buzzing was so intense, it had become a shrill quavery hiss, like air escaping through a puncture. Vaguely, he rubbed behind his ears as if he could make it go away. *Quit it*, he thought, addressing it for the first time. *Danger's gone.*

The glass had mostly fallen near the window. Mrs. Cecchetti would be furious; he hoped she wouldn't make him pay for it; it was hardly his fault if people went around throwing rocks. Only where *was* the rock? It occurred him that he should not be walking around bare-ass naked with no curtains. This was probably the sort of thing his mother imagined him doing in New York. He put the heel of his hand to the back of his ear, pressed hard. If anything, the hiss grew louder, as if outraged by his effort to silence it.

When he saw the bullet, he wondered, *But how did that get here?* It lay on the floor in the small hallway that led to the kitchen. It had taken off quite a chunk of doorframe.

Reality came, mundane in its clarity. Someone had shot through his window.

No, someone had tried to kill him.

The buzzing was rattling his teeth. He found it hard to stand. He told himself he was only shaking because he was bare-ass naked and it was cold. Really cold.

Then he remembered it was June.

Hurriedly, he went to the bathroom, slapped his face, groin, and armpits with a wet cloth. Then he dressed, pulled on his shoes, and fled the apartment.

Chapter Nineteen

The desk clerk at the Ritz was reluctant to call the Fitzgeralds' suite; the couple was having a party. Markey could see his appearance made the desk clerk nervous. His hands had been shaking as he dressed, and he had missed a button or two on his shirt. His hair was barely combed. Markey wanted to tell the man his hands were not working right, that he had done the best he could, but he knew: He did not look sound.

But there had been complaints about the party, and Markey hinted that if he could speak with Mrs. Fitzgerald, things might quiet down. The clerk, eager for a solution, handed over the phone.

His nerves drawing tighter and tighter, Markey waited as the phone was set down and picked up by half a dozen drunken guests. He heard Zelda's name shouted, muffled repetitions of his request to speak with her, shrieks of laughter that might be in response to his request or something else entirely. He rubbed his fingers along the inside of his palm, pressed his nails against the ball of his thumb. Finally, he heard her voice: "Now is this Santa Claus or Babe Ruth? Either way, if you don't come bearing gin, don't bother!"

He told her he was neither. He told her he had no gin. He told her he couldn't face people right now. Could she possibly come down? He would be outside. Then he handed the phone back to the desk clerk and went out to the street. Hands in his pockets, he paced. Then he stopped dead at the sight of Zelda coming through the revolving doors. He was astonished to see her. Yet he had never doubted that she would come.

Now that she was here, he felt he could sit down, which he did on the pavement.

Apparently familiar with people collapsing on the sidewalk, Zelda hurried to pick him up. He sensed her smelling his breath, was glad there was only toothpaste. But an explanation was required.

"I think," he said slowly, "I may be losing my mind. It feels like it's breaking."

"I see." She crouched beside him. "Did something happen or it just came on you?"

"They shot at my apartment. A bullet came through my window."

"Someone tried to kill you?"

"Yes!" He laughed because she'd gotten it so quick. "That is precisely what happened. They—"

He couldn't stop laughing. Her hand on his arm was blessedly warm; he almost started crying at the sight of it. *Thank you*, he thought. *Thank you.* He had started shivering again. The mosquito whine in his ear intensified.

"I'll get Scott."

"No, don't." He clung onto her wrist, loathing himself but

clinging all the same. "I'm sorry, I know it's very wrong of me, but I'd prefer just . . ."

He couldn't say *you*. But he thought it hard and prayed she'd see it.

Glancing up at the hotel entrance, she said, "Would you like to walk? I'm not so sure that doorman's the friendly one."

Markey looked. "He doesn't seem friendly." In fact, the man was pointedly waving his hand across his leg as if brushing off dirt. *Move on.*

"No, there's a nice one and a mean one, and that's the mean one. Let's get you up."

He looked back at the monumental hotel, all the way up to the top floor. "You don't mind leaving . . . ?"

She shook her head. "Everyone's having the same old conversation, and Scott's making a fool of himself over Beadsie Bankhead."

Startled, he was about to say Scott needed his nose punched when she added gaily, "I was ready to go out the window with boredom anyway, and here you are, so where shall we go?"

They were unsure as to where. Markey felt badly in need of a drink, but he didn't want to be seen with a woman famously the wife of another man, and the speakeasies he knew were full of reporters. In the end, they went where nobody went, at least not in the middle of the night, and that was the plaza in front of the library on Fifth Avenue and Forty-Second Street. Looking at the vast marble temple to literature, Markey wondered how many of Fitzgerald's books would be on its shelves one day. Two imposing lion statues stood guard at either end of the stairs. He sat at the base of one of the lions while Zelda did a sort of hopscotch dance up and down the stairs. He watched as she grew in confidence, moving from the stairs to the plaza. Her arms were raised, her expression grave and inward. She twirled, legs strong, back straight. In the sketchy moonlight, she was a burst of bright gold and milky diaphanous silk. Sun and clouds. She used the space fearlessly, rejoicing in its openness. But she was isolated and exposed, and it worried him. He kept a close eye on the roof, the low stone walls, the trees for signs of movement. The electric hum in his feet and hands returned. The tightness in his chest made his breath clutch up; his heart was so tired and sore from pounding so hard, it occurred to him it might quit.

But Zelda's joy was reassuring. She was not scared, and it seemed an insult to her for him to be. He forgot to be vigilant. The bees in his body and mind quieted, went to sleep.

When she was finished, she sat down on the stairs beside him, and he told her about coming home to find Griswold murdered.

Drawing her knees up, she hugged them. "The thing is," she said, "I can see Viola shooting Elwell. But I don't see her shooting you or your neighbor. She seems like a girl that's got one shot in her."

He nodded in agreement. "I don't see her making a habit of it. And she was in Newport when Griswold was killed."

"Whoever it is has killed two men. How come they missed you?"

"Three dead bodies would be a lot to overlook. I think they just wanted me to know they know where I live."

"So you'd stop writing about Elwell?"

He shrugged: *Maybe.*

"Why not warn you off at the beginning?"

"Because the story's changed. I started off writing about the girl in the green dress and Viola Kraus. But my last article was on Griswold and the APL."

But the article hadn't run yet, he realized. It would be in the morning edition a few hours from now. So, how would anyone know what was in it? Who had he spoken to? The countess, Rhodes, Gus Schaeffer. Who had, now that he thought of it, not wanted him to mention the APL . . .

"The what?" asked Zelda.

"The American Protective League." Instinctively, he knew leagues, along with guilds, unions, and associations, would be of little interest to her. "Spies who hunted people seen as disloyal during the war. Elwell worked for them. So did Griswold."

"Why does the killer care if you write about some league?"

"Because this murder is not a love story gone wrong, it's about what Elwell did during the war." Or perhaps more recently, if what Dottie said was true.

He said, "The killer could be someone who's angry at the APL. Or the APL could be cleaning house of its troublesome agents. From what I understand, some of them used their power for ill or personal gain. If it comes out Elwell was a member, people might start looking into what he did with that badge."

"And your vile neighbor?"

"Shot to shut him up. I think Griswold was keeping an eye on Elwell, either to protect him because someone was out to get him or because Elwell was a loose cannon who had money troubles. Never a good thing for an organization that deals in secrets."

He looked at Zelda, who said, "I prefer the love story."

She stood, looked up at the lion. "Give me a boost."

Now used to her quicksilver turns, he knew not to fight it. He knelt, braided his fingers together, and held them out to her. Slipping off her shoes, she placed her foot in his joined hands. He said, "Ready?" She said, "Ready." He rose and she with him. He felt her weight for a moment; then she was gone. The next thing he knew, she was seated on the beast's back. Triumphant, she smiled down at him. He knew she was making a point of her splendor, but she was splendid all the same.

Leaning forward, she draped herself over the lion's neck, resting her chin on its mane. "Tell me—did the flowers work?"

"For Mrs. Larsen? Yes."

"You talk to those other women?"

"I did." He thought of poor Katherine Rhodes and Amelia Hardy. Amelia Hardy's husband, the one who worked in gas, where was he these days?

"How about that girl in the green dress? Maybe she's a German *spy* out for revenge." The gleam in her eye reminded him she thought the spy story pure bunk.

"According to Griswold's diary, she left an hour after she arrived at Elwell's house. She does work at the *Frolic*, but it turns out she's just an attractive girl in a nice dress. I would like you to come down now. You're making me nervous."

Zelda waved her feet. "Oh, but attractive girls in nice dresses matter enormously."

"Yes, they do, but please come down."

"Why?" Sitting up, she took hold of the lion's ears, arched her back.

"Because I don't want to explain to Scott Fitzgerald why I let the woman he loves break her neck."

Making a show of obedience, she swung her legs over the other side and slid down. She gave him her hand for balance, a strangely helpless gesture, given her boldness a minute ago. He beat back the urge to hold on to it.

"Should we go back?" he asked. "I feel I've taken enough of your evening."

They began walking back to the hotel. But Zelda dawdled, distracted by the store windows on Fifth Avenue. Finding one she liked, she pulled him beside her, positioning them so their reflections appeared in the glass. A stiff lacquered man and a frozen flapper with a bee-stung mouth stood lofty and unaware of them. It reminded Markey of many a New York party.

Zelda posed, watching herself as she swooned, laughed, and took fright. "I'd like to be in movies. My mother was going to be an actress."

"Isn't your father a judge?" In his mind, the two did not go together.

"Yes, he is. Judge Anthony Dickinson Sayre. He wanted to marry my mother, but she ran off to Philadelphia to audition for the Barrymore company. They accepted her, too. Only *her* father was running for office, and he thought a daughter married to a respectable lawyer would be better for him politically. He dragged her back to Kentucky, and that was that."

He was about to say that the consolations of children and married life must compensate. Then he remembered Zelda's rage at the buried women at the cemetery and thought better of it.

Peering at her likeness, she said, "It's like with photographs when they make a mistake and there's two images, one sort of like a shadow over the other."

"And they tell you it's the ghost of your great-aunt Clara."

"Sometimes at parties, I end up watching myself, and that's what it's like. I vibrate intensely, like when you pluck a string and it becomes a blur? Or when I talk, there's an echo. It gets so I'm not sure which one is which."

"That sounds unnerving."

"Oh, no, it's entirely suitable, even fashionable." She spun to punctuate the point. "This town is more a reflection of itself than anything real. When people talk about New York, they're really talking about themselves being in New York, like the city's a mirror they like to see themselves in."

Or everything's a mirror to you, he thought affectionately. Zelda deserved mirrors; she deserved all the light. He worked to hold that image of her dancing along the marble stairs because he wanted to keep it. Then he remembered the way she and Scott had played word games at the *Frolic*, captivated by each other. They reflected each other perfectly.

Pointing, she cried, "Don't you think I'd look extraordinary in that squirrel coat?"

"I think you'd look eaten by a squirrel." Gleeful, she swatted him. Recalling Scott's embarrassment at the florist's, he added, "And I might suggest, be gentle on the family purse."

This she greeted with a bright "Ishkabibble."

She consented to walk alongside him for another block or two. But at Forty-Third Street, she veered left, saying, "Actually—I'm tired of Princeton boys at the moment."

All Princeton boys, he wondered, or just the one? Remembering the kisses bestowed at the party, he said carefully, "They seem very fond of you."

"They're not fond, they're fascinated. I don't think any of them has ever met an actual girl before. Sometimes I feel like something in a cage, surrounded by children. 'What'll it do? Poke at it, make it do a trick.' I do not mind turning the occasional somersault, but I didn't come to New York to amaze college boys."

He knew she was a girl who deeply enjoyed the spectacle she created. But her frustration felt sincere. "You miss home?"

"I don't have the time to miss anything." Then, "Sometimes. You miss it?"

He thought. Was *missing* the word? "I don't know. Sometimes I feel like old Aunt Clara."

"Shall I fetch you a shawl?" she teased.

Somehow, they had reached Times Square. The night sky was a blaze of neon and names: Loews, Arrow, Maxwell House, some lights so strong they created rivers of illumination across the pavement, caught the black tops of taxi cabs. The whole world was liquid with light. The shimmer, the irregular beat of current—every so often, a light would flicker, then blaze back—the rush of people, the obnoxious honk and sad fade of car horns created a universe of there and gone.

"Well, look at us," she said, twirling among the lights.

"Look at us," he agreed. "How'd we ever get here?"

He offered his arm and she took it, saying, "Well, God bless harebrained boys who insist on being interesting."

He smiled to acknowledge the compliment. But the fickle light and her talk of reflections had put it in his head and he heard himself admit, "You know, the war's probably the biggest thing I'll ever do in my life, but it didn't make me the person I thought I'd be. I feel like that harebrained boy died in France, but I came back anyway. Seems like he should be here or I should there—one of us is in the wrong place."

She nodded but made no comment. He couldn't tell: Did she understand so well she didn't need to ask what sort of person he'd hoped to be? He himself was not exactly sure, but cheering and confetti had been involved. Speeches made by him, a beautiful woman nearby. And money, flowing so that he never even had to think about it. A secure place in the world. No, a secure *and* exalted place. Whatever the living version of those statues was, that's what he had wanted.

Then she asked, "When you said your mind felt like it was breaking—what was that like?"

It was like their first meeting when she asked how many people he'd been to bed with, the question so personal yet posed so casually. His first impulse was to brush it away. Then he exhaled.

"You remember that night at the *Frolic?*"

"When you got fidgety and strange."

He nodded, accepting the words. "It was the balloons. The popping. Ever since"—he waved a finger to indicate France—"one bang and everything in me starts humming like a live wire, sparking and snapping. If I can't get out of the situation, then I'm fairly convinced I'm going to die." He tried to say it lightly, as if expressing a preference for black coffee.

"Balloons mean you're going to die."

"I am aware that it is untrue. Even when it's happening, I know. I tell myself this is not real . . ."

"But?"

He took a deep breath. This was the dangerous thing to confess and he spoke quickly. "But I can't *feel* it's not real. The buzzing gets so loud, the fear . . ."

There, he'd said it.

". . . gets so strong, I worry I'll . . ." Raising his hands, he flared his fingers, blew out air.

"Explode."

"Sure." It was as good a word as any. "And I know they're just balloons and the buzzing sound is lying to me, but—"

"You're trapped in your mind."

"Yes." He looked at her, surprised she had said it so simply, as if it were a thing everyone felt. "Yes."

"You should write about that. There's more money in fiction."

"I have a story I'm thinking about," he said, pleased that he was already doing as she suggested. "It's about a doctor. One day he's operating. He's about to make the incision and he hears a buzzing. Like a warning. So he makes a different cut and saves his patient. After that, anytime he's in danger of doing the wrong thing, the hissing starts, just behind his right ear."

"Then what?"

"I don't know yet, I haven't figured that part out."

He was about to ask why she had asked about broken brains when she said, "Here's what I don't understand: If you're so scared of dying or exploding or whatever, why go running after that girl when you thought she'd killed a man?"

He tried to make a joke of it. "I guess it didn't seem the worst way to go."

"Do you want to go?" she demanded.

"I . . ." How to explain it, both the terror and the dreadful pull? "No, but sometimes death feels like seeing someone out of the corner of your eye and you won't feel right until you meet them. Nothing else feels as true, I guess."

"It's funny, isn't it? How danger makes people passionate? Even if you know someone's going to destroy you, you can't help it. We yearn to feel that obliteration, to be *consumed* by love."

"Well, if that's the case . . ."

Then he stopped. She had been kind. He shouldn't repay her with judgment.

"What? Go ahead."

"No, I . . . All right, here it is. If you're so consumed—and I pay you the compliment of believing that's true—why do you mess Scott around by kissing other men? You say he doesn't mind, but I think he does mind it . . ."

He had intended to ask about Scott's trifling with another woman; why he had attacked Zelda, he wasn't sure. And yet he found himself waiting for the answer.

Dropping his arm, she said, "Don't be so Victorian. I never want to be one of those sticky little wives, going, 'Dearest, may I? Darling, use your fork.' People are always saying women civilize men. Well, I don't want to civilize anybody, I want to be one of the savages, they have more fun. If I want to kiss a man because I like his tie, I shall. A woman should be able to kiss a man beautifully, even romantically, without it meaning she wants to become his wife or mistress. But what you really mean is why didn't I kiss you."

He did a fair imitation of a laugh. "No . . ."

She waved off his no with a light hand. "And on the subject of husbands and wives, I want to point out that Miss Kraus may have been in Newport, but her former husband, Mr. Victor von Schlegell, was *not*."

He was about to say, *Now I know girls are fond of love stories*, when he was struck by the word *mister*. Because Elwell had not said *Mister* when he addressed Von Schlegell.

He had said *Herr*.

Markey had dismissed this point when Zelda first made it. But if Elwell belonged to the APL, the gibe had a different weight. And

Von Schlegell's taunt: *It seems we can't keep away from each other.* Zelda had assumed he was talking to his former wife, but perhaps not. The more Markey thought about it, the more he wondered if the fellow club members were romantic rivals at all.

As they rounded the corner, the Ritz came into view. Markey could see tired revelers spilling out of the doors. Some of them were no doubt friends of the Fitzgeralds. A drunk in a tuxedo slammed into Markey. Throwing "Sorry, sorry" over his shoulder, he lurched down the block, followed by a few straggling compatriots, one of whom looked back at Markey and hooted. Zelda watched them, amused.

When they reached the entrance, she asked, "Head stopped buzzing?"

"More or less."

"I'm glad they didn't get you. Don't let 'em get you."

"You neither."

He hadn't thought much before saying it, considering it a pleasantry along the lines of *Nice seeing you.* But the words seemed to strike her hard. For just a moment, her brave swagger faltered; the dazzling halo of self-belief dimmed. He saw a thing he had never seen in her before: uncertainty. And—it took him a moment—grief.

He was on the verge of saying *It'll be all right* when she brightened back up and said, "You need to stop thinking about the war, Morris Markey. There is too much life to enjoy. You're a big man, act like it. If you're going to be here, *be* here."

Marching back to the Ritz, she ran up the steps. At the top, she turned and shouted, "Do you know what I'm going to do?"

"What?"

"I'm going to find you that girl in the green dress."

"I might be over her," he called back.

"Oh, no, you're not. Not till the day you die."

Chapter Twenty

Mrs. Cecchetti was pleased to see him. She had seen the broken window that morning when she went to sweep the front stoop. Concerned, she had knocked on his door and worried when he did not answer.

"I hope you don't mind," she said. "I went inside. I wanted to make sure you weren't . . . ."

"Of course."

She looked him up and down. Markey knew he looked less than fresh. Finally, she said, "It's a good thing you work late."

"Yes." He wondered how to ask her if he might have a new mattress.

She said, "They're coming next week to replace the window. I'm afraid I had to put plywood in for now. But the bars will keep people out. And it's summer, so . . . ."

"I'll appreciate the air," he assured her.

"Why is this happening, Mr. Markey? Who is doing this?"

Looking at the tiny Italian woman who had worked so hard to own a building and make her way in this country because she believed it to be a safe place with laws, Markey, tired as he was, felt invigorated by outrage. It should *not* be happening, and the person who was doing it must be made to stop. And, if he had his way, hurt—badly—for the pain they'd caused. He had found it hard to work up much anger over Elwell or Griswold, or even the threat to his own life. But Mrs. Cecchetti was frightened, and that was just plain wrong.

"I'm going to find out," he promised.

He bathed and changed clothes. Then he drank several cups of coffee and made notes, holding his eyes open with the heel of his hand at times.

Until now, he had assumed that Elwell's murder was connected to his amorous pursuits—"sexitis," as the sham minister had said. That he had been shot because he chased one woman too many or a woman with the wrong husband. But what if it was not so much the wives Elwell was interested in but their husbands. It would explain the odd now-ardent, now-indifferent courtship he had carried out with Viola Kraus, as well as his friendliness to the husbands observed by both Rhodes and the countess. Elwell had obviously wooed Amelia Hardy to watch the countess, dropping her as soon as the countess was released from jail. If he had only pursued Viola to spy on her husband, it made sense that once she had divorced that husband, there was no need to carry on the pretense of an affair.

Dottie had told him that the APL had been started by a rich businessman. The Studio Club seemed like a place where those men could do deals—and perhaps conduct other business—they wouldn't want people knowing about. Like spying.

Or doing what businessmen did best: getting rich by selling

to anyone who would buy, no matter what side of the war they were on.

Why would Elwell target Von Schlegell? Was it just his Germanic last name? Or had he been doing business with people he shouldn't? What was Von Schlegell's business? He couldn't remember.

There was also Walter Lewisohn to consider. Elwell could have courted Viola as a way to acquaint himself with her brother-in-law. He tried to recall what Schaeffer had said about the Lewisohn fortune but only remembered vague words like *banking* and *real estate*. Markey didn't know much about either, but he knew someone who did. He would pay a call at Edwin Pond Parker's office at Paine Webber. He wanted to make sure Spook was all right anyway.

He had once asked Spook how he knew what a stock was worth. "It's worth what people are willing to pay for it." Thinking he had asked the wrong question, Markey said, "No, I mean its value." Spook repeated, "Its value is what people are willing to pay for it." "How do they know what to pay for?" asked Markey.

"Well, if something's valuable, you've got to pay more to own it," said Spook.

Knowing there was a contradiction but unable to articulate it, Markey shook his head. Spook took out his handkerchief and noisily blew his nose. Then he held it out to Markey.

"One of a kind. The linen made in England, its contents produced domestically. Seeing as we're friends, I can let you in on the ground floor." Markey said no thanks.

He was relieved to find Spook at his desk—relieved to find him at all, frankly. "Did you make it home last night?" he asked, his tone more accusatory than he'd intended.

Spook looked at him cockeyed. "Aw, Ma, you don't have to worry about me, I got a gal."

"I know you do. She was worried sick."

Spook raised his eyebrows to indicate disbelief.

"She *was*."

"And I'm sure she gathered her pals round the table and told them all about it. 'George, Mr. Benchley, listen to what my ridiculous husband did this time.'"

"So stay home and she won't have stories to tell."

"I think she's fucking Benchley. It's just my opinion, of course, but I have been known to be right from time to time."

"Are you drunk?"

"Are you kidding?" Then he dropped the air of jovial spite. "What do you want?"

I want you to rejoin the living, thought Markey. But that wasn't why he'd come. "Walter Lewisohn."

"What about him?"

"Do you know anything about his politics?"

"All for the greater good of Walter Lewisohn, and a boot in the face of anyone who says otherwise. He's only human. Well, maybe that's too kind . . ."

"Does he belong to any organizations that you know of?"

"You know, Walt and I used to be great pals, but we've lost touch somehow."

"Stockbrokers in general, do they join political groups?"

Seeing that Markey wasn't going to drop the subject, Spook considered. "Not really. These fellows write a check."

"How'd Lewisohn do during the war, do you know?"

"Generally, those who had it got more of it. I assume he was no exception."

"Did he ever invest in things like munitions, steel . . . ?"

"The family's in banking. I assume they invest in everything."

Markey fell back in his chair, frustrated. Spook was right. The Lewisohn holdings were probably so extensive, it would be difficult to prove any specific benefit the war might have brought them. On the other hand, they would have no reason to want America out of the conflict—and so no quarrel with the APL, an organization dedicated to making sure the war had all the bodies it needed. And by all accounts, Elwell and Lewisohn had been friendly enough. Lewisohn had even found Elwell a place to live. What was the landlord's name again? Sand . . . no, Sandler. Bernard Sandler.

Von Schlegell was a different story, however. Both Dottie and the countess had said the APL could cast a wide net, sometimes based on last names alone.

"Spook, have you ever come in contact with a fellow named Victor von Schlegell?"

"Other than in the pages of your esteemed publication? No."

"You don't know what his business is, do you?"

Spook shook his head.

"Is there any sort of manual I could look at? Like a telephone directory for who sells what? Say you've got a client who wants to invest in saltwater taffy, how do you find the big names in taffy?"

Leaning down, Spook opened a lower drawer in his desk, pulled out a fat volume that, by the look of its pristine spine, hadn't been opened much. He pushed it across the desk to Markey. "Have fun." Then he got up and began straightening his tie.

"Where are you going?" asked Markey.

"Lunch."

"It's not even noon."

Spook didn't answer, using the window as a mirror to comb his hair. Turning, he clicked his heels and spread his arms wide. "There—the spitting image of a young man with a future, wouldn't you say?"

And when Markey didn't answer, "Oh, well, I tried."

As Spook left, Markey said to his back, "Stay away from the damned oven, would you?" Spook stopped a moment, then kept walking as if he hadn't heard.

The Broker's Guide to Better Business was as riveting as its title promised. Some of the companies' products were clear-cut—real estate, department stores, precious metals. Others less so. Not every company was publicly traded, he realized. Smaller arms firms for example. Others, like US Steel, were so large it was impossible to identify an individual who might have caught Elwell's suspicions. Besides, Frick and Morgan were both dead.

What else sold well in wartime? Oil, lead . . .

Then he remembered Scott's joke, how he had remarked to Von Schlegell, *So you're in rubbers.* He recalled feeling suffocated by the mask meant to protect him from gas, the acrid chemical smell of the material—rubber. His father, patting one of the army vehicles that rolled down Main Street during a victory parade. *Farewell, horse of the Light Brigade. Here's the new cavalry.* Spook at the wheel of the ambulance, the tires so often stuck in the mud. More rubber.

Turning to the *R*s, he found United and Globe Rubber. The name, an apparent combination of *United States* and *global*, intrigued him. It had many, many vice presidents, probably most of them a relative or college pal of someone. Nonetheless, he dutifully read down the list. The names began to blur. But when the name appeared, it leapt out at him right away. It was so theatrical.

Victor von Schlegell.

Or . . . VVS.

He jotted down the address of United and Globe Rubber. It was 120 Broadway. Not far at all.

He did not expect to see Victor von Schlegell in person. He counted it as a victory that a secretary in a navy-blue suit came down to the lobby to tell him Mr. Von Schlegell was not available and to inquire as to the nature of his business. Handing her his card, he said, "My name is Morris Markey. I'm with the *Daily News*. I'm writing a piece about the industries that won the war for America. I'm a veteran myself, and I know firsthand how vital rubber was to the war effort."

"Mr. Von Schlegell is a busy man, but you can speak with our press department."

"I was also interested if he had personally experienced any anti-German sentiment." She gave him an odd look. "So many loyal and upstanding Americans came under unfair suspicion during the war years. Someone like Mr. Von Schlegell would be an excellent reminder not to judge people by their surnames."

"Our press department can be reached at Stuyvesant-0717."

She headed back to the bank of elevators. But he noticed that she kept his card.

By afternoon, the coffee had worn off. Markey realized if he did not sleep for several hours, he would be the next person on his block carried out on a stretcher. His thoughts were gummy, his memory such that it was difficult to distinguish memory from dreams. Had Zelda actually climbed on top of the library lion? What had she said about New York? It had been astute, and now he couldn't remember it. He thought of calling to ask her, then decided probably best for several reasons not to.

When Mrs. Cecchetti informed him a policeman was waiting to speak with him, he was so tired he said, "Truly, I don't know anything about Mr. Griswold." Only to be told the policeman wanted to ask him about who might have shot through his window.

The officer was very young and slapped his notebook against the palm of his hand in a way Markey found irritating. In turn, the officer was annoyed he'd had to wait so long to speak to Markey. Stepping into Markey's apartment, he said "Um, hm, um, hm" several times as he looked about the floor and at the boarded-up window.

"You sleep here?" He pointed to the bed.

Markey nodded.

The officer indicated the bullet, still on the floor. "Shot landed here?"

Markey bit his tongue on sarcasm. "Yes, sir."

The officer prowled about the room, pretending to notice things. Annoyed that he was being kept awake for this, Markey said, "It's just a guess, but it seems to me the shot came from some distance. Normally, that caliber gun, bullet doesn't stop until it runs into something. Like a wall."

"How'd you know what caliber gun it is?"

"Joe Elwell was shot with a .45. This bullet looks like a .45. What's the make on the gun that killed Arthur Griswold, do you know?"

Now the officer was looking at him with hostility. Rather than admit he didn't know, he flipped the pages of his notebook. "You didn't get along with Griswold, is that right?"

"As I told the other officer, he didn't get along with anybody." He was about to say, *Ask Mr. Siegel.* But he didn't want to expose his neighbors to the same foolishness.

Instead, he asked the officer, "Did you know Arthur Griswold was a member of the APL?"

"What's the APL?"

His tone was offhand; he didn't care. Markey changed up his questions. "Does it interest you that he was murdered in the same way as Joseph Elwell? Also a member of the APL?"

"Does it interest you?"

Markey almost said, *Do you actually want to do your job or just look like you're doing it?* But his father had always told him to be polite to police officers.

"Yes, it does interest me, given that both those men lived near me and all three of us were shot at."

"Now that *is* interesting, that you lived near both the murdered men."

Markey was about to tell him straight out not to be an idiot. Then he realized, at the time Griswold had been shot, he himself had been passed out at a party where all the other guests were equally unconscious and so incapable of providing him with an alibi. He had been wandering the streets of New York, euphoric and alone. Mrs. Larsen would attest that he had approached her just after Elwell had been shot. Why had he offered help when no one else did? Why had he taken such an interest? It was said murderers liked to revisit the scene of the crime.

Also, he had let too much time pass before answering.

Pointing to the glass on the floor, he said, "The shot came from outside."

"Did you have company that night? Someone who could vouch for you?"

"Of course I didn't. Are you saying you think I shot out my own window?"

The officer shrugged. Markey almost told him to smell his mattress. But there was no proof that it was fear piss and not liquor piss.

It felt peculiar to be looked at as a murderer. You began to question: Did you do it? Perhaps so, if someone could see you that way. Fogged, he thought of Viola Kraus, Walter Lewisohn, now Victor von Schlegell. All three had seen Elwell that night; all three might have wanted to kill him. Why weren't the police looking at any of them?

His room gave him the answer. Because they didn't live in cellar apartments with soiled mattresses and broken glass on the floor.

"You're a long way from home," said the officer.

"So are a lot of people in this city."

"Your landlady says you served in the war."

Markey remembered that the *Herald* had been pushing the story of a soldier equipped with an army-issue pistol as the shooter. Dislike for the policeman clarified his thinking. "Yes, I did. First lieutenant with the American Red Cross. Unless you have further questions, I need to get some sleep."

"It's three in the afternoon."

He nodded to the window. "Well, I didn't rest so easy last night."

"And yet you were out and about all day."

"I went to talk to Victor von Schlegell, Viola Kraus's former husband, if you must know. His secretary will tell you I was there."

"All *day*?"

Markey remembered Spook. Spook, who was sick, who had been out all night and now was God knew where. He didn't want the police jumping on him. Spook had enough problems.

"I saw my broker at Paine Webber." Spook would know to cover for him if it came to it.

"You have investments." The policeman looked at the wreck of the apartment.

"I'm considering some. What do you think of pogo sticks? I hear they're the next big thing."

The officer ambled to the door. "Don't change addresses. In case we need to speak to you again."

"I look forward to that with enormous anticipation," said Markey.

Pulling off his clothes, he surveyed the bed. If he flipped it, it should be all right. Only when he pulled back the covers did he see that Mrs. Cecchetti had already given him a new mattress. Composing a thank-you letter in his head, he fell asleep.

He slept hard. So hard it was work. Plunging into the darkest depths of unconsciousness, unencumbered by reality, his mind conjured the monstrous and miraculous. He was in the ditch, but Johnson was quiet, sleeping, Markey decided. The shooting had stopped, the smoke had cleared, the sun arrived. Markey stood, his legs aching from the long crouch, and stretched. Then he climbed out. There was a vast meadow before him and he started walking. A lion padded into view, its tail stiff and twitching as Zelda danced. Markey watched, unsure if he was the lion or himself watching. Then he was not watching but joining, and even in his dream, he wondered how he could know what this felt like because he had never felt it, the weight of another body, being inside and having someone inside. But he knew: This would be exactly how it felt. The lion was heavy; prone and on his back, Markey kept expecting the animal to take his head in its mouth, but it didn't. With delight, he saw that the lion's fur and Zelda's hair were the same gold. He turned his head to tell her, knowing it would please her. He felt a gentle kiss behind his right ear; then the knocking started. The carpenters were back at work. He needed to keep an eye on them, so he woke up.

It was not the carpenters, but Mrs. Cecchetti. She was sorry, she knew he was tired, but the young lady had called *again* and she couldn't have the phone tied up that way.

"I understand," said Markey, who didn't. "Forgive me, what time is it?"

"It's noon." Her raised eyebrow added *the next day*.

"I see." He took the slip of paper from her, smiled at the number. "I'll call her back now. My apologies, Mrs. Cecchetti."

He dressed slowly to give himself time to clear the dream from his mind. When he was ready, he went upstairs to the telephone.

When he reached Zelda, she cried, "Markey! You have to come to tea this afternoon. Scott and I went back to the *Frolic* last night. I realized we've never sat through the whole show because there's usually so much else going on. There were these two dancers: Maurice Mouvet and Leonora Hughes. She'll be coming, too, by the way."

"Who'll be coming?"

"Miss Hughes."

He felt irritated; Zelda could be sloppy, pulling in this person and that when they weren't to the point. ". . . Why?"

"Why?" Zelda echoed his irritation, doubling it. "Because Leonora Hughes is your girl in the green dress. Now hurry up. We'll be in the Palm Room."

CHAPTER TWENTY-ONE

The two ladies were not difficult to spot, being by far the youngest and loveliest people in the room. They sat by a window in the exact center of the restaurant, probably placed there by a maître d' as proof that the hotel was not merely a haven for walrus-faced men with muttonchops and ladies with lorgnettes and bustles. As Markey approached, he thought Zelda looked especially fresh in a rose frock, her gold hair just visible below the line of an apple-green cloche. Her companion was a red-haired sylph with a tilted nose, a delicately molded chin, full mouth, and blue eyes that, when they slid up to meet his, made him feel as if she had drawn her long, elegant hand across his fly.

It was her. The girl in the dollar-green dress.

He extended his hand. "Miss Hughes. A pleasure to see you again."

She hesitated, then burst out laughing. "I'm sorry, Mr. Markey. I meet an awful lot of men; you'll have to remind me."

He knew it was foolish to exonerate someone of murder because you liked the way they laughed. But he was tempted. Her appearance might be the last word in sophistication, but her accent, he knew from the newsroom, was Brooklyn, and just as Park Avenue had notes of pretension and phoniness, Flatbush had the sound of forthright and true. If she had shot Elwell, she'd be the first to admit it and she'd probably had a good reason.

That last thought, he chided himself, might have been inspired more by those eyes than her accent. He should sharpen up.

Zelda explained, "Scott and I saw Leonora dance last night. She is *wondrous*." And when Miss Hughes demurred, she insisted, "No, you are. You would be ideal to play the girl in the movie they're making of *Paradise*. And I must know who designed that green dress you wore."

Artless, she said to Markey, "Leonora and her partner do a dance where he's a banker and she's . . . well, you're money, aren't you? That's what the costume is supposed to be? Green and silver, like, oh, confetti made of money." She raised an eyebrow to remind Markey of his description. "So alluring, dancing just out of reach as he chases her all over the stage."

"Does he win her in the end?" Markey asked.

Miss Hughes smiled; she had the most charming gap between her front teeth. "I thought you'd seen the show, Mr. Markey."

"Regrettably, no. I live across the street from Joseph Elwell. I saw you with him the night before his murder."

"The gangly fellow with the big eyes and dropped jaw." She turned to Zelda. "So, this isn't about the movie for *This Side of Paradise*."

"It can be both," said Zelda.

"But it isn't. Goodbye, Mr. Markey."

As she stood, Markey said softly, "Miss Hughes, all I know right now is that you were with Mr. Elwell hours before he was shot. So, that's all I can write. I'd really like to write a different story."

He felt bad scaring her—he knew from Griswold's diary that she'd left Elwell's house an hour later—but she was a woman with a strong self-protective streak, and he had to break through that. Her fingers were tight around the strap of her black beaded purse. Taking in their beauty—they were long and sensitive—he realized he had seen them more recently than the night of Elwell's murder. One finger, to be precise, perfect and eloquent as it was raised high from behind a curtain.

"I should also mention that I'm the fellow who dragged Walter Lewisohn out of your dressing room."

"The one who knocked him on his ass?"

He nodded.

That got a slight smile, and when Zelda put in, "Mr. Markey is a good man, Miss Hughes. I know for a fact he only wants to write nice things about you," the dancer returned to her seat. But she bundled herself up, crossing her arms and legs and keeping one eye on the door. Nervous lady, thought Markey, despite the tough talk.

He said, "Why don't we start with your story?"

"Me? I'm a dancer who started off as a telephone operator. I've made a couple of movies. I don't have a husband. I'm one of eight kids. My parents still live in Flatbush. You understand what I'm saying?"

He nodded. She was a regular girl and she was looking to survive. "I won't use your name if you don't want me to. But people should know why you went home with Joseph Elwell that night."

She sighed, conceding the point. "Walter Lewisohn is, shall we say, sweet on me. It happens. Stage-door Johnnies, they show up with flowers, offer to take you out on the town. They're usually harmless, and the ones that aren't, I have a nail file in my purse."

"But Lewisohn is a different case," guessed Markey.

"Six months ago, Maurice and I start dancing at the *Frolic*. Lewisohn sees the show, tells me he's very interested in my career. I start getting invitations to his parties. I don't think the wife is so happy about it, but she doesn't complain. Although she and her sister usually spend the evenings giving me dirty looks."

"How does Walter spend the evening?" asked Markey.

"Different kind of look. He wants dance lessons."

Pert, Zelda asked, "And is he a good student?"

"His foxtrot's lousy, his tango is worse, and that's all I know."

He asked, "So why are you frightened?"

"Rich men are not always tethered to reality. How could they be? But with Lewisohn, it goes deeper. I don't think he's right in the head. The second time I ever saw him, he asked me to marry him. And he wasn't drunk. Just crazy."

Markey remembered the odd way the man had watched the ladies of the *Frolic*, his eyes glazed as if he were staring at a meal rather than a person. He also remembered the millionaire's congenial promise to gut him.

"But you did accept his invitations," he said, knowing readers would wonder.

"He said he could get me back into movies. Don't spread it around, but Maurice Mouvet's got TB. He's not long for the dance world—or any world. I need to work."

"Oh, but you don't," said Zelda, distressed. "You're so lovely, don't wear yourself out with labor and ambition."

Markey sensed Miss Hughes summoning patience. He had the feeling that were Zelda not so childishly sincere in her admiration, she might get an unkind response from a woman who'd worked her way up from telephone operator to Ziegfeld dancer.

"Well," she said finally, "if I found a man like Scott Fitzgerald, I'm sure I wouldn't worry. But there aren't so many of them."

She then adjusted herself so her back was to Zelda. Markey registered the snub.

So did Zelda. Eyebrows raised, she plucked sharply at her napkin, as if giving it a piece of her mind.

"What happened the night of the murder?" he asked. "Why did you go home with Mr. Elwell? You weren't part of the divorce party."

"No, I was not," she said shortly. "Walter had begged me to come to the party at the Ritz they were having for Viola. I said I had to work. Which I did, but also he was starting to scare me. In his own head, he had decided things needed to progress."

Zelda was noisily turning her spoon over on the table. To placate her, Markey asked Zelda, "Was it Walter's idea to go on to the *Frolic* after the Ritz that night?"

She set down the spoon. "Yes, it was."

"I wouldn't go to the divorce party, so Walter brought the party to the *Frolic*," said Miss Hughes. "After our number, Maurice needed some ice for his hip. I went to get it from the bar and ran into Walter. He accused me of lying to him, leading him on. He said I didn't love him the way he loved me. I don't know if you know this about men, Mr. Markey, but most of you have inflated ideas about your own attractiveness."

"I don't, believe me."

"He grabbed my arm, hard. Nearly pulled it out of the socket. First time he ever got rough."

"You should have broken a bottle over his nasty little head," said Zelda.

A slight edge to her voice, Leonora Hughes said, "I didn't want to make a scene at a place where I work. Especially not with one of the richest men in New York. Fortunately, that's when Mr. Elwell showed up and asked if I wanted to dance."

"He saw you were in trouble," said Markey.

"I guess so. Also, I had the feeling he wanted to get away from Miss Kraus. He said, 'These people are mad without being the least bit interesting. Shall we save ourselves and leave them to drown?' I said that sounded swell to me. He said, 'To the lifeboat, then.' I had finished for the night, and by that time, I didn't care if they fired me."

"Did Walter Lewisohn see you leave with Joseph Elwell?"

"Sure he did. Elwell had to pry Walter's hands off me. And I made it very clear I was going and he was not to follow me."

Further proof that Viola had lied when she said she and the Lewisohns had left before Elwell. That did not surprise him. What surprised him was the reason behind the lie: not to protect herself, but to protect her brother-in-law.

Miss Hughes said regretfully, "I thought it was a smart idea to tell Walter I was leaving. I never thought what happened would happen. I should have, though."

"Has Lewisohn done that before, followed you?"

"He's turned up at my apartment many times."

"Did you call the police?"

"My landlord called the police on him twice. Cops show up, find out it's Walter Lewisohn, they apologize to *him* for the embarrassment, then tell my landlord not to bother them with frivolous calls."

"Do you know if Walter Lewisohn owns a gun, Miss Hughes?"

"I wouldn't be surprised."

He sensed she believed the millionaire had killed Elwell. But she wasn't yet prepared to say so, and a direct question would put her off. As he tried to think of a comfortably circuitous route, Zelda, tired of being left out of the conversation, asked, "Weren't you worried Elwell had his own reasons for playing knight in shining armor?"

"He was very much the gentleman, as it happens. He gave me a brandy. Asked about my career. Complimented my dress, suggested I visit Lanvin when I was next in Paris. We talked about the movies. He said I should think about moving out to California. Even gave me some names. He was a nice man."

"So, you never went upstairs," said Markey, thinking of the pink boudoir.

"No. He didn't seem the least interested. He really did just want to get away from Miss Kraus and the Lewisohns. Frankly, I think he was tired. He wasn't a young man, once you saw him in the light."

"No, he wasn't. And . . . was there a phone call at some point?"

Leonora Hughes had relaxed as she told the story of her rescue. Now she became uneasy. "There was."

"Viola Kraus?" guessed Zelda.

"No, Walter. He demanded to speak with me, and Mr. Elwell told him I was indisposed. He also told Walter, and I quote, that he was 'entirely delusional' and why didn't he leave me be? Which was good of him, but maybe not so wise. That's why I left and went to a girlfriend's. I didn't want Walter coming around and making trouble."

So someone had persuaded Viola to "confess" to making the 2:30 phone call. Selma or Walter, it hardly mattered which.

It was time to come to the point. "Miss Hughes, don't you think it likely—"

Crisply, she interrupted him. "I don't know."

"—that Mr. Lewisohn—"

"I don't know."

"—did come to Elwell's house—"

"You going to make me say it again?"

Stymied, he rearranged his argument. "If your position is what I think it is, do you think it's wise to leave a man like that at liberty?"

"Do you understand what his family is in this town? How many people they have cleaning up for them?"

Having been asked to do just that by Selma Lewisohn at the *Frolic* and accused the police of doing the same, he did. "But—"

"I'm not saying what you want me to for the papers. It's not worth my life."

Zelda said scornfully, "You can't be scared of that little dump of a man."

Miss Hughes snapped, "Only a stupid person wouldn't be, Mrs. Fitzgerald. Because that little dump is not right in the head. I don't mean 'ha-ha, what a gas' not right, I mean sick. At one of Lewisohn's parties, a waiter came around with canapés. Deviled eggs with caviar. He offered one to Mr. Lewisohn. Mr. Lewisohn, as it happens, does not like eggs. Of any kind. He took it personally. He also took the tray and slammed it into the waiter's head. Then, when the man was down, he kicked him hard. Right in the gut. I don't have to tell you everyone else at the party just went on drinking their champagne. They probably slipped the waiter something afterward, but you can't slip a corpse a hundred bucks."

"Has Lewisohn personally threatened you, Miss Hughes?"

She lit a cigarette, hand shaking. "Right now, he's staying away because enough people saw me leave with Elwell, he knows it doesn't do him any good to remind people he's been making a fool of himself over me. But if I start pointing fingers, it's a different story."

He wondered if she had already been slipped a hundred bucks. Or more. He couldn't blame her for being scared of Walter Lewisohn. Rich and violent was an intimidating proposition. But he couldn't get past the fact that she knew Lewisohn was dangerous—and for that very reason refused to do the thing that could stop him being a danger to others.

"But how will you feel if he does it again?"

That gave her pause, Markey could see. But she said, "I am far from the first person to let Walter Lewisohn get away with something. Let the wife do it. He's got brothers and sisters. Or . . . here's an idea, let the police do their job."

"They can't do their job if people don't tell them what they need to know."

"Are you a big fan of the police, Mr. Markey?"

Before he could answer, Zelda announced, "Here's what *I* am *not* a fan of: people who say, 'I'm scared.'"

To the idle listener, Zelda might sound as if she was calling for justice. Or integrity, civic duty. But Markey knew she wasn't. The word *scared* had offended her to the very core. She had admired Miss Hughes as a dancer and a fellow beauty, a woman ready to carry her banner forth into the world without fear of consequence. Here, she had the opportunity to make a grand and glorious gesture and she was refusing. Zelda might have forgiven Miss Hughes's refusal to accuse Walter Lewisohn had the dancer said she loved him or didn't believe him guilty. But she could not abide fear being the reason. Nor could she abide being ignored.

Leonora Hughes stubbed out her cigarette, saying, "What can I say? Most of the time, I like living."

"*Just* living? You might as well be dead."

Markey did not attend much theater, but he knew Zelda had delivered her line poorly, raising her voice on *dead* like a schoolgirl attempting Joan of Arc. She was too aware that it *was* a line, too conscious of how it was received. Miss Hughes, he saw, had had enough.

She said to Zelda. "So, you liked the show, Mrs. Fitzgerald."

It was not the challenge Zelda had expected and she shook her head.

"You and Mr. Fitzgerald come a lot, don't you? Sure, we see you. You know how we think of you backstage? That drunk, obnoxious couple that can't seem to get it through their heads that they're not the star attraction."

To Markey, she explained, "They don't watch the show, they think they are the show. Not only do they talk all through the acts, they yell at the performers, all kinds of cute comebacks, because they're just so *amusing*. The other night when he tried to join the show? That wasn't the first time. This one"—she cocked a thumb at Zelda—"likes to imitate the dancers. Sometimes it's almost sweet. Mostly, it's sad."

She stood, purse in hand. "Nice meeting you again, Mr. Markey.

I wish you luck. If you put my name in your paper, I know some very mean lawyers."

Markey glanced at Zelda. His heart broke to see her stunned and bewildered, as if someone had struck her. He knew his next words should be spoken in her defense. But he had one more question.

Quietly, he asked, "What was that waiter's name, Miss Hughes?"

For a moment, she hesitated. "I heard someone call him Chester. The Lewisohns use Acme catering for their parties. Maybe that'll help you."

Markey nodded his thanks.

He waited as long as he could. Then, when it couldn't be avoided, he faced Zelda. Her jaw was set, her cheeks mottled, her eyes keen and rageful. She had been humiliated, and he did not know what to say; he would not have thought she could be humiliated.

"I don't think I like your girl in green. I do not like her at all."

"Zelda, she's just—"

"She's flinty and she's mean. I wish I hadn't found her."

She stood up, but her legs were unsteady. How much had she had to drink? he wondered. Then realized, nothing. But something was coursing through her so intense and poisonous, it put her off balance. He assured her it would just take him a moment to pay the bill, but she tore out of the tearoom as if she hadn't heard him.

After settling, he went to the suite and knocked on the door. He called her name several times. She did not answer. He said he was sorry. Very sorry.

The door opened. Scott appeared. "We agree. You are a sorry individual."

"If I could—"

"If you could, then you would have. But you didn't, so you can't. See how that works? The damage is done. Go away, Markey."

Fitzgerald shut the door.

Chapter Twenty-Two

Markey thought of waiting. He thought of calling. Putting a note under the door. Sending flowers—buckets of hyacinths—to atone. He knew he had felt worse in his life, but he couldn't remember when. Two days ago, Zelda had literally picked him up off the pavement. In return, he had let her be brutally insulted without saying a word on her behalf. Briefly, he mourned the loss of the girl in the dollar-green dress, the fantasy of her, anyway. In the light of day, Leonora Hughes was still ravishing. But she was also real, with ambitions and troubles, things that made her laugh and things that worked her nerves; she was a busy woman, with far more to do than dance eternally in his imagination. She required a man with money and power and he was neither, so he bid her farewell. Then remembered he had lost something far more substantial and felt rotten all over again.

He did, however, follow up Miss Hughes's tip and head over to Acme catering. He told the manager he had recently been to a party where he'd spilled a drink on the rug and a waiter named Chester had been so skillful in getting out the stain, it had saved him buying his host a new rug. A tip was in order; would they be willing to help him find the man?

Chester was a lithe, good-looking fellow who lived along the newly built 7 train in Queens that took many an actor and dancer from a room they could afford to their dream employment on Broadway. Chester did remember Walter Lewisohn. He insisted the millionaire's assault was no great matter—all in a day's work. But Markey noticed the man's fingers lay protectively over his ribs, and he winced when the late-afternoon sun hit his eyes. He asked Chester if he was in a show right now and he answered, "No, everything's still a little . . ."

Markey nodded so the man wouldn't have to say the word *painful*.

"I'm having trouble remembering the steps," Chester confessed. "I must be getting old."

"A blow to the head can do that," said Markey. "Usually goes away, but maybe see a doctor."

As he left, Markey paused on the stairs, "You really weren't scared when Walter Lewisohn took after you?"

"I didn't say I wasn't scared," said Chester. "Only that it didn't matter."

"So, how did you feel?"

"Truly? I thought I was going to die."

"Thank you. I hope you find your feet. Let me know when you get in a show. I have a friend who's a drama critic, I'll send her over." Although given what Dottie wrote about most shows, that might not be a blessing.

Returning to the office, he wrote about Chester, the waiter who wished to be a dancer, only he couldn't move quite right after being smashed in the head with a silver platter by someone who'd had the world handed to him on just such a surface. He said he couldn't give the smasher's name, but the assault was particularly ironic, as he was known to love the theater.

> There are men in this city who have much and want more. They want everything there is to have, particularly if it is feminine and attractive. There is a dancer at the *Midnight Frolic* who is both those things and a great deal more. She has had the misfortune to be noticed by one of these men. I won't add to her misfortune by revealing her name.
>
> The night before he died, Joseph Elwell did this woman a kindness. Six hours later, he was shot and killed in his own home. Captain Arthur Carey says a woman could not have shot Joseph Elwell and we will take his word for it this time.
>
> But did jealousy over a woman inspire a man to shoot Elwell? A man who feels he has a right to everything and everyone that's desirable and who might not have had a silver platter on hand the night in question?
>
> Maybe District Attorney Swann should take a ride on the 7 train.

"Did the waiter take money?" Gus Schaeffer asked when he'd read the story.

"Yes. Wouldn't you?"

"Why'd he open his mouth, then?"

"He didn't. He said it was no big deal, only he can't move so well these days. And that's all I wrote."

Schaeffer glanced up at him.

"You said rich people doing bad things was good for the paper," Markey reminded him.

"I did, I did." Schaeffer frowned at the article. "I'm just not sure about accusing Lewisohn, especially when neither of these individuals will be quoted by name."

"I never said it was Lewisohn. People will know it's him because they know he likes the theater. Dozens of people have witnessed this man being a menace. We're not telling the city anything it doesn't know. It just puts a fire under Swann."

"Would you put your name on it?"

"You offering me a byline?"

"No. I was just curious." He looked up. "By the way, I hear they shot out your window. You still living there?"

"I guess so. My summer house is being redecorated."

Gus Schaeffer didn't smile. Instead, he read over the article again. "Okay, let's go with it."

The girl at the front desk knocked at the door to tell Markey, "Phone call for you."

"Man or woman?"

"Man. Says he's from the Studio Club."

"More fancy friends?" guessed Schaeffer.

"We'll see." Going to the phone, he said, "Yes, this is Morris Markey."

"Mr. Markey!"

He had expected to hear Rhodes. But this voice was altogether more jovial, more arrogant; he addressed Markey as he would the maître d' at his favorite restaurant. It was the voice of a wealthy man used to conning people. But it wasn't the strangled growl of Walter Lewisohn. Lewisohn would have had lawyers call. And they wouldn't be friendly.

He said, "Forgive me, I—"

A laugh came over the line. "Oh, of course. I forget we've never met. The way you write about all of us, I feel you know us so well. This is Victor von Schlegell, Mr. Markey."

"I see. I've been wanting to talk to you."

"Isn't that fortunate, I've been wanting to talk to you."

A long pause, which Markey understood to be the other man keeping the upper hand. He asked, "Well, how would we do that?"

"I thought you might come to the Studio Club. Now that you know where it is. Say, tomorrow evening?"

Markey had a sudden image of himself up against a basement wall, being pummeled to pulp by William Rhodes. "Does it have to be the club?"

"Oh, I think so. In honor of Joe, we'll even have a few rubbers of bridge, what do you say?"

United Rubber, in fact, thought Markey. "That sounds fine. Except I don't have a partner."

Von Schlegell tutted. "Don't you? What about that enchanting young lady you've been squiring around town? Mrs. Fitzgerald."

Parsing the level of threat in his question, Markey said, "The woman you refer to is married. I haven't been squiring."

"Still—bring her along. But leave Mr. Fitzgerald at home. I have no desire to talk about Minnesota."

"They wanted me?"

In the Fitzgerald suite, Zelda sat on the sofa, radiant with excitement. Scott stood behind the sofa, a good deal less thrilled. On the single occasion Markey had the nerve to meet his eye, Fitzgerald looked murderous.

"The Red Baron asked for me?" She wanted to hear it again.

"Yes, but that doesn't mean you have to go."

Zelda cried, "Of *course* I'm going to go," as Scott said, "Of course she's not going."

Not for the first time, Markey questioned why he'd come. He could easily have told Von Schlegell Zelda didn't play bridge. Made Scott out to be a jealous monster. He could have said the couple was out of town and he had no way of finding them. So why hadn't he?

Because he knew it would please Zelda to be asked. And he knew that after the things Leonora Hughes had said to her, she needed the chance to show herself the woman she believed herself to be. Her spirit had taken a blow because of him and he wanted to make it up to her. It had taken tracking down a poster of the *Frolic*, one that advertised Hughes and Mouvet, and drawing an enormous mustache on Hughes. In addition, he had written, *Also appearing: Morris Markey as Cowardly Swine.* Then: *VVS called. He wants to see us.* He had slid it under the Fitzgeralds' door and waited.

Zelda stood up. "I'm going."

Trying to make the peace, Markey said to Scott, "It's theater. Von Schlegell invited me to play bridge because he wants to find out what I know about Elwell's involvement with the APL. Zelda's just part of the performance. We'll play a few rounds, then I'll send her home in a taxi."

"I don't want to be sent home," Zelda objected.

"I'll come with you," said Scott with the sudden energy of a solution. "Markey can partner Von Schlegell, I'll partner you . . ."

Zelda shook her head. "We make terrible bridge partners, and besides—"

She looked at Markey.

"I'm the one they asked for. Not you."

Scott sighed. Rubbed his eyes hard. "Markey, perhaps you and I could step outside for a moment?"

Zelda turned. "Why?"

"Because this is private," he said, with sunny, supreme confidence. "Boy stuff. Men conspire to protect their womenfolk because their women are precious to them. You must be patient with our weakness and self-aggrandizing. We are beasts, we can't help it."

Half charmed, Zelda opened her mouth, but Scott said seriously, "I mean it." And Markey saw that he did.

Taking Markey down the outside hall and around the corner, he said, "Who is this guy? Von Schlegell. I know he's from Minnesota, but is he really a businessman or a gangster or . . . ?"

"I don't think he's a gangster. I think Elwell suspected him of profiteering and selling war material to the other side."

"And Von Schlegell killed Elwell?"

Markey thought of Rhodes. "Or had him killed, yes. Either because Elwell had something on him he was about to reveal. Or because Von Schlegell still loves Viola and thinks Elwell had it coming for wrecking their marriage. Maybe it was a mix of business and pleasure, I don't know."

"Regardless, I don't want Zelda in that room."

"I understand your concern, but I don't think he's a man to shoot women . . ."

"You don't understand." Scott laid a hand on his chest: *Be silent, let me explain.* "Zelda is . . ."

Fitzgerald gathered himself as he prepared to describe his wife.

"When Zelda plays bridge, she simply imagines what God wants her to play, then, if it's the wrong card, says, 'Oh, my, I meant to play hearts.' Beyond that, she does not dissemble. She does not keep her own counsel. And she is not wise, nor prudent, nor tactful, nor . . . She is entirely capable of accusing Von Schlegell of murder in between bids. And I have *concerns* as to what happens should she do that."

"She's not stupid."

"I never said she was. She's unspeakably brave, which can have the same effect. She does not . . ."

Scott paused to compose his words.

"She does not care for the parameters of reality. Things that can harm her, she does not consent to see as a danger. This is a woman who leaps off high cliffs when she does not know the water's depth. That's not metaphor, it is fact. It is magnificent. It's . . ."

Markey understood. Several things, but chiefly that Fitzgerald was genuinely anguished at the thought of his wife coming to harm. That he loved her and considered her care. Markey had not known that. Probably he hadn't wanted to.

"You're right," he said. "I'm sorry, I shouldn't have . . ."

Scott's brow cleared. He smiled in relief. "Thank you."

"Of course. I'll just slip away . . ."

"And I'll explain it to Zelda."

They were both nodding when he heard, "I'm ready, Mr. Markey. Let's go."

Zelda, in pink and gold, stood before them, adjusting her gloves. She turned her miraculous green eyes on him, then on her husband.

"I said I'm ready."

Defeated, Scott gestured to the elevator. "The lady has spoken."

In the taxi, Zelda was strangely quiet, staring out the window. Her concentration was so intense it was like sitting close to an open fire; even at a distance, you felt the heat singe the delicate hairs on your skin. At one point, he said, "Nothing will go wrong, but if it does . . ." She cut him off with a shake of the head. Either she didn't want to think of what might go wrong or she didn't want him telling her what to do if it did.

This time, there were no Cadillacs lined up outside the Upper East Side brownstone. It was dusk, the street oddly deserted. Markey looked to the other brownstones on the block. The windows were all dark, the curtains drawn. He wondered, had the Studio bought all the other houses on the street so that they could do what they wished free of scrutiny?

No, that was childish. This was just a club for men who liked to drink and gamble without their wives saying, *Henry, that's enough.*

Still, his hands were cold and his breathing shallow. Feeling lightheaded, he took care to fill his lungs before they started up the stairs. The hiss came, like a copperhead in the grass. He looked to Zelda and thought her profile, with the expansive pale cheek, hawk eyes, and broad cheekbones, very fine. If you were going to die next to someone, she would be an excellent choice.

But of course they weren't going to die.

"I should warn you," he murmured, "I'm a poor bridge player."

"I think there'll be a lot of games played tonight. You're bound to be good at one of them."

He rang the bell. The door opened, and a butler welcomed them with a blank expression and neutral tone that suggested that, if asked later, he would deny ever having seen them. The entry hall was narrow, illuminated from a crystal chandelier that cast a cold light on the black-and-white-tile floor below. From behind closed doors on either side, Markey could hear the laughter of men, the clink of ice, the thrum of a roulette wheel, and the snap of cards.

Victor von Schlegell appeared at the top of the stairs.

"Mr. Markey. Mrs. Fitzgerald. Welcome to the Studio Club."

Serene, Zelda said, "It seems we can't keep away from each other."

Chapter Twenty-Three

It was difficult not to like Victor von Schlegell. He had all the attributes—blond, elegant, wealthy—that granted a man the right to arrogance. And yet he greeted Markey with enthusiasm, saying, "I probably shouldn't admit this, but on occasion, I do pick up a copy of the *Daily News*. It's marvelously entertaining. And you're the best thing in it."

"I don't see how you can know which pieces are mine."

"The subject! Viola told me you were writing about poor Elwell. And the style, too, of course. You've your own particular way with words. You notice things—that's rare. Yes, I know which pieces are yours."

Markey wanted to ask Von Schlegell how he managed to convey threat in a compliment. It seemed a good skill to have.

Moving to Zelda, Von Schlegell said, "Mrs. Fitzgerald."

As he kissed her hand, she said "Von," startling him.

"That's what your friends call you, isn't it?" she asked. "Or perhaps we're not friends."

"I hope we will be," he said. "But you may call me Victor. Come, let's go upstairs."

They followed Victor up the carpeted staircase—no sound of footsteps, Markey noted, no clue they were here. He wondered about Victor's reasons for inviting Zelda. Had he been attracted to her that night at the Ritz? Or did he want Markey to have a point of vulnerability? In a fight, it was better not to have someone to worry over. Although Zelda was more of a fighter than Von Schlegell might suppose.

Victor led them to a small, elegant room on the third floor. A man was already seated at a green baize card table; he rose as they came in. He seemed blandly forgettable—of middle height, with hair of a wet-sand color some would call blond and some brown. And yet Markey felt he had seen him before. Beside him, he sensed Zelda assessing the stranger. When she did not acknowledge him, Markey knew she hadn't figured him out either.

But when the fellow thrust his hand out in greeting, Markey remembered. At Elwell's funeral, this man had offered that same handshake to the grieving father.

Why had he been at the funeral? Why was he here now?

Victor said, "May I present William Barnes, director of the Studio Club?"

Zelda said it was a pleasure. Mr. Barnes twinkled. "We don't generally permit women to enter the Studio Club, Mrs. Fitzgerald. But when Mr. Von Schlegell suggested it, I didn't see how I could pass up the chance to meet you."

"I don't see how you could either," agreed Zelda.

By his accent, Barnes was British. At first, that surprised Markey. Then, thinking of something Spook had told him about British interests during the war, he thought it made sense.

A drinks cart was rolled in. A bottle of champagne was produced. As the waiter removed the cork, Markey said, "Mr. Rhodes. You're wearing different livery this evening."

A linen napkin wrapped around his hand, the chauffeur gave the cork a twist. "I'm a family man. Doesn't make sense to pass up extra work."

"You can understand that, Mr. Markey," said Victor. "I know reporters don't get paid much."

An elegant setup for a bribe, thought Markey. "Actually, I come from money. An uncle on my mother's side made a fortune in seahorses."

"They make marvelous pets," said Zelda.

The four of them sat, Markey and Zelda quickly taking seats opposite each other to signal that they were partners. Victor admitted defeat with a charming smile. "How disappointing. Barnes, it seems you and I must play together."

He took up the deck of cards and began shuffling. Markey watched the man's practiced hands fold the cards again and again with a soft rustle. "What are we playing for?"

"The truth," said Victor pleasantly. "If you win, I tell you who shot Joseph Elwell and why."

"And if you win?" asked Zelda.

"I prefer not to show my hand entirely," said Victor. He dealt the cards, laying the last on the table with a gentle snap.

Markey knew the dealer was the first to bid. Usually they passed, unless they had a particularly strong hand.

"Two clubs," announced Victor.

It was a strong bid, almost aggressive. Markey himself had two clubs, both poor. But he had four spades: the queen, jack, ten, and five. He held his cards so that four fingers were visible to Zelda—had she been looking. But she was studying her own cards intently. "Two spades," he said, signaling to her that he had decent cards.

"Three clubs," said Barnes.

Markey raised his eyebrows at Zelda. If Barnes had clubs as well, Markey had to hope she had spades or a strong hand in another suit.

"Pass," she said, theatrically suppressing a yawn.

Victor became the declarer. Zelda had the dummy hand, which meant she laid her cards face up on the table and Markey played for her. She had several clubs. When Victor raised an eyebrow, she said, "Oh, are these clubs? You see, I call them trefoils."

As they began slapping down cards, Markey asked, "How did you know Mr. Elwell, Mr. Barnes?"

"Through the Studio."

"Nice of you to attend his funeral. It's a long trip."

"Barnes was representing the club," said Victor.

"What kind of work do you do?" Markey asked. He knew enough about bridge to know that casual conversation was usually frowned upon. But he hadn't been asked here to play cards. He was surprised at how many tricks he was winning. Victor turned out to have a poor hand. Or else his mind wasn't really on the game.

"I manage the Studio," said Barnes. "Plus this and that."

"Is 'this' bootlegging?" asked Markey. "'That' a little side work for the government? British or otherwise?"

"It's this and it's that," said Barnes. "I also worked for Joseph Elwell in certain capacities."

"Yes, Rhodes tells me you recommended him to Elwell."

"I always like to place people who've served their country. It's the least we can do."

"'We'?" asked Markey. "Does the APL run its own employment agency these days?"

Markey and Zelda claimed the last two tricks. "Nicely done," said Victor, noting the score on the pad under THEY. "One game to you, Mr. Markey. And Mrs. Fitzgerald, of course."

As another hand was dealt, Victor changed the subject. "May I take your recent article to mean that you've abandoned this insane notion that Viola is guilty of murder?"

"Well, if you go around leaving cut-up pink kimonos in dead men's apartments," said Zelda, "questions will be asked."

Playing the seven of diamonds, Victor sighed. "Viola was so upset when you published that nonsense about her being engaged to Elwell." Here a look of friendly rebuke. Markey *had* gone over the line, but man to man, they could admit women were oversensitive.

Markey played the nine, taking the trick. "I published it because she told me so."

He waited to see if Victor would argue. Instead, the rubber magnate said, in a low, confidential voice, "But you can see *why* she would say that."

This time the charm was too thick; Markey rebelled. "No, I can't see why a woman would go around saying she was engaged to a man she wasn't engaged to. Only to change her story a few days later and say she barely knew him."

"Viola doesn't always think clearly. The moment she heard Elwell had been murdered, she worried that the police would think she—or someone close to her—was the murderer." Victor raised an eyebrow. "Her first instinct was to say how close she was with him. But once she discovered that the police knew about the other women, she decided it was better to say he was just an old family friend."

"So what was she, really?" Zelda asked.

"An unhappy woman looking for a life rope. Like most Casanovas, Joseph Elwell was astute when it came to sniffing out vulnerable women. Viola was miserable married to me. But she dreaded being alone, especially at her age. Elwell flirted with her, flattered her. He would not have been her first or even tenth choice for a husband. But it was reassuring to think she could go from being Mrs. Von Schlegell to Mrs. Elwell if she found herself alone for too long."

Markey said, "You said she worried the police would suspect someone close to her."

Victor nodded.

"Would that someone be a member of the party at the *Midnight Frolic?*"

"Just so."

Markey waited. He knew Victor wanted him to show his hand by guessing the identity of the protected person.

Victor played the ten of diamonds, Zelda the jack.

Markey smiled. He was out of diamonds. He laid down the king of spades, winning the trick.

Victor said, "Barnes, I believe you're bad luck for me. Would you mind withdrawing so I might choose another partner?"

Barnes rose, saying, "Of course."

"I don't believe that's done, changing partners," said Zelda.

"Neither is pretending you thought clubs were trefoils," said Victor. "Ah, here she is."

On some level, Markey had expected it. If Victor wanted to play bridge to gain an advantage in the death of Joseph Elwell, it only made sense for the woman who was the brains behind the master of society bridge to be involved. And really, hadn't he always suspected Helen Elwell wasn't at her lawyer's that morning?

But the woman taking the chair beside him was not Helen Elwell.

It was Selma Lewisohn.

Chapter Twenty-Four

Zelda realized first. "That's a mean trick to play on a little sister."

As Selma slid into her chair, Markey noted the change in the opera singer since that night at the *Frolic*. It was as if she'd had a blood transfusion. Her movements were freer; her slenderness was no longer starved and angular. Her colors had returned, from the pink in her cheek to the coffee-brown sheen of her hair. Lady Macbeth was still present. But there was a touch of Cleopatra as well. This was a woman who lived in anticipation rather than dread. Given the chance, he thought she might even giggle. He watched the space between her and Victor. They did not look at each other. But in their resolute denial of the other's presence, there was complicity.

When had it started? he wondered. When Selma realized she was married to a madman, which must have been on her honeymoon?

Or when Victor decided he needed the added insurance of the other sister's loyalty to fend off Elwell's efforts to trap him? Maybe they were just two people caught in bad marriages. That happened, too, from time to time.

But none of it explained what Selma Lewisohn was doing here this evening.

Victor took up the deck. Zelda said, "I believe it's Mr. Markey's turn to deal. As we won the last game."

As Markey shuffled, she leaned across the table and said, "Selma, I hope you'll forgive my very rude question, but did you shoot Joseph Elwell? I wouldn't blame you, given the way he treated your sister. But given the way *you're* treating your sister, I confess, I am confused."

Selma smiled condescendingly. "I imagine you often are."

Victor confided, "Viola and I were never happy, Mrs. Fitzgerald."

"Well, how could she be when you're rolling around with her sister? Did you shoot Elwell, Selma? 'Cause if so, we can all go home. I don't even like bridge that much. I would like another drink, though." She snapped prettily at Rhodes.

"I did not shoot Joseph Elwell," Selma told the table as if she were sharing a choice piece of gossip.

Markey finished shuffling and offered the deck to Victor to cut. Markey began to deal. "Then I'm guessing you have something you want to tell us about Walter Lewisohn."

For a few moments, everyone examined their cards. Zelda met his eye. Perhaps no one else would see it, but there was an energy about her. She had an excellent hand.

Zelda said to Selma, "Love is so strange, isn't it? Von, I never would have guessed you would have a passion for someone as . . . well, as distasteful as you, Selma, forgive me. You're just not a natural object of romantic yearning. But the heart is an unpredictable thing. Everyone is a queen to someone, I suppose. How long have the two of you been smitten?"

Love, passion, romantic, yearning, heart, smitten—Zelda had six hearts, one of them the queen. Markey himself had four, including the ace. He didn't want to give away the strength of their position, so he bid three hearts, meaning they aimed to win at least nine tricks. Zelda won the auction. Markey had the dummy hand this time and Zelda played his cards, leaving him free to converse.

Selma turned to him, saying, "You're correct, Mr. Markey. We do have something to tell you about Walter Lewisohn. And that is that he is a very dangerous man."

"Yes, my gut remembers." Markey looked to Victor. "But I don't see your interest here. Or, rather, I do, but it could be one of a number of things."

"I treated Viola shabbily. But I still care for her—at least enough not to want to see her punished for someone else's crime. Walter has been getting away with things since he was a small, spoiled child. Indulgence has only emboldened him. If he's allowed to get away with murder, it may become one of the things he thinks he can do with impunity, the way he now cheats on his wife or defrauds his business partners."

"Walter Lewisohn is not unique among wealthy men in getting away with things."

"Lewisohn's behavior goes far beyond the crass entitlements of his class."

"He's insane," said Selma.

Victor added, "Everyone who deals with him knows this, but no one will say a word because of his money."

"Then why did Walter kill Elwell?" asked Zelda, sounding bored. She had run off five heart tricks in a row. Markey smiled, thinking she was annoyed by the lack of challenge.

"Because he was madly in love with a dancer named Leonora Hughes. He hounded her, harassed her . . ."

"Oh, for heaven's sake, the showgirl saw her opportunity,"

muttered Selma. Victor shot her a look. She was to stick to the narrative: Walter was the villain here.

"In a way, it is our fault," Victor confessed. "We looked the other way. Took our consolations where we could find them." He smiled warmly at Selma, who reached across the table to put her hand in his. "Walter and his temper, we said. Walter and his foolish passions. But this time, it got out of hand."

Markey said, "As opposed to the time he bashed a waiter in the head and destroyed his career."

Victor and Selma let go of each other, giving the same slight frown; they knew it would look better to care about the waiter, but they did not remember him, and what they did not remember, they resented being told to care about.

Markey said, "Leonora Hughes did tell me that Walter frightened her that night at the *Frolic*. She said Elwell rescued her by taking her to his house. But she didn't say a word about Walter killing him. Even when I pushed her." He hoped that gave the dancer some protection.

Victor said, "Yes, unfortunately for Joe, he did the chivalrous thing for once. Walter, in his insanity, thought Joe was robbing him of Leonora. If he could ensnare Viola, surely Leonora would fall prey to his charms as well."

"And so he went around the next morning and shot him." Victor nodded. Markey looked at Selma. "Is that why you sent me backstage that night to fetch Mr. Lewisohn? You wanted me to see his obsession with Miss Hughes without it coming back to you."

"No," Zelda corrected. "She wanted to sic her crazy husband on you so you'd stop writing about Viola."

"Oh, that's right—either way it would have worked out for you," Markey said to Selma. "Clever."

"I think you're being very cruel," said Selma Lewisohn.

Markey laughed. Then apologized. Then laughed again.

Regaining control of himself, he asked, "Why come to us now?"

Victor took over. "Because we are afraid he may do it again."

"You're afraid he'll shoot you if he finds out you've been messing with his wife," said Zelda. "I wouldn't worry—I don't think he cares for her nearly as much as he does Leonora."

"With a man like Walter Lewisohn, it's about possession. Selma wishes to build a life without him. We worry he may kill her, if she tries to leave. Or Miss Hughes, if she continues to refuse him."

Remembering Leonora's intense fear, Markey found Victor's point believable. "Then it seems to me you should be talking to Captain Carey or the DA."

"You think they don't know?" Victor tutted over Markey's naivete. "To those men, doing the right thing presents a greater peril than staying silent. If they go after Lewisohn, the family donations to the DA's campaign will stop. People in power will put pressure on Carey to find reasons not to charge him. Even if it does come to trial, Walter can plead Viola's heartbreak, in which case he might be acquitted."

"So?"

"So the story has to change," said Selma. "The public must bring its own pressure to bear. The potential jurors must be made aware of how dangerous Walter is. Rather than worry their careers will suffer if they charge him, Carey and Swann must be made to see their careers will be made if they bring him to justice."

Victor said, "Now, I wonder, what sort of writer is capable of telling that story?"

Markey said, "You're probably thinking of a writer who's wondering why Walter Lewisohn would kill Arthur Griswold."

Selma shot a look at Victor. "Who is Arthur Griswold?"

"Other than the subject of Mr. Markey's latest article, I haven't the slightest idea," said Victor. Markey almost believed him.

"My upstairs neighbor. He was shot as he was taking the air at his window. Someone also shot through my window. Same gun. Now, you can argue that was Lewisohn or one of his people trying to scare me off because I was writing about him. But how would he know to shoot Arthur Griswold? Griswold liked to keep an eye on the block. But Lewisohn doesn't strike me as an observant man unless beautiful women are involved."

Selma and Victor did not quite look at each other. But he could sense that Griswold was a complication they had not anticipated.

Selma played the jack of hearts. "I know nothing about Arthur Griswold. But if Walter has tried to kill you once, Mr. Markey, then you'd better start taking us seriously. My sister and I will be leaving for France soon. We no longer think it safe to be around my husband."

"That's a wise move," said Zelda. "Given that you're both suspects in a murder. Do you know, Mr. Markey, I'm wondering if Viola didn't do it after all. Selma, maybe you do love your little sister if you can go to all this trouble to make us think Walter did it."

Victor said, "Come now, you've met Viola. Do you really think such a petite woman could fire a .45-caliber weapon? I can assure you, Viola has never even thought of owning such a thing."

"I believe you," said Markey. He said to Selma, "In fact, I probably owe your sister an apology."

With a triumphant cry, Zelda played her queen, bringing the round to an end. Victor said with a thin smile, "It appears you've won the rubber. I would offer to tell you the truth, but you see, of course, I already have."

"Perhaps, as the winners, we can dictate new terms," said Markey.

"And those would be what?" asked Selma Lewisohn.

"I tell you the truth," said Markey.

Chapter Twenty-Five

"No! No, no, no . . ."

"Zelda, I just think it's better if I talk to Von Schlegell alone."

A finger to her lip, Zelda focused on the ceiling, as she tried to come up with the precise word. Then it came to her: *"No."*

"I'm going to accuse him, and I don't want you around when I do because it's better if he thinks you have no idea he's a suspect."

They were talking in a corner of a cramped hallway. Victor, Selma, and Rhodes were still in the gaming room. Markey was trying to keep his voice low. Zelda was not.

"You are not sending me home in a taxi. You are not stuffing me in some little women's chitchat corner. You even try it and I will bite you."

"I am not trying to . . . put you anywhere. I want you to talk to

Selma about Walter and her affair with Victor. Divide." He sliced the air with his hand. "Conquer."

Zelda flapped a finger between them. "*We* are being divided and conquered . . ."

The door opened. Victor stepped into the hallway. "Mr. Markey, shall you and I have a cigar on the balcony? The ladies can have a quiet drink downstairs."

Markey said "Yes" as Zelda said, "I love cigars."

Selma emerged. Striding toward them, she slid her arm through Zelda's and said, "Come, Mrs. Fitzgerald, let's leave them. I so want to hear more about your husband. What is he working on now?"

Unwillingly, Zelda let the other woman drag her toward the stairs. As they began to descend, she caught Markey's eye and snapped her jaws to remind him.

"Such an original young woman," said Victor.

Markey did believe Zelda could get something out of Selma, and he had told the truth about not wanting her to hear what he had to say to Victor. If things did go wrong, he'd prefer one of them to have a way out. He'd also prefer it if Victor hadn't chosen the balcony, but you couldn't have everything. It was only three floors.

Offered a cigar, he declined. "Your business is rubber, isn't it?"

A pause, covered by the lighting of a cigar and the first inhale and exhale. "Yes, that's right."

"I imagine you did well during the war."

"Certainly United Rubber was proud to stand with the country in the war effort."

"How does that work?" Markey asked, as if the question had never occurred to him. "The government made it a crime to do business with Germany in 1917 with the Trading with the Enemy Act. Confiscated a lot of property and business interests like Bayer Chemical. So do you tell your customers in Bavaria, 'Sorry, we can't sell to you anymore'? Does the government compensate you for the loss, buy up all your stock . . . ?"

Victor smiled as if Markey's questions were too simplistic for him to answer. "As I'm sure you know, England controls most of the world's rubber supplies through its colonies in Africa and Asia."

"Oh, that's right. I imagine England wasn't keen on selling to Germany."

"No."

"No, now that I recall, Germany got pretty desperate for raw materials. The Allied naval blockade was very effective in limiting supplies. The Germans were running trucks on steel tires at one point. The Allies were lucky because, as you say, England's loyal colonies. And we Americans, we're so ingenious, we've learned to make synthetic rubber. Is that your line, Victor?"

"I'm just a vice president."

"Then you probably know that the government created the Motor Transport Committee to centralize synthetic rubber production. That's how important it was to the war effort. But what you might not know—at least you'll pretend not to—was that in 1915, England was running out of glass. Guess where they make glass. Germany—you're right! So the English made a deal with Germany, their *enemy*, to exchange glass for rubber. Certain English companies—you know, the ones that needed glass and the ones that sold rubber—were all for it. But it had to be kept secret, otherwise London's mothers would tear government ministers limb from limb. Supposedly, nothing came of it. But that's what you would say if you were providing war material to a country slaughtering an entire generation of your people."

"I don't understand why you're telling me this story," said Victor.

"I'm telling you this story because those English war profiteers are just the kind of men Joseph Elwell would have hated. And call me cynical, but I suspect you'll find profiteers the world over. Even in this fine country. Elwell was an agent in the American Protective League. Anyone who refused to serve or covertly supported

Germany, he was authorized to have them arrested. Apparently, he was angry over his financial loss when the Bolsheviks pulled Russia out of the war. It made him irrationally suspicious, the sort of man who might, say, call an American with a Germanic name 'Herr.'"

"Your point?"

"Well, I'm just wondering if I misjudged Elwell. I saw him as a rich, feckless cad who toyed with married women. He'd string them along, flirt with them, have them to his home. But at a certain point, usually when they left their husbands, he seemed to lose interest."

"This is not unusual."

"No, especially if it was the husbands he was interested in all along. See, I wonder if he only courted Viola to find out how your rubber business was doing. If his passion for Mrs. Hardy wasn't inspired by the fact that he suspected her sister of spying for Germany. He taught bridge to the Princess Dalla Patra Hassan El Kamel. Now, she's said to be the niece of the current khedive of Egypt—am I saying that right?"

"The British made him a sultan, so I can't imagine he resents them very much."

"But up until 1914, Egypt was part of the Ottoman Empire. At the very start of the war, they sided with Germany and Austria-Hungary. And not all of them appreciated the Brits coming in and taking over. Gordon and Kitchener aren't always the best ambassadors for His Majesty. Which makes me wonder if the princess was detained on Elwell's report. Sure, the police said she stole a stickpin and stiffed the hotel. But better to say it's a matter of theft and unpaid debts so there's no diplomatic unpleasantness."

"What an exciting world you live in, Mr. Markey. Spies! International intrigue! Cloaks, daggers . . ."

"Rubber sold to the highest bidder. At the cost of American lives."

"If I understand you right, you are accusing me of selling synthetic rubber to the Germans."

"Yes, sir."

"Remind me, how do I get past those naval blockades?"

"I wonder if your friend Barnes had something to do with that. That man reeks of dirty government business."

"And Barnes and I killed Joseph Elwell now, in 1920, because . . . ?"

"Because your company produces something that's very valuable to the American military, and whatever you did during the war, the government would like to forget it. Most of the APL has moved on to other targets. Unions, Communists. But Joseph Elwell was still fighting the old war."

"And your neighbor? What was his name again?"

"Arthur Griswold. Like Elwell, he was a zealot. I don't know if Elwell asked him to keep an eye on the house in case unwanted visitors came by or he did it on his own initiative. Either way, he saw something he shouldn't have."

"Ah, the person who killed Joseph Elwell—who is that, exactly? Which fair lady with the key?"

"No lady at all. I would guess it was one of two men. Rhodes, the chauffeur, who originally told me about the keys, neglecting to mention he had one himself . . ."

"Or?"

"You seem on very good terms with your divorced wife. Certainly on good terms with her sister. You could have gotten the key from either of them."

Victor von Schlegell took a long drag on his cigar. "Do you know what is most painful to me, in all this?"

"What?"

"That a fine young man like you, who did the right thing, who served his country, came back so . . . twisted." He turned, a sorrowful expression on his face. "You spoke of Joseph Elwell fighting the old war. But you're the one who can't let go, Mr. Markey. Everything in your life becomes a vast conspiracy—"

"No, just this."

"—to justify your feelings of rage and betrayal by the country that sent you and so many others to die. You've decided it was all a lie. Bad men made money. Good men died for nothing. Your parents, their whole generation—"

"Leave my parents out of it, please."

"We have all . . . lied to you. Cheated you."

Markey had been about to give an easy no. The word *cheated* threw him. He had been very clear in his thinking. Now he was struggling to assert his story.

"Someone shot at me when I started writing about the American Protective League . . ."

"No, someone shot at you *before* your APL article came out." Victor gestured to him with the cigar. "I'm right about that, aren't I, Mr. Markey? Your article on Arthur Griswold came out the morning of June 19th."

"Strange that you know that."

"You visited my office that same day."

Or, thought Markey, Rhodes reported that the job was done. Or at least attempted.

He asked Victor, "So, who do you think tried to kill me?"

"Walter Lewisohn, of course. The day before, you—you, Mr. Markey—had exposed Viola as the owner of the pink kimono. Selma tells me Walter threatened you once for writing about Viola."

"Did Selma tell you she didn't do a thing about it? That she makes a habit of looking the other way when her husband attacks people?"

"She's terrified of him. That's not hard to imagine, is it?"

No. He hated it to admit it, but it was not. True, it was easier to envision—and to care about—Leonora Hughes's terror. But in either case, there were two women frightened of Walter Lewisohn. Not to mention that man out in Queens.

"Mr. Markey, I'm not a perfect man, by any means. But you've seen Walter with Miss Hughes. You saw what he was like. It wasn't attraction. It was obsession. Talk to Selma. She will tell you stories that will make your hair stand on end."

"All that proves is she married poorly and should get a divorce. Doesn't prove her husband murdered Joseph Elwell."

"She is also prepared to say that she does not know her husband's whereabouts the morning of the murder."

"'Prepared to say' doesn't sound quite the same as 'tell the truth.' If Mrs. Lewisohn wants to get rid of her husband, she can do it without me."

"Then you must also speak with Ludlow Bentham, Walter's secretary. I'll arrange it."

"I'd rather not speak to people who've made arrangements with you."

He'd pushed it. Victor demanded, "Do you want to know who killed Elwell or not? Do you want to write this story or not?"

Those were two different things, thought Markey.

"I want to write the right story. The truth," he added lamely. What was it about this city that made you feel so juvenile saying words like that? Or maybe it was the times. Truth, purity, faith, all that seemed rather outdated. Or . . . exposed, the word came to him, as not being what your old father said they were.

"If you want the truth," said Victor, "then you talk to Walter's secretary. He has nothing to gain by turning in the man who pays him."

Unless you're paying him more, thought Markey.

"Help us put a dangerous man away. Help me"—the man put a hand to his heart—"help two women I care for very deeply feel safe again."

Markey wanted to tell Victor he was out of the Lewisohn business and walk away. Then he remembered Leonora Hughes saying, *I am far from the first person to let Walter Lewisohn get away with something.* He did not want to be yet another man who let Lewisohn terrify women.

"I'll talk to the secretary. I can't promise what I'll write."

"Of course not. I'm very grateful—"

"Don't be. I appreciate your time, Victor. And I appreciate you letting us win at bridge."

Victor attempted to look puzzled.

"I'm a poor player, but I know enough about the game to know when someone's bidding badly. You wanted to tell me your story, I understand."

As he turned to go back inside, he heard Victor say, "Yes, you'll want to get Mrs. Fitzgerald back to her husband. After all, we can't have a scandal."

Markey stopped. "Oh, I see. That's why you invited her. If things didn't go your way, you'd try blackmail. Well, you can try. But I warn you, Zelda Fitzgerald is not Viola Kraus, a woman so worried about what people will say, she has to lie her way through life. She's not Selma Lewisohn or Mrs. Elwell or your mother or her mother or mine. She doesn't scare and she doesn't shame. I imagine that terrifies you."

Then he went to find Zelda at the bar.

Chapter Twenty-Six

The parting was elaborately polite. Zelda thanked Victor for returning Markey in one piece. Victor thanked her for noticing. Selma, employing her skills as an operatic personality, thanked Markey for hearing her plight. He thanked her for her forbearance and had no idea what he meant by that. Then he thanked Victor for the game and the information. "I hope you'll do what's right," said Victor.

"Yes," said Selma.

"I hope so, too," said Markey.

"I hope we can get a taxi," said Zelda, neatly putting an end to the niceties.

Markey was apprehensive as they made their way down the stairs. He insisted Zelda walk ahead of him, then worried the attack would come from the front. Rhodes was nowhere to be seen.

Neither was Barnes. Between his shoulder blades, he felt the itch of expectation. A sudden shove and the wrench of his neck. He listened for the clamor of wealthy drunken men but did not hear it. Had all those revelers left? That seemed unlikely. And ominous.

Zelda whispered, "You know, I don't think they're going to kill us."

"Let's wait until we're in the taxi to decide that."

The doorman was very good at his job, finding them a cab straightaway. Even that, Markey found suspicious. Had the car been waiting around the corner, ready to appear as they left? He imagined the driver turning, shooting them both, then heading for the river. Then the cabbie asked "Where to?" in a speedy, impatient tone, and he felt back in the real world and his nerves began to ease.

Gazing out the window, he tried to reconstruct his theory of war profiteering, the conviction that Rhodes, under orders from Von Schlegell and Barnes, had killed Elwell, then Griswold, and shot through his window. But the story kept falling away like a poorly built sandcastle.

"She really did want to be a singer."

From the other side of the taxi, Zelda's voice, strangely subdued. Reluctant, he turned from the window. "Who? Selma?"

She nodded. "Her family thought it unsuitable, so she married Lewisohn instead."

"Didn't he make her a singer? I thought she was Madame something or other."

"It's difficult if your husband's always losing his head and chasing showgirls. She hasn't sung in years."

As Zelda related the stories Selma had fed her, Markey listened with half an ear. All of it was sordid, none of it a surprise. All he could think was that it gave Selma Lewisohn a very good motive to frame her husband.

He said, "She could leave him."

"And live on what?"

He knew he sounded callous, but he was trying to build his story, and he didn't want Von Schlegell and Selma's version in his ears. Had it really been Walter who called at 2:30 in the morning? Leonora Hughes said so, and he thought she was solid citizenry. But she attended Selma Lewisohn's parties. The two women knew each other. How hard would it have been for Selma to persuade her to say Walter had called and not Viola? Given how frightened the dancer was of Lewisohn, not very. On the other hand, she was frightened of him for good reason . . .

Then Zelda said, "I'm amazed to say I feel a bit sorry for her."

"Why? She seems to have found a replacement."

"That's just a distraction. She knows she can never marry Victor—what would Viola say?" She leaned forward, trying to catch his eye. "You're being very unkind."

"I don't like being used."

"Are you saying you *don't* believe Walter is guilty?"

"I believe people want us to believe he's guilty."

"Did you not hear what I told you about Selma?"

"Do you not see she's sleeping with her sister's husband?"

"I don't see what that's got to do with it."

"It means she's a liar."

"They're *all* liars."

"Right. They're all liars and we'd be fools to believe them." His voice had risen. Struggling for calm, he said, "So that doesn't matter. What does matter is who killed Joseph Elwell—"

"And that person is Walter Lewisohn," insisted Zelda.

"Did he also shoot at me? And Arthur Griswold?"

"Who cares about Arthur Griswold?"

Retreating to her side of the seat, she folded her arms to signal the argument was over; she'd won and she'd appreciate it if he realized that.

After a few minutes, she said in a bright, brittle voice, "Where are we celebrating?"

"We're not, I have to write the article . . ."

She dismissed this with a shrug. "You can do that tomorrow. We'll pick up Scott on the way. Maybe the Plaza, we can rent a room. Did I tell you about the time Scott left all the taps running in the bathroom? Or—no! Let's dance. I feel in the mood to dance."

Struggling to be gracious, he said, "Thank you, truly, but I have to write the—"

"You do not have to. We did it, we solved it." When he didn't respond, she pushed him with both hands.

He shook his head: *I have to write.*

She pushed him again. Markey could feel she wanted him to come at her, one way or another, and he held himself at a distance, one arm braced against the door, the other along the back of the seat.

They were at the Ritz. Zelda started out of the taxi, then stopped when she realized he wasn't coming. With surprising fury, she yanked his arm, striking fast enough that he was caught off guard. He fell on his side, glasses askew. For a long moment, they stared at each other. He tried to show her he didn't understand her anger, but the look she gave him said his incomprehension enraged her all the more.

Then she ran into the hotel. Remembering he had promised Scott he would take care of her, Markey threw money at the driver and ran after her.

He found her turning helplessly in the lobby. She stood on tiptoe, arms raised and agitated, as if willing herself to take off. Several guests stared at her in bemused fascination: This lovely young thing—what were they called, flappers?—what had worked her into such a fury? And what would she do next? The energy was both familiar to him and not. He had seen her sudden and unpredictable before, but this was desperate.

"I want music," she said.

He said carefully, "I don't think it's here in the lobby."

She charged toward . . . He didn't know what she was running to, but he caught her by the arm. "Let's find Scott."

"No!" she shouted. "I want music. I need to dance."

Now the onlookers were less benevolent. Zelda glared back at them. *You don't know how to live*, her look seemed to say, *why do you even bother?* So wild was her mood, it felt necessary to contain her somehow, so he pulled her to him, adopting the posture of a dance partner.

"We'll find you music," he assured her. "We'll dance."

The desk clerk stepped in to say, "Fred Waring and the Pennsylvanians are playing in the Persian Room."

Zelda snarled, "Go away." The clerk retreated, almost bowing.

"Fred Waring and the Pennsylvanians in the Persian Room," cried Markey as if it were just the thing. "I've never seen a Persian room or heard a Pennsylvanian. We'll get Scott . . ."

"You don't want to dance. Let go of me," snapped Zelda, struggling to get free. She was very strong. He had to work to hold her. He felt bad, as if he were hurting her somehow by not letting her throw herself God knew where. Now she seemed barely aware of the people in the lobby and she only understood him as a detested tether, something to fight and throw off.

He gave her a little distance, but kept a firm hold of her wrists. "Let's go upstairs."

She screamed *"No."* Once, then again in case he hadn't heard it. "You don't want to dance, you don't want to do anything, you just want to write. So why don't you *go* on then and *write?*"

She shrieked the last word as if it were an embarrassing obscenity. Frantic, he wrapped himself around her, with a vague purpose of comforting and muffling. He put a hand to the back of her head so that she wouldn't scream at him again and murmured, "Come on now, I'm sorry. You're tremendous and you're right, I'm sorry . . ."

Suddenly all her weight was on him. Her eyes were open, but she had a distant, lost look of someone in a stupor. He told himself she probably hadn't slept much in the past few days. He got her into an elevator. People gave them dirty looks; leaning heavily against him, Zelda looked passed out. As he guided her down the hall to her suite, he realized he had not the slightest idea what he would do if Scott was not there.

Thankfully he was. Saying, "Darling girl, what has he done to you?" he gathered Zelda up and took her to the bedroom. Over his shoulder, he instructed Markey to wait.

Markey did wait. He waited sitting. He waited pacing. He waited wondering if he should say he was going now. Then he saw that Scott had been working. As a distraction, he looked over the pages. Some of the lines sounded familiar: *A woman should be able to kiss a man beautifully and romantically without any desire to be either his wife or his mistress . . . I don't want just words. If that's all you have for me, you'd better go.* Zelda had said these words, he realized. And here they were as Scott's.

Then he read, "*Once I wanted something and got it. It was the only thing I ever wanted badly, Dot. And when I got it, it turned to dust in my hands.*"

This, he knew, Zelda had not said. The words disturbed him. He wished he hadn't read them. Markey understood instinctively that the thing Fitzgerald had wanted, the thing that had proved so profoundly lacking, was success. Markey felt as if the novelist had taken him aside to whisper in his ear, *There is no peace. There is no security, no point at which you know you belong and will always belong. No point at which you feel loved and know you will always be loved. Success doesn't give you any of that. The only thing worse than success is failure. You never reach the summit. You just keep climbing to escape that plunge to the bottom.*

But what caused him the greatest despair was that Fitzgerald had the power to reveal something he hadn't even suspected before, yet now understood it to be one of the fundamental truths of his own life. Before this moment, he would have refused to admit he envied Fitzgerald. He hadn't quite allowed into his mind the reality that the pretty Princeton boy had everything he himself wanted—and that Fitzgerald had obtained it with an ease that suggested that if Markey didn't have success by now, it would never be granted him. Because he didn't have what it took. He wasn't good enough.

And Fitzgerald was. For all his charm and beauty and audacity, the man really was that gifted. For a moment, the chasm between what he could do and Fitzgerald could do was unbearable.

For a few moments, Markey paced. Considered fleeing. Then, in the paper and sharpened pencils, the way to settle his nerves became clear. Sitting down, he took a sheet of paper and began writing the story Victor and Selma had told him.

A few minutes later, Scott emerged, jaw set, hands in his pockets. "Management called. I gather she shocked a few tourists in the lobby."

"She was upset."

"Screaming?"

"Her voice was raised, I wouldn't say screaming."

He waited for Scott to ask what had upset his wife. When he didn't, he supplied, "Everything was fine at the bridge game. It was when we were coming home in the taxi . . ."

Scott cut him off with a slice of his hand. "It happens. She gets excited. Then she gets frustrated. Then angry. And it happens."

"What does?"

Scott sat heavily. "I told you, she jumps off a cliff."

"I understand."

"No, you don't. And that's part of the problem. I don't understand either, just to be clear. But at least I'm not completely *ignorant*."

Ignorant—there was a lot in that one word, thought Markey. Success, money, Princeton, origin.

Fitzgerald raised his hand above his head, holding it level. "She starts here," he said, "and ends here." The hand fell to his side as if someone had cut a nerve. "It's a steep fall and it makes her pretty dizzy."

"You lead a pretty dizzy life," said Markey, telling himself Fitzgerald deserved that for *ignorant.*

"I know." Scott nodded, no longer confrontational. "I know. I have to do something about that. What do you think about Connecticut?"

"I know nothing about Connecticut."

Scott issued an "Ah" that suggested that again, Markey had failed him. Markey's eye fell on the pages Fitzgerald had been working on. In the mood for a counterattack, he said, "Do you use what she says?"

"Sure. I'd be crazy not to. Who else is so perfectly the woman of right now? You think we're the leaders of this red-hot jazz revolution? We're not. It's women who've changed. You want to write about now, you write about them."

"But they're her words. She doesn't mind?"

"Not at all, she's flattered. As she should be." He gave Markey a sharp look. "You did the same. That quip about writing on a man's sleeve? That was her, wasn't it?"

Markey conceded it was.

"Well, then."

As if exhausted by the subject of his wife, Fitzgerald picked up Markey's half-written article. For a moment, he read. A slight twitch of the lips indicated respect. "Zelda said you'd gotten the story. She's right."

"I suppose."

"Yet you seem more pitiful than usual. What's the matter, Markey? Vertigo?"

The words were mocking, but the tone was not. For the first time since they'd met, Markey felt Fitzgerald had remembered he was also a writer. "I have *a* story. But I don't know if it's true."

"Oh." Scott nodded gravely. Then whispered, "Does that matter?"

"Newspapers, it matters. Or it's supposed to."

"I find if a story is beautiful enough, dazzling enough, people want to believe it, and that makes it true. Or as good as makes no difference."

"This isn't a beautiful story."

"But it makes sense to people," Fitzgerald hazarded. "It feels true."

"I think it will. And maybe it is true on some level, I don't know. It's a *good* story," he said, suddenly defensive.

"Of course. Because it is only partly true. Illusion gives color to the world, Markey. People like people who tell them a good story. They're inordinately grateful." He smiled, his gleaming handsomeness reminding Markey that the rewards for telling a good story were considerable.

Then Fitzgerald became serious. "Look, Markey, do me a favor. Leave Zelda alone for a bit. A long bit. I'm not saying forever, but if you choose to hear it that way, that's fine. You got the story—true, not true—just . . . let Zelda be. If you don't mind."

The writer's hands bobbed between his knees. The tension in his fingers reminded Markey of Zelda's light wave the night of the library, her serene assertion that he'd wanted her to kiss him, his stammering denial, and the brief agitated feeling that he'd missed his chance. He had told her Fitzgerald minded—and he had been right.

Borrowing a speech from somewhere, he said, "I would like to make it clear that Mrs. Fitzgerald views me solely as a friend."

"*Friend?*" Suddenly Fitzgerald was relaxed and smiling. Settling back on the sofa, he said, "You're Zelda's rag doll. One day, she'll drop you somewhere and feel bad for about five minutes. Oh, I see—"

He tilted his head.

"You think you're the only one."

Markey remembered the party, which, up until now, he had considered the best night of his life. He remembered the men around Scott, all dressed like him, all with the same complacent air of collegiate cultural supremacy. He remembered Zelda kissing each one of them, their brief, private expressions of pleasure, one shy, one smug, one even possessive. One of those men, he now realized, had lent her the Packard they drove to the funeral. Why had he done so? Because she had gone on adventures with him, too. With all of them.

He allowed his pain and confusion to show.

Rising, Scott put a hand on his shoulder—encouragement or ballast as he stood up, Markey couldn't tell. "She gets bored."

As Scott let go of his shoulder, his hand landed flat and gentle on Markey's head. Markey felt his scalp shifted this way and that as the great writer—the youngest Scribner's had ever published—tousled his hair in benevolent contempt.

"Good night, Markey."

The next morning, he visited Walter Lewisohn's office and asked to speak to Ludlow, the secretary. Ludlow was not only available; he was extremely helpful, confirming that Walter had been late to the office that day and showing Markey where he'd noted that in his diary. He also reported that Lewisohn had seemed quite frantic when he arrived.

On Lewisohn's schedule for that day was a one o'clock appointment with Joseph Elwell. When questioned, he had told the police he had learned the bridge master was dead when he telephoned the house shortly after one to inquire why he was late. Markey reflected that this explained why Viola had lied about going to the house that morning. Not only did she not wish to be revealed as the woman who kept lingerie at the dead man's home, she knew it would expose Lewisohn's claim that he had made a one PM call to the Elwell house as a lie. If she knew Elwell was dead hours before, Selma and Walter would have known it, too.

And the key? Walter might have gotten one from his good friend Bernard Sandler, Elwell's frustrated landlord. Or else Elwell decided that the millionaire was of no real threat to him and let him in. Either way, Lewisohn had gotten into the house first thing that morning.

As for which jealous lover had made the 2:30 AM phone call—Walter or Viola—it hardly mattered. But he suspected Leonora had told the truth that it had been Walter.

Markey went to Gus Schaeffer's office and presented him with two articles. He could tell from the speed and focus of Schaeffer's eyes as they moved over the article about Lewisohn that the editor was pleased.

Then Schaeffer moved on to the second piece. After one paragraph, he asked, "What's this shit?"

"It's not shit, it's true. Elwell was a member of the American Protective League. So was Arthur Griswold. Both men ended up dead in their home with a bullet through their brain. I like the chauffeur for it, but I don't know yet."

Schaeffer slapped the Lewisohn piece. "Yes, you do. It's all here."

"What's *there* is that Lewisohn is crazy and wasn't where he was supposed to be on the morning in question. That he was obsessed with Leonora Hughes, who went home with Elwell that night."

"And he's a wealthy man and the police are covering for him." Schaeffer laid a finger on the Lewisohn piece, said not unkindly, "This is a story."

"Yes, sir, I suspect that's just what it is."

Schaeffer tapped the APL piece like the wrong key on a piano. "*This* is not. Not yet. You don't have it, I can't run it. This—"

A gentle hand on the Lewisohn piece.

"This I'll put your name on."

Markey found himself smiling. Schaeffer took his smile as acquiescence, which it was, not that it was needed. But Markey could have told him that it was the smile of a man whose faith in God had been restored. That he had remembered being in church as a boy and hearing Matthew 4:8–10, the story of Christ in the wilderness.

> Again, the devil taketh him up into an exceeding high mountain, and sheweth him all the kingdoms of the world, and the glory of them; And saith unto him, All these things will I give thee, if thou wilt fall down and worship me. At which point, Jesus had said, Get thee hence, Satan.

It had made Markey tremendously anxious because, even at the age of seven, he sensed that if he was offered a place of honor in a vast and mighty kingdom, he'd take it without blinking. Now, in Gus Schaeffer's office, he smiled to think that he had known himself well from an early age. He smiled because although he had failed this time, and would again, there could be forgiveness. Because if Satan existed, his creator must as well.

The next day, the Lewisohn story ran. Markey owned the front page—the headline; images of Elwell, Viola, Selma, Leonora Hughes, and Walter Lewisohn. Inside, his article over a two-page spread. His name in bold black type. He spent the day in bed, pitching a wadded-up piece of paper at the ceiling, trying to raise the ghost of Arthur Griswold.

He did also go out and buy several copies of the paper. When he returned to 237 West Seventieth, he found his landlady and neighbors on the stoop, eager to congratulate him. They all had questions. And he enjoyed answering them.

The following day, it was announced that Walter Lewisohn had entered the Blythewood Sanitarium for the Insane in Greenwich, Connecticut. The reason: strain over recent investment losses. Markey wrote it up, not even wincing as he made insinuations he did not believe. It was a good story. He no longer noticed when his story was the only thing on the front page—it had happened so often—although the sight of his own name under the headlines eased something in him. Johnson had been gone from his dreams for a while, and he couldn't recall the last time the buzzing had taken hold.

He sent a note to Leonora Hughes: *I hope recent events give you some peace. Yrs Markey.*

A week later, a card arrived: *When a man has been a jackass, it's only right to admit it. Present yourself at the Plaza tomorrow and I shall present my ass for kicking. SF*

With it were a dozen hyacinths.

Chapter Twenty-Seven

The next night at the Plaza, champagne and laughter flowed freely. Had he looked out the window, Markey would have seen the vast sweep of Central Park, a Vanderbilt mansion, and General Sherman astride his horse and felt not the slightest bit intimidated. But he had no time to linger at windows. The moment he walked through the door, he had been greeted by a roar of recognition and had not stopped talking since.

"What I think you have to understand about the Walter Lewisohns of the world is they don't believe anyone can touch them. From a very young age, he was raised to think he was special. That what he wanted, he should have. He wanted Leonora Hughes, and he wasn't going to let Joseph Elwell take her away from him."

"But what about Viola Kraus?"

The question came from one of the fellows at the edge of the group that surrounded him. It was a large crowd. Everyone knew: If you wanted to know the latest on the murder that gripped New York, you went to Morris Markey.

Directing his attention over the heads of the other listeners, he said, "You mean, did Viola Kraus kill Joseph Elwell?"

The man nodded.

"For a time it seemed possible. The two were intimate. She had hoped to marry him."

As he paused for effect, he realized that, more and more, he was using the accent that once had seemed such a liability; now it marked him out as different. Singular. As did his height. Zelda was standing across the room; he glanced over to see if she had noticed he was at the party. He felt confident that Scott's invitation was a recognition of his success. But he had the quiet hope that Zelda had put him up to it.

But she had made no move toward him since he'd arrived. Scott had waved, but Zelda had been looking elsewhere. Now she and Scott were regaling their own audience with their plans to storm the movie world. They were to play themselves in the movie of *This Side of Paradise*—or play the characters that were supposed to be them. Markey wasn't sure.

But his audience was waiting. Resuming his story of Viola Kraus's hopes, he said, "She was intimate with him. However, I think we've seen that Mr. Elwell kept intimate company with about half the ladies of New York, give or take a dozen." He got his laugh. "And while I disagree with Captain Carey when he says a woman couldn't have handled the recoil on a .45—"

Deliberately, he used words like *recoil* and *.45*, knowing this group might be unfamiliar with guns.

"—Viola Kraus is a petite woman. You don't see it in the newspaper images, but I have met her, and I feel it unlikely that she would own such a weapon, much less be able to fire it with any accuracy. No, the importance of Viola Kraus to the story is that Walter Lewisohn had seen her leave her husband for Joseph Elwell. That made him understand that Elwell had much to offer women. In Lewisohn's deranged mind, once Leonora Hughes had fallen under Elwell's spell, she would never be his. Elwell had seduced his sister-in-law, now he was seducing the object of his fantasy. It was not to be borne."

Too much, that *not to be borne*? From the avid expressions all around him, it seemed not.

Then a girl with honey-blond hair asked, "Do you think Walter Lewisohn did the shooting himself?"

"Yes. Yes, I do. And here's why. When he died, Elwell was completely relaxed. If he felt any danger at all, he was at pains not to show it. He was in his robe, casually looking through his mail when he was killed. That's rather provocative, isn't it? You admit a guest to your home, then look at your mail as he speaks to you?"

Markey hoped the girl would answer with a yes that could cover any number of things. But then a man pushed his way to the front, saying, "Elwell might have done the same if it were Bernard Sandler, the landlord. And Sandler would have the keys."

The man was old for this gathering, nearing forty, and he looked worn, his thin hair barely covering his scalp, an old-fashioned goatee on his chin. He seemed to know the goatee was unbecoming because he scratched at it with quivering fingers. Markey was dismayed to hear that he sounded Southern.

"You might think so. But one time when Sandler called upon Mr. Elwell, he was refused admittance by Mrs. Larsen, who claimed Elwell was out. Sandler specifically said he didn't have the keys."

"Well, he would say that, wouldn't he? If everyone in the city knows the person who shot Elwell had keys to his house, you wouldn't admit having a set."

The man's hands shook. His eyes were red-rimmed. Whatever he needed, he was running low. Through gritted teeth, Markey said, "The person who shot Joseph Elwell did not need keys. Because Elwell mistook his madness for buffoonery and let him in the door."

"But Sandler..."

Markey was done being polite. "Bernard Sandler has an alibi, provided by his wife, Bertha, who says that at the time of the murder, he was consuming a plate of eggs and bacon. Bernard Sandler has no motive whatsoever for murdering Joseph Elwell. Whereas Walter Lewisohn, in his own distorted view, had considerable provocation. Now if you'll excuse me..."

As he crossed the room, he smiled in response to the nods and waves that came his way. He clocked names: Woollcott and Wilson—whom even he now knew to be Bunny.

He had kept his distance from the Fitzgeralds all evening. Now he felt he could greet them without awkwardness. Scott's gibe about rag dolls had hurt at the time. But now he felt it was better that he understood things as they were—and he hoped Zelda would see that he did. As he approached, Scott acknowledged him with a raise of his glass. But Zelda issued a short sigh and folded her arms; clearly he was not yet forgiven for his refusal to dance the night of the bridge game.

"Ah, just the man," said Scott. "We are talking about the war." He announced this as if it were a marvelous new restaurant and Markey was the only one who had dined there.

Markey smiled. Then he saw that the other gentleman included in the "we" was Robert Benchley, and the single thing he could think of was Spook's crude remark about Benchley and Dottie.

"Have you read Benchley's 'An Eminently Safe Citizen'?" Scott asked.

Benchley demurred; he seemed a modest man. Likable, thought Markey sadly.

Noisily encouraged by Scott, Benchley explained, "It was about a man named Horace Peters who ended up on a list of people seen as having pro-German sympathies. He went to Germantown Military School, you see."

The word *German* caused Markey to focus, as if someone had turned up the sound on what Benchley was saying. "Really."

Benchley waved his drink to underscore the point. "Horace Peters's actual crime was that he was a pacifist. But the APL—sorry, that's the American Protective League—put his name right next to Emma Goldman's."

"Benchley's a pacifist," said Scott. "Markey here was with the Red Cross . . ."

"Oh!" Benchley toasted him. "Well, that's fine."

"Thank you." Damn it, the man really was likable.

"You know, *I* was accused of spying for Germany." Markey saw with irritation that the jittery gentleman who had pressed him about Bernard Sandler had joined them. "You write one little book on Nietzsche, and suddenly you're the Kaiser's man."

His desperation to charm was as noticeable and appealing as damp armpits. Markey saw Scott and Benchley smile to themselves. Anxious to distract them, Markey was about to ask Benchley what reaction he'd had from the Peters article when Zelda broke in, saying in a high, excited voice, "Do you know, I feel like *everyone* is famous? The people who aren't well-known, they were all killed off in the war or something."

It was, he thought, typical of her: outrageous and childish. But at least she was smiling at him. He opened his mouth to answer.

Then she said, "Markey, aren't you sad you didn't die in the war? Do you feel sometimes maybe you should have?"

Scott said, "*Zelda.*"

On her toes, almost off the floor, she said, "Oh, yes—congratulations, of course, on all your great success. You'll have to remind me: What did you actually do? You . . . *reported.*" She said the word as if it were foreign. "It must be so strange, to be dependent on other people to be interesting and do things so you have a story to tell. I, personally, cannot imagine that."

Stunned, he stared at her. He did partly understand. They had left her out of the conversation. Scott had stopped responding to her demand: *Tell 'em 'bout* . . . If Zelda could not be the center of the conversation, she wanted no part in it. So she had regained their attention the only way she knew how: to be shocking, intimate, irreverent.

But she had also taken a thing he had shared with her, a shame he did not speak of, and tossed it up in the air like so much confetti. A brief, happy distraction—utterly meaningless and, once it had fallen to earth, a mess to clean up.

Astonishingly, it was Scott who came to his rescue, saying, "Yes, it is quite a success! Mr. Byline! Your name in print at last."

"But how long *shall* it last?" said the unkempt Southerner who fancied himself a wit. "You'll have to be looking for your next corpse if you want to stay in business."

"Somehow, in New York, I don't think I'll run short of people asking to be killed." Markey did a double take at the wit. "Why, here's one right now."

The laughter was raucous; he had won the moment. But Zelda, he noticed, was not laughing. She was lost in her own thoughts, none of which seemed happy. His success in trouncing the interloper made him feel generous, and he tried to draw her back into the conversation, saying, "Perhaps we can agree there's some room for existence between famous and dead."

The men waited for her to be gay and charming. When she stayed silent, Scott diagnosed, "Mrs. Fitzgerald requires a drink."

She flared, genuinely angry. "Mrs. Fitzgerald requires air. Air that isn't *hot*."

As she turned on her heel, Scott said to Markey, "I believe you're the gasbag to whom she refers."

Markey rather thought it was all of them together. But it gave him the chance he wanted, so he said, "Then I should make my apologies."

"Make mine, too," Scott called after him. "There's a good man."

He found her in one of the bathrooms. In fact, in the bathtub. It was dry and she had her clothes on, but he wasn't sure how long those conditions would last. The tub was a massive thing, white and shining. One arm curled above her head, Zelda lay red and gold at the center of its blinding brightness, haloed as if a flashbulb had just exploded. Her feet were bare; the shoes lay in disparate corners. Clearly she had kicked them off with some force.

"Do you like hotel bathrooms?" she asked him. "I find them highly erotic."

He lowered the toilet seat and sat down. "Did we annoy you?"

She widened her eyes: *Yes*.

"Did I annoy you?"

"You've got all famous now. Famous and pompous. Acting like one of those clever stupid people going 'I did *words*, and my words are best, and oh, my words.'"

"On the subject of words, yours were fairly vicious."

"Oh, well, *ice cream* then, if you want nice. I should tell you I didn't think much of your last articles."

"No?" He kept his voice light so she wouldn't know she had kicked out the platform on which he now rested his entire self-worth. "I thought you'd be pleased. You said Lewisohn was guilty."

"I never *cared* about Lewisohn." She jerked her head to face him. "I care that you didn't put me in the story. You acted like it was all you."

"I didn't put myself in."

"Your *name* is on it." The accusation echoed jarringly in the tight, tiled room.

"But I wrote it."

"You wouldn't have anything to write if it weren't for me. I got you Viola, I got you the car to the funeral, we took you to the *Frolic*, we played bridge. I even found that odious girl in the green dress. You wouldn't *have* any of this if it weren't for me."

He felt she was overstating it, but he now understood the cause of her poisonous behavior. She had been overlooked and it hurt her.

"I know, I'm very grateful."

"I didn't see a thank-you."

"Thank you. Truly. I mean it." He took her hand, as if to impress his feelings on her skin. "You're . . ."

"What?" It was, he thought, the same expression he had seen in the taxi as she took in the cheering crowds. But what she was to him was too complicated a thing to confess in a bathroom with her husband just through the door.

He let go of her hand. "You're Zelda Fitzgerald."

The title didn't seem to please her. Her eyes went dull. She drew her knees under her chin, rubbed a finger over her kneecap. After a long moment, she said, "I'll tell you something, it is a lot of work bein' Zelda Fitzgerald."

"No one does it better."

A fleeting smile. "I give 'em a good show, don't I?"

But she had become distant, as if he were just another member of the audience and she found him a bore. Awkward, he tried, "More than a show . . ."

She cut him off, saying in a strange, detached voice, "No, it's all right. You mustn't confuse me with someone in search of some dreadful *purpose* in life. I'm really only good at lighthearted pursuits. I'm terribly lazy and quite selfish. I think a lot about myself, yes, but nothing else is nearly as interesting. Most people don't bear thinking about, I find. Whereas I never cease to fascinate."

She had settled her hands in her lap. Now she stretched out her leg, drawing her bare foot down the tile, stroking it with her big toe.

He was uncertain as to her mood; it seemed dangerous to contradict her, dangerous to agree. Finally, he said, "I think that's a paltry summation of someone with a much grander spirit. There's lots you could do . . ."

"No," she said firmly as if she had expected the argument. "There are things I might be good at, but much nicer to *think* I could do something better than anything else than try and be disappointed."

She fixed her foot on the hot-water tap, her toes playing over the spokes. She looked so intent that Markey worried she would twist it by accident, drenching herself. He put his hand over the tap, felt her toes wiggling under his palm.

"I worry you'll ruin your dress," he said as an excuse.

"Scott will buy me another." Now she was fighting him to turn on the water, her foot twisting with purpose.

"That one is especially becoming, it'd be a shame to get water all over it."

"I *love* water. If I could live in water, I'd be entirely happy. You can move right through it like it's not even there, but it raises you up at the same time. I wish to be immersed. I want to float . . ."

She kicked at his hand. But he held firm, keeping the taps shut. She glared at him.

"That's the hot tap, you'll burn yourself."

"I don't care. I want hot water. I feel desperate for warmth." She felt along the tub's pristine surface as if it were a busted radiator. "I need something around me. Something . . ."

Furious, she threw an elbow at the tub's porcelain wall, slammed her feet under the faucet so hard he worried she'd break a bone.

Drawing into herself, she clutched her arms. "It's *freezing* in here. It's cold and it's hard and . . . too shiny, it hurts my eyes. I don't know why it's always so frigid in these hotels . . ."

He held out his hand. "Well, come out then."

"No, you get in." She sat up, hands on the rim of the tub. "You get in here with me."

Thinking this was more naughtiness, he half smiled: *Come on now.*

But she was insistent, saying, "You're my friend and you should be in here with me. Not leaving me alone."

". . . I won't fit."

Immediately, she lay down, pressing herself against the side. "You will. I'll make room. See?" She gestured to the empty space. "You can fit."

He was about to gently explain that it was impossible and that she should know that without him explaining when the sight of her, open and needful, reminded him of the time she had crouched beside him on the curb outside the Ritz. When he had been shaking and miserable for reasons she could not have understood and yet she had come. She had put her hands on him, walked with him, been with him.

He climbed in. Half squatting, he turned, seeking the best place to sit, worried he would trample her dress. Zelda was delighted, crying, "You are ab*surd*ly oversized."

"Well, I warned you.

"No, I like it, you stay that way."

At first, he kept his knees bent, but Zelda said no, so he sat up higher and extended his legs. Once settled, he saw the appeal; there was something pleasing about the smooth, slippery perfection of the porcelain, the faint echo of an empty tub; one felt rather grand and imperial. He straightened a bit, thinking, *Valet, my robe . . .*

Zelda sensed him preening; in a windy, self-important voice, she quoted, "'Elwell mistook his *mahd*ness for buf*foon*ery.'"

"All right, that was probably overdone."

"Horrifically overdone. I thought: Who is he trying to be?"

Grinning, he drawled, "That there Lewusohn banged on the do-ah and chicken chaser Elwell let him in cos he didn't know no better. Then Lewusohn took that .45-caliber automatic and SHOT him, right through the haid."

"Right through his bald old head."

"Bang."

She laughed. Pointed at him with a cocked thumb and forefinger. "Bang."

Then she lay alongside him, stretching herself with a sigh of "Oh, *yes*." He felt her body ease, become soft. She did not so much curl around him as flow over him. She was right about water, he thought vaguely, the weight and buoyancy. Her head was on his shoulder, her arm across his middle. He kept his left hand over the side of the tub. There wasn't much he could do with his right hand; it seemed natural to place it on her head. Still, he felt compelled to observe, "This is a strange and awkward place."

"It is. But we can do it. That's a thing about here, it gets chilly and unpleasant. They have these winters."

"They do."

"I hate cold. You better stay."

"I will. I'll stay."

"Good."

But her *oh, yes* had been the first time he had heard a woman sensually pleased, and he could not shake its effect. He could smell the spice of her hair, the warmth where her arm met her breast. The crown of her brow seemed just below his lips. He crossed his legs, looked out at the bathroom. It was an antiseptic space, he told himself, a doctor's office.

She lifted her head. "Markey's worried."

"No, Markey's fine."

"*Are* you?" She peered at him, smiling. The hand so quiet a moment ago began to play over his ribs. "I'm going to do it . . ."

"No, you are not."

"That thing you're scared of, I am."

She pecked him on the mouth. It was quick and sudden, like a pinch, and he barely had time for a disappointed *oh* when she popped her eyes, mouth agape to exclaim, "Oh, my! Oh, no! Has society collapsed?"

She actually looked left, then right. "I do not believe it has. And I do not believe I have turned to salt. Have you?" She prodded his chest with two fingers. "I don't believe so. Nor do I believe that a scarlet *A* has appeared on my flesh, but maybe I should look . . ."

Later he would tell himself that he kissed her because her voice was rising and people would hear. That he knew a dare when it was issued. Above all, he was tired of hearing that she did not believe; he wanted to hear that she did. So he threaded his fingers through the sunlight of her hair, shut his eyes, and kissed her. And for a few moments, it seemed she did believe and life really was as perfect as it was ever going to be.

Then the sound of laughter broke through the door, a man's voice, and her lips thinned against his and her body trembled with mirth. Because Scott had said something and she had been listening for him the whole time? Or because she found his ardor flattering, even touching, but nothing more than that. *Beautifully and romantically*, he remembered. *Means nothing.*

He broke. Said with as much wry dignity as he could muster, "This doesn't matter, does it?"

She gave him a quizzical look. "It's just nice . . . fun . . ."

Frowning, she plucked at his shirt button, which annoyed him because if it came off, she wasn't sewing it back on. He looked down at his long, stiff legs, feet toes up. That tombstone: *Here lies Zelda's rag doll.*

He pushed her hand away. Too hard; now she knew he was angry. She made a noise of bitter amusement.

He began moving to extricate himself. But she was partly on top of him and the tub was deep, the surface slippery and uncertain. A fall would be dangerous. It seemed every time he got purchase, she moved so he was back down. Was she doing it on purpose? He couldn't tell. Clenching his teeth, he tried to lift himself. But he could not get his arms free, his legs untangled. His head was lower than it had been and his throat was crunched, making it hard to breathe. She was on top of him, fingers tight in his hair. Certain she was about to slam his head against the cast iron, he managed, "Zelda, I need to get out. I just need . . ."

"Oh, for God's sake." Suddenly she was up and stepping over him. His head free, he watched as she bent down to find her shoes. Then she stood, her eyes hard on him as she lifted one foot, then the other to put them back on. Then something in her eyes told him she no longer saw him at all. When she went to the door, he had a premonition that this would be the last time they knew each other, and he threw at her, "Goodbye, Mrs. Fitzgerald."

He waited for her to correct him. *Zelda.*

She looked at him and he would forever wish she hadn't. She was sad, not for any loss on her part, but his stupidity. Then she left him.

He allowed himself to think what a messy business it would have been. The mechanics simply wouldn't have worked. They hadn't even locked the door. He let some time pass. He had the confused notion that he had to stay at the party because people would talk if he did not. They would say he had made a clumsy pass and she had turned him down with a laugh. Which perhaps was what had happened, although it hadn't felt like it at the time.

Slipping back into the room, he glanced about, expecting to see pity. Or mockery. But, as usual, everyone was listening to Scott.

"You've got this fellow in an enormous house," he said. "He's rich, but no one seems to know where the money comes from. All sorts of fantastic stories about him. There are rumors of women, many women. But perhaps there's one he loves above all others? Then, one day, he's found in that fabulous house, a bullet through his brain. Murdered by a man who believed he was fooling around with the woman he loved."

Scott was telling the Elwell story, making it his own. He told it skillfully, Markey conceded.

But he was weary of skill, even his own, as meager as it might be compared to Fitzgerald's. Comparisons, another thing he was weary of. All those—what had Zelda called them? *Clever stupid people.* He was weary of her, too. And Scott. It was time to go.

He was almost at the door when a man stumbled into him, giggling at his own drunken clumsiness. It was the sad, needful Virginian. The man brightened at the sight of Markey. Markey cursed himself for not getting out just that bit sooner.

"Willard Huntington Wright. Fellow writer and Virginian."

The gentleman held out his hand. Taking it, Markey prayed that was all they would ever have in common. "What do you write?"

"Oh, everything. Art mostly. Now Elwell—that's a good story. Locked room, shades of Poe's 'Murders in the Rue Morgue.' And we're all locked in, one way or another, aren't we?"

". . . Poetic," said Markey, unsure—and uncaring—whether Wright was joking or not. He looked for someone who might take this man off his hands, but the other party guests looked pointedly away.

Guilty over how much he despised this man, he said, "I'm very sorry. About the APL and all that, that must have been . . ."

"Oh, no." Suddenly embarrassed, Wright stepped back, clearing the path to the exit. "You were almost out, I dragged you back. My apologies. Best of luck."

"You, too," said Markey and left.

CHAPTER TWENTY-EIGHT

For a long time, he wandered. At times, memories of that midnight walk with Zelda came to him. Ruthlessly he put them aside. He did not want to remember that she was capable of sympathy, that she had ever understood him. Better to think she had always been a pretty, silly, over-admired girl with a ridiculously high opinion of herself, all because she had happened to marry . . . oh, yes, the greatest writer of his generation. Well, they could both rot.

It was dawn by the time he finally got back to West Seventieth Street. Exhausted, he stared up at 244, thought how astonishing it was that only a few weeks ago, he had staggered across Joseph Elwell, at least the illusion of him, a sophisticated man of the world about to spend the night with a glowing, erotic fantasy. When, in reality, he was a tired old man helping a woman escape a pervert.

Probably one of the more decent things he'd done in his life and it got him killed.

The sight of Jost Otten, in his cap and white jacket, carrying his bottles of milk, was so wholesome and everyday that Markey felt tears come to his eyes. Raising a hand, he called, "Morning, Mr. Otten!"

"Morning, Mr. Markey. You've been out late."

"I have. Too late. I need a good long sleep."

So pleasant was the sight of Jost Otten and his milk that Markey lingered, watching as Otten trotted up the steps of the building next door. Opening the front door, he disappeared for a moment. Then reemerged, his basket lighter by two bottles.

"You know you're lucky," said Markey, "that you didn't have one of the Elwell keys. You would have been dragged into that mess."

"I used to," said the milkman. "But they changed the locks after the burglary."

"Burglary." Markey felt groggy from a long night. Burglary seemed important, but he couldn't say why.

"Yeah, about a month before"—Otten jerked his head at the building to indicate the murder—"a couple of thieves got in through the cellar. Took some cash, jewelry, a vase, I think. After that, they put in new locks and Elwell had the only set of keys. Well, him and Mrs. Larsen, but that was it."

Markey smiled as he remembered his early article. Five women! Five keys! The whole city, at least in his fantasy, buzzing about those women and their keys. The five husbands who might have discovered those keys and used them to get in and shoot the man who despoiled their marriage.

When all along, there had been only one.

No, two.

Well, he thought, wheeling toward his own door, if he'd gotten it wrong, his name hadn't been on those early pieces, so who cared?

Everyone knew Walter Lewisohn had done it, and if he was ever fool enough to come out of the lunatic asylum, they'd nab him. Stories moved fast. No one would remember that he'd gotten the number of keys wrong. Still, to remember for next time, talk to the milkman. Milkmen knew everything.

Then, as he fumbled for his own keys, he realized the number of keys was not the only thing he'd gotten wrong.

He told himself no. Told himself he was tired. When you never went to bed, the world started to feel upside down. Day was night, night was day. He would sleep. Then he would wake up and remember that tiny detail that would reveal how wrong he was.

Hours later, he woke up and searched his mind for that tiny detail. He didn't find it.

Over and over, the story of the two keys came together the same way.

In the late afternoon, he went to the Larsens' home.

Standing outside, he thought how often reporters had written that Mrs. Larsen was married to a butcher. It was a detail that underscored her solid middle-class decency. You could rely on the word of a woman married to a man who provided families with their meat for supper. Except they should never have relied on the word of Mrs. Larsen. Or her memory. Again and again, she had forgotten things. Hidden evidence. Evaded . . .

Lied.

Mr. Larsen was cutting chops from a side of pig when he came in. He gave Markey no more than a glance before going back to his work. But Mrs. Larsen immediately came around the counter to welcome him. For the first time ever, he thought, she seemed pleased to see him.

He said, "My editor suggested I go back and talk to the people who cared about Joseph Elwell. He said we don't pay enough attention to the ones who grieve once the circus moves on. Would you have time for coffee—and maybe one or two of those excellent sausages?"

He sat in the small kitchen upstairs while she fried the sausages and put the coffee on to boil. "You once told me to find another job," he reminded her. "You said newspapers were no way to make a living. Or no way to live, I can't remember."

"I was wrong." She set the plate before him. "You exposed Walter Lewisohn for killing Mr. Elwell. He is locked somewhere he cannot do more harm. Even if he does not go to jail, you did a good thing."

She took the seat opposite, supervising as he cut up his food. He was glad he did not have to look her in the eye as he said, "Yes, I can imagine you think so. Since you're the one who actually killed Joseph Elwell."

Her chin had been resting on her clasped hands. Now she raised it to take a deep breath. She stretched her fingers, then folded them again. Resettling herself, she said, "There have been so many stories about this murder. A lot of them have been wrong."

He nodded. "And I wrote a fair number of them. It must have been worrying, realizing you had a reporter with irregular hours living right across the street. But then you saw that you could use it—me—to your advantage. I don't say that to accuse. It's my fault. I should have been more careful about my sources. That's why I'd like to get the story right this time. If only for myself."

"And why do you feel this is . . . 'getting it right'?"

"The keys, Mrs. Larsen. So many women—not to mention their husbands—had good reason to want Elwell dead. But I couldn't figure out how they'd gotten inside. The doors were locked. The windows were locked. Mr. Elwell had a habit of keeping people out when he didn't want to see them. I knew that from the way he avoided Bernard Sandler when he was trying to evict him."

As he said it, he realized that had been another detail she had given him. Had that been a lie as well?

"How did this wronged woman or enraged husband get in? Even if they were able to get in, how did they get out, locking the door behind them? That's why I thought that beautiful woman in the green dress shot him."

"You sold newspapers with that woman in the green dress."

"Yes, we did. And we sold a lot of newspapers with Viola Kraus and the other women with keys. Five women with keys. That's what Rhodes told me and you didn't dispute it. But I never did find the fifth. Until now."

She tilted her head. "I don't think we know, do we? All the women to whom Mr. Elwell gave keys. Viola Kraus . . ."

"As you know very well, the locks were changed after the burglary. Only two people had the new keys. Joseph Elwell had one set. You had the other. Rhodes never came into the house, he didn't need keys. Elwell wouldn't have trusted him anyway. He did trust you—unfortunately for him."

"But a woman could not have shot this gun."

She was not particularly alarmed, he noticed. She spoke calmly, as if they were discussing someone else. As if he was not accusing her of murder.

He said, "I thought it foolish of Carey to say a woman couldn't fire a .45 with accuracy. Myself, I've always found it a big puppy dog of a gun. It's heavy, jumps a bit. But nothing you can't handle if you're prepared. And I suspect you were prepared. You're a calm, deliberate person, Mrs. Larsen. Not the kind to act in haste."

"The kimono?" Neatly, she placed another of his stories before him, blocking his accusation.

"Yes, the kimono. I doubted myself for days about that pink kimono. You said you found it under the bed. But I didn't recall seeing it under either bed. How bad must my eyesight be?"

"You were not in the rooms very long."

"No, but I would have noticed a pink kimono left under the

bed as if someone had worn it the night before." He paused. "All I found was a number of robes and undergarments hung up neatly in the closet. So, I must confess, Mrs. Larsen, pride makes me wonder if, after the murder, someone took the pink kimono off a hanger and tossed it in the closet for the police to find."

"I think it's more likely the police did this themselves, to show they were working hard on the case."

"And they snipped off the initials as well?"

She shrugged; what did she know of police practices?

"Because that's a clue that might have helped them solve the murder. Which, contrary to popular opinion, police prefer to do if it's not too much trouble. Oh, sure, the press rejoiced because there's nothing more tantalizing than a missing monogram on a piece of lingerie. That was the point, wasn't it? Getting us all chasing after that delightful detail?"

She shook her head, maintaining the pretense that they were speaking of a third, deranged individual.

"Whose initials were they, Mrs. Larsen? It wasn't 'VVS,' was it."

As if suddenly tired of the game, she admitted, "There were no initials."

Markey lifted his head in a half nod. "But by cutting a bit out to make people think there might be, you had everyone asking the wrong questions."

"The wrong questions were asked, certainly."

"Joseph Elwell was never romantically interested in any of those women, was he?"

"I told you, he was a gentleman."

"I don't think that's what you call a man who seduces vulnerable women so he can get information on their friends and family for the American Protective League."

"I'm sorry?"

"Oh, you've heard of the League, I know you have, Mrs. Larsen. You know how I know?"

She shook her head slightly.

"Because when you gave me Mrs. Hardy's name, you didn't mention that she had a sister. A sister whose photograph was also in Elwell's bedroom collection. And the reason you didn't tell me that is that you knew the countess might tell me about the APL and you didn't want any connection made between Elwell's murder and the war. You thought Mrs. Hardy wouldn't say anything because she believed Elwell was innocent of accusing her sister. Which of course he wasn't."

"I told you, Mrs. Hardy is not a bright woman."

"At first, it seemed a bit far-fetched. Could all these women really be working for Germany? Now I can believe the Countess Szinswaska would do any number of things to survive. Princess Dalla has family connections to people with reason to support Germany. But Viola Kraus? What connection would she have to the war? Then I remembered that Mrs. Elwell told me a very interesting thing. She said bridge is so popular because it's a game for partners. Couples. You take on a lady as a student, sooner or later, you end up at a card table with her husband. Victor von Schlegell is a vice president of United Rubber. He's also a member of the Studio Club. I can't prove it, but I'm fairly sure if the government opened up the books on United Rubber, they'd find some lost inventory that somehow ended up in Germany. I think that's what Elwell was really looking into when he started romancing Viola. But he liked keeping those photographs as proof of his success in spy catching. He was a vain man."

"Yes."

He took a deep breath. "But I don't think you're a spy, Mrs. Larsen. Sweden was neutral during the war. Your husband isn't rich or well-connected. So why did you kill Joseph Elwell?"

She didn't answer, sitting contained and distant, as if she were in another room. He noticed that her gaze had settled on a calendar on the wall. It was from a dry goods store and he saw nothing remarkable about it until he realized it was from the year 1918. He could think of only one reason someone would keep a two-year-old calendar: to remember something from that year. A loss. She was too young to have a son of fighting age. Her husband was downstairs and he seemed intact—outwardly at least.

The sharp pop of steel landing on wood as the cleaver struck made him jump ever so slightly. Then it came to him.

"Is Mr. Larsen your first husband?"

"No, he is not."

He took that in. "Funny, the *Herald* had it right for once."

This startled her out of her disinterested pose. He said, "Don't you remember—I bet you do, it must have worried you—when the *Herald* ran a story speculating that an ex-soldier had shot Elwell?"

He saw from the faint crease in her brow that she did.

"This particular .45 was only issued to the military. Until recently, it wasn't available to the public." He paused. "I assume your first husband was given one in the army."

"A man who knew him brought it back. He thought I would want it to remember him by. I said to him, 'Anders hated guns. He was gentle. A little fearful, even. Why would I want to remember him with a weapon he hated?'"

Remembering what Dottie had told him about the APL's slacker raids, he asked, "Where did the APL agents get him, Mrs. Larsen? The movie theater? Work?"

"They took him as we were leaving church."

Her eyes went still, and he knew the memory had taken hold of her. Feeling he was moving on ice and had just heard the sharp crack of warning, he moved the conversation away from her husband, asking, "Did Viola Kraus really come to the house that morning? Or was 'Miss Wilson' entirely your invention?"

"She did come. She was worried she had left something indelicate behind. She is a scattered sort of woman."

"That gave you the idea to leave a kimono where the police could find it."

She nodded.

"But that was dangerous, wasn't it? You showed yourself a liar. I couldn't figure out why you'd do that. And then I realized that kimono showed up right before Arthur Griswold was killed. You knew you were going to kill him and you wanted everyone focused on something else. There's nothing tantalizing about Arthur Griswold, especially when you put him up against a lady's undergarment. One thing I am curious about."

She nodded: *Go on*.

"Did you kill Griswold because he was APL? Or because he saw something he shouldn't have?"

"That woman you were so obsessed with—the girl in the green dress."

He nodded.

"Griswold was the only one who knew she did not stay the night. That she left an hour after she arrived. Furthermore, Miss Kraus's Packard is noisy. It has woken him in the past. He was suspicious that he did not hear it prior to the shooting. It took a few days, but he drew his conclusions."

"Did the two men know each other, Mrs. Larsen? Were they working together?"

"No," she scoffed. "In Griswold's mind, perhaps. Some people cannot let go of what they see as their best years. They hang on, pretending they are still the brave young men they probably never were. Sometimes it gets them killed. I did not think I had anger left in me. But when he waved his finger at me even as he demanded money to keep silent—"

In Swedish, she said something contemptuous. It gave him satisfaction to learn that Griswold had been a worm through and through. Had she shot him from Elwell's house? She did, after all, have the key, and the police had stopped interviewing people on the premises at the time.

But remembering the crowds of thrill seekers, he thought it more likely that she had used the chaos they created as cover. Griswold would have been watching from the window. No one would expect a shot. The policeman had told him once the gun was fired, everyone ran screaming. No one would have been looking for the shooter in that moment. Even if they had, who would have suspected a quiet, soberly dressed woman? Viola Kraus, the most beautiful woman in New York, they would have noticed. But an older married woman like Mrs. Larsen could be invisible. And perhaps she had left off her black straw hat, distorting the image everyone knew, making them believe she was a different person entirely by changing one superficial detail.

"Then you shot through my window a few nights later. Forgive my curiosity, but did you mean to kill me?"

"You keep such late hours, who would expect you to be home?"

Meaning she thought he would be out and only wanted to warn him off? He wanted to think so, but he was probably being sentimental.

"Also," she said, "you were with the Red Cross. So, for the people you helped."

"You're a good shot," he told her.

"Thank you. My father took me duck hunting many times. It was something he shared with his children."

"Mine, too. You worked for Elwell for some time. Did you take the job meaning to kill him?"

"Of course not. I felt fortunate to find work with a wealthy American who had good manners."

"What changed your mind?"

She crossed her arms around her middle, leaning forward as if a pain had taken hold. "One morning, he had been out late. I do not think he even went to bed. He was still in his evening clothes. He was very . . . merry. He even invited me to have a drink with him. I said no, of course. But I would sit with him, out of politeness.

"We had never spoken of my husband. I didn't even think he knew that I was married before. But then he says, 'I'm very sorry, you know.' I said, 'For what are you sorry?' 'Your husband,' he said, 'that you lost him.'"

Something like a smile crossed her face. "I was about to say thank you. That's when he said, 'But better to die than live as a coward.' He said it twice. 'Better to die than live as a coward.'"

Markey reflected that if Elwell had been sober enough to see in Marie Larsen what he saw now, he would have run for the hills.

"I said I did not think so. That my husband was not a coward. To which, he said, 'Yes, he lived up to his responsibilities. And we've done all right by you, too.'"

Remembering Rhodes and the mysterious Barnes, Markey said, "Meaning they got you the job working for him."

"Yes. It took me a long time to understand what he meant by that 'we.' I thought he meant America. Then, one day, I was tidying his bureau and I found this little pin. A badge. It was the same one worn by the men who arrested my husband on the steps of the church. And from then on, I kept thinking of my husband's face, the . . . fear, the grief. More than dying, he was afraid of killing. After that, whenever I saw Joseph Ewell, I compared my husband's face to his. So often, Elwell was drunk. Smiling. With his white tie and his playing cards. Talking of responsibility. Of cowardice. He, who never did anything but send men to death because he lost a little money."

Her voice rose as she said, "And that he thought he had done me a *kindness* . . ."

She collected herself, shrugged. "So."

He considered what to ask next. About the murders themselves, he understood everything he needed to. But he was still curious about her. It seemed to him that there was a Mrs. Larsen before Joseph Elwell had fatally boasted of sending her husband to death and a Mrs. Larsen after. But did she think so? How did one live with hope and purpose when you understood how quickly and pointlessly life could end?

"How do you manage, Mrs. Larsen? What do you think of it? If you think of it . . ."

Of course she had, coming to her own concise conclusion. Her voice distant, she said, "Killing that man is my atonement."

"Atonement?"

"Yes. It was my idea to come to this country. 'There is more work,' I said, 'more opportunity.' But if we had stayed in Sweden, my husband would have lived. My country stays out of wars, it does not throw away men's lives so carelessly. Even those who come back, they are . . ." She shook her head. "Sometimes I imagine my husband saying to me, 'But this is not the way.' But then I think what he must have gone through, the things he would have seen and maybe done. That he died alone . . ."

The thought of her husband brought her close to breaking. Her eyes were wide, seeing something not in the room. Then she swallowed.

"And I think someone must be punished for that. It is my atonement that I am the one to do it. It kills you a little to take a life. I cannot . . . I cannot feel what I should. It is either rage or nothing. Fire or ash."

For a moment, she sat, puzzled by what she had become. Then she said to him, "When my husband died, someone wrote to me from the Red Cross. They said he died peacefully. That someone was with him. I believed that with all my heart for a very long time. Then, one day, I realized, no, they lied. Of course they lied, what else would they say?"

He nodded, unable to tell her otherwise. For a long while, they were quiet. He suspected that she was done killing. But he was not sure enough to tell her he would have to write her story. It seemed wiser to pretend he would keep her secret. He prepared to leave the table.

"They won't believe you," she said.

Startled that she had guessed, he said, "All the same."

"But your name, it's on all these newspaper articles accusing Walter Lewisohn. Before him, you accused Viola Kraus. You cannot now turn around and say, 'Oh, I was wrong. Again.' What do you think Lewisohn will do to you when he's released?"

"I don't imagine they will release him. No one is in a hurry to have him back."

But it was a disquieting thought. The Kraus sisters had fled to Europe. Their need to keep Lewisohn caged was not as imperative as it had been. And as mad and disgraced as Lewisohn was, he still had friends.

The word *disgraced* stung; he forced himself to be honest as to why. He recalled himself bloviating at that party. Several parties. To go back after all that, to say, *No, I was wrong*—his career would be finished.

"Also," said Marie Larsen, "anyone can see that there is something wrong with you."

Perhaps because her voice was gentle, he took it as sympathy. She was only telling him something he suspected was true. Not that there was something wrong with him—that he knew to be true—but that people could see it. It was like someone quietly alerting you that your fly was undone, only his brokenness could not be discreetly buttoned up. Perhaps that was why Zelda had told him to be big. Because she saw it as the only recourse when you were a bit funny in the head, as they might say back home. It was, he decided, sound advice.

He said, "I know. But I'm not wrong about this."

"Does that matter?"

The question landed like a medicine ball against his chest and he struggled. Matter—what did it mean to matter? It meant he would do something. Expose Marie Larsen, exonerate Walter Lewisohn. It would be the right thing. And yet it felt wrong.

Or maybe he wanted to believe it was wrong because he really didn't want to write one more article about Joseph Elwell. Not this one. He knew, in his gut, it was not the story people wanted to hear. Gus Schaeffer would be so disappointed. He did smile at the thought of breaking that man's beef-jerky heart.

He needed sleep. Hours and hours, days and days of it.

"You can write what you want," said Marie Larsen. "But you will look like a liar. Captain Carey will look like a fool. The district attorney will be embarrassed."

"Sure. But truth matters."

Did it, though? Hadn't Fitzgerald told him, if a story is beautiful enough, people will want to believe it and that makes it true?

Zelda, eyes on him, insisting, *I just think it's awful not to matter.* Then she'd ripped his heart out for a joke. But she'd never really included him among the people who mattered. That was a club of two.

Why *should* he care, he thought querulously. He'd gotten what he wanted out of the story: fame, to be blunt. Success. That was the currency of the times. Yes, the truth shall set you free, but whom would he liberate? Walter Lewisohn, a man who should spend the rest of his life locked up? Whom was he defending? Elwell and Griswold? Fakes and frauds. Cheats, charlatans.

He thought of the Elwell boy, who had been cheated by his father. Perhaps he should nudge the world a little in the right direction for his sake.

But that was just hubris on his part. You could only make the world right if you believed you could, and he was too old for that now.

Now I got the crazy blues . . .

Oh, that face, that strange, wonderful double face. Eggs and spinach. Rivers of light in the darkness and reflections upon reflections upon reflections until it all became something of a house of mirrors and who knew what was real or right? *We keep you clean in Muscatine!* Was it true? Did it matter?

He looked at his plate. He hadn't finished his food. But he no longer felt hungry; the memory of the butcher slamming the cleaver into the pig's carcass, the animal's dead limbs trembling under the impact, was too vivid.

Still, to be polite, he said, "They really are fine sausages, Mrs. Larsen."

For the first time, he noticed that she had not eaten. He thought of the memories she lived with, the images that had killed her appetite, not just for mercy but for life. Everyone had praised her mature demeanor. No one had guessed it was arid despair. She had said she could not feel as she should, and he suspected she could no longer feel at all. There was very little point to putting this woman in jail. Even if there were a point, he didn't think he could bring himself to do it.

As he thought of how to thank her for breakfast, he thought of his grandfather's funeral repast—a meal taken as people shared stories of the deceased. Most of those stories were a bit of truth with a generous dose of fibbing—as a courtesy to the living. Markey hadn't liked his grandfather. He thought him a mean man. But you couldn't say that, of course. You made it nice. Otherwise the pain would be unbearable.

It wouldn't be the first time he'd lied about somebody's death.

"Thank you," he told her, "for the repast."

Chapter Twenty-Nine

Markey had not been in the habit of going to the Morgue; it seemed a thing for more established reporters with their news feeds already well grooved, the stories sluicing down the shoot from the old sources at predictable times. He had always felt too pressed to spend half an hour with men he saw as his rivals.

But after he spoke with Marie Larsen, he took a stool at the bar. He knew what his room would feel like, and he dreaded the emptiness of it. He would lie on the bed, waiting for something else to smash through the window. Oh, he would try to fight back; he would imagine he was on that couch at the Ritz, a blanket high and free overhead before it settled comfortingly over him. Or snug in the tub with Zelda, laughing about bald old heads. He would try and get that dream back, and it wouldn't come. Or it would turn sour and disturbing. Better to be here.

After a little while, Frank came over to talk. He had had a win at the track and wanted to explain in detail how he'd managed it. He seemed pleased to see Markey, as if his earlier absence had been noted, even resented. After a drink, Markey decided he liked Frank more than he had. He even liked Hal Meyers when he arrived. More drinks were ordered.

He was drunk for several days. He liked it and wondered why he had not thought of this before. Only men drank at the Morgue, and not a single one of them was glamorous or well-dressed. Liquor made everyone brilliant, especially himself, and he felt inordinately fond of everyone he met. It was, he told himself, the first time he hadn't felt lonely since coming to New York.

One day, he heard a Georgia accent and presented himself to the fellow with "Welcome to the small but influential union of Southern drinkers." Then he noticed the man had steel where his ankle should be and toasted him, "And to the Union of Those of Us with Missing Parts."

His name was Laurence Stallings. He worked for the *World*.

"You should stop by," he said. "I've read you. You're good with words."

"I am fond of words," Markey allowed. "I like them. And I like stories. I like . . . taking the words, picking the best ones, putting them in the right order but a little unexpected, so there's some style?"

Stallings nodded.

"And I do like telling a story."

"So what's the story on why you've been here three days straight?"

Markey blinked. His new best friend had been here for three days and he had missed him? Putting a finger somewhere in the vicinity of his lips, he whispered, "I'm waiting for a story to die."

Stallings nodded with more understanding than he had expected. "Something you wrote?"

"No, something I did not write. And I don't want to write. And"—before the other man could ask—"something I do not want to tell. If I stay here long enough, people will find another story to care about and I can write something else."

"You getting paid not to tell the story?"

Appalled, Markey shook his head. "No," he said, sounding almost sober to himself. "No. It's not that. It's . . ."

"You got a story wrong," said Stallings. "Now you've got the truth and it makes you look bad and might get you fired."

His tone was matter-of-fact. It was something, he seemed to suggest, that happened to most, and it *might* not be the end of the world.

Markey nodded, explaining, "And the right people got punished with the wrong story, and the wrong people will be punished with the right one." He could probably kiss that *World* job goodbye. But it seemed important to say. It felt honest and that felt pretty good.

"Well, that's more interesting than most," said Stallings. "Usually, it's about a woman."

"Oh, well, that, too."

He felt the other man's hand land on his back, give it a gentle rub, then a thump between the shoulder blades. He heard him suggest a sandwich and some coffee. He thought *No* but found himself nodding. He let the man guide him off the barstool, minding his own feet as Stallings took up his cane. For a moment, he worried: There was friendship, there was kindness, and there was pity. The first two were fine, but he didn't want anything to do with the third. He looked doubtfully at the door. It was ill-fitting; the light from outside leaked into the darkened speakeasy through the chinks. It felt cold and threatening. Beyond that door was a blindingly bright chaotic space where you were not guaranteed kindness, as you were here. Here there was always someone who understood the need to float a little below the surface. He felt the old need to run tingling at the back of his knees, heard the warning hiss in his ear.

Stallings guided him a step or two; then Markey balked. Transfixed by the light, he panicked at the thought of the door opening, the brightness flooding in, acid and relentless. Something bad was beyond it, he felt certain. Something he could only think of as the end.

"It's out there," he managed by way of explanation.

"It is," said Stallings. "But I don't think it's coming for you today."

It took a few months. Markey stayed with the *Daily News*, but began dreaming of moving on to the *World*. When he got the story of a wife of a Long Island dentist who caught her husband cheating with one of his patients and shot him, he started to think of himself as the writer on the Wheelock case, no longer the Elwell writer. He rented the parlor apartment at Mrs. Cecchetti's. He took his breakfast regularly at the lunch counter nearby. And one day, he saw a young woman with dark brown hair seated at the lunch counter reading *This Side of Paradise*, a frown of concentration on her face. Something about the freshness of her white hat with a hydrangea-blue band told him she was not a city girl.

He thought to begin, *I know the author*, then follow up with a story—not the stripping off at the *Frolic*, something only he could tell. *He once helped me buy flowers. He even tried to pay for them, but the hotel wouldn't extend his credit. They've gone to Connecticut so he can finish the next novel . . .*

Instead, he said, "I haven't read it. What do you think?"

Startled, she looked up. There was that brief moment of assessment: Did his looks appeal? Did he seem a nice man? Before she confessed, "I'm not sure. I *think* it's brilliant . . ."

"That's the general opinion."

"Most books, they're well written, but they don't feel so vitally true the way this one does. And the way he writes about women—they're so vivid and original. I can't say they feel like anyone I've ever met. But I feel I ought to try and be just like them."

"May I?" He gestured to the seat next to her.

"By all means. You're not a born-and-bred New Yorker."

"You don't sound so Park Avenue yourself."

They exchanged names. She was Helen Turman. What had brought them to New York: He said newspapers; she said Barnard, from which she had recently graduated. Hometowns: He said Virginia; she was from Atlanta.

"I worked in Atlanta," he told her. "For the *Journal*."

Suddenly alight, she said, "I know you. Well, I know of you. You're the one who got stabbed."

It was so odd to have his party story recited by someone else, it took him a moment to say, "I am."

"Only you were lucky because the next fellow got shot."

". . . He did. How . . ."

"My little brother told me when I went home for Easter. He was terribly impressed." Crossing her hands on her knee, she leaned back to survey him properly. "*My*—you're Morris Markey."

"For better and worse."

For a few moments, they sipped their coffee. He said, "I'll tell you something so long as you don't pass it on to your brother."

"Not a word."

"The fellow didn't really shoot the second reporter, he just shot out a window and squealed a bit."

"Why'd you tell people the other reporter had been shot?" He was relieved to see she was amused.

"Made for a better story. He did cut me, though." He rolled up his shirt cuff, held out his arm. "There, you can see the fearsome scar."

She gave it a good long look, even running a light finger over the ridge with a concern that made him feel he ought to point out that it was barely noticeable. Then he decided that might make her feel awkward and maybe he should let her be concerned if she were so inclined.

"Well," she said, "I'm glad you told me the truth."

"Me, too."

EPILOGUE

HALIFAX, VIRGINIA
1950

"I beg your pardon."

The coroner George Abney looked up to see a woman standing at the door. She wore a simple, correct dress, the kind one might wear to receive old friends for an afternoon visit. Her hair was combed; she'd recently had it set, and it rose high off her forehead, with only a few threads of gray through the dark brown. But the loss showed in her face. Her eyes were dull. Her mouth and forehead were deeply lined as if someone had carved into her skin with a knife. She kept one hand on the door as if she might topple.

"Please accept my condolences, Mrs. Markey."

"What are you doing in my husband's study?" Her gaze wandered about the darkened room. He sensed that with every part of it—desk, chair, the piles of magazines, the lamp, her husband's letter opener—memories came. They were not happy memories.

Helen Markey had the reputation of being an intelligent woman. She knew the difficulties presented by the way her husband had died; if she hadn't, the police had made her aware of them by interviewing her, her daughter, and the daughter's fiancé extensively.

"Your husband was a fine writer," he said, making conversation. "Quite the reader, too." He nodded to *The Great Gatsby* spread on the arm of the chair.

"Yes. He had never read Fitzgerald before. He felt it was time."

The coroner nodded. All he knew of Fitzgerald was that he had died in Hollywood a while back and was considered a flash in the pan. Curious about the dead man's state of mind, he asked, "Did he say why it was time, Mrs. Markey?"

"I think because he got a free copy when he was a war correspondent in the Pacific," she said dryly. "Their paths crossed once or twice when Morris was first in New York. And he was very upset by the death of Mrs. Fitzgerald a few years ago. But that was such a tragedy, it would distress anyone."

"I'm not familiar with what happened to her."

"I gather she was mentally unstable. She was in an institution in North Carolina, Highland Hospital. It sounds like a dreadful place, they locked the women in their rooms at night, put chains on the windows, padlocks on the doors. One night, the building caught fire. Poor Mrs. Fitzgerald was trapped. She died along with eight other women. Morris was appalled when he read the news. He became fixated on the fact that she had no way to escape. For a time, he talked about writing an article about safety precautions that actually endanger people."

On a short sigh, she said, "I confess, I got a little irritated by it. Harping on someone trapped in their home—there were times I felt he was making a point."

Abney was intrigued that Mrs. Markey would allude to her husband's unhappiness, given the circumstances. She had to know if

Abney entered a verdict of suicide, the insurance company wouldn't pay. But perhaps she preferred that to the alternative.

He glanced out the window. The daughter had emerged from the house, the Caldwell boy following her. The couple held hands, stretching their arms to stay connected even at a distance. Bill Caldwell's mother was the talkative type. She had a lot to say about the Markeys. She was a tetchy woman, easily offended. The son took after her.

Careful to keep his voice neutral, he said, "I can't imagine a man dissatisfied in such a well-kept home as this."

She gave a brief, brittle smile of a woman who had been grieving long before the actual death. "Did you ever meet my husband, Dr. Abney?"

"Not that I recall."

"Oh, you would remember if you had. Morris was . . . he was a big man. The sort of man who had been everywhere, done everything, and could tell a fine story about it—usually over a drink. Or several. He could tell how he walked straight into a murdered woman's apartment and took her sister out for a gin rickey to get the whole sordid story. If you wanted to know how they make yat ko mein at Port Arthur, he could tell you. Or how the clock at the Metropolitan Tower works, he could tell you. Most boys will take you dancing, or out for a meal, or the movies. When we first met, Morris took me walking all over the city. He showed me the Tombs, Hart's Island, the docks where the Cunard Line came in. He promised we would go to Europe, the Far East—and he kept that promise. I once joked that he seemed to think that if he stayed put, it would be the end of him. And I never saw a worse driver in my life. Reckless, fast . . ." She waved a hand: *Enough said.*

"Could it be that he was running from something, Mrs. Markey?"

"And it caught up with him in Halifax? No, Dr. Abney. At least not in the way you're thinking."

Gesturing to the typewriter, Abney asked, "Do you know why he would be writing about the murder of . . ." He had to look at the page to recall the name. "Joseph Elwell?"

It was clear from her expression, she didn't. "It was one of his first big stories, but Lord, that was ages ago."

"From his article, I gather they weren't sure if it was murder or suicide."

Understanding that he had come to the point, she lit a cigarette. "What does my husband say?"

"In the article? Suicide. He says the housekeeper covered it up by hiding the gun so everyone thought it was murder, but the man's own actions brought him to that point long before. He feels what she did was wrong. But he understood her motives."

"That sounds like Morris. He wasn't fond of outrage or judgment."

Abney felt she was making a point about people who judge. Taking off his glasses, he made a show of cleaning them. "Would you say it's significant that your husband was writing about suicide just before he died?"

"I think it's far more significant that my husband was a heavy drinker and that rifle hung on two loose hooks on the wall. It's my view that Morris staggered, put a hand out to steady himself, and knocked the rifle down by accident. It hit the ground and it fired."

Mrs. Markey had told him a good story—the only story that would keep one person in this house—or perhaps two—out of the electric chair *and* ensure the insurance company paid out. But it didn't fit the facts as he saw them.

"The difficulty is that it doesn't *look* like an accident, Mrs. Markey. A man shot with a rifle behind the right ear . . ."

"Are you saying I shot my husband, Dr. Abney?" Her voice was numb; she was too exhausted to take offense.

He gestured to the young people outside. "Word was your

husband wasn't all that pleased by his daughter marrying a small-town Virginia boy with no education."

"That's absurd. Sue's just graduated college. She hopes to be a writer. Morris worried she'd feel stuck as a wife in a small town. 'Buried' was the word he used. Bill's mother got it into her head that it was Bill we objected to when it most certainly was not. Morris himself was a small-town Virginia boy. Didn't even graduate high school."

"Maybe he wanted more for his child."

"Yes, and we gave it to her. A fine education at Barnard."

And yet, thought Abney, despite the crushingly expensive degree, the girl ended up right back in the place her father had worked so hard to leave behind.

He said, "Mrs. Markey, let's pretend I'm a writer. I'm going to tell a story about your husband's death. Of course I want it to be true. I don't see any point in causing more pain if the only person we're hurting is some fellow at the insurance company who has to write the check. But I need to know how your husband ended up with a rifle bullet behind his right ear without someone else putting it there."

Mrs. Markey finished her cigarette. Then she rose and went to the bookcase. Abney thought she placed her palms on the books' spines as if they were her husband's body and she was urging him to stay. Then she saw what she wanted. Standing on tiptoe, she pulled a volume from the row and handed it to him. Abney looked at the cover. *Short Stories As You Like Them.*

"'The Strange Noise of Dr. Beldoon.' Morris didn't write much fiction. He'd be the first to say he wasn't very good at it. But this story was important to him. As he would have explained to you, probably in far greater detail than you might wish, it is possible for a man to shoot himself this way. All he has to do is set the rifle up—you'll remember the .22 doesn't have a slanted butt, it's straight. He holds the barrel in one hand, leans down like so"—she inclined her body—"then fits the muzzle behind his ear and pulls the trigger."

She straightened. "This is my husband's suicide note, Dr. Abney. He wrote it in 1939."

She seemed to expect him to read it. So he did. It was the tale of a doctor. One day, as he was operating on a patient, he heard a hissing sound. He understood it to be a warning that he was about to make a mistake. From then on, the hissing alerted him whenever there was danger. At first, he rejoiced in the success it gave him. But he grew dependent on it, alienated from the world around him. Loved ones said he had become strange. He resolved to be free of the noise by destroying it. So he got a gun, took careful aim at "the spot where the noise was hiding," and pulled the trigger. That spot was just behind the man's right ear.

Mrs. Markey said quietly, "Sometimes when he got agitated, Morris would describe a buzzing or hissing sensation in his head. He said it started after the first war."

Fingering the page in the typewriter, she added, "Funny, I met Morris shortly after the Elwell murder. He had a byline, was clearly destined for greatness. Well, that's what we thought, but then we were very young. He seemed to me a supremely confident young man. Back from the war, curious, eager for life. How could you not feel the future was yours — you'd earned it, hadn't you?"

She smiled for a moment, then stopped. "But the cracks were there. Morris was good at hiding them, but after a time, they were plainly visible. The drinking. The fits of temper. Then he got a story wrong and the magazine had to print a retraction. That was the beginning of the end." For a moment, she struggled. "Writers don't have pensions. But he always said, no matter how bad it got, that he would make sure Sue and I were taken care of." Then she met Abney's gaze. "That it would look like an accident."

Abney had seen too many young servicemen unable to stay out

of fights and bars to doubt her. "I'm deeply sorry, Mrs. Markey. Always a shame when we have to send young men off to war."

"You might think so. I don't know that Morris would. Morris's family didn't have money. He knew he wanted something different but had no idea what it looked like or how to get it. He once told me about the day the parade came to town—that's what he called it, as if it were a day of national importance. Everyone turned out to watch the young men in uniform marching with rifles on their shoulders. Brass band. Boy scouts, waving flags bigger than they were. Pretty girls, of course. Morris was nineteen, working for the railroad. A man with a bullhorn rode by on a truck, shouting 'Who's ready? Who's worthy?' He saw Morris on the curb, pointed to him—in front of the whole town, mind you—and said, 'I see you, young man. I know you're ready.'" She looked up. "Well—it's that moment, isn't it? When the world notices you. Morris said a whole new vision of what his life might be unfurled before his eyes. He leapt at it without a second thought." Her gaze fell on *The Great Gatsby*. "I imagine the Fitzgeralds felt the same thing when they laid eyes on each other."

She took up *Gatsby*, laying it gently on top of a pile of books. Then she set her husband's short story back on the shelf. "Sometimes I imagine Morris's life if the parade had not come to town. He might have worked for the railroad like his father. Never gone to war. His mind might have stayed quiet, without the frenetic buzz of past pain. But it's not what he would have chosen. They might all have led calmer, steadier lives, but they didn't live in calm, steady times. Imagine—Mr. Fitzgerald could have been an advertising executive enjoying his martini lunches, Mrs. Fitzgerald a Montgomery housewife, Mrs. Parker a critic who never wrote a line of poetry. But then we wouldn't have 'Resumé.' We wouldn't have *Gatsby*. We wouldn't have Morris's *New Yorker* articles, revealing the city they knew." Abney heard a note of defiance as she placed her husband's name alongside the rest. "At least we can credit them with giving their era its color, its charm, and its truth. It's not a terrible legacy."

Abney murmured no, it wasn't. He personally thought of the '20s as a time when a lot of broken people drank too much, spent too much, and pleasured themselves into early graves. But looking at the copy of *Gatsby*, he knew most would disagree. Especially if they didn't live through it.

"I think what you're telling me, Mrs. Markey, is that your husband was getting older. Not as widely read as he once was. No longer able to travel or afford life in the city that made his reputation. He was ill. In pain. He drank. And he kept a gun in the house. The word 'careless' comes to my mind. How about yours?"

She knew it was the best he could offer and she nodded.

"All right, then," said Abney and left her alone in the house with her husband's stories.

AUTHOR'S NOTE

> I doubt if you are the most original writer living, but I doubt whether anybody is. . . . The greatest living writer is Morris Markey.
>
> —E. B. White in a letter to James Thurber

In 1950, former *New Yorker* writer Morris Markey dashed off a piece for *Esquire* on the 1920 death of Joseph Bowne Elwell, who had been found in his New York town house, shot through the head. "Was it suicide—or murder?" Markey wondered. The same question would be asked later that year when Markey was found shot through the head in his home under suspicious circumstances. Neither death has been officially solved.

That part of *The Girl in the Green Dress* is true. Other parts are not.

Markey and Zelda never met. Remarkably, at a time when every writer encountered Scott and Zelda Fitzgerald, there is no record of any meeting between them and Morris Markey. They had acquaintances in common: Fitzgerald dined on separate occasions with two of Markey's close friends, James Thurber and James M. Cain. Another good friend, Laurence Stallings, wrote what Fitzgerald considered the only intelligent review of *The Great Gatsby*. But Zelda and Markey moved in different circles, she artistic, he journalistic. (Some writers moved in both, such as Dorothy Parker.)

The Elwell case is not a front-runner in the "murders that inspired *Gatsby*" stakes, although Jonathan Goodman makes a decent case for it in *The Slaying of Joseph Bowne Elwell*. At the time of the murder, the Fitzgeralds had decamped to Connecticut. Morris Markey was not yet in New York; he arrived a year later, having already married Helen Turman in Atlanta (where he was indeed stabbed by a manic lawyer). My account of the murder of Joseph Elwell makes full use of the tabloid headlines and should not be taken as definitive. But the "cast of characters"—Viola Kraus, the Lewisohns, Victor von Schlegell, Leonora Hughes, and Marie Larsen—are based in fact, as is Marie Larsen's role in hiding the pink kimono and the "gallery of beautiful women" found in Elwell's home. Lewisohn did go mad and was committed to an asylum, but it was years after the murder. The affair between Selma and Victor is my invention. The chauffeur—whose real name was Edward or Edwin Rhodes—did not drive Elwell home that night. A cabdriver remembers taking him home with two men and a woman; I omitted the two men. The theory that Lewisohn killed Elwell in a jealous fit concerning Leonora Hughes comes from Jonathan Goodman's book. My theory that Mrs. Larsen killed Elwell is rooted in two things: Elwell was a member of the APL, and she would have had keys. Her husband did serve but was not killed. The Griswold character is pure fiction. But at this time, another member of the APL was shot and killed in his New Jersey home, which led to speculation that the murders were connected. If so, it was never proved.

Markey served in World War I. His passport in 1918 cites the

Red Cross. He wrote for several papers, including the *Daily News*, before moving on to *The New Yorker* in 1925. (The process of reporting at that time was not as it's described in the novel. Markey's raw report would have likely been polished by a rewrite man rather than negotiated directly with an editor.) My portrait of him is based largely on his early *New Yorker* pieces. They give a sense of a young man wandering the city, delighted by its spectacle, from Communist rallies to the Bathtub Orgy Trial. The tone is cheerful, skeptical, and resolutely unshockable. As a reporter, he had a reputation as a graceful, original stylist—and a man who could be loose with his facts. While he fiercely denied this, in 1934, his article on the soundness of North Dakota banks was found "erroneous," forcing *The Saturday Evening Post* to print a retraction. Still, in the opinion of Ben Yagoda, author of *About Town: The New Yorker and the World It Made*, "Markey's articles did more than anything else to establish *The New Yorker* as a magazine that could be serious as well as light. He explored every stratum of society, and his presence as 'I' or 'we' in nearly all his pieces gave them an authority that the conventional reporting of the day usually lacked." Perhaps E. B. White was sarcastic when he called Markey the "greatest living writer." Or perhaps he was sincere.

And then there is Zelda.

From Fitzgerald to Zelda herself, many gifted writers have tried to capture this mesmerizing, charismatic, and confounding human being. She can be hard to see through the lens of people's fixation with her charms. How crazy was she? How sexy? Was her accent heavy or nonexistent? To borrow an observation from Sarah Murphy, she was *young*. She candidly confessed to thinking mostly about herself. This novel depicts Zelda at the start of her marriage, when she took her first step into the public consciousness. High-energy, confident, capricious, brilliantly intuitive, she is just beginning to suspect that she can live a wildly unconventional life but still get trapped in the identity of "Mrs." The Fitzgerald marriage was volatile from its earliest days. Zelda often went off on adventures with Scott's friends and formed at least one mildly romantic attachment. It didn't seem a stretch to imagine her careening around with a fellow Southerner also new to the city.

So what killed Morris Markey? His mother and James Thurber believed it was an accident. Cain suspected it was murder. Markey's wife told the police it was an accident, then confessed to Cain it was suicide, brought on by illness, pain, and financial difficulties.

The letters of Thurber and Cain reveal a more boisterous, self-destructive character than the shy young man of my book. Zelda and the real Markey shared a certain panache and appetite for risk. (Thurber would have fallen over laughing at the thought of a Morris Markey unable to command a room.) Cain recalls a gregarious, warmhearted man, but a prickly and combative one, given to fits of temper that grew worse over time. Thurber's brother remembers Markey as restless and fidgety. Thurber affectionately recalls his terrible driving, as well as a passionate desire to be known as interesting. It's not clear what kind of war Markey had; his fictional nightmare is based on a trauma experienced by Edwin Pond Parker Jr. But these traits, combined with the heavy drinking, indicated possible PTSD.

Strangely enough, I gave my Morris Markey fits of buzzing when in the grip of an anxiety attack before reading his 1939 story "The Strange Noise of Dr. Beldoon," in which the protagonist hears hissing when under stress. That he frees himself of the hissing by shooting himself at precisely the spot the bullet entered Markey's skull eleven years later decides his death as a suicide in my opinion.

In his article on Joseph Elwell, Markey theorizes that the bridge expert committed suicide. He suggests that Mrs. Larsen, accustomed to tidying up Elwell's messes, found the gun near the body and cleared it away to avoid the disgrace. It seems unlikely to me;

if so, why wouldn't she admit it at the same time she admitted to hiding the pink kimono, thereby sparing the police more work and the suspects the investigation?

But clearly suicide was on Markey's mind. In the piece, he warns the reader:

> The next time you have an empty .45 automatic around the house, try holding it with both hands at arm's length, and pointing it at your brow, and pressing the trigger with your thumb.
>
> Be sure it is empty. Because it certainly would work.

Works Consulted

The Slaying of Joseph Bowne Elwell by Jonathan Goodman
Zelda by Nancy Milford
Zelda Fitzgerald: Her Voice in Paradise by Sally Cline
Some Unfinished Chaos: The Lives of F. Scott Fitzgerald by Arthur Krystal
Invented Lives: F. Scott and Zelda Fitzgerald by James R. Mellow
Exiles from Paradise: Zelda and Scott Fitzgerald by Sara Mayfield
The Crack-Up by F. Scott Fitzgerald
The letters of James M. Cain held at the Library of Congress
Cain: The Biography of James M. Cain by Roy Hoopes
The Thurber Letters edited by Harrison Kinney and Rosemary A. Thurber
James Thurber: His Life and Times by Harrison Kinney
That's New York! by Morris Markey
"The Strange Noise of Dr. Beldoon" by Morris Markey
Various articles in *The New Yorker, Esquire, Harper's*, and others by Morris Markey

ACKNOWLEDGMENTS

It's a nerve-wracking thing to take on the Fitzgeralds. I am grateful to my writers group for their invaluable guidance and support. Heartfelt thank-yous go to Sandra Newman, Clare McHugh, Colette Willis, Sam Amir Toosi, Mark Becker, Concetta Panzariello, and Rob Edelstein. I am deeply in the debt of early readers Karen Odden, Elizabeth Kerri Mahon, and Elizabeth Mannion. Special gratitude goes to Kate and Craig Hohl for attempting to explain the game of bridge to me and checking my work for errors. If errors remain, they're mine, not theirs. Thank you to Dallas Brech for his thoughts on how someone could shoot themselves in the back of the head with a rifle.

As always, I thank my editor, Catherine Richards, who listened patiently to my endless theories on the death of Morris Markey. Her assistant, Kelly Stone, kept the project on track. I am intensely grateful to production editor Ginny Perrin for her eagle-eyed read of the manuscript. Special shout-out to designers David Rotstein, Rowen Davis, and Meryl Levavi for their gorgeous work.

This was an emotionally challenging book to write, requiring patience and a generous spirit from friends and especially family.

Thank you to Josh and Griffin for putting up with me. A special thank-you to Larry Weiss and Peggy Florin for their willingness to indulge my odd obsessions. It is not everyone who will buy a signed Morris Markey letter off eBay for you. Or come so faithfully to every book launch.

Finally, the book is dedicated to my agent, Victoria Skurnick, for understanding all my reasons for being scared to write Zelda Fitzgerald and telling me to do it anyway. A great agent and an even better friend. Thank you for proving F. Scott Fitzgerald wrong. There are second acts, and you gave me mine.

ABOUT THE AUTHOR

Mariah Fredericks was born, raised, and still lives in New York City. She graduated from Vassar College with a degree in history. She is the author of the Jane Prescott mystery series, which has twice been nominated for the Mary Higgins Clark Award. *The Lindbergh Nanny*, her first standalone novel, was nominated for the Agatha and Anthony Awards.